The Lines We Cross

Rachel Tork

For all the 'soft fire' girls. Know that it's okay to embrace that part of yourself—there are many different kinds of strength.

Trigger Warnings

Conversations and flashbacks involving the death of a sibling, conversations about pregnancy loss, sexual assault, brief gun violence, accidental pregnancy

3 Years Prior

Julian hated Fridays.

They held the promise of a weekend full of work and the empty quiet of his shitty, one-bedroom apartment. Not that he really wanted to socialize or go out. Several of his colleagues had tried to get him to go to the bar, and he'd refused each offer. One of them, a woman with very straight teeth and aggressively blonde hair, had been particularly adamant. He had a hunch she had wanted more from him than a friendly round of drinks. Not that it mattered—he didn't have the time for a relationship, nor did he really want one.

Yet still, on this particular day, he dreaded heading back home. His shoes clicked on the linoleum floors of Sierra Hill University's music building as he walked towards the exit. A group of girls hurried past him, giggling as they rushed down the hall behind him. When he pushed the glass door open and approached the concrete steps that led to the courtyard beyond, he paused.

A girl was sitting about halfway down the steps, her head on her knees. From where he stood, he could only see two fiery auburn braids and a thin frame shaking slightly with silent sobs. An odd, catching feeling tugged somewhere in his chest, and he swallowed, trying to banish it. He had made it a few steps past her before the girl let out a small, muffled noise, as if she was trying to hide that she was crying.

His jaw tightened. He couldn't just leave her here, crying and alone. It wasn't right. He really should be on his way, but against his better judgment, he paused and turned to face her. She didn't even look up as he asked, "Are you alright?"

Her head remained down, ignoring him, but he felt the need to ensure she was fine, so he spoke again. "Hello?"

The girl made a soft, sniffling noise and finally raised her head. A small, long-unwanted feeling began to drag itself up from deep in his chest as he met her eyes. They were a clear, icy shade of blue, clouded just slightly by the tears. He watched as those eyes widened incrementally as she observed him, took him in. God, he was suddenly being swallowed whole by those large, blue eyes.

Stop, he begged her silently. *Stop looking at me like...that.*

He was glad when she finally spoke, insisting in a thick voice that she was fine. Still, her words bothered him. She was clearly not.

"You don't look fine." His words were clipped and maybe a tad rude. He hoped the hint of regret didn't show on his face.

The girl's shoulders lifted in a shrug. Her full lips parted before she spoke, and it took everything in him to keep his gaze from lingering on her mouth as she replied with a soft fire, "What's it to you?"

Nothing; it should mean nothing to me. Except there's this weird feeling somewhere in my chest that's making me think I need to make sure you're alright. Not to mention the fact that you're the most beautiful woman I've ever seen, and if I was a weaker man, I might just ask to kiss you. Which you'd definitely refuse, but still...

He didn't say any of that, instead schooling his expression into what he hoped was merely mild concern and raising his brow in question at her rebuttal. But whatever she saw on his face caused her lower lip to momentarily tremble and her eyes to fill with more tears. He couldn't help but move closer to her then, carefully crouching, still slightly below her.

"Did your teacher yell at you or something?"

The question sounded stupid as soon as it left his mouth, but he needed to know how to help her.

The girl let out a dry, humorless chuckle that caused his chest to tighten.

"Yes, but that's not an unusual occurrence," she replied.

"So, something else?" His voice pitched lower—quieter.

"I don't know you," she said.

That was entirely true, but somehow, he felt it would take very little for him to memorize her, to know her completely and wholly. The most disconcerting part of it all was that he thought she might be able to know him too.

"I know. You just looked..." He searched for a word and lamely came up with, "Sad."

The girl rubbed her eyes. "Just today."

He wanted to ask why. *Why today? Who or what made*

you look so hopeless? Feeling helpless and a little stupid, he reached into his rucksack and fished for a pack of tissues. He always carried one around with him, just in case. He hated seeing people cry. He had since the last time he'd seen his mother, blotchy-faced and getting into a cab.

For a few agonizingly long seconds, the red-headed girl just stared at the tissue in his hand. The moment felt like a decision, the flip of a coin, which was ridiculous. His tissue was not going to fix or begin anything.

Finally, she took the tissue, mumbling a thanks. He forced himself to look away from her then, instead peering out at the setting sun. The sky was perfect today, painted like some enormous, celestial canvas.

"A sunset such as this is like a beautiful song for our eyes."

His mouth twitched at the bittersweet memory—of his tenth birthday, when his mother had woken him up early and they'd left Edinburgh by dawn, spending all day exploring the Highlands. When evening came, they'd sat by the loch and watched the colors spread out all around them.

"You like sunsets or something?"

The girl's voice startled him out of the memory, but it wasn't an unwelcome intrusion. Instead, she only felt like a part of the beauty of it all. He couldn't help but stare at her, her auburn hair aflame in the orange-hued glow of the sky.

"Very much so," he told her. Even though she didn't know why, telling her that felt like sharing a hidden piece of himself. It was a part he so rarely showed to anyone. It was why, after a few more seconds of gazing at her, he looked back at the sunset.

It was odd how comfortable he suddenly felt. She was a

complete stranger—he didn't even know her name, nor did she know his. It didn't feel important, though. Not yet.

Her breath shuddered and slowed behind him as she began to calm down. Minutes passed, and the sun began to dip below the horizon, a chill setting in around them. A wave of something that felt like nerves fluttered in his stomach as he stood and offered his hand. The feeling intensified and turned to disappointment as she shook her head.

He found himself insisting, "It's cold."

The girl gazed out at the sky growing darker by the minute. When she looked back at him, her voice was softer, almost gentle, as she told him, "You probably have somewhere to be. But thanks for the tissue."

He swallowed, warring emotions telling him to leave, to stay, to insist. He must've been fairly transparent, because she spoke again.

"I'll be fine. I just... I'm going to try and look for a few stars."

She was—

He was...

He was in far too deep already. It was time to leave. She did not want someone like him in her life. No one did. He couldn't afford to feel anything beyond this moment.

Forcing himself to move, he made his way past where she still sat huddled on the cold stone steps. But he couldn't resist the question.

"So, stars are your sunsets?"

Are you just like me? Am I imagining this, or are you truly real?

The girl glanced back at him. The lights from the buildings beyond reflected in her eyes, and she smiled faintly as she said, "Something like that."

He froze, the world suddenly feeling all too real. He felt like he was looking at his entire life as he stared at the girl.

In the end, it was precisely why he tore his gaze from hers and walked away.

The Beginning

"The Elevator"—Lizzy McAlpine

"Mess It Up"—Gracie Abrams

"Cold Cold Cold"—Cage the Elephant

"Two Birds"—Regina Spektor

"The John Wayne"—Little Green Cars

"Burned"—Grace VanderWaal

"Dancing With Our Hands Tied"—Taylor Swift

Chapter 1
Sleepless Nights & Stars

THE EMAIL CAME ONLY a week before the semester began. It was short and to the point, mostly because Rowan assumed it had been all the sender could manage in his state. This particular email, read on a Monday morning in early August, caused a cataclysmic tremor to rip through her life. It was the beginning of a coming disaster, really.

She had come to Grandview University's Belton School of Music quite specifically for John Higgins. Seeing an email from him wasn't unexpected. It was the content that caused her to nearly drop her steaming cup of tea all over the cheap carpet of her new apartment.

Dear Ms. Evans,

With great regret, I must inform you that I have fallen ill quite suddenly and will be unable to be present for the current academic year. The department has filled my position with a very capable replacement, Dr. Julian Lynch. I have attached a link to his résumé should you like to view it. I wish you all the best and good luck.

Sincerely,

John D. Higgins

Rowan was a bit surprised the email came from Higgins himself, but she was even more shocked at the prospect of a completely new professor in his place. She had spent months networking, auditioning, and emailing to find the perfect mentor for her graduate studies. Hell, she had foregone an offer at fucking *Juilliard* because Higgins had seemed so perfect. Not to mention, Grandview was close enough to home that she could keep an eye on her mom if need be, though far enough away that she could forgo coming home on the weekends. Not that she'd have time anyway; such was the nature of music school. She'd learned at least that much in undergrad.

But now, she was being essentially forced to learn under someone she had never heard of and knew almost nothing about. Seeing as Grandview had to fill the position so quickly and abruptly, maybe this Julian Lynch person wasn't even that capable, despite Higgins' claim.

She should have looked at his résumé, but she couldn't bring herself to open the attachment, not at least before she met the man. What if he was completely lackluster? Rowan knew she was probably being a bit pretentious about the whole thing, but coming to Grandview was a big deal. She didn't want it to be ruined by some half-rate fill-in.

Staring at herself in the bathroom mirror, where her pacing had taken her, she nearly slapped herself.

It was fine.

It would be fine.

Fuck.

"Christ, Julian, it's just drinks."

Julian rolled his eyes, and though Ethan couldn't see it, his friend must have somehow sensed the gesture, because he scoffed into the phone.

"Lighten up, man," Ethan said. "I have to go, I have a quick meeting, but I expect to see your sorry ass at Francesca's in an hour. I'll even buy you a beer."

"Mm, tempting," Julian muttered.

Ethan only snorted and ended the call, leaving Julian alone in his apartment. The place was nice enough. Nothing high-end; rent wasn't entirely cheap fairly close to the city. He didn't really care either way. It was simply a place for him to sleep, eat, and shower. Starting tomorrow, most of his time would be spent at the university.

Landing the job was a fluke on his end. When Sierra Hill had decided not to renew his contract last year thanks to department budget cuts, he'd scraped by well enough in a professional ensemble. But just a month ago, Ethan had contacted him with a "huge opportunity".

It was, to be fair, and even Julian was surprised that he'd actually *landed* the teaching position at Grandview. "Temporary for now" is what he'd been told, but he'd had several calls with the man he was replacing, and John Higgins had assured Julian that, sadly, he would likely not return due to his poor health. Like most things in Julian's life, it was bittersweet.

John Higgins was well-respected in the community, and to replace him like this felt both honorable and shifty at the same time.

The most daunting factor in all of it had come in the form of the graduate student files he'd been sent two weeks ago. Sure, it was intimidating to fill the shoes of the man all the students had *thought* they would be receiving as an advisor and teacher, but that wasn't what had caused him to nearly drop the papers on the floor of the staff office. It was the blurry photo on the front page of the third student file.

Rowan Evans, it had read. Staring back at him, with a pasted-on smile, was the very girl who had haunted him for the past three years. No matter what he'd tried to do to erase her, she had always shown up—in quiet moments, in dreams, in the way the stars blinked at him on late, sleepless nights.

He knew it was stupid. They'd barely spoken that day, and he was certain she wouldn't recognize or remember him.

Which was good.

Besides, if she was far from his reach before, she was completely lost to him now. She was going to be his student, so he was going to have to shove his feelings aside completely.

A drink—or a few—was sounding better by the second. In the end, he begrudgingly headed to the bar Ethan had named. As soon as he stepped in, he heard Ethan's booming voice call, "Julian! Come on over!"

Phenomenal. Ethan was—unsurprisingly—already drunk, which likely meant Julian would be hauling his ass home tonight.

Sitting around a table with Ethan were four other people,

presumably the professors Ethan told Julian would be attending tonight. A thin, older woman scrutinized Julian, her gaze scanning him, as if checking if he was fit for the job. Next to her, a man who looked about Ethan's age gave Julian a goofy grin and a thumbs-up. And to the left of him, an ancient-looking man was deep in conversation with a woman wearing the ugliest green glasses Julian had ever seen—not that he was going to tell her that.

All the professors were dressed smartly, despite being here at a bar. Ethan slapped the seat next to him and said, "Sit. I'll buy you a drink."

Julian nodded at the others as he made his way over and sat down. Ethan meandered towards the bar, and the younger man stuck out a hand and said, "I'm Leopold. But please, call me Leo."

Julian shook his hand and said politely, "Nice to meet you."

"Penny Thea." The thin woman nodded. "And that's Bill Smith and Miranda Lark," she added, waving her hand airily in the direction of the two others. "Welcome to Grandview."

"Thanks," Julian said just as Ethan returned, setting a beer down in front of him.

"Drink," Ethan ordered, laughing.

Penny raised a brow and scolded, "Really, Ethan?"

Ethan grinned. "Let me just tell you all now—Julian is a *very* serious person. It gets boring pretty damn quickly."

"So, is he less serious when not sober?" Leo asked, chuckling as he took a sip of his drink.

"Hardly," Julian replied, shooting a glare at Ethan.

Penny rolled her eyes, seemingly ignoring Ethan and Leo

as she asked, "So, Julian, how do the incoming students look? I know you're taking over John's grads."

"Ah," Julian began. "I am. They look... interesting."

Ethan's brows rose. "And what the hell is that supposed to mean?"

"I just mean it's a pretty mixed group," Julian amended.

Penny nodded. "Did you get a chance to see any of them play?"

"I listened to recordings of all their senior recitals," Julian told her.

Bill and Miranda turned their attention to Julian then as Miranda asked, "Any standouts? I conduct the orchestra, so I've already evaluated them, but I'm curious what your thoughts are. Especially the wind group, given that's what you'll be teaching."

Julian swallowed. There *had* been a standout, and he was fairly sure Miranda Lark knew that, given which flutist she had selected for the first chair position. Still, the woman held his gaze, waiting.

His reply wasn't a conflict of interest, yet somehow, it felt odd as he replied, "There's a girl... a flute player. Rowan Evans."

Both Miranda and Penny smiled, so it seemed he'd answered correctly. Penny sighed and said, "I nearly got her once John fell ill, but he recommended the girl study under you."

"Ah, apologies then," Julian replied.

Penny laughed softly. "None needed. I've seen your work, Julian. I'm sure she'll excel with you."

"She just needs..." Miranda rubbed two fingers together.

"A spark. Just a bit of kindling, and I think she'll explode into a supernova."

"Her playing was slightly..." Julian trailed off, not sure what word he was looking for.

Penny stepped in and said, "It felt just a tad heavy. Too heavy, like the playing carried something she needed to let go of."

Tear-filled blue eyes swam in Julian's mind. "That's a good way of putting it," he said.

"She'll be fine," Ethan cut in. "Pretty girl like her will soar when put in the right environment. Let's just hope Julian can cultivate it."

Miranda rolled her eyes, and even Leo snorted.

"Really?" Penny deadpanned. "And what does beauty have to do with her talent?"

Ethan shrugged. "We put on performances. It doesn't hurt if the performer is nice to look at as well as nice to listen to."

A sudden wave of irritation washed over Julian at his friend's words. Sure, Ethan was often crass, but now wasn't the time. Rowan Evans was off limits to all of them, but especially to Ethan. Julian had seen how he'd treated his past girlfriends—nothing devious, just a whole lot of cheating and lying.

Bill lightened the tense moment by saying, "Well, I do hope my audiences appreciate the bald spot and wrinkles."

Leo laughed, and the rest of the night fell into easy chitchat. Julian didn't entirely hate it, actually finding himself enjoying parts of the conversations. When Ethan had one too many drinks, Julian dragged him out of the bar and into his car.

"You're lucky you got her," Ethan said with a lazy grin as Julian pulled out of the parking lot.

"Got who?"

Ethan snorted. "Don't play dumb, Julian. Rowan Evans. I mean, the term's not even started yet, and she's the talk of the department. Not to mention, she won't be hard to look at."

"Ethan," Julian warned. "Don't."

"Why not? She's not my student."

Julian tightened his jaw, and Ethan laughed. "Damn! Have I finally hit a nerve?"

"Just...leave my students out of your escapades," Julian gritted out.

"And why should I do that?"

Julian turned off the main road into the parking garage of Ethan's fancy apartment complex. "Because I don't want any drama," he replied stiffly.

"Sure," Ethan drawled. "But just know," he jabbed a finger at Julian's chest, "I see right through it. I have no idea how you know this girl, but—"

"Ethan—enough."

Ethan put his hands up but added one last thing before he got out of the car. "While you're holding onto your restraint, just keep in mind that I can dare to cross lines you assuredly cannot."

He slammed the door, punctuating his words as he strode away. Julian gritted his teeth, watching Ethan go. His friend likely wouldn't remember or care about half of what he said in the morning. Ethan was stupid when he was drunk.

Still, Julian couldn't shake the feeling that the coming term was going to be anything but normal.

Chapter 2
An Original Piece

A WEEK later from the day she had received the fateful email, Rowan approached the geometric building that housed Grandview's music program. It was perched on the edge of Lake Michigan, practically leaning out over the shimmering water. The sun was shining, the air warm around her, though it cooled slightly by the lakefront—typical Chicagoland weather for August. Next to her, her best friend, Amelia, said her name loudly.

"Row."

Rowan turned her head slightly, biting the inside of her cheek. Amelia had her hands on her narrow hips, glaring at Rowan. Though she was a good three or four inches shorter, Amelia's personality made up for it with vigor. She pushed a strand of raven-black hair behind her ear as she said, "You've been quiet. Things are never good when you're this quiet."

"I'm always quiet," Rowan commented dryly.

Amelia rolled her eyes. "You know what I mean."

Rowan raised a brow and muttered, "Not sure I do."

"*Row.* You may be naturally stoic, but you are not normally this sullen, especially on a day like today. We're here, together! I mean, who would've thought we would both end up at the same grad school? It's pretty much a miracle."

She gave an encouraging smile that Rowan tried and failed to return.

Amelia stopped with a sigh a few young and rather terrified-looking students passing by.

"Okay, I know this isn't ideal, but we looked Dr. Lynch up. Yeah, he's young, but his credentials looked good, like really good for his age. I thought we were over the super bad nerves at least."

Amelia was right. Dr. Julian Lynch looked like he couldn't be past thirty-five in the blurry photo that had just been posted two days ago to the university website. When she'd finally looked at his resume, she discovered he'd earned his undergraduate degree at the prestigious Irene University, then both his master's and doctorate at none other than the Juilliard School of Music. He'd also taught briefly at the University of Sierra Hill, where Rowan had gone for her undergraduate degree with Amelia. She was surprised she'd never crossed paths with him there. Maybe he'd only taught entry-level theory classes or something.

Rowan glanced at Amelia, an expectant look on her friend's face, and said with a huff, "I'm fine."

Amelia nodded. "You are. I know it was a disappointment about Dr. Higgins, but I don't think the department would hire someone incompetent."

"Maybe in a time crunch, they would," Rowan muttered.

She glanced down at her worn leather watch. "We should go, or we'll both be late."

Amelia promptly took Rowan's hand and pulled her towards the building that would be their home for the next two years, the place where they would eat, sleep, and breathe classical repertoire. Rowan would spend hours alone there in practice rooms, with only her silver-plated flute for company. Well, and Dr. Lynch too, apparently.

Once they were inside, they parted ways. Both of them had lessons this morning at nine, doubling as their initial meetings with their graduate advisors—which was, for Rowan, of course, Dr. Lynch.

Rowan already knew where to go; she had scouted the entire building over the summer. She patted her tightly braided auburn hair, checked that the fly of her jeans wasn't open, and glanced at the matte black instrument case she carried alongside her bag.

She was ready.

The door to the practice room was closed when she arrived. For a moment, she hesitated before just deciding to just go in. It was nine o'clock already, after all.

She took a deep breath and pushed the door open. The first thing she saw was a head, ducked and staring at papers in a manila folder. Deep brown eyes, so dark they were almost black, snapped up to hers as soon as he realized she had entered the room. Wavy, dark hair framed a sharp, olive-toned face. He almost looked familiar.

"Rowan Evans," he stated flatly in a slightly accented voice. British, maybe?

She cleared her throat. "Yes. I imagine you're Dr. Lynch?"

He stood, towering over her even though she was nearly five-nine. He wore a dark button-up with black pants to match. As he scrutinized her, he casually slid his hands into his pockets.

After staring at her for a few moments, he spoke again, "It's rude not to knock if the door is closed. And 'professor' is fine."

Something about him was so strangely familiar...but what was it?

She fidgeted slightly. "Well, *Professor*, my schedule says our lessons start at nine a.m., so I figured you were ready."

"Don't assume," he admonished.

She lifted her chin slightly, already sensing the air of superiority he carried. She wasn't one to be shoved around. She respected teachers who respected her. It had caused some conflict in the past, but it always did her more good than bad.

"I didn't," she replied evenly. "We're supposed to start at nine. I arrived exactly then. If you wanted to push back our meeting time, I'm fairly certain you have my school email address. I check it regularly."

Something flashed across his expression, his eyes darkening further.

"Careful," he said, his voice low. "You are not the teacher here."

She smiled coolly. "No, I'm not, but I've always understood mentor-mentee relationships to be reciprocal."

He narrowed his eyes then sat down.

"Scales," he clipped out. "Now."

She hid her surprise. She thought they'd speak more before he had her play—thought he would actually advise her like he was supposed to. Still, she didn't hesitate before setting her bag and instrument case down on a small table near the door. She quickly assembled her flute, checking that it was tuned by ear. She adjusted it once then faced Professor Lynch and ran through several scales.

"Chromatic!" he barked out as he played along on the piano. "Quickly."

She did so with ease, her fingers delicately playing over the softly clicking keys. When she was done, she lowered the mouthpiece.

"Do you have something prepared?" he questioned.

She raised a brow. "I didn't realize this was an audition."

Professor Lynch thinned his full lips and replied, "I've never heard you play, at least not in person. I think it's appropriate that you show me what I'll be working with."

"Did you listen to my senior undergrad recording?" she asked.

He nodded, silent and waiting.

She pursed her lips and raised her flute to her mouth. She played a section of the same piece she had for her recital: *Sonata in A Minor* by Bach. Professor Lynch watched her with a flat expression, showing no indication of what he thought about her playing or the piece she'd chosen.

Once she was finished, he leaned back slightly, seeming to consider something. Finally, he said, "You could be good. Exceptional, even."

She was still and silent, waiting for him to elaborate. Her

heart beat furiously, with both the adrenaline of the piece she'd just finished and the suspense of what he would say next.

He leaned forward then, resting his forearms on his knees and looking at her with a sort of calculating expression. "Why music?"

She blinked, taken aback. "You mean why did I decide to pursue it professionally or...?"

He shrugged. "That's one way to put it, but not quite what I mean. I want you to tell me why you picked up a flute in the first place. Why, unlike so many other students who dropped off after high school band or even undergrad, you stuck with it. Why do you play?"

She shifted, a little uncomfortable and unsure how to answer the question. She'd picked up the flute because her sister, Alex, had. They'd gone to lessons together and had both taken band almost all the way through high school. That is, until Alex couldn't. Music had been her sister's dream.

Rowan couldn't let it die.

Except there was no way she was telling Professor Lynch, a man she'd just met, all of that. So instead, she answered, "I just love playing."

He smiled, but it was void of warmth, almost mocking.

"You just... love playing," he repeated, turning the words over in his mouth.

She shrugged.

He sat back again and sighed. "Whatever your reason is, it isn't strong enough. Your technique is good and you have excellent breath support and style, but you have no spark. No passion. Without those elements, it's like I'm watching a washed-out old recording."

Her cheeks warmed. "I'm not sure I understand," she said as evenly as she could.

He scrutinized her, and for a moment, something flickered in his eyes, a fleeting expression she couldn't quite interpret. Then, he stood, walking over to the piano bench in the corner where an instrument case sat. He opened it and quickly assembled his flute, tuned it, then faced her.

He met her eyes as he began to play. Surprisingly, she didn't recognize the piece. It was quick-moving yet emotional and deep-reaching, as if the notes touched her very soul. He hardly looked away from her as he crescendo-ed and eased delicately off a run. By the time he finished, her hands were nearly shaking with the impact of what she'd just heard. The feelings rushing through her were almost too much, and she had to make a conscious effort to keep her breathing even.

He was silent as he lowered the instrument from his mouth, watching her. After several long, quiet moments, he finally asked, "Do you understand now?"

She opened her mouth then closed it. When she spoke again, she asked in a crackling voice, "What piece was that?"

"An original," he replied immediately.

"You mean, you wrote it?"

He nodded. "But the composition didn't matter, not really. I think you see that, yes?"

She took a deep breath. "I understand."

He tilted his head slightly as he looked at her and then said in a low voice, "*That* is what you're missing. I don't care how you find it, but if this is going to work, if *you* are going to work as a professional musician, you need to find it."

She bit her lip and muttered, "Alright."

"Lesson over. Try to come back with something better next time," he snarked.

She raised a brow but decided against a retort, cleaning then packing up her instrument. She swung her bag over her shoulder and dared a last glance back at Professor Lynch. He met her eyes but quickly looked away.

As soon as she stepped out of the practice room, she slumped against the wall. She hadn't felt as alive as she had in that practice room in a long, long time.

Chapter 3
The Spark

INSTANT RAMEN BURNED Rowan's tongue as she scarfed down her dinner. Next to her, on their hand-me-down couch, Amelia did the same. Her friend's usually sleek pixie cut had puffed out a bit on the sides due to the stress of the day.

"So, apparently," Amelia said between bites of noodles, "everyone is hot for your teacher."

Rowan coughed, nearly choking, and Amelia clapped her on the back.

"*What?*" she was finally able to demand.

Amelia nodded enthusiastically. "He's among one of the youngest professors to ever teach here, apparently. Not to mention, he's supposedly brilliant. I heard some guy babbling about it in the coffee shop on campus, how he's never heard a flutist play like that."

"Was the guy one of his students?"

Amelia nodded. "Yeah, uh... His name was Jake or Jared or something like that. The dude who came from Berklee. Like, the one in Boston."

Rowan nodded with her. "I see. And was Jake the one who was hot for Professor Lynch?"

Amelia shook her head. "Nah. Well...maybe. It was mostly this group of girls. One of them was a student of his, and she had somehow snagged a picture of him. They were passing it around like it was porn or something."

Rowan made a face. "That's creepy."

Amelia shrugged. "Maybe. But I asked to see it, because why not, and they weren't exactly wrong to be lusting after him."

"Lusting?" Rowan snorted.

Amelia shoved at her shoulder and said, "Okay, my word choice is not the point. What I'm trying to get out of you is, what was he like? Was he as hot and young and brilliant as everyone says?"

Rowan set her cup of half-eaten noodles down on the coffee table and pressed her lips together. Amelia was watching her carefully as she said, "Well, he *is* young, for a professor. He played some crazy original piece for me—"

"What!" Amelia immediately squeaked. "Wait, he composes too?"

Rowan rolled her eyes. "Chill, Ami. He was just trying to show me how incompetent I am compared to him. Honestly, it was kind of an arrogant move."

"How was his playing?"

Rowan sighed. "Really brilliant. But I mean, that much is to be expected. I don't know; he was honestly kind of an ass."

"But?" Amelia pushed.

"But nothing," Rowan said as she swallowed. "He's my

teacher. I'll put up with his moods and he'll help me improve my technique."

Amelia narrowed her eyes. "You seem very nonchalant about this. Almost too nonchalant."

Truthfully, Rowan was trying to conceal some of her feelings about Professor Lynch, about the way his playing made her breathless and his eyes had barely left hers throughout the entire lesson. And how, when it was over, she'd felt like she was coming down from some euphoric high, nearly collapsing, jelly-legged, against the wall outside the room. But Amelia didn't need to know that. No one did. She herself needed to let it go.

"He's attractive, alright," Rowan conceded. "But he was also rude and lacked a general sense of mutual respect— which I guess isn't surprising, given his age and what he's achieved."

Amelia nodded thoughtfully then smiled widely and chuckled. "Well, I guess it doesn't matter if he's hot. He's your teacher and advisor, so...totally off-limits. At least you'll get a nice view in addition to your lessons."

Rowan rolled her eyes and stood, depositing the rest of her uneaten ramen in the trash. Amelia shouted, "Hey! I could've eaten that!"

Rowan turned and winced. "Oops, sorry."

Amelia set her empty cup down and sighed. "It's okay. Oh, I forgot to ask, is it okay if Sam comes over later?"

Rowan glanced at the digital clock above the oven. It was already 7:35, and Samuel, Amelia's boyfriend of four years, lived in the city, where he worked.

"He's on his way already," Amelia explained. "Sorry, it

was kind of last minute. His jazz group's practice was canceled."

Rowan smiled tightly. "It's fine. You two can have the apartment to yourself for a while. I'm heading back to practice for a bit."

Amelia lounged back on the couch as she called, "Have fun!" Rowan chuckled dryly, disappearing into her room momentarily to grab her bag and instrument case.

She debated whether to bring a light jacket, since it could get a little chilly at night on the lakeside. In the end, she decided it would be more of a hassle to carry around than it was worth. She slipped on her long-ago broken-in Oxford shoes and adjusted her braids a bit before slipping her earbuds in. Most music students listened to the pieces they were currently working on in a constant stream. She did so often enough, but right now, she just wanted to listen to the soothing tones of her favorite indie-folk artist.

Amelia waved at her as she clicked open their apartment door and left. It was a good twenty-minute walk to the Mitchell Center, and she relished every moment of it.

The best song of the album came on just as she pushed open the heavy door to the entrance. She sighed and paused it, immediately hearing the faint sounds of other students hitting the practice rooms.

She thankfully found an empty one and pulled her earbuds out as she shut the door behind her. Once she'd assembled and tuned her flute, she ran through a few scales to warm up. She paused when she was done, thinking about Professor Lynch's words.

"You have no spark, no passion."

Her anger resurfaced at the memory. Of course, she had passion. She wouldn't be here if she didn't. She wouldn't have worked her entire life for this without it.

She began to play in earnest, but her fingers slipped as she barreled through a run. She let out a huff of annoyed air, causing a screech to ring through the cramped room. She lowered her flute and swore softly, then, once again, louder.

Her reason for playing was none of his damn business. It was good enough. *She* was good enough. That much, she'd been told, multiple times, by multiple teachers, all of whom were probably better than him.

She began to play again, and she stayed in the practice room as late as she could, until her fingers were cramping and a headache bloomed behind her temple from the bright fluorescents.

Once midnight finally rolled around, she gathered her things and stepped out into the empty hall. Her lip wobbled momentarily with exhaustion and pent-up emotion. Then, she turned and left the building, walking home alone.

A week later, Rowan stifled several yawns in her repertoire studies class. The professor shot her a dirty look as she left, which she ignored. She couldn't exactly help her yawning.

After she'd escaped the classroom, she headed out of the music building to the nearby on-campus coffee shop, where she was meeting Amelia for an early lunch. Her friend was bleary-eyed and already nursing a coffee when Rowan arrived.

"Hey," she croaked.

Rowan smiled. "What time did Sam leave last night?"

He'd come over again—another "canceled" jazz band practice. Rowan was beginning to suspect he was just skipping them to see Amelia. She didn't necessarily blame him and wasn't entirely surprised. Sam had struggled with intense burnout near the end of undergrad. Now, he worked a job totally unrelated to his degree. Maybe the jazz group was just a last-ditch effort to make all those years in the practice rooms worth it.

Amelia looked a little sheepish as she replied, "I don't know... Maybe two? I feel horrible about it since he has work today. But every time he went to leave, I whined like a stupid, needy baby."

Rowan patted Amelia on the shoulder. "You're in love and not used to being apart. It's okay. I'm going to order. I'll be right back."

Amelia nodded and Rowan got in line, drumming her fingers against her arm. When she arrived at the register, a girl with blue streaks in her hair asked for her order.

"A medium earl-gray latte, please," Rowan said absent-mindedly.

She nearly ordered the same thing every time she went to coffee shops. The tea lattes were less likely to give her headaches or make her hands shake. The girl smiled, and Rowan reluctantly handed over her card, draining more funds from her already-dwindling bank account. 'Starving artist' wasn't just an empty term.

Once she'd paid, she walked over to the counter to wait for her drink. Next to her, a boy with straw-blond hair and oval-shaped glasses tapped his fingers against the counter. Probably another music major, given the tapping.

He glanced at her and asked, "You're in the grad program, yeah?"

She looked at him and replied, "If you mean the music school, then yeah, I am."

He smiled broadly and offered a hand to shake. She gingerly took it as he said, "I'm Jake. I'm also in the grad program."

She nodded. "What do you play?"

He let go of her hand. "Flute."

"Ah," she said.

He looked at her quizzically. "Have you heard of me or something?"

She laughed softly. "Not really. I just mean, my friend overheard that you're working with Professor Lynch too."

Jake grabbed his coffee from the counter just as hers arrived as well. She took it, curling her hands around the warm cup. She moved to make her way back to Amelia, but Jake asked, "Do you like him? The professor?"

She glanced back and shrugged.

Jake chuckled. "Yeah, me too. Brilliant, but kind of an ass."

"Really?"

They both froze. Approaching from behind Jake was, naturally, Professor Lynch. She hadn't even seen him enter the coffee shop. Jake closed his eyes and swore softly before turning and saying, "Hi, Professor Lynch."

Professor Lynch barely looked at Jake before his gaze flicked to Rowan.

"I know what Quinn thinks of me now, but I'm curious what the shrug meant, Evans."

His tone was cool and even, as if he didn't really care. Rowan wasn't even sure why he was asking.

Jake opened his mouth, probably to protest or apologize, but Professor Lynch cut in. "Save it."

Jake's face turned beet-red as he shut his mouth. Rowan glanced over to where Amelia sat, gawking. She was just thinking about the best way to escape when Professor Lynch chuckled, grabbing his coffee order from the counter.

"See you in thirty minutes," he said and then strode out of the coffee shop.

"*Shit,*" she muttered as she watched him go.

"Indeed," Jake agreed. "Good luck trying to get through your lesson."

She glared at him. "At least I didn't call him an ass."

He held up his hands in defense. "I didn't know he was *right there.*"

She rolled her eyes and walked over to the table where Amelia sat, nearly collapsing in the plastic chair across from her as Amelia snorted. "Well, that was awkward."

Rowan took a calming sip of her latte and shook her head. "That was disastrous. He already doesn't like me, and now..." She groaned. "Now, this lesson is going to be torture."

"At least he didn't look like he wanted to murder you, like he did when he looked at Jake," Amelia consoled.

Rowan shook her head. "He told me I had no passion,

Ami. That watching me play was like watching some washed-out recording. And now this."

Amelia took a sip of her coffee, some sugary concoction topped with whipped cream and sprinkles. "I'm sorry, Row. You're good, no matter what Professor McHotty says."

Rowan glared at her. "Seriously?"

Amelia shrugged. "He looked mad, but like, sexy mad. And he was also kind of staring at you."

Rowan snorted. "What happened to 'off-limits?'"

"Oh, he definitely is, especially for you, being his student and all, but it's fun to daydream."

"You watch too many rom-coms."

Amelia glanced at her watch and chirped, "I know. I gotta go. Good luck with—"

"Don't say it."

"McHotty."

Rowan swatted at her. As she left, Amelia blew a kiss at Rowan before disappearing outside. Once she was gone, Rowan grabbed the earbuds from her backpack and fiddled with them before pushing them into her ears. She sat back, sipping her latte and trying to calm her thoughts. Around her, students chatted and laughed. A few had their heads buried in laptops or were simply staring blankly at the wall, already feeling burnout on week two of the semester.

Her allotted ten minutes passed much too quickly, and she sighed, taking a few last sips of her drink before tossing the empty cup in the trash and heading out the door. She walked the short distance back to the music building and arrived just in time in front of the closed practice room door. She sucked in a sharp pull of air then knocked.

"Come in," a voice, *his* voice, called.

She pushed open the door. Professor Lynch was seated at the piano bench, staring at the keys. He didn't even look up as he said, "Not so hard to knock, yes?"

She swallowed the urge to call him an ass and opted for nodding silently. He looked up at her and sighed.

"So," she began. "Um, what are we going to start with?"

He scrutinized her and then asked, "The piece you played last time, play it again."

She gleaned his unspoken words—*play it again but better.*

Nodding, she assembled her instrument. He played a few keys as she tuned it, making sure she was exactly on pitch. Then, he waited.

She lifted her flute to her mouth and tried to imagine Alex's beaming face. She tried, and failed, to conjure up an image of the face nearly identical to hers; the same freckles, the same blue eyes, the same full mouth, the sharp-tipped noise. It was as if she could recall those details, but putting them together was impossible. Hearing her sister's laugh was impossible too.

About a minute passed before she realized she had just been standing there, her flute pressed to her lips, Professor Lynch staring at her with a single brow raised.

"Any day now, Evans," he mused.

She swallowed and took a shaky breath, but Alex's absence was suddenly so glaring, she couldn't hear the music anymore, or even remember the correct fingerings. She lowered her instrument and shook her head, muttering, "I'm sorry. Just a moment. I—"

"Do you think this kind of behavior would be acceptable in a professional setting?" Professor Lynch asked, standing.

She lowered her gaze, refusing to look at him as he towered over her.

"No," she said softly.

"Then why are you assuming it is acceptable with me?"

"Jake was right."

The words were out of her mouth before she could stop them. Her eyes darted up to see Professor Lynch had gone still, a shadow over his face.

"Really?" he murmured. "And tell me, has your mediocrely gifted boyfriend achieved anything by insulting his teachers? Has he obtained a doctorate or played in a professional ensemble?"

"No," she muttered. "And he's not my boyfriend. I hardly know him."

"I don't give a shit about your personal life," Professor Lynch said coolly. "As long as it doesn't interfere with your performance. Which, just a moment ago, it seemed to be very much doing."

She raised her chin and looked him fully in the eyes as she said quietly, but not weakly, "I understand you hold the power here. I understand that you think you can treat me like crap because of that power. I can also see you are talented and brilliant at what you do, that you treat people poorly because you think you're better than them. And it's probably true that you're more gifted than me. It's definitely true that you've achieved more than I have. But I am not stupid, and all I ask is that you don't treat me like I am. Push me, berate me on matters of musical technique, tell me I am not doing enough, that I could do better, but do not treat me like I am some kind of punching bag for your arrogance."

Professor Lynch stared at her. His features flickered and his mouth parted slightly as his chest rose and fell, his hands clenching at his sides. She waited for the dismissal or warning, but instead, she watched his long, slender fingers unfurl. A muscle in his jaw flickered, and then he said, "There's some spark. Play now."

She lifted her flute to her mouth. As she played, she let the fire in her belly fuel the crescendos. When the ending neared and softer notes began to float through the room, she finally saw Alex's face. It was mostly just her eyes, bright and alive, crinkled at the sides as if she was smiling.

Rowan was breathless by the time she lowered her flute. Professor Lynch nodded once, curtly, and said, "Better."

She was reeling from the memory of Alex and the lingering anger at the man standing before her. All she wanted to do was run from the room, but the clock read that they had ten minutes left in the lesson, and she doubted he would let her go early.

Which was why she didn't move when he said, "I have a meeting in a different part of campus in twenty minutes. We're done for today. Next time, be prepared to work on more technical elements. We won't pick up a piece again until later in the term."

She stared at him blankly, and he cocked his head to the side. "Did you hear me, Evans?"

She unfroze and muttered an apology, quickly cleaning and then packing up her flute. She left the room without looking back, heading out of the music building. She had a two-hour break and knew she should spend it holed up in the practice room she'd reserved this morning, but she couldn't bring herself to do anything but head home, wanting to simply curl up on the couch for a little while and stare at nothing.

Her gaze was downcast as she approached the crosswalk that led her off campus and to the neighborhood where her apartment complex was. She heard a beep, and without even glancing up, she stepped off the sidewalk and onto the road.

Everything that followed happened slowly, as if she was moving through still water.

She saw the bus nearly in front of her first and felt her body seize up, preparing instinctually for the impact—for the bone crunching crash and her blood spilling her life out onto the pavement. But just as her mind flashed to her mother and Alex, an arm looped around her waist, pulling her flush against a hard body, tugging them both back to the sidewalk just in time. She stumbled, and so did the person behind her, but somehow, they managed to keep both of them from falling to the ground.

Someone said something from what felt like far off, and she blinked rapidly, her body beginning to shake. The arm was still around her middle, though the person quickly let go, and she was turned around by deft hands gripping her shoulders.

"What the hell, Evans?" Professor Lynch shouted in her face as he shook her shoulders. His face was flushed, pink tingeing the sharp peaks of his cheekbones, almost as if he was angry.

She opened her mouth, but nothing came out, her body

beginning to tremble. Something warm dripped from her nose, and she lifted her fingers to her face. They came back bloody.

"Evans?" Professor Lynch was still shaking her. "You're bleeding! What—"

"I get nosebleeds sometimes, when I'm really anxious or stressed," she muttered hollowly, hardly looking at him, instead staring at the crimson staining her fingers.

He was still holding her shoulders when a familiar voice exclaimed, "Row! Oh my God, what happened?"

He immediately released her as Amelia came into view. Amelia looked from Professor Lynch to Rowan, a questioning look in her eyes.

Professor Lynch clenched his jaw as he spoke. "Your friend just nearly walked in front of a bus."

Amelia's eyes widened, and she muttered, "Holy shit. Oh, fuck. I mean—crap. Sorry, professor."

Professor Lynch hardly acknowledged Amelia's outburst. Instead, he glared at Rowan and demanded, "Are you always that careless?"

Rowan finally found her voice again and replied, "I just didn't see it."

Professor Lynch closed his eyes briefly and breathed in through his nose, then opened his eyes again and pulled a pack of tissues from his bag, holding one out to her. She blinked as she saw it, and suddenly, she realized why he'd looked so familiar.

He was the man who'd sat with her nearly three years ago, when she'd cried on the anniversary of Alex's death. The person who'd said he loved sunsets and asked if stars were *her* sunsets. He was the very same man she'd thought about for months and months after. She wondered if he knew, if he even remembered.

She took the tissue and held it up to her bleeding nose.

"Thanks," she said, her voice muffled from behind the tissue. "And sorry."

"Just be more careful," he said gruffly before walking away.

Once he was out of earshot, Amelia turned to her and questioned, "What the hell just happened?"

Rowan adjusted her bag. "Nothing. I was just stupid and didn't look before crossing the street. He must've been just behind me and pulled me back before I became human pulp under that bus."

Amelia's hazel eyes were wide as saucers as she demanded, "Are you alright, though?"

Rowan nodded. "Besides the bloody nose, I'm fine."

"Thank God Professor Lynch was there," Amelia muttered, adding, "He seemed mad or something."

Rowan shrugged. "He's kind of intense in general. That might've just been his face."

Amelia huffed out a breath. "You looked at him funny when he gave you the tissue."

Rowan bit her cheek and nodded.

"I think I may have met him before."

Chapter 4
Moody Professors with Savior Complexes

Julian had been sure he'd been on his way to cleansing his mind of Rowan Evans. She could just be another student, as unremarkable and plainly human as every other one of his grads. There were no supernovas exploding around her. The idea he'd had of that girl from the steps was merely a figment of his imagination.

But then, she nearly walked into moving traffic.

He could still feel the soft warmth of her body beneath his hands as he strode away from her, listening to her speak in low tones to her friend.

The girl had a knack for attracting trouble, truthfully the least of all being the bus. Earlier, in the coffee shop, it had taken no small amount of self-control not to shove the boy away from her. The boy, Jake Quinn, had been accused of terrible things in the past, according to his record. But the situation had been neatly resolved with Daddy's money, and the girl who had accused him of assault was shut up and shoved away. Why Grandview had decided to admit him,

Julian had no idea. Probably some patriarchal bullshit about second chances.

But he had to play nice, according to Grandview, even if he had seen the glint in Jake's eye when he looked at Rowan.

Rowan, who he already felt intensely protective of. Rowan, who he could not move any closer to. Rowan, the fucking problem he could not fix. He wasn't sure he honestly even wanted to. Even if she left him in turmoil, at least he was thinking of her, despite the stark truth that he shouldn't be. It was a feat that was becoming all the more difficult.

It wasn't until he'd made it back to his office that he realized he had completely forgotten the meeting he was supposed to be attending right at that very moment. He ran a hand over his face and then leaned his forehead against the cool wall, a string of curses falling from his mouth.

He was in such deep, unending shit.

Amelia had a few free hours, so she joined Rowan at home, fretting over her nose and checking that she was otherwise alright. Once the blood had mostly dried and Amelia was sure she wasn't about to drop dead, she finally asked, "How do you know him?"

Rowan fidgeted, and Amelia's mouth dropped open.

"Wait... Please don't tell me you two hooked up at some point before you realized he was your teacher? Oh my God—"

"No, Ami. Just…no. That did not happen."

Amelia still seemed unconvinced, so Rowan clarified, "You know how I get on her—on Alex's anniversary."

Amelia's features softened into a mix of pity and understanding as she nodded.

"Well, on that day the third year of undergrad, I was kind of crying alone on the steps of the music building. Some guy asked if I was okay and gave me a tissue."

Amelia's brows shot up. "Sooo, you think Professor Lynch is the mysterious guy you've been pining after since like forever?"

"What? I never told you I was pining—"

Amelia chuckled, cutting her off. "You don't remember, do you?"

"What?" Rowan asked, uneasy.

Amelia grinned. "Christmas Eve of senior year, you came home with me, remember?"

Rowan nodded.

"And we got super drunk on spiced wine."

"Mhmm."

"And you told me about this gorgeous, dark-haired stranger. About how he was so mysterious and elusive and no guy would ever compare."

Rowan froze and muttered, "Oh God."

Amelia reached for her mug of tea and took a sip before she said, "I thought you'd been in a secret relationship or something."

Rowan shook her head. "Ugh, I am so stupid. Please forget all of this."

Amelia set her mug down and paused, looking like she

wanted to say something. Finally, she asked, "Do you still have feelings for him?"

"No, of course not," Rowan answered, a tad too quickly.

Amelia nodded and said slowly, "Good. Because that's *definitely* off-limits. I'm usually a fan of the forbidden love trope, but this...this might be too far, at least while you're his student."

"I know."

"But," Amelia shifted on the couch, "I will say one last thing about it. Professor McHotty looked *awfully* concerned about you earlier."

"Of course he was. I nearly got hit by a bus," Rowan interjected.

"I know, I know. There was just something...intense about how he was looking at you. I don't know."

Rowan shrugged, trying desperately to brush off Amelia's words.

"I told you," she said, "that's just his face."

Amelia gave her a long, searching look before standing and heading to the kitchen. She put her empty mug in the dishwasher and said, "I have to go. You?"

Rowan nodded. "Yeah, I have orchestra practice in, like, half an hour."

They both freshened up, Rowan changing into a non-bloody shirt, and then they headed out the door back towards campus. They parted ways at the entrance to the music building, and Rowan made her way to the lofty auditorium. She sat down gingerly in the principal spot, not wanting to draw too much attention to herself. Jake was the second chair, and to his left were two other flutists, both girls, one of whom also had a piccolo in front of her.

The conductor, who Rowan already knew to be Professor Savannah Lark, entered, and they all stood. She smiled at them, her graying hair pulled back into a severe bun, pine-green glasses sitting atop her nose.

"Welcome!" her raspy voice filled the room.

They all nodded in acknowledgment before she went into a rather drawn-out speech about the importance of orchestra, the prestige of the auditorium they sat in, and the talent she couldn't wait to see. After that, they warmed up, and then Professor Lark handed out a few additional packets of sheet music.

"Now," she said, "I'd like to hear just a few short sections from our soloists for this term. Just to feel out the air." She smiled. "Who would like to start?"

Rowan felt her hand lift of its own accord. Professor Lark's gaze landed on her, and she nodded.

"Go ahead. Rowan Evans, yes?"

"Yes, Professor," Rowan said, attempting to keep her heartbeats slow.

She raised her flute to her mouth, but just before she started, she saw a figure near the back of the auditorium. Well, a few figures, all professors, among them, Professor Lynch, who watched intently.

She took a breath and began.

She let the somber tone of the music take her to another place; to rainy days spent sitting in hard hospital chairs. A storm brewed outside... No, inside of her. The beeping of machines kept time, as did the shallow, labored breaths of her dying sister lying next to her. A crack of thunder boomed, and her sister sucked in a trembling breath.

"It's okay, Alex. Just some thunder," she said, and her sister smiled weakly, taking her hand.

The fast-moving end of the piece pushed those breaths in and out of her sister's body, and she was almost afraid that if she stopped playing, the breaths would stop coming.

Except it didn't matter.

Alex was dead.

She de-crescendo-ed on the last note and then lowered her flute. Wide eyes stared at her from all around, and Professor Lark began to clap slowly as the professors in the back of the room joined in for a moment too. Once the noise died down, Rowan sat back in her chair, and Professor Lark chuckled. "Well, who wants to follow that?"

It took a few moments, but a cellist volunteered. Once the small solos were played, they began to dive into a piece they'd perform at the end of the semester. Rowan was still reeling from the memories that had played in her mind during her solo. Jake kept glancing sidelong at her too, but she ignored him.

As soon as Professor Lark dismissed them, Rowan made a beeline for the door, only to nearly crash right into Professor Lynch.

"Are you always this careless?" he scoffed, steadying her for the second time that day, his hands gentle on her shoulders to keep her from tumbling over.

"Only when I know there are moody professors with savior complexes around."

The words came out before she could stop them, something

that seemed to happen a lot around him. Again, she expected to be reprimanded, but surprisingly, the corner of his mouth twitched, almost as if he thought what she'd said was funny.

Then, a gruff voice from behind her said, "My, my, Julian, you've got quite the handful there."

She turned to see who she assumed was another professor. He had red hair a shade lighter than hers, and he looked just slightly older than Professor Lynch.

She stared at the man for a moment before he chuckled. "Hello, Ms. Evans. That solo was quite impressive. I must say, I'm quite jealous that Julian has such a gifted student on his hands."

She gave him a tight smile as he extended a large hand.

"My name is Ethan, but I suppose Professor Petrarch works fine too, if that's more comfortable for you."

She shook his hand. "Nice to meet you, Professor."

Professor Petrarch let go, then glanced down at his expensive-looking watch. "I have a lesson in five minutes, but I hope to see more of you, Ms. Evans."

He patted Professor Lynch on the shoulder and then strode away, his dress shoes clicking on the linoleum floor.

"What instrument does he play?" she asked.

"Oboe."

"Do you know him well?"

"He's a friend. He helped me get the job."

She nodded, cleared her throat, and said, "Did you need something, Professor?"

"No."

"Okay..." She backed away a bit. "I'll be going then."

He stared at her before saying, "Be careful. I won't be around with my 'savior complex' every time you almost walk into moving traffic."

She winced a bit. "Sorry about that."

He shook his head just as someone called, "Hey, Rowan!"

She turned to see Jake emerging from the auditorium. When she looked back at Professor Lynch, his demeanor had instantly chilled.

"Next week," he said to her in parting.

She nodded at him as Jake reached her. As Professor Lynch walked away, she saw him clench his hands into fists at his sides. She didn't allow her thoughts to linger on that.

"Hey, uh, Rowan?"

She glanced at Jake as he spoke to her.

"Yeah?"

Jake shifted on his feet a little awkwardly as he asked, "Um, well, I was just wondering if you wanted to go to dinner sometime?"

She blinked. Was he actually asking her on a date? Already? They'd hardly just met.

"Oh," she managed. "Well, I..." She trailed off then cleared her throat and said, "You're super nice, Jake, but I'm not really interested in a relationship right now. Just trying to focus on music and all."

Jake looked crestfallen and almost a little irritated, but he just replied, "Okay, uh, yeah. It's cool. I mean, I get it."

She nodded, relieved. "Okay, um, no hard feelings, okay?"

He looked like maybe he had some, but he just said, "Sure, yeah."

She awkwardly tipped her head at him and then walked away. When she arrived in the wing holding the practice rooms, several students were milling about in the lounge area just outside the rooms.

She stared longingly at one of the empty couches but made a beeline to the room she'd reserved before she could change her mind. Professor Lynch had told her they'd work more on technical exercises next week, so she put aside playing any pieces for now.

Three hours later, she emerged, bleary-eyed and hungry. Before heading home, she slumped down on the couch she'd been eyeing earlier and closed her eyes briefly.

"Long day?"

She opened her eyes and started as she saw Professor Lynch lingering next to the small counter containing a coffee maker and a microwave.

"What are you doing here?" she questioned.

He gestured to the coffee maker. "Free caffeine."

She raised a brow. "That's for us broke college students, not cushy professors."

Professor Lynch chuckled and said dryly, "I hate to break it to you, but being a musician is always a little financially shaky. Besides, I'm new and a last-minute replacement. No tenure for me."

"Ah," she said. "So...essentially, you're a broke-ass college student like the rest of us?"

He shrugged. "Fortunately, I'm no longer a student."

She sighed as he filled a paper cup with stale coffee and

took a sip. Of course, he drank it black. Over the edge of the lid, he stated more than asked, "You rejected Quinn."

A small laugh escaped her. "It's very rude to eavesdrop."

He shook his head. "No, I stopped to tie my shoe. I may have lingered longer than necessary, but why would I miss a good show?"

"You think me awkwardly rejecting Jake Quinn is a show? Sad life," she said.

She didn't really know where this easy, almost teasing, conversation blooming between them was coming from, but she didn't necessarily hate it. It was better than the cold tension from last week.

Something dark and stormy flickered over Professor Lynch's face, but it was entirely fleeting. He walked over to the chair that faced the couch she was slumped on. He sat down and leaned back, sipping his coffee.

"Don't you have an office?" she asked.

He nodded but said nothing.

She bit the inside of her cheek and sighed. "Well, I should get home. I have ramen to eat and music to transpose."

Professor Lynch nodded again, silently, his expression doing nothing to betray what he was thinking.

"Okay... Uh, goodnight," she ventured.

She stood and walked towards the hall that led away from the lounge. But just before she left him behind completely, Professor Lynch called out, "Evans."

She turned and met his brown eyes. She swore she saw a small crack in his even demeanor as he ran a hand through his dark hair and said, "Be careful. Look before you cross the street and all."

She smiled slightly. "Will do."

Then, she left, leaving him to sip his coffee in the student's lounge.

As the days passed, two things became quite clear to Julian.

One, he could not work on his compositions—could not play, or write, or even think of them—without Rowan Evans popping into his head.

And two, that was going to be a major problem.

He needed to be able to think clearly when it came to music. Not that he ever really had—everything he'd ever done successfully had been driven by passion and heated whims. Which, he supposed, made sense at the moment.

He wanted her. He knew that. He probably *had* known that for a long time now. But under no circumstances would he be the one to do anything about it.

At first, the idea of her had simply been a soft, fleeting afternoon thought, a lapse in his mental slideshow because he'd become tired and needed another cup of coffee. But now, barely a few weeks into the semester, the thoughts had taken a turn. He was going down a road he did not want to go down. She didn't deserve to have her teacher thinking of her in *this* way. It was just the kind of behavior he had always found disgusting. God, this was all his fucking fault, and no one could ever, ever know. It was bad enough that Ethan suspected.

He had to snuff it out.

The heat.

The want.

The need and hope and desire...

But the fact of the matter was, she was becoming his jailor, and she had absolutely no idea.

The remainder of Rowan's week was fairly uneventful. Busy, but mundane. She just had practice and class, as well as finally beginning lessons for a couple of undergraduate students. Teaching got her the meager stipend that paid her rent and *sometimes* kept her fed.

When the time came for another lesson with Professor Lynch, she tried to quell the stupid pounding of her heart as she knocked on the closed door to the practice room.

"Come in," he called from inside.

She could already tell he was in a mood by the shortness of his tone. So much for the progress they had made last week. He hardly looked at her as she assembled her flute then ordered her to begin scales.

She obeyed, glancing at him as she played. And for a few short moments, the look shared between them was...

God, the way he stared at her sometimes. She felt as if she was on the edge of something both terrifying and exhilarating. There was the promise of a freefall in his eyes, and she was constantly fighting to resist it. Somehow, she had the feeling he was doing exactly the same.

But suddenly, he broke the spell as he barked out, "Stop."

Lowering her flute, she waited for him to correct whatever fault he'd found in her playing. He stood from his seat and declared, "You're sloppy today."

He didn't explain further, and she cocked her head. "How so?"

"Poor breath support. And Jesus, Evans, have you slept at all this past week? If you don't get adequate rest, it will affect your performance."

She shrugged. "Grad school. No time for sleep. But I'll try to focus on my breath more."

His jaw clenched, and he shook his head. "I thought you were serious about music."

She froze. "Of course I am."

"If you were, you'd take the time to maintain your body and mind."

"My *mind*?"

"Yes. You're distracted! Your eyes are bloodshot. I won't allow you to show up to lessons like this."

"I am not distracted!"

"Do not raise your voice around me!" he bellowed, his composure cracking.

She flared her nostrils. "That respect goes both ways."

"I am your teacher."

"And you're being an—"

"Do *not* say what I think you're going to."

"Asshole," she finished, breathing heavily.

His cheeks were tinged pink, his chest rising and falling quickly, his hands clenched at his sides.

"You dare?" he breathed, stepping closer to her.

She curled her mouth. "I do."

His gaze flicked downward, and her heart began to pound in her chest as it landed on her lips. The room felt too hot, and they were so close. But she wasn't done. She *wanted* to make him angry. She craved the rage in his eyes and the heat of his closeness.

When she moved next, it was hardly driven by reason. Only by pure instinct and some sort of wild urge which she could only interpret as an actual death wish on her part.

She tilted her head up and heard him suck in a sharp breath just before she pressed her mouth to his in a searing, angry kiss. Her hand rested on his chest, pressing up against the soft material of his gray sweater. For a moment, his hands remained clenched at his sides, but after a few seconds, she felt his fingers brushing against her hip, then tightening there. For the first few seconds of the kiss, his mouth remained still. She thought he might've been shocked. But then, he inhaled sharply against her lips and everything changed. His hand tightened further and his lips parted, then moved against hers in a rhythm that was far from clumsy. He knew how to kiss... But it was more than that.

So many of her first kisses had been awkward because she hadn't known her partner and their quirks or needs. This was *technically* just a kiss, but the way he teased the seam of her lower lip with his tongue and then sucked slightly there had a wave of heat rushing through her and then growing into an inferno. He kissed her like he was desperate for her, and it only intensified when she made a small noise, almost a whimper, and his lips against hers became near-bruising.

Some faraway part of her was screaming that this was inappropriate, that she should stop, that *he* should be stopping *her*. This should stop, this should stop, but...

He pulled back abruptly, staring at her with wild, dark eyes. Her hand was still resting on his chest, and she could feel his heart pounding beneath it.

"Step away," he breathed after a moment.

She held his gaze as she did so and waited for the dismissal, or perhaps angry words, or even threats. Instead, he just stared, his hands once again clenched tightly at his sides.

"Are you going to report this?" she finally asked.

Professor Lynch closed his eyes and laughed tightly. When he opened them again, he said, "As you have so clearly stated, I am the one holding the power in this room. If anything, I should be asking you if you'll report *me*, which you are within your full right to do, of course. In fact, I expect it."

"I won't," she said softly. "I kissed you."

He shook his head. "I didn't stop you either."

"I'm not a child," she hissed.

Professor Lynch glared at her. "You're my student."

A palpable tension lingered in the air between them for a few moments. Her flute was still in her hand, the one that hadn't been pressed to his chest. She swallowed and began to clean it then pack it away in the case.

Just before she went to open the door, Professor Lynch said quietly, "Evans."

She turned and found him looking at her with a mix of

wariness and what she thought might've been lingering desire.

"You can report me. You probably should. We shouldn't... I shouldn't teach you anymore."

"Why?" she asked in a voice barely above a whisper.

"Evans," he said, his tone almost exasperated. "You know why."

She shrugged and left him standing alone in the practice room.

Chapter 5
Why You Play

WHEN SHE GOT HOME HALF an hour later, Amelia was sitting on the couch, staring quizzically at a piece of sheet music. She looked up as Rowan entered, and her gaze immediately sharpened.

"Row," she said, her tone accusatory.

Rowan cleared her throat, setting down her bag. "What did I do?"

Amelia raised a brow. "You look...different."

"Different how?" she panned, lingering near the kitchen counter.

Amelia stood and walked closer to her, her gaze skirting over Rowan's face before she asked, "Were you with someone?"

Rowan choked out a laugh. "Why would you think that?"

"I know you, Row."

"That's hardly an explanation."

"Row. You were supposed to be at your weekly lesson with Professor Lynch, so—" Amelia's breath caught in her throat and her eyes grew wide. "Wait... Oh my God, did you and Professor Lynch—?"

"No! No, of course not. I..." She took a breath, trying desperately to think of an excuse. "It was just someone random. I'll probably never see him again."

"So you skipped your lesson?"

"Uh, yeah."

Amelia didn't look entirely convinced. "Won't Professor Lynch be angry with you for skipping?"

"Probably... Definitely," she amended. "I'll go to his office and apologize tomorrow."

It was a good excuse to see him again. Plus, they did need to talk, that was for sure.

Amelia sighed. "I don't envy you. He scares me."

Rowan nodded, her voice a little faint as she said, "Yeah."

Julian stared at the ceiling of his apartment, his back flat on the couch and an untouched glass of vodka and ice on the coffee table next to him. He had pulled out the liquor thinking he would need it to get through the night, but quickly, he realized that he neither should drink nor wanted to. He had a mountain of untouched work to get through before morning came. That would be a distraction enough.

He just needed to not—

Think.

He couldn't think about the heat flashing in her eyes, the

way she had stepped closer to him, how his heart had pounded in his chest the moment her feet lifted. He needed to stop replaying how his control had frayed in seconds and that he had been moments from showing her just how much he wanted her. God, the fucking smell of her, the soft curve of her hips, the way her breath caught as he forced himself to pull away.

Whether he wanted it or not, he knew today would replay in his mind for a long, long time, until he leashed himself and got this damn thing under control or until one of them gave in again. Because today, it had been both of them. He wished that didn't feel so satisfying, knowing she felt even a fraction of the same way.

But he couldn't go on thinking like this. It was now his responsibility to snuff it out. He should say something, get her away from him, but the idea of not seeing her regularly— well, he was a selfish man.

He let out a heavy sigh, sitting up and snatching up the glass of vodka. He stared at it, held it in his hand for a moment, before striding to the kitchen and dumping it out. But as soon as he was sitting at his desk, staring at the pile of work, he regretted it.

A slideshow of images and words from the past few weeks found their way to the forefront of his mind, and he clenched his hand into a tight fist.

"Do not treat me like I am some kind of punching bag for your arrogance."

"Only when I know there are moody professors with savior complexes around."

"You're being an asshole."

God, that *mouth*. She infuriated him, mostly just because of the way her words lit him up. She appeared soft at first, but Rowan Evans had a fire underneath her. That spark was going to be the death of him, or at least of his restraint.

He rubbed his temple. It was already nine and he was nowhere near finishing up for the night.

By the time he laid down in bed, it was well after midnight, and again, wide awake, he stared at the ceiling. His thoughts kept drifting to places he did not want them to, to the taste of her, to the way her hand had begun to curl in the material of his sweater, the slight flush of her cheeks when he had pulled back, the fiery mix of anger and heat still in her eyes.

Then, further... The sounds he might be able to wring from her. How his name would sound on her lips—because he would make her *scream* it. He would take such good care of her, make her come at least twice before he even let her touch him.

He didn't even realize how hard he was until he was already stroking himself. A shuddering gasp escaped his lips, the sound half regret and half relief that he was finally letting himself do this as he thought of her. He knew it was nothing close to the way it would feel if it were her hands on his cock, but it would have to do.

By the time he came, his ears ringing and the memory of her at the forefront of his mind, he already felt that heavy remorse. Fear, too, because he knew that something was forever changed between them after today, and he didn't know where that landed him.

Deep in trouble, he supposed.

That night, Rowan lay awake in bed. She often lost sleep when she was anxious or her mind was over-occupied, but Julian—Professor Lynch—was right. She was tired and worn down, and it was barely October. If she was going to make it through the next two years, she needed to find some balance.

Balance that did *not* include kissing professors. She knew he was right when he said she should report the incident, or at least request to be given a different teacher for her private lessons. But he was brilliant, even if he was arrogant. He was probably the best chance for her success as a musician if what had happened between them didn't destroy everything first.

She rolled over in bed, and her mind wandered to the way his lips had felt on hers, the way his heart had thudded beneath her palm as she rested it on his chest, the warm, cinnamony smell of him.

She needed to stop. She couldn't go on thinking like this, not if she wanted to make sure things could be kept professional.

Eventually, she drifted off. Hours later, when her alarm sounded and she jolted awake, she felt her cheeks warm.

Her dreams had been anything but innocent, filled with *him*. Even if she could control her imagination during waking hours, her unconscious mind had laid itself open to every thought she had tried to tamp down.

"Row!" Amelia called. "Get up!"

Rowan let out a disgruntled noise and dragged herself from her bed, which was just a mattress resting atop the cheaply carpeted floor. She couldn't currently afford a bed frame or a headboard.

She pulled off her oversized t-shirt and dressed quickly in dark jeans and a mossy green button-up. Amelia was in their shared bathroom when she ducked in.

"I'm done. Go ahead," Amelia said, shuffling past her as she dragged a brush through her dark hair.

"Thanks," Rowan muttered, lathering soap in her hands and quickly scrubbing at her face. Then, mechanically and half-asleep, she brushed her teeth and braided her hair. She didn't bother with makeup these days.

On their way out, Amelia grabbed two granola bars from the cabinet, slapping one into Rowan's hand once the front door was locked.

"Eat as we walk," she ordered, and Rowan unfurled the wrapper.

It was windy today, cooler than it had been up to this point in the year. Autumn was on its way, with the promise of cold days ahead. They both scarfed down the granola bars before they even crossed the road leading to campus. Rowan made a point to look both ways.

Once they'd reached the music building, they parted ways, Amelia attempting to smooth down her wind-blown hair. Rowan headed to the orchestra room, thankful to find that Professor Lynch was not lingering in the back today.

Professor Lark gave Rowan a warm smile as she took her seat while one of the other flutists gave Rowan a dirty look.

So her solo playing the other day *had* attracted more than just good attention.

Jake took a seat next to her, and she gave him an awkward half-smile.

"Hi," he began, but Professor Lark was already shouting at them to begin warmups.

The two-hour period passed slowly. Rowan spent the whole time thinking about her planned excursion to Professor Lynch's office at lunchtime. She supposed he might not be there—he had been out at the coffee shop during lunch the other day. She could have scheduled an actual office hour with him, but that felt odd to do for the conversation she was planning to have.

Not that it was anything big. She just wanted to clear things up, tell him that the other day had been a mistake on her part, that she was sorry, and that it wouldn't happen again.

By the end of orchestra practice, nervous butterflies flitted around in her stomach, and she felt slightly sick. She packed up her flute, ignoring Jake's not-so-covert staring, and then headed out. Professor Lynch's office wasn't far, and when she stopped in front of the door to it, she found the wood bare aside from a nameplate. Many of the other professors had photos or posters on their doors, but on his...nothing. She supposed it was because he was new.

Taking a deep breath, she rapped against the door a few times, half-hoping he wasn't there. But sure enough, she heard his deep voice call, "Come in!"

Curling one trembling hand around her instrument case handle, she opened the door.

His gaze immediately snapped to hers as she stepped into the office. There was a plate in front of him, the crumbs of what might have been a sandwich remaining, and a paper cup of black coffee between his hands. He straightened, having been lounging back in the office chair. It was odd to see him like this, relaxed. Or, at least, he had been.

He set the cup of coffee down on his desk, his mouth forming a thin line.

She shut the door behind her and took a deep breath before saying, "I need to talk to you."

"I see," he said evenly, his voice nearly void of emotion.

"I..." She fidgeted her fingers. "I wanted to say that I still want you to teach me. Because I think you're my best chance of success, and I'm not going to let a...mistake compromise that."

His eyes flashed, but he nodded slowly, though he still didn't say anything.

"Things will be professional from now on. I know they always should have been, but that was just a slight. A moment. It won't happen again."

He leaned back slightly in his chair, watching her.

"Okay, so...we're good?" she ventured.

He stood suddenly, stalking over to her, and she stiffened as he brushed past her to open the door.

"We're good," he said.

She took the open door as his dismissal.

"See you—"

But he'd already closed the door in her face.

Asshole.

She almost said the word aloud, but then she remembered where that had gotten them last time. She ran a hand over her face and then headed for the practice rooms.

The next Monday morning, Julian sat in the practice room, ten minutes before nine o'clock. For ten minutes, he was frozen like an idiot, his hands poised over the piano keys, unable to play. He felt trapped, somewhere between his wishes, her wishes, and his restraint. When she came into his office, he should have told her to leave and never come back. He should have denied her request and told her he had already spoken to someone. She needed to stay far, far away from him. And yet, he had been unable to do anything but stare at her as she said the kiss had been a mistake. It was, of course, but hearing it from her stung more than he wanted to admit.

A knock sounded on the door, jolting him out of his thoughts. He cleared his throat and called, "Come in."

His hands were still hovering about the keys when she entered, silently walking to the far side of the room and assembling her instrument. Without speaking to or even looking at her, he played a few notes so she could tune.

"Scales," he bit out, his back still mostly to her.

Finally, his fingers danced across the keys as she played along with him. God, playing with her felt like...

It was more than the heat and the want. It was that feeling that had caught in his chest on the steps of a different university all those years ago. It was much more dangerous than even the kiss they'd shared a few days prior. This was a thread that ran much deeper, the line that had always drawn him to her, even when he thought he would likely never see her again. It was the connection he could not bring himself to snap.

The litany of scales ended, and he finally forced himself to turn and look at her. It only made things worse, because as their eyes met, hers widened incrementally. A dusting of pink caressed her cheeks, and her lips parted. He couldn't help but track the movement. It was a reflex now, to notice these things.

"Are you going to participate in the end-of-term recital?" he finally forced himself to ask after a moment.

"I think so," she said, and he didn't fail to notice the slight rasp in her voice.

"What piece do you plan to play?" he asked stiffly.

"I don't know."

"You don't know?"

This, the rudeness and mockery, was all to keep her at bay. To keep distance, even if it meant she hated him and thought he was an ass. Even if it made him hate himself a little bit too. Of course, there was still a part of him that desperately wanted her to succeed. Because for all his turmoil, there was still the fact that she was an extraordinary musician. Perhaps that was his biggest problem in all of this. He wanted to see her soar like she deserved to—like she needed to—and he knew he could help push her to do that, but not if he let things unravel any more than they already had.

So, he took a slight step forward, ready to scold her again. A double-edged sword, ready to put up walls between them and push her toward her undoubtedly bright future in one fell swoop. But before he could speak, she cut in and said, "I know. I need to take this more seriously."

He narrowed his eyes thoughtfully. "You never gave me a good reason."

He watched as her grip on her flute tightened and her cheeks flushed again as she challenged boldly, "About what?"

"About why you play."

He needed to know, and perhaps, she needed to say it. He had a hunch it was part of what was holding her back still.

She looked away from him, her eyes trained on the wall. "It doesn't matter."

He didn't mean to, but he took another step closer to her, urging her to break as he said in a low voice, "It always matters. It matters most of all."

"Why do you play?" she dared, looking at him again and raising her brow.

It still surprised him sometimes, her boldness, and it took him a moment to tamp the equal feelings of irritation and maddening want that rose with that surprise. But as soon as he had, he replied as smoothly as possible, "My mother and father are both professional musicians. I grew up with music in my soul. There was never another route for me. Not necessarily because they wanted it for me, but because it was a part of me I could and will never separate myself from."

The words were true, laid bare before her. He supposed

he had relayed them to people before, but never quite so starkly.

She swallowed, and he followed the bob of her throat. "I see."

He waited for her to finally explain further, and she sighed heavily. A dimness entered her eyes, one he immediately hated. The fire in her was all but extinguished as she spoke.

"My twin sister. She played. We played together."

He creased his brow. "Played?"

Her gaze fell to the floor. "She's...dead. Cancer, when we were eighteen."

A roaring entered his mind. Eighteen—so achingly young to encounter so great a loss. It explained a lot about her.

"So," he began as gently as he could, "you play for her?"

Rowan squared her shoulders. "I play because she can't. Music was Alex's dream. It was our dream. I play for both of us."

He paused for a moment then said honestly, "I'm sorry."

"It's fine," she muttered, glancing at her feet.

"Death is never fine. It just is," he said quietly.

Death had torn his family apart once. Not in the same way, since the loss of his grandmother at her old age had been expected, but he still remembered the feeling of the world falling out from under his feet, so soon after his mother and father had split.

Rowan looked up at him, her eyes widening slightly. She seemed to be on the cusp of asking him something. Maybe she wanted to know who he had lost. But in the end, she shut her parted lips and squared her shoulders.

"We should continue," she said, the words closing a door between them, though her voice was still soft —understanding.

He nodded and stepped away from her, his fingers curling into fists at his sides. It was all he could do not to reach out and comfort her, but it was obvious she didn't want his touch. Not that he could give it to her anyway.

She avoided his gaze for the rest of the lesson.

Chapter 6
Never Change

Rowan essentially lived in the practice rooms for the next week and even through the weekend. In her lesson on Thursday, Professor Lynch had been a little less cool after their conversation on Monday, but he still scolded her for her lack of self-care and called her technique sloppy.

She was going to prove him wrong. She wouldn't be sloppy—she would be perfect. For herself, for him, and for Alex, she knew she could be exceptional.

The next Monday rolled around, and she knocked on the door to the practice room.

"Come in, Evans," she heard Professor Lynch say from the other side.

She opened the door to find he had dragged a chair in and had set it up in front of the piano bench where he was sitting. Warily, she set her bag and case down on the small table near the door. As soon as she began to open her instrument case, Professor Lynch said, "Not yet."

She pursed her lips and took a breath before turning.

"What are we doing today?" she ventured.

He stretched his long fingers. "I'm advising you. I realized we haven't had a conversation about your career goals yet, which is part of my job."

She nodded. "Okay. Uh, should I sit?"

He gave her a pointed look. "That is what I brought the chair in for."

"Right," she muttered, taking a seat.

He cocked his head at her and asked, "What do you want to do with music?"

She huffed out a laugh. "*That* is a loaded question."

"Why?"

She shrugged. "Most people are still a little unsure, even the other grad students."

"Okay," he said. "Then let's figure it out."

She glanced at her hands. "I think I want to play professionally. I don't think I'd be a good teacher."

"Why?" he asked, and she looked up.

"I don't know if I'd find much satisfaction or fulfillment from it. Playing is what I love. As much as I like hearing other people play, I don't think being a mentor would give me the same feeling."

Professor Lynch nodded. "That's understandable. And it's good that you've figured that out and are being honest with yourself about it. A lot of people revert to teaching because it can be a more stable profession, even if it's not what they really want to do."

"What about you? I mean, do you teach because you love it?" she asked boldly.

He leaned forward a little, and she tried to hide the catch

of her breath by clearing her throat as he said, "I do very few things without passion, Evans."

Her mind took that exact moment to remember the kiss between them, the way his hands had moved to her hips, just for a moment, before he'd broken away, almost as if he'd wanted it.

She swore his pupils were slightly larger as she said quietly, "I see." He sat back, a muscle in his jaw flickering. She cleared her throat again and asked, "Do you have any suggestions or insights on getting into the professional world?"

He sighed heavily. "I won't lie to you, it's not an easy profession. It requires a lot of work and nearly all your energy. You have a bachelor's degree from a very good music school, and you'll be getting your master's from an even better one. That will help. While you're here, try to make connections with other students and professors. Connections are your friends."

"Have you ever played in a professional symphony?" she asked.

He nodded. "Two, but neither for a very long time."

"And you compose?"

"I do. It was my first love as a musician."

"Is there anything you can't do?" she said lightly.

He shifted, cracking his fingers. "Don't be fooled into thinking I have it all. Music is my life, but, as with many people in positions like mine, that is all we have."

"And is it enough?" she dared.

He searched her gaze and replied, "Most of the time. You'll need to wager what's worth it and what isn't. That's something that's not talked about with music students enough."

"Do you mean, what we're willing to give up?"

He nodded. "Exactly, Evans."

She glanced at the clock on the wall behind him. Twenty more minutes. He followed her gaze and drawled, "Am I boring you?"

"No, you're distracting me."

The words fell out of her mouth before she could stop them. His features sharpened, and he said, "You shouldn't say things like that."

She looked away, toeing at a loose thread in the carpet with her foot.

"I'm aware. Sorry."

He sighed heavily and stood, his arm brushing her shoulder as he walked past her. She held a shiver back and asked, "Are we ending early?"

"I think that would be best. For now," he replied.

She gathered her things and opened the door, only turning to say, "Okay. Um... See you on Thursday."

He didn't reply, shutting the door in her face. But just before it closed, she caught sight of his left hand curled into a tight fist at his side.

On Wednesday afternoon, Julian entered his office to find

Ethan sprawled in his chair, smirking at him. Julian shut the door and said flatly, "What is it, Ethan?"

Truthfully, he had been avoiding his friend. It was easier than lying to his face. Besides, Ethan was annoyingly observant. He would know something was amiss. Maybe he already did, given the shit-eating grin he was wearing.

"Nothing," Ethan drawled. "Just checking in on my friend, seeing how you're adjusting to the job and its... requirements. The rules and all can be difficult, I know."

Julian clenched his jaw so tightly, his teeth hurt, but he forced himself to sound uncaring as he said, "I'm adjusting just fine."

Ethan nodded, sitting up straighter in the chair. "I'm sure. There's a reason they hired you, after all. But I'm curious to know how things are going with a certain grad student."

Julian sighed through his nose. There was no use playing dumb now. It would only make him look more suspicious.

"If you're referring to Rowan Evans, things are going fine. She's headstrong, often to her own detriment, but she is also just as talented as everyone thought she would be."

Ethan chuckled. "I picked up on that the other day—her fire. But I'm curious to know why she called you her savior."

"She nearly walked into moving traffic. I happened to be around to keep that from happening."

Ethan barked out a laugh. "My, my, savior indeed, Julian."

Julian made a low noise of acknowledgment then tried to steer the conversation away from *her*, asking, "And how's your group of students this semester?"

"Oh, no," Ethan said, shaking his head. "We are not done talking about you. Or her."

"Why do you give a shit?" Julian snapped, his patience fraying.

Ethan's eyes flashed. "There it is. I wondered how much I'd have to push to get you to show it."

Julian didn't trust himself to say anything for a moment. By the time he'd opened his mouth, Ethan had stood, striding towards him as he spoke.

"She obviously has a taste for more...mature men. Maybe I can help you out? Fulfill her desires while also drawing her attention away from you. It might make things easier if she's not looking at you like she wants you to fuck her all the time—"

Julian shoved Ethan against the wall as he snarled, "Enough."

Ethan only laughed, not looking at all perturbed by the fact that Julian had him pinned.

"Too far?" Ethan said, raising a single brow.

"She is a *student*," Julian snapped, releasing him. "Not one of your escapades."

"But one of yours, perhaps?"

Julian rolled his jaw. "Just stay away from her, Ethan."

Ethan only shrugged. "You know me." He chuckled under his breath. "I always want what I can't have."

He slipped out of the office before Julian could get in another word. It took no small amount of self-control not to run after him and punch his stupid face for his horrible words.

Ethan had always been a great friend. He was funny and

supportive and was an exceptional musician. But when it came to his treatment of women, Julian had always felt uncomfortable. He hadn't even realized it until after they were both out of Juilliard. He knew it was a stupid excuse, but by that point, he'd valued Ethan's friendship enough to look past it.

But this, what he suggested he wanted to do to Rowan...

It made Julian's vision flash red, and it had nothing to do with feeling any sense of ownership over her. It was just that she was fiery and alive and bright, and he had seen time and time again how Ethan had snuffed out the light in other girls. That could not happen to her. He wouldn't let it. It was bad enough to see the sadness settle over her when she talked about her sister.

If he put some further distance up between them, it would probably help. Because the fucked-up part of this was that Ethan probably didn't even really want her. Not for her. No, it was just as he said. He wanted what he couldn't have, and even more, he wanted to take what he thought Julian himself wanted. But she wasn't some toy on the playground. Her future was at stake here, and he would be damned if he let Ethan ruin that for her.

But he needed a second to breathe.

The email canceling their lesson tomorrow was composed and sent before he could overthink it. It was unprofessional to do so, but it would also be unprofessional to see her when he was feeling like this.

He'd get it under control—these *feelings*. He had to. By this point, he knew he would do anything for her, even if it meant letting go completely.

Rowan got an email from Professor Lynch on Wednesday evening informing her he had something come up and that he would have to miss their lesson. She scolded herself silently for feeling disappointed and went to campus early anyway to practice on her own. Besides attending classes and teaching her two undergrad students, she continued to live in the practice rooms, hardly stopping to eat or stretch. She knew she was probably pushing it, especially so early in the semester, with so much time left to go, but she couldn't help it.

She couldn't fail. And if she wasn't constantly working, she *was* failing.

When Monday rolled around again and she showed up for her lesson with Professor Lynch, his back was to her as he sat at the piano bench, staring at the keys.

"Apologies about Thursday," he said. "Something came up with a colleague. An... impromptu meeting."

"Everything okay?" she asked wearily.

She watched his shoulders shrug. "Nothing major, and nothing you need to worry about."

Then, he turned, and she saw a varying range of emotions play out on his face as he took her in. Shock, anger, maybe even a hint of hunger. She waited for him to say something. She knew she looked like shit.

Finally, he shook his head and muttered, "Evans, come on."

She raised a brow. "Something wrong?"

His nostrils flared as he bit out, "I think you are very aware how exhausted you look. You are not going to make it through your degree if you keep pushing yourself like this."

"Why do you care, just as long as I do what I'm supposed to and I get better?"

He stood, walking over to her and stopping only a foot or two away. "Because one, I am your advisor. I am here to make sure you succeed and thrive. And two, because you are not going to get better like this. There's a difference between working hard and working yourself to death."

"Everyone is tired," she deflected. "It's just how grad school is."

"Okay, well, have you ever considered that maybe you shouldn't care what 'everyone' is doing or thinking?"

She narrowed her eyes. "Of course. I don't care what people think. I do what I want, what makes me feel alive. It's why I kept playing even when I felt like dying."

His stern expression faltered, but only for a moment. "Good. Then stop taking every piece of criticism you're given and turning it in on yourself. You won't make it if you keep doing that. Whether it's burnout or a breakdown, you will fail if you keep going like this."

This time, she stepped closer and said sharply, "How very encouraging, Professor."

"I'm just being honest with you, Evans," he shot back.

"I will not fail," she hissed.

"Who are you doing this for?" he asked, tilting his head. "Because if it's for anyone but yourself—"

"Don't you dare insinuate I'm only doing this for my

sister or for you or for God knows who else!" she shouted. "I am *nothing* without music. Nothing."

She was breathing heavily, her slightly shaking hands splayed at her sides.

"Evans," Professor Lynch said carefully. "Take a breath. I didn't mean to insinuate anything."

"Didn't you?" she hissed.

He shook his head. "I'm sorry. Why don't you take the rest of the lesson and go cool down? Or eat something other than coffee."

She scoffed. "I don't need you to take care of me. I can continue."

He shut his eyes and muttered, "Evans, you are trying my patience."

"Good."

He opened his eyes, shaking his head. "Just go. Come back on Thursday with a little more sleep, and we'll work then."

"Fine," she said shortly, grabbing her things and storming to the door. But she paused, turning and adding, "This is how I am. Don't expect me to change just because you think it's the right way."

He ran a hand through his hair. "I would never ask you to change. I would never want that."

She hardly let the words register, hardly let them hit, before walking out the door.

Chapter 7
Jealous

THE NEXT TWO months flew by in a blur of classes, orchestra, practice, and tension-filled lessons. Rowan avoided Professor Lynch as much as she could outside of their private meeting times. She knew Amelia suspected something was up with her, and she often asked if Rowan needed to "talk." Rowan always pushed her friend off.

A week before the holiday break, Rowan stood in the cramped lesson room, Professor Lynch pacing around her.

"Are you ready?" he was asking her. For the end-of-term recital, that was.

She nodded, holding his gaze. "I am. As much as I can be."

"Not good enough, then." His words were short, his tone impatient. He was in even more of a mood than usual today.

She raised her chin slightly, her instrument poised in her hands. "No, I'm ready."

He took a step towards her.

"Prove it, Evans."

She cocked her head, moving closer to him as she challenged, "Haven't I already, Professor?"

"There is always more you can prove," he said, his tone edged.

They were so close now, they nearly shared breath. Her chin tilted up to meet his darkened gaze.

"And what exactly do you want me to prove?" she dared.

His gaze flicked to her throat, to her mouth, as her lips parted.

"Step away, Evans," he said quietly.

It was the same thing he'd said to her months ago, after she'd kissed him. Now, they were teetering that edge again. Maybe they had been this entire time. She didn't want to obey—a mix of a desire to rebel against his orders and a desire for him.

Because she still felt it all—the want and the simmering heat between them. She had only avoided succumbing to it again by telling herself he didn't want her, that she was just another student to him. It was a lie she fed herself each day— because she'd learned to read between the lines of his scathing words and demands. He was good at maintaining the ruse most of the time, so much so that she sometimes thought the lie to be true. But when she played and their eyes met, she saw it: the crack in his composure, just barely revealing what was beneath. But he would always hide it away quickly, his hands tightening at his sides.

She tilted her mouth to the side in a half-smile as she looked at him now. "You first," she retorted.

A muscle jumped in his jaw, and his gaze lingered heavily on her as he moved away.

"We're done for today," he said, a bit of roughness catching in his voice. "Be ready for Friday."

She nodded, packed up her flute, and left without a glance back at him. She immediately bolted for a bathroom and splashed cold water across her face.

After Rowan left, Julian lingered in the practice room, slumped on the piano bench. The invisible barrier he had built between them these last two months had come dangerously close to shattering today. It was always like this, teetering on the edge. He'd think he had everything under control, and then she would snap at him or play a particularly moving section of a piece. It was as if an invisible string connected them, drawing him closer to her near-constantly, unaware of the impossibilities. At least winter break was approaching. Maybe some separation would clear his head.

He jolted as he heard a crash from the hall outside. Quickly, he stood, rushing out to see one of his other students, Helen, sprawled on the floor, surrounded by papers she had seemingly dropped when she fell.

Approaching her, he extended a hand to help her up, just as he saw Rowan on the other side of the hall. Their gazes clashed as Helen took his hand and breathed, "Thank you."

"It's not a problem. Are you alright?" he asked her, though his gaze was still on Rowan.

"I'm fine," Helen half-giggled.

"You're sure?" he asked her distractedly.

Her smile didn't falter as she nodded. Quickly, he let go of her hand and began to help her gather her things. When he looked back at Rowan, she was already striding away—but not before he saw the flush on her cheeks and the look in her eyes. He wasn't quite sure what her expression meant, but he could guess.

He suddenly needed to know.

"Be careful," he muttered to Helen before striding down the hall.

He reached the door just before Rowan shut it. A wild urge had him pushing against it before she could, sweeping into the room after her. He was breathing a little heavily, though it had little to do with hurrying down the hall.

They stared at each other for a long, tense moment.

Finally, she said in a hoarse voice, "You should go."

"Why are you upset?" he asked, moving her way.

She shook her head. "I'm not."

"Yes, you are," he breathed, instinct taking over almost completely now.

She retreated a step, then another, until he practically had her backed against the far wall. But she didn't look afraid as he said in a low voice, "You saw me helping Helen, and you looked angry."

"Not true," she whispered, but he knew they could both hear the lie.

"Evans. Tell me why," he demanded, his hands bracing on the wall on either side of her head. He just wanted her to *say* it, despite the fact he could see it written plainly across her features.

She huffed out a breath. "Because it..." She shook her head. "Because it made me jealous."

"Jealous?" he murmured, his lashes lowering. "Why?"

"So many questions," she deflected, her gaze darting across his features.

He waited. He knew this was wrong, but he couldn't relent now, not until she admitted it to him.

"I was jealous because she giggled and looked at you with fuck-me eyes," she said boldly.

"Fuck-me eyes?" he repeated, a questioning lilt to his tone, even as a thrill ran through his entire body.

They were so close now, his nose nearly brushed hers. This near to her, memories of that kiss from months ago pushed to the forefront of his mind. She smelled the same, like roses with a hint of vanilla. Her eyes were wide, pupils large and dark as she held his gaze, but he couldn't help looking at her mouth as she moved her head to look more directly at him.

He needed to step away, but he felt powerless when it came to her, only able to move closer. The tips of their noses brushed, and he shuddered, the subtle touch doing much more to him than it should have.

In a last-ditch effort, his forehead fell against hers, and he closed his eyes as he murmured, "I'm trying to be good, Evans. God above, I have *been* trying."

"And if I don't want you to be good?"

He opened his eyes and pulled back slightly to look at her. "Don't say things like that."

"Or what?"

Warring emotions battled within him as he sucked in a short breath. "Or I might do something like this."

And then, he kissed her.

Her mouth was so soft against his, and for a moment, the kiss was sweet, chaste, even. That was, until she opened her mouth, and he couldn't help the groan that escaped him as he swept his tongue in, tasting her. She reached up one of her hands and twined it in his hair. He liked that more than he wanted to admit.

She braced her other hand on his chest, pushing against the material of his sweater, but he wanted more. He wanted her bare skin against his in whatever way he could get it.

His hands were still braced on either side of her, but he moved one of them to cradle her cheek, his thumb trailing down her jaw to her neck. He deepened the kiss, and she pressed herself against him, impossibly closer. The feel of her, nearly writhing in his hands, was almost too much. Another low noise dragged itself up from deep in his chest. He was about two seconds from making this much more inappropriate than it already was. He needed to pull away, but she was intoxicating, urging him on with those small, breathy sounds and her damn hands running over him.

She nipped at his bottom lip, and it was all he could do to pull back and hiss, *"Fuck."*

She stared at him, and she was still close enough that he could see the dilating of her pupils. He stepped back further, running a hand through his hair, mussed by her hands. For a moment, he just stared at the piano backed up against the wall, trying to take deep breaths.

He still wasn't quite sure what had overcome him. Something near-feral had tugged him into this room. It was awful, the way he had cornered her. He had to fix this, or at least mend whatever remained of professionalism between them. It wasn't fair to her not to do so, especially as Ethan's face flashed in his mind. His friend had backed up in the last eight weeks, and Julian could only guess it was because he had too.

When he finally looked back at her, he opened his mouth —to say what, he did not know—but she cut him off. "I know, I know. You're already regretting this."

"I wish I didn't have to," he said roughly, and he meant it.

She only nodded.

He lifted a hand, ghosting her cheek. She watched him, barely breathing, and then, he let it fall, turned, and left her alone in the practice room.

A few nights later, Rowan stood in front of her dirty bedroom mirror and frowned. She wore a simple black dress, her fiery hair pulled back from her face in an elegant bun, thanks to Amelia. Her friend had also darkened Rowan's eyes with eyeliner and mascara, making her look older somehow.

"What's with the face?" Amelia asked from behind her, walking into her room without knocking.

Rowan turned. "Is it too much?"

"What?"

She shrugged. "The makeup, the hair. I don't know. it doesn't feel like me."

Amelia grinned. "That's because tonight is for dressing up, for being someone you're normally not. Maybe you'll even catch the eye of that secret admirer you won't tell me about."

Rowan rolled her eyes, though a pit formed in her stomach. Professor Lynch was sure to be there tonight, and maybe that was mostly why she was nervous about looking like this. She didn't want him to think she was trying to impress anyone but herself tonight.

Amelia must've seen the warring emotions play out on her face, because she sighed and said, "You'll have to tell me eventually. Or I'll find out myself. I'm observant, you know."

Apparently, not observant enough, Rowan thought. Then, she straightened her shoulders and turned. "We should go. I don't want to be late."

Amelia nodded. "Agreed. And maybe when we get home, we can down a bottle of rosé together."

"So you can ply all my secrets out of me? No way," Rowan chided.

Amelia choked out a laugh just as someone knocked on the front door. Rowan furrowed her brow.

"Who is that?"

"Oh, shit, sorry," Amelia said. "I forgot to tell you: Sam quit the jazz group. Said everyone was too stuck-up for no good reason. But anyway, he's coming tonight. So...I guess no rosé later. Well, not with just you and me, at least."

Rowan raised a brow. "He quit?"

Amelia shushed her. "Not a word about it, okay? I think he feels a little guilty."

Rowan put her hands up, and Amelia pranced out of the

room to get the door. Rowan heard it open, and Samuel's deep voice filled the living room beyond.

"You in there, Row?" he called, and she poked her head out of her bedroom.

He grinned as he saw her, his long brown hair already mussed from the windy day. She walked over and gave him a quick hug. Mischief flickered in his light-green eyes as he said, "So...Ami tells me you have a secret lover."

Rowan glared at Amelia. "Seriously?"

"Hey, hey," Samuel said. "No need to get all upset about it. We're just curious, right, Ami?"

Amelia shrugged as Rowan continued to glare at her.

"What? We are," her friend said.

Rowan let out an exasperated sigh. "Okay, we need to go or we'll be late. And I need to warm up."

Amelia headed for the door and Rowan and Samuel followed. Amelia handed her a jacket before they stepped outside. Wind threatened at the hair coiled atop Rowan's head, and a light smattering of rain misted her face.

"Can't you drive us?" she said to Samuel.

He shook his head. "Parking will be a nightmare, and it's not free."

She rolled her eyes, and they soldiered on through the cold. By the time they reached the music building where the auditorium was, they were all shivering and damp. Rowan and Amelia made a beeline for the women's restroom to fix their hair and makeup while Samuel waited dutifully outside in the hall.

Amelia helped adjust Rowan's hair and dragged her thumbs under her eyes to get rid of the shadows of makeup there. Then, she stood back, hands on her hips, and said, "Alright. You look good as new."

"Thanks," Rowan muttered, and Amelia chuckled.

"Take a compliment for once, Row."

Rowan said nothing, waiting for Amelia to finish smoothing down her hair and applying a fresh coat of lipstick. She played piano, so she didn't need to worry about getting makeup on her instrument. Not that she was playing tonight anyway. Jazz ensemble's optional concert was next week, and Amelia was going home for the break before then. She was just here to support Rowan tonight, as was Samuel.

Once they returned to Samuel in the hall, he turned to Rowan and said, "Hey, Row, I just met your teacher."

Rowan froze up a little but quickly righted herself. "Oh, really?"

Samuel nodded. "Yeah, he seemed really cool. Brilliant too. You're lucky to have a teacher like that."

"He wasn't rude?" Amelia asked.

Samuel furrowed his brow. "No, not at all. He seemed pretty friendly to me."

"Really?" Amelia said. "Rowan always paints him to be such an ass."

"Because he is," Rowan muttered.

Amelia snorted and gave her a little shove. "Go get ready. You don't want to be late."

Samuel was looking at Rowan a little funny, so she decided it was indeed a good time to go. She hurried to the backstage area, instrument case in hand. When she got there, she was greeted by Jake, who turned from his spot where he'd been talking to Helen.

"Hey, Rowan!"

She gave a small smile. "Hi, Jake. You ready for tonight?"

He chuckled. "Definitely. Though I doubt *he* will think so."

She had a feeling she knew who *he* was. And, of course, as usual, *he* took that exact moment to appear.

"For once, Quinn, you appear to be correct in your assumptions," Professor Lynch drawled.

Jake turned and said warily, "Hi, Professor."

Professor Lynch met Rowan's eyes briefly before looking back at Jake and Helen. "You all need to warm up. The recital starts in ten minutes, and if I remember, Quinn, you're up first."

Jake's cheeks colored a bit, but he nodded. Professor Lynch led them to a small side room with a piano, and the three of them, along with a few others who'd tagged along, assembled their instruments. He played a few notes as they tuned. Once everyone was set, they filed out of the room.

Just before Rowan was about to leave, Professor Lynch called, "Evans."

She paused then turned.

He was dressed in a dark suit and his hair had been pulled back in a bun, a few of the loose waves framing his face. His eyes were intent as he looked at her, leaning forward on the piano bench, and she felt strangely as though she was looking at the calm before a storm.

"Yes?" she asked.

He cocked his head slightly. "You're ready?"

"Of course, I am."

"Remember what we talked about. About the reason you play. Keep that in mind tonight."

She lifted her chin. "Don't worry. I'll be sure to impress all your colleagues."

His eyes flashed, and he said quietly, "You are one of the most talented musicians in this program. Am I wrong to want others to see that?"

She leashed the flicker of emotion that sparked in her at the praise. "I suppose not. Especially when your job depends on it."

Then, she turned and left him sitting alone in the room.

Rowan's performance was near the end of the recital, and she waited in the back for nearly an hour. She re-tuned her instrument once more before Helen finished her piece, and then, it was time.

She stepped out onto the stage, the lights blinding. Her steps were even and light as she took her place on the still-warm chair. The audience waited with bated breath. She lifted her flute to her mouth, pausing for just a moment.

Be with me, sister, she thought.

And then, she began to play.

Every note, every run, every crescendo and quick move-ment of her fingers across the keys was for Alex. It was like an offering up to some pagan gods, an offering to everything she had been before her other half had left. She smelled her sister's floral perfume, smelled the antiseptic of the hospital she'd spent her last days in. She smelled the rain on the day Alex died. It thundered in her ears, driving out all sound, all light or semblance of the room around her.

In and out. Breath after breath. The uneven rise of a thin chest. The beeping of a machine. Her mother's breath catching in her throat as the beeping dragged out long. Too long. And the rising stopped. Her mother sobbed. And Rowan felt nothing, absolutely nothing, before the explosion. Before the red wave of violence filled her vision. Before her world fractured into *now* and *before*.

And then, she stopped living.

Because *she* stopped breathing.

The last crescendo of the piece soared, crested, and fell, until all that remained was a low, vibrating note.

Then, nothing.

Nothing, until the crowd exploded into clapping, thunderous in her ears. The stage lights fractured in her eyes, and she tried to see into the audience as she bowed. When she raised her head, all she was able to make out was Julian Lynch, standing in his seat, near the front with the other professors. He gave her a slight nod.

You did it, he seemed to say.

She turned and hurried off the stage.

"Deep End"—Holly Humberstone

"I know it won't work"—Gracie Abrams

"Salt"—RY X

"Only"—RY X

"hate to be lame"—Lizzy McAlpine, FINNEAS

"To Love Someone"—Benson Boone

"I miss you, I'm sorry"—Gracie Abrams

"Waiting Room"—Phoebe Bridgers

"The Last Time"—Taylor Swift, Gary Lightbody

Chapter 8
Christmas Lights & Margaritas

ONCE THE CONCERT WAS FINISHED, about half an hour after Rowan had performed, she filed onto the stage with the other musicians as they gave one final bow. Then, they headed backstage again. Jake caught her before she could make a beeline for the hall.

"Hey, Rowan, that was amazing," he said. "Like, really amazing."

She smiled. "Thanks, Jake. You did great too."

"A couple of us are going out for drinks. You want to come?" he asked earnestly.

She bit her lip. She *should* go, but that hole in her chest was currently a gaping wound—

"She'd love to go," Rowan heard Amelia say from behind her. "And so would we."

Rowan turned as Amelia hurtled for her, hugging her tight. "Row, that was amazing!" Amelia squealed.

"Great job, Row," Samuel said, patting her shoulder. "Who's this?"

She followed Samuel's eyes to where they landed on Jake. "This is Jake. He's a student of Professor Lynch's too."

"Ah, I see," Samuel said. "Nice to meet you, Jake. I'm Sam, Amelia's boyfriend."

He reached out a hand, and Jake shook it with a grin. "So, you guys want to go get a drink?" Jake asked.

Amelia sighed. "Please. I haven't gone out drinking since before term started."

Jake chuckled. "Same. This program is insane. Brilliant, but insane."

"Tell me about it," Amelia said.

Rowan shot Amelia a look, trying to convey that she just wanted to go home, but Amelia ignored her, probably on purpose. Instead, Amelia took her hand, dragging her out of the backstage area as Jake and Samuel talked. They were outside before Rowan knew it, walking to one of the nearby train stations, along with Helen and some other guy Rowan thought might be a cellist. She hadn't even seen Professor Lynch before leaving, and she wasn't sure why it disappointed her.

The cellist introduced himself as Daniel from Wisconsin, and Rowan shook his slightly sweaty hand. They boarded quickly, Amelia sat next to Rowan, and then they were off.

"God, it's freezing," Amelia said, though she was still grinning.

Jake laughed. "I'm used to it. Boston is the same, if not worse."

They got off a few minutes later, spilling onto a street that consisted of a strip of bars and restaurants and headed for a bar that Jake claimed had karaoke.

Samuel bought himself, Rowan, and Amelia two rounds of tequila shots, and they downed them quickly. As the alcohol took over, Rowan was suddenly glad she'd come with. She bought a strawberry margarita and drank it fast enough that Amelia said in her ear, "You good?"

"Why?" she shouted over the noise of the bar.

Another group of college kids had just piled into the bar, the dim lighting obscuring their faces in shadow. Christmas lights hung all around, their multicolored glow filling the space, along with a few mini-Christmas trees and bundles of mistletoe.

"You don't usually drink this fast unless you're trying to get drunk," Amelia said back.

Rowan gave her a look. "And what else would I be *trying* to do?"

Amelia snorted. "Fine, fine. Have your fun, just be careful. I'm going to go dance with Sam, but find me if you need anything," she said, pointing in the general direction of a raised platform where people were indeed dancing.

No karaoke was in sight, so it seemed that Jake had been mistaken. Thankfully.

Rowan ordered another strawberry margarita, and as she speedily sucked it down, the Christmas lights began to fracture. There had been lights like these strung around the hospital the Christmas right before Alex had died. Her sister had loved them. Rowan remembered wheeling her down to the main level so she could see the tree in the lobby...

She stood abruptly. It was too hot and too loud in here. Her heart sped up, and her hands began to shake as she pushed out the front door. Cold hair hit her square in the face, and she embraced the sting of it. She walked down the street, wrapping her arms around herself, the thin jacket she had on doing little to shield her from the wind. It began to rain, and her vision blurred the lights of the cars flashing by.

Gasping, she braced a hand against the brick wall beside her and doubled over. She could hardly tell if the rain was causing the wetness on her cheeks or if it was her tears.

"Evans?"

She lifted her head as an alarmed voice said her name. Through her blurred vision and the rain, she saw none other than Professor Lynch standing just outside what was probably a restaurant.

"I do not need you to save me again," she slurred out. "So please, go back to your fancy-pants professor dinner."

He furrowed his dark brows and took a step towards her, the rain running in rivulets down his face. "You're drunk," he stated.

"And what if I am?" she said, her hand still braced against the wall.

Professor Lynch was moving towards her carefully, as if she was a scared colt.

"Evans," he said her name again, softer this time.

She couldn't hold back the sob that clawed up from her throat. She didn't want him to hear it, but it was inevitable— her pained voice. She fell back on the wall and slid down to the cold, wet concrete of the sidewalk. He sank down with her and held out a hand.

"Go away," she choked out.

He didn't pull his hand back. "Evans. I am not leaving you drunk and alone in the rain at night. Not like this."

She stared at his hand, stared and stared at the steadiness of it. Stared at it as she thought about all that taking it meant. She didn't want help or pity. She never had—had refused the therapists and the pills and stuffed her pillow into her mouth so no one would hear her crying at night.

"Take my hand, Rowan," he said.

She didn't know if it was his use of her first name or the alcohol in her veins that broke down her final shields, but she took his hand, somehow warm even in the freezing rain. He hauled her up and she shuddered, another sob working its way up her throat.

She stumbled and he caught her in his arms. And then, somehow, she was curled against his chest, her head right above his heart. It took a moment, but his arms wrapped around her.

"Shh, Evans," he murmured. "It's alright."

"It's f-fine," she stammered.

"Yes, it's fine," he repeated softly, the lie quiet and apparent.

He pulled back. "You're shaking. You need to get out of the rain, or you'll get sick."

"My friends..." She trailed off.

"Your friends who let you wander off in the rain, alone and drunk?" he challenged.

"They were just having fun. I didn't want to bother them," she rasped, swaying a bit.

He eyed her. "Where are they?"

"Who?"

He narrowed his eyes. "Your friends. How many drinks did you have?"

"None of your damn business," she muttered, her words slurring again as she swayed.

The world flipped over on itself as her vision crossed and felt herself falling. Seemingly far off, she heard Professor Lynch swear and vaguely felt someone catch her before she could hit the ground. After that, everything faded out.

The rain had turned into snow by the time he figured out what the hell to do. Rowan's phone was dead, so he couldn't even attempt to contact the "friends" she had mentioned. Friends who apparently thought to let her drink this much and then wander out onto the streets alone. Friends, who seemed blissfully unaware of the turmoil eating at her.

He knew it was bad—had seen the pain of loss in her eyes on several occasions—but tonight, he finally understood the depth of it. Rowan Evans held herself together in pieces so the rest of the world might move by the same as it had before. Never disturbing anyone, never asking for help, just...surviving.

But now, she was still unconscious in his arms after nearly passing out face first onto the sidewalk. He had half a mind to take her to the emergency room, but she seemed to be breathing fine, just drunk and overworked. It wasn't the first time he'd seen a musician reach this point.

Eventually, when she didn't wake, he had taken her around the corner to his car, at least to get her out of the snow and ice. When she *still* remained unconscious, he finally texted Ethan and told him he would send him the amount he owed for the dinner he had barely touched.

He entirely wasn't sure what had propelled him to walk out into the rain. It was as unexplainable as most things when it came to Rowan Evans.

She muttered and twitched as he drove, and he tried not to feel like he was kidnapping her. Technically, this was against her conscious will, but he had absolutely no idea what else to do.

When they finally arrived at his apartment and he went to set her down on the couch, she whimpered softly, clinging to his wet shirt. He tightened his jaw, ignoring the feelings that stirred in him, and gently disentangled her, arranging her on the cushions with a blanket and heater. She was shivering, even in her sleep.

Then, after lighting a candle, he settled into the armchair to the side of the couch and waited.

Chapter 9
When Rain Turns to Snow

WHEN ROWAN AWOKE, she was still wearing her wet clothes but was wrapped in a heavy blanket. Heat was blowing in her face and the light was dim. It smelled like cinnamon and cloves.

She groaned, lifting her head to see Professor Lynch sitting in a worn maroon armchair, staring at a flickering candle on the coffee table in front of her. He turned to look at her as she winced against the pounding in her head.

"Where am I?" she croaked, glancing at the space heater in front of her then around the room. It was unfamiliar to her, yet it felt homey. Posters and pictures were scattered on the walls and lights were strung up around the edges of the room. No tree, though. Beyond lay a small kitchen, a mug of forgotten tea or coffee sitting on the counter. Black coffee, if she was a betting woman.

"My apartment," Professor Lynch said, gesturing around the general area.

"Um, why?" she managed to ask.

He narrowed his eyes. "You passed out on me. Your phone was dead, so I couldn't contact your 'friends.' I didn't really have a choice but to take you here. I wasn't about to leave you on the street."

"Oh," was all she could think to say.

He sighed, standing up and cracking his fingers. "'Oh' is right. Can you stand?"

She looked at him. "Are you kicking me out?"

He raised a brow. "I probably should. But you're still shaking because of your wet clothes."

She was, she realized.

"I don't have anything to change into," she muttered.

"You can borrow something of mine, and then we'll see about getting you home," he said simply.

She sat up a little, adjusting her dress so she didn't flash him. The couch beneath her was damp, and she bit her lip and said, "Sorry. About getting the couch wet."

He shrugged. "It's fine. It's old anyways."

She swung her legs around the edge, her feet landing on a plush carpet. As she stood, her vision swam. Professor Lynch was at her side immediately, grabbing her arm to steady her.

"All good?" he murmured.

She ignored the way the rumble of his voice spread down to her toes, curling them into the carpet. Taking a deep breath, she replied, "Fine."

He let go of her, and she followed him to a bathroom.

"I'll be right back with clothes," he said a bit awkwardly before he disappeared into what she assumed was his bedroom.

She waited, still shivering, her arms wrapped around

herself. The bathroom was clean and neatly organized, with little shelves that housed various self-care products. So, Professor Lynch was an organization junkie. She couldn't say it really surprised her.

A moment later, he returned, a bundle of clothes in his arms. She took them with a muttered, "Thanks," and then shut the door to the bathroom so she could change.

First, she used the bathroom—she'd needed to pee since she'd woken up. Then, she examined the clothes he'd given her: a t-shirt, way too big for her, and sweatpants that she would probably have to roll up at the ankles. Plus, a pair of socks and boxer shorts.

Her underwear *was* wet, but the thought of wearing his was...interesting, to say the least. It was thoughtful that he'd even remembered to include them.

She sighed and dressed quickly, ignoring the scent of cinnamon that clung to the clothes. The smell of him was explained by that scented candle in the living room. He must burn them all the time.

She quickly splashed water on her face, trying to clear away some of the smeared makeup. Her hair was still half-up and tangled. She let it fall and combed her fingers through it in an attempt to tame it. Eventually, she managed to pull it back into a single braid.

Then, she took a deep breath, gathered her wet clothes, and stepped out back into the living room. He was sitting in that armchair again, his fingers tapping on the side of it. Just musician things. She didn't doubt that he was always thinking about composition and rhythm.

He looked up as she walked towards him. Seeing her wet

clothes bundled in her arms, he stood, muttering, "I'll get you a bag for those."

He swept past her and into the kitchen, reappearing with a plastic grocery bag. She dumped her wet clothes into it and fidgeted a bit.

"What time is it?" she finally asked.

"Almost two in the morning," he replied, and she could hear the tinge of exhaustion in his tone. She glanced outside to see that the freezing rain from earlier had turned into a heavy snowfall. She bit her lip.

"Is it... How far away are we from campus?"

"About twenty minutes."

She took a breath. "If it's not safe to drive because of the snow..." She trailed off.

Understanding dawned on his face, and he glanced outside too, muttering, "Of course."

She wasn't really sure what that meant but said, "Just since the plows probably haven't been out yet. I can sleep on the couch."

He took a breath, his chest expanding in the t-shirt he wore. "Alright, fine."

"And can I have my phone? Amelia, my roommate, is probably freaking out."

He blinked. "Of course. I put it on a charger an hour ago, so it should turn on now."

"Thanks," she said, the word rasping from her throat.

She tracked his movements as he walked over to the kitchen again and retrieved her phone. As soon as she turned it on, the screen lit up with over twenty notifications, mostly from Amelia, some from Samuel.

Rowan, where are you??

Row, please pick up!!!

HOLY FUCK ARE YOU ALIVE??!?

ROWAN EVANS PICK UP YOUR DAMN PHONE NOW!!

She quickly texted Amelia: *I'm alive. I'm sorry.*

A call from Amelia almost immediately popped up on her screen.

"You should probably take that," Professor Lynch said quietly.

She pursed her lips and nodded, answering the call and lifting the phone to her ear.

"Holy crap, Rowan, where are you?" Amelia's voice shouted at her.

"Keep your voice down, Ami. I have a massive headache," she answered.

"Where are you?" Amelia's voice was flat, but Rowan could hear the worry tingeing every word.

"I'm safe. I'm fine," she replied.

"Row, one minute you were there at the bar, and then I looked, and you were just *gone*. I thought someone had taken you or something. And then you weren't picking up your phone, and I swear to God, I thought you might be fucking dead. It's snowing like crazy now and..." Amelia's voice broke off.

"I'm sorry, Ami. Seriously, this is all my fault. But I'm okay. I just went out for some air and then..." She took a breath, thinking about how to say this. "I... Well, I walked a block or two, and Professor Lynch found me in the rain just before I fainted. My phone was dead at that point, so he didn't really have any choice but to, uh, take me to his apartment. I just woke up, like, twenty minutes ago."

"You're at Professor Lynch's fucking apartment?" Amelia's voice rose.

Rowan's eyes flicked to where he was sitting, watching her intently. She looked away as she said, "Yeah. I'll be home in the morning. It's not safe to drive because of the snow."

"Uh-huh."

"Ami," Rowan hissed.

"You're having a sleepover with your teacher, then?"

"Not a..." She huffed out a breath. "I am just staying on the couch until the morning, and then I will be back. Goodnight."

"You better not disappear again."

"I won't. Goodnight, Ami."

"Tell him I say hi," Amelia said, and even over the phone, Rowan could hear the gleam of mischief in her tone.

"Goodnight," she said and cut the call.

She sighed, and Professor Lynch asked, "Everything alright?"

"Yeah. She was pretty freaked out, but, yeah. We're good."

He stood from the armchair and glanced at the couch, his brows furrowed.

"What?" she asked.

"It's probably still wet."

Her mind went completely blank for a moment, but she somehow managed to say, "Do you have a guest room? Or like a blow-up mattress or something?"

Slowly, he shook his head.

"You don't entertain people often here, do you?"

"I don't 'entertain' people much at all," he said dryly.

She thinned her lips and said, "Well, I guess I can sleep on the floor."

He shook his head. "No."

She raised a brow. "Then what exactly are you proposing?"

"I'll sleep on the floor. You can have the bed."

Her brows rose before she could stop them. Sleep in the bed? *His* bed, where he slept every night?

"We need to sleep," he said. "Or at least, I do. I have work to do tomorrow."

She opened her mouth then closed it, still unsure of what to say.

"Evans. It's just a bed. Go to sleep," he clipped out.

Her brain finally decided to work, and she said, "The floor isn't very comfortable."

"I'll manage."

Then, without waiting for her to decide, he walked towards what she assumed was the bedroom and flicked on a lamp. After a moment's pause, she followed him inside to find another neat but cozy room. A salt lamp sat on the table on the other side of the bed. He glanced at it and asked, "On or off?"

"On," she replied instantly.

Alex had loved salt lamps—and candles and Christmas lights.

There was a bookshelf on one end of the room, and a music stand sat next to the window on the other end. A small desk was opposite to the bed, covered in neat stacks of papers

—sheet music, she realized, with compositions drawn by hand. He *had* said he composed.

He pulled back the comforter and fluffed the pillows. He was... fussing, she realized.

"There. Is that fine?" he asked, completely serious as he glanced between her and the bed.

She nodded silently, walking over to the bed. He stepped aside and she sat down, pulling the sheets back. Christ, they smelled like him. Clean, but like him. She tried not to shudder as she lay down. He leaned over and turned off the lamp on the bedside table nearest to her.

"Goodnight, Evans," he said.

She nodded into the pillows and whispered, "Goodnight."

He stared at her for a moment in the dark before leaving the room. She closed her eyes, her head still aching, and fell asleep.

Chapter 10
Just for Tonight

"Be with me, sister."

"Always."

"Promise?"

"Forever."

"Even when I'm dead and gone?"

"Even then."

Rowan was crying as she woke up, heaving sobs that she could not control. She had not dreamt of Alex for three years. She had blocked her sister so thoroughly from her mind that it never happened. But tonight, with the performance, then the rain, and the salt lamp beside her...

Footsteps sounded, and the door flung open.

"Rowan?"

Professor Lynch's voice was alarmed as it cut through the still, heavy air around her. She could only sob, "Fuck, fuck, *fuck*."

He was at her side in seconds, kneeling at the side of the bed.

"What's wrong?" he demanded. "Are you hurt? Does something—"

"No," she cut him off. "I just..." She sucked in a shaky breath. "I'm sorry. I shouldn't keep doing this. It's just... You sometimes remind me of her."

His tense features fell slightly. "Your sister."

She nodded. "Only parts of you. The passion for music, the lights you have in here... She loved light like this. 'Soft light,' she called it."

"Anything else?" he asked hoarsely.

She looked down at her hands and said in a voice barely above a whisper, "I love my friends, but there was only ever one person who made me...feel. Not many people get me, the way I think and see the world. But Alex did. For a long time, she might have been the only one."

"And you think I do?"

She forced herself to look at him as she said, "Stars are my sunsets. I see her in them. Even when the light has gone, they're like little specks of hope in the sky."

His jaw tightened, and she shrugged. "I think you remember. And you probably don't care, but I want you to know that I felt seen that day in a way I hadn't in a long, long time. It pulled me back from a ledge I'd been nearing for a while."

He wasn't looking at her as he said roughly, "I care."

She took a shuddering breath and dared to say, "I don't want to sleep alone."

He looked at her sharply, but she held his hard gaze.

"Just sleep," she whispered after a moment.

He closed his eyes, the lids fluttering shut like delicate bird's wings. When he opened them, onyx irises met hers, and he nodded.

She hardly breathed as he walked over to the other side of the bed and climbed in. At first, he was stiff, lying near the edge of the mattress. But after a moment, he moved closer.

"Just for tonight," he whispered as he pulled his arms around her.

"I know," she replied, laying her head on his chest.

His heartbeat was steady and thundering against her ear. Her palm rested against the hard contours of his chest, and she traced her fingers over the lines of muscle. She both felt and heard him suck in a breath as he murmured, "Careful."

She continued, letting her fingers ghost his collarbone and then the curve of his neck, listening in fascination as his heartbeat began to speed up. As her hand brushed against his jawline, his hand caught hers.

"Evans," he whispered. "We can't."

"Technically," she breathed, "this is already very inappropriate."

His hands tightened around hers, and he took a long breath.

"Just for tonight," she said softly, raising her head to look at him.

His face was shadowed, lit only by the salt lamp and the

whisper of dawn outside. She didn't break his gaze as she slid her hand—their hands—along his cheek. He let his hand fall away as she traced his cheekbones down to his lips. Her thumb ghosted over them, and she felt warm, quick breath against her fingers. He swallowed as she adjusted so their noses were brushing.

She waited. She wanted him to make the final call. They'd crossed this line before, but not quite like this. Not in this raw, vulnerable way. Not in a bed, not in his home. Not completely alone.

He closed his eyes, and she watched as he tried to leash himself and do what he thought was right. When he opened them, she saw the decision already written across his features. His lips brushed hers, gently at first, and she shuddered.

"You drive me mad, Evans," he murmured against her mouth. "You have no idea."

"I think I do," she said. Then, she leaned in and whispered in his ear, "You are everything I have been trying not to feel all these years."

His eyes were wide as she pulled back to look at him.

"I can't give anything to you," he said hoarsely.

She nodded. "I know."

There was a moment of silence, charged, heavy silence, loaded with all the words they couldn't say. And then, his expression shifted into something hungry and carnal. She curled her hand in the material of his t-shirt and sucked in a breath just before he kissed her.

It wasn't soft or sweet, but it wasn't hurried either. Emotions surged through her, red-hot and burning right to her core. His hands trailed up her back, one of them gently tugging her hair free from the braid. He threaded his fingers through the damp strands, and she shifted into his lap and...

He groaned as she ground against him. A fire was beginning to consume her, desire spiking along every inch of her body as she felt him hard beneath her. She moved her hips again, and he hissed, "Rowan."

"Yes?" she breathed.

"You know..." He let out a ragged sound that tore through every last boundary she had assembled between them these past months. "You know what you're doing."

"Maybe I do," she said, dipping her head and letting her teeth graze his neck before flicking her tongue over his skin.

"Fucking hell," he said as she kissed her way up his jaw.

Her peaked nipples brushed up his chest, aching and sensitive. His hand slipped just under the oversized shirt, thumbs brushing against her bare stomach.

"We need to stop," he muttered against her mouth as she kissed him again.

She didn't respond this time; she only moved her hips against him again. The hand in her hair gently tilted her head back, exposing her neck to him. She felt his lips move down her jaw, and then he sucked gently on the sensitive skin just above her shoulder.

And then, he moved lower, his mouth grazing her collarbone. She let out a soft moan, and his hand on her bare hip tightened. Her back arched as his mouth moved even lower, brushing against the fabric covering her breasts.

She moved to pull the shirt off, and he paused her, looking at her with something cautious in his gaze.

"You do that and..." He swallowed. "I really don't know if I'll be able to stop."

"I don't want you to," she said.

She pulled the shirt off so her torso was bare before him. She heard him suck in a breath as she tossed the shirt to the ground.

His hands slid up her sides, leaving goosebumps in their wake. His eyes were wide in the near-dark as he murmured, "You are so beautiful."

"Your turn," she dared, not letting his words wash over her fully.

He didn't protest this time, hardly breaking her gaze as he dragged off his t-shirt, revealing a thin, muscled chest and abdomen. She ran a hand over his bare skin, and he shuddered. She leaned in and nipped at his lip, just as she had a day ago in the practice room, but this time, he did not push her away. Instead, he made a low sound and then flipped her over expertly so she was beneath him. Instantly, her legs curled around his narrow hips. He began to move, and she matched him, cursing the fabric of the sweatpants between them.

He dipped his head, and she gasped as his mouth closed around one of her nipples, sucking deeply. He let his teeth catch a little, and she couldn't help the loud moan that escaped her. But the sound only seemed to drive him further, his hand drifting down.

He looked up at her, pausing just before he dipped his hand under the rolled waistband of the sweatpants she wore.

"You're sure?" he rasped.

"Don't stop," was all she could manage to say.

His hands slipped clean under both the sweatpants and the boxers, and he swore quietly as his fingers brushed against her core.

"You're already so wet," he murmured.

She felt her cheeks color a bit at the crassness of his words, but nevertheless, she moved her hips, grinding against his fingers. He sucked in a breath as he teased her, sliding his fingers up and down her slit.

She made a low, whining noise, and he chuckled softly, the sound deliciously dark.

"Who knew you'd be so needy?" he said.

She only nipped at his lip again. He kissed her deeply as he brushed his fingers against her clit, and her back arched again. He swore again and slipped his fingers inside her. As he curled them, a low moan escaped her.

"That's it," he murmured as she began to move. "Ride my fingers, Evans."

"I—can't," she gasped, the sensations blasting through her, each touch a wildfire to her body and soul.

"Yes, you can," he said steadily, moving his thumb to just the right spot.

She shattered, a crescendo, up, up, and up...

She soared, and then the wave crested, and she fell in a freefall, crashing into pieces back onto the bed.

He had watched her through the entirety of it, and somewhere in her mind, she knew she should probably feel self-conscious. But she couldn't, not with the heavy intensity in his eyes and the gentle brush of his fingers against her thigh.

"We can... We should probably stop here," he said quietly.

She stared at him, a hole forming itself again in her chest as she realized everything she'd be losing once she left, the way things would have to fall back into their proper places. So she whispered, "No."

"Evans."

"This is all we get. This is all. I want...I want to remember something more."

His breath caught at her words, and she almost thought he was going to say no and make her leave. But then, he leaned down and caught her lips with his. Momentarily, he pulled back and she half-prepared herself for him to stop entirely. But instead, he lifted his fingers to his mouth, still covered in her, and licked them clean, his eyes dark and intent on her still. She swallowed hard, her cheeks aflame with desire and the smallest hint of self-consciousness at what he'd just done. After, he laced his fingers with hers, their interlocked hands pressed to either side of her. He kissed her again and she could taste herself on his lips, but she didn't find herself put off by it. If anything, the whole thing had just turned her on even more.

He broke the kiss for just a moment to look at her and whisper, "You're sure?"

"I'm positive," she said.

He let go of her hands and reached over her to the bedside table. When she heard the crinkle of a wrapper and realized what he was doing, her cheeks warmed. She hadn't even thought of condoms, not through the hazy blur of the night and the fiery touches. She supposed it was good that one of them was responsible.

He smiled slightly at her, at the expression on her face, and asked, "You're not a virgin, are you?"

"No. But would you care?" she dared.

He shook his head slightly, leaning back down over her, sliding down their remaining clothes as he said, "No. I would just be gentler."

Her lips parted in...surprise? She wasn't even quite sure. But then, he was kissing her again, his cock at her entrance, and every coherent thought flew out of her head.

He pushed into her slowly, giving her time to adjust to his size. A soft moan escaped both of them at the same time, and his hands gripped hers. His head fell to the juncture of her neck and shoulder as he began to move, slowly at first.

When he looked at her again, there was a wild darkness in his eyes that probably should have scared her, but it only made her want him more.

"I'm about to not be so gentle," he rasped.

She held his gaze. "Don't be."

It was all the permission he needed. Both their movements became near frenzied, their shared breaths ragged. Her hands ended up pinned above her, and she let out a loud moan, the sound only encouraging him.

She had never done this—fucked quite like this. It was a release of months' worth of tension, and yet, it didn't feel simply physical. There was the vein of something else beneath the need and the urgency, a feeling that made her both want to run and never let go of him.

He kissed her again, and she pulled her wrists from his grasp, needing to touch him. He didn't stop her, a low groan escaping him as she threaded her fingers through his hair. With one hand, he gripped her thigh, deepening the angle. With the other, he fisted in the sheets next to her as his hips snapped against hers.

"Please," she gasped.

He let out a ragged sound, his fingers tightening on her leg, but never hurting. When his hand drifted further up again, to where their bodies were joined, she gasped, "I already..."

He brushed his fingers against her swollen clit. "And?"

Words escaped her after that. He kept a steady rhythm, even as he touched her, even as he began to lose control. It was as if her pleasure was all that mattered here. The thought nearly sent her to the edge all on its own. But what really did it in the end was his voice.

"Are you ready?" he rasped.

She could barely speak, but managed, "I want to come together."

"I know... Just tell me—"

She was already free falling by that point. He made a sound, some garbled mix of curses and praises and then, with one last thrust, his body seized up, a sound that she swore was her name escaping him.

He slowed, finally stilling. Their heavy breaths were the only sound in the still, quiet air of the bedroom. Outside, dawn was creeping further up the horizon, staining it a pale pink. He pulled out, and a small sound escaped her. He kissed her brow, and her heart broke a little at the simple gesture of affection. For a moment, they just laid there, his head on the pillow just below her shoulder, one of his hands in hers. She hadn't even realized he'd taken it.

"I should get you home soon," he eventually murmured.

"I know," she said. "I know."

He raised his head. "I'll be right back. Bathroom."

She nodded, her eyes fluttering shut as he rolled off the bed. She heard his soft footsteps, and then the bathroom door clicked shut. A few minutes later, she heard him come back. Her eyes were still shut.

"Rowan."

There was something in his voice that made her open her eyes right away. She turned her head to look at him, standing in boxer shorts and a t-shirt he must have grabbed on his way out. His hands were slack at his sides, his face tight.

"What?" she asked, sitting up slightly.

He pursed his lips and then sighed and said, "The condom broke."

For a moment, she just stared at him. And then, in between that moment and the next, she began to laugh. He looked at her incredulously as she giggled.

"Evans, this is not a joke," he said crossly.

She took a deep breath, trying to calm herself. Finally, she managed to say, "I know. Sorry, it's just kind of hilarious. I sleep with my professor and—" Her own laugh cut her off.

"Do you need the morning-after pill?" he asked, his voice flat as she continued to giggle.

She managed to calm herself enough to say, with the shake of her head, "No. It's fine. I take birth control."

Relief visibly washed over him as his shoulders loosened. "Oh," he said. "Okay, good."

She sighed through her nose, dragging a hand across her face as the last of the giggles escaped her.

"It's still not funny," he muttered, walking over to the other side of the room where a small dresser sat.

"It's kind of funny," she said.

He glared at her, though his expression became slightly glazed as the sheet fell and revealed her bare torso. He cleared his throat and turned, opening the drawer and pulling out a fresh set of clothes. He tossed them at her, and she caught them as she stood, feeling slightly self-conscious.

He watched her intently and then said, "I meant what I said. You're beautiful."

She looked away and shrugged. "Doesn't matter, does it?"

She glanced back at him to see his jaw clench.

"I suppose not," he said after a moment, though she had the distinct feeling the words were forced.

She walked lightly over to the bathroom. Once she was inside with the door shut, she stared at herself in the mirror for a moment, a little disbelieving.

She had just fucked Julian Lynch.

Her teacher.

It was like something out of one of the movies Amelia watched. It was comical, hilarious even. Preposterous. Stupid. Forbidden.

She sighed and used the bathroom and dressed in the fresh clothes, rolling the sweatpants up at the ankles again. Then, she braided back her hair, rinsed her mouth with water, and opened the door.

He was already dressed and waiting in the living room. Waiting to take her home, she supposed. It was nearly six a.m. The plows had probably been out by now. There were no more excuses to stay here.

Silently, she walked over to the couch and shoved on her ballet flats over the socks she wore. She probably looked ridiculous in the dress shoes and too-big clothes.

Amelia was going to give her hell for this. It would take a lot to keep her from suspecting anything had happened.

"Are you ready?"

She cleared her throat. "Yeah, let's go."

He glanced at her bare arms and walked over to the coat closet by the door, pulling out two jackets and handing her one of them. She took it wordlessly and grabbed the bag of her wet clothes. Then, they headed out into the empty hall. It smelled faintly of cigarettes, but it was clean and well-lit, free of the ever-lingering smells of food and weed that haunted her apartment complex's halls.

They walked in silence down the single flight of stairs to the parking lot. The frigid air hit her square in the face, and a shiver immediately racked her body.

"Cold?" he asked, his brow furrowing as he looked at her.

She took a shuddering breath. "Yeah. I get cold easily."

He nodded but didn't say anything. Though she noticed that as soon as they got in the car, he cranked the heat all the way up. Unsurprisingly, he turned the radio to a classical music station.

"What's your address?" he asked, his voice roughened by the cold air outside.

She told him, and he entered it into his phone, setting the directions up then pulling out of the lot. She stared out the window as he drove, watching the wintry landscape fly by.

Finally, he broke the silence, saying, "You did well last night at the concert. Everyone was very impressed."

She glanced sidelong at him. "And were you?"

"What?"

"Impressed?"

Something flickered across his expression, something that almost seemed sad, as he said, "I was. You found it. The spark."

"It nearly broke me. Drove me to drink like I did and walk alone in the rain."

He nodded and said softly, "I know. The best of us are consumed by madness, nearly driven to it by the music. You'll have to find a way to balance it eventually."

She chewed on her lip. No one had ever explained it to her like that.

A few minutes later, they reached her parking lot, and she rummaged around in the bag of her clothes, pulling her key from the pocket of her still-wet jacket.

"Okay, well... This is me."

"Really?"

She made a face. "Don't be an ass."

"Oh, but I am."

She rolled her eyes. "You don't think I don't know that? You make poor Jake nearly piss his pants every time you talk."

His expression darkened slightly. "Good."

She let out a scoff and reached for the door handle, but he caught her wrist. She turned her head to look at him. He opened his mouth then closed it.

"What?" she asked softly.

He shook his head, his jaw shifting.

"Nothing, Evans. You should go. Your roommate is probably still worried."

She helped his gaze for a moment longer before she said, "Alright. Drive safe. I'll...see you later."

He looked away as she climbed out of the car. She turned and didn't look back as she headed for the apartment building.

Chapter 11
Beautiful, Delusional Fools

TO HIS OWN SURPRISE, Julian made it home without crashing his car. He was immensely distracted, and the roads weren't exactly dry. He hardly even registered getting out of his car and making his way back upstairs to his apartment. In fact, he only realized he was home when he slumped down on the couch and realized it was still a little damp.

From the rain-soaked clothes Rowan had been wearing.

Because less than an hour ago, she had been here in his apartment.

On his couch.

In his bed.

Touching him and—

He swore softly under his breath. He should be exhausted after the near-sleepless night, but he was wide awake, his body buzzing with half-wild energy. Even if he had the restraint to try, he couldn't shut out the memories. Still, despite the fact that it had barely been an hour ago, everything that had happened felt increasingly far away. It was just too far-fetched. She was far too beautiful. He was a fool.

And they were both delusional.

Still, sprawled on the damp couch cushions, he let himself sink into the daydream for just a little bit longer, let himself remember her soft curves and the fiery spark in her eyes warming the icy blue of her irises. Before long, his thoughts wandered further, to far less innocent places. Then again, she hadn't exactly been innocent. He had seen the reflection of his own dark desire in her eyes—the hint of wild, searing passion that he had never once found with another.

Drunk on the thought of her, a tidal wave of heat swept through him. But getting off, even to the now very-real memories, quite suddenly wasn't enough. He wanted her hands wrapped around his cock, wanted to taste her in other ways that he hadn't taken the time to, wanted her to taste him.

He wanted her in a thousand more ways he could never let himself have.

Eventually, still half-hard from the memories and unable to think straight, he forced himself to stand. Make a cup of coffee. Drink it. Get dressed.

He resolved to go to campus and work today. His apartment held too many reminders of her still, and he wouldn't be able to focus on anything but her. Even if it was all he wanted to do.

As soon as Rowan opened the front door, she heard rustling and a small shout from Amelia. When her friend emerged into the living room, a sleepy-looking Samuel trailing after her, she froze, her eyes trailing over Rowan.

"Where are your clothes?" she asked slowly.

Rowan held up the plastic bag.

Amelia's brows rose. "And I suppose those are...his?"

Rowan sighed. "Ami, mine were soaking wet. I was cold."

"Oh, really?"

"Yes, really."

Amelia narrowed her eyes and took a step closer to Rowan, cocking her head.

"What?" Rowan sighed.

Amelia glanced at Samuel, some unspoken words passing between them. Then, she turned back to Rowan and asked, point blank, "Did you fuck him?"

Rowan had known this was probably coming, had known how this would look. Though she hated lying to her friend, she shook her head and said, "No. I didn't."

"You're sure?"

"Um, would there be a situation where I wasn't sure?"

"Yeah, a situation where you fucked him."

Rowan rolled her eyes. "It didn't happen. Can I please go shower?"

"Where did you sleep?"

Rowan gave Amelia a look. "On the couch, like I told you over the phone."

"And where did he sleep?"

"In his bed in the other room."

Amelia's face pinched up, and Rowan knew she was thinking. Finally, she relented. "Alright. I believe you. You can go shower."

"Wow, thanks, Mom," Rowan shot back, heading for her bedroom to retrieve her own clean clothes.

But just before she shut the door, she saw Samuel looking at her contemplatively, as if he saw right through the lie she'd told and was deciding whether to push the issue or not.

Amelia went home later that day, Samuel going with her. She didn't nag too much about Rowan's "sleepover," as she kept calling it, but still, she caught the edge of suspicion in her tone a few times. She could only hope Samuel wouldn't raise any alarms.

Rowan had already decided she was staying at the apartment for most of the break. She tentatively planned to go home and see her mom at least once. She would see if that actually happened. Amelia had, of course, offered for Rowan to come home with her, but Rowan had turned down the offer this year, wanting to stay back and focus on music over the break.

So, a few hours later, she was alone in the deafening

silence of the apartment. Eventually, after eating a sad cup of ramen, she decided to go to the practice rooms before they closed for the holidays.

After grabbing her instrument and bundling up in a coat and hat, she headed for campus. When she arrived, it was nearly empty, so quiet that she could hear the soaring voices of a few vocal majors in the practice rooms down the hall. Other solitary students, avoiding going home for one reason or another.

She headed to an empty practice room and set up. She stayed for nearly two hours, until her fingers were aching and her sleepless night began to catch up with her. She was in desperate need of coffee, and today of all days, she'd succumb to it over her usual tea latte.

She left the practice room, and just as she was about to head down the main stairwell and back outside, someone called her name. She turned to see Jake striding towards her, a goofy knit hat on his head.

"What are you doing here?" he said in a way of greeting.

She forced a smile. "Oh, just practicing. I'm not going home until later, so I figured I'd get some hours in before campus closed for the week," she half-lied.

He scoffed. "Practicing? You should be taking a break after your performance last night. It was really phenomenal, Rowan. I was super impressed."

Everyone was very impressed.

She banished Julian's voice from her head and forced herself to cheerfully say, "Thanks, Jake. That's really nice of you to say."

He smiled and took a step closer to her. She tried to conceal the way her body stiffened as he crowded her space.

"Hey, uh, Rowan," he said, quieter now. "I meant to talk to you more last night. It's why I asked you out to drink. But you disappeared."

She nodded and managed to say, "Sorry."

He tilted his head. "Why did you leave?"

"I just needed air," she said tightly.

"I wanted to do this," he said. He was so close to her, close enough that she could smell his too-strong aftershave and see the places where his razor must have nicked.

"Jake, I don't want—"

He shoved her lightly against the wall, and a puff of air escaped her before he shoved his mouth against hers. She pushed against him.

"Jake, stop."

"Shh, Rowan," he muttered.

She squirmed in his hold, her heart racing. His mouth was roaming her jaw, and tears of desperation began to sting at her eyes as she screwed them shut and said, louder this time, "Stop!"

"Rowan, I know you want—"

And then, he was dragged away from her abruptly.

"She said no!" she heard an all too familiar voice shout.

Her eyes flew open, and she saw Julian gripping Jake by the shoulders, shaking him. Jake squirmed in his grasp as he said, "Professor, it was just a misunderstanding—"

"I could have your sorry ass dismissed from this program in an instant, Quinn," Julian growled.

"Please," Jake squeaked. "Please, I was just confused."

Julian shoved Jake up against the wall and shouted, "And what is confusing about the word 'stop?'"

A few people had gathered. One of them, she recognized as Professor Petrarch. He rushed towards them and said, "Julian, what's going on?"

Julian finally let go of Jake, his eyes tracking his every movement. Rowan had begun to tremble slightly.

"Quinn just assaulted Evans," Julian spat.

Jake spoke up again. "I didn't. It was just—"

"Enough," Julian cut Jake off.

Professor Petrarch let out a breath, running a hand through his hair. He turned to Rowan and asked, "Rowan, can you tell me what just happened?"

She swallowed hard as Julian's attention finally swung to hers. His onyx eyes were icy as they met hers, but she could have sworn she saw something else in his expression. A small crack, revealing endless, roiling waves of fury.

Looking back at Professor Petrarch, she said hoarsely, "I was just leaving. Jake kissed me, and I told him to stop."

Professor Petrarch's mouth thinned. "And he didn't?"

She met Julian's eyes again briefly before looking back at Professor Petrarch and whispering, "No. Not until Professor Lynch showed up."

Professor Petrarch sighed, glancing at a ruddy-faced Jake warily.

"Okay. Okay," the professor said. "Mr. Quinn, come with me. Julian, can you take care of Ms. Evans?"

Julian nodded, crossing his arms over his chest and glaring at Jake.

"Come with me," he said to her.

She avoided Jake's imploring stare as she followed Julian to his office. As soon as they were inside and the door was closed, he met her eyes. There was a soft fire in his voice as he asked, "Are you alright?"

She fisted her trembling hands. "I'm fine. Really, nothing happened. Jake shouldn't be kicked out of the program."

"And what if I hadn't shown up?"

She clenched her fists harder, willing them to stop shaking, but it was spreading up her limbs, making her legs quiver where she stood.

"Well, you did. It's fine."

"It's not."

She closed her eyes. When she opened them, Julian took a slow, tentative step towards her. He reached out a hand, pausing, waiting for her approval.

"I'm fine," she whispered.

He gently took her arm and guided her to the chair in front of his desk as he knelt in front of her.

"Do you want to fill out a Title IX form?" he asked softly.

She took a deep breath. "You think I should."

"It's completely up to you."

And then, Julian simply waited, not saying anything more, not encouraging her or pressuring her. He just let her think.

Finally, she took a breath and said, "I need to think about it more. But I don't...I don't think it's something I want to deal with right now."

"Whatever you feel comfortable with is fine," he said softly. "It's completely your decision. If you think about it later and want me to do more, let me know, and I can direct you to the right office. For now, you should probably go home and rest."

She swallowed and nodded once. But to go...where she would be alone. Where he would not be. Where he would *never* be. She'd known that last night. That the whole time, it was only temporary. But she still found herself fumbling for a way to make it work. It couldn't, of course, not if he wanted to keep his job and she wanted to keep him as a teacher, both of which were essential for their individual successes.

"Evans, are you alright?" he asked.

She cleared her throat. "I'm fine. I should get going."

He nodded, his brow creased. "I'm sure your friend is waiting."

She shook her head. "No... Amelia's gone home for the break."

He looked at her strangely. "You'll be alone?"

"Yup," she said as casually as she could.

He fisted his hands, and she watched his chest rise and fall deeply. He was considering something, possibly even fighting something in himself.

"Do you need someone to walk you back?" he finally asked. "I can ask one of my colleagues, one of the women, if they're free?"

"I'm fine," she said. "It's a short walk."

"Are you sure?"

She stood, grabbing her instrument case and bag. "I'm sure. I guess I'll see you when term starts up again."

He furrowed his brow and again, nodded.

"Alright. Merry Christmas, Jul—Professor Lynch."

She felt her cheeks warm at the slip-up, but he didn't look

irritated. He just tilted his head and said softly, "Merry Christmas, Evans. Be safe."

"Always," she said, and he blinked.

She turned and walked out of the office and down the hall. It wasn't until she was out of the building and halfway to the main road crossing that she heard him call her name.

"Evans!"

She turned around and met his eyes. He had thrown on a coat and grabbed his bag. His hair was already windblown, his cheeks tinged pink with the cold.

"You shouldn't walk alone," he said after a moment of silence. "Not after what just happened."

She knew this was dangerous. He had to know it too, that the chance of a repeat of last night happening was very likely if he followed her home. But she didn't fight him on it. In fact, she wanted someone—no, *him*—here right now, with her. So, she simply said, "Alright."

He closed the distance between them, and they began to walk in a comfortable silence. When they got to the crosswalk, he made a show of looking both ways once the *walk* light flashed.

"I know," she muttered. "I look both ways now."

He raised a brow at her. "Good."

The rest of the way, the silence that fell between them became charged and tense. She kept wanting to speak, and she had a feeling he felt the same. When they finally reached her building, he paused. "I'll walk you to your door."

She took a shallow breath and replied, "Okay."

When they did get to her door, he just stood there, and she knew, again, he was grappling with himself.

"You can come in. If you want?" she said tentatively.

He sucked in a breath. "I just... You shouldn't be alone tonight. You should have someone there for you."

"I thought that wasn't supposed to be you."

He ran a hand over his face. "It's not."

"But?"

He huffed out a breath. "I won't stay long."

She hid her smile as she ducked inside, flicking on the light in the small, cramped entrance hall. The apartment was still messy from the chaos of the semester—cleaning it was one of her priorities over the break.

"Sorry," she muttered, toeing aside the pile of shoes that nearly blocked the way.

He laughed softly. "And I thought I was messy in college."

She rolled her eyes as she took off her coat and chucked off her shoes. "We can't all be clean freaks."

He cocked his head. "Is that what you think of me?"

"Maybe."

This felt natural, the easy banter they were not supposed to be able to have. She didn't say that, though, because she didn't want to break the spell.

"Make yourself at home," she said. "I'm going to make tea. Do you want some?"

He surveyed the couch, and as he sat down, he said, "Sure, thank you."

"Mint or green?"

"Mint," he replied easily, craning his neck to look at the photos on the couch side table.

"Most of those are Amelia's," she called from the kitchen as she started the hot water in a kettle.

He didn't reply, and when she emerged back into the living room, he was holding a frame. Her stomach sank instantly as she recognized which one it was.

"This is her," he stated, glancing between Rowan and the photo.

It was a picture of Rowan and Alex at seventeen. It had been taken after a music competition and was the last good photo they'd taken before Alex had gotten sick.

Rowan could only nod.

"She looked like you."

She shrugged. "We are—were twins."

Julian nodded. "I... It's not the same, I know. But I do get it, the shift in the way you talk about her. My parents got divorced when I was fifteen, right after we moved to the States. My mom pretty much bailed completely on us after that."

She pursed her lips. "I'm sorry."

He shrugged. "It happens."

The kettle began to wail, and she hurried back into the kitchen and poured the hot water into two mugs, the tea bags floating up atop the steaming liquid.

When she returned, carrying the mugs, she asked Julian, "What does she play? Your mother."

He furrowed his brow. "Flute. It's why I decided to play it. My father plays the clarinet and my sister, Lena, plays bassoon."

"Ah, so you're one of those mega-gifted musical families."

"I suppose," he said dryly.

"Where are you from?" she asked, sitting down next to him on the worn couch. "Before you came to the States, I mean."

He took a sip of the tea, then said, "Edinburgh. But we traveled around a lot because of my parents' playing."

"Was that hard?"

He took another sip of tea and then said, "Well, I didn't really have friends growing up. My sister and I stuck together, though, so it was fine."

"Are you still close with her?"

He looked a little uncomfortable, shifting as he said, "Not...exactly. We got into a bad fight after my mom left. She blamed my dad, and I stood up for him. I thought he was the victim."

"And was he not?"

He glanced at her over his mug. "You're very forward, Evans."

She took a sip of tea, and it nearly burnt her tongue. Then, she shrugged and said, "I'm just curious. You don't have to answer if you don't want to."

Julian paused for a moment. "I found out a few years later that he'd cheated on her with a woman who played in the symphony they were in."

Her brows raised. "Damn. That's rough."

Julian blew out a breath. "Yeah." Then, he glanced at the photo and asked, "What was she like?"

Rowan forced herself to breathe and take another sip of tea before she said, "Alex was like...all the good parts of me and none of the bad. She was shy but funny, and she hardly ever cried or got stressed. I used to call her a cool cucumber.

Our dad was never around. He and Mom were never married, so Alex used to make a joke that every time I got sad or angry, it was all to be blamed on my 'daddy issues.'"

"And do you have…"

"Daddy issues?" she snorted. "No. Honestly, it sounds like you have more than I do. I never really knew the man, so there wasn't anything to miss."

"Well, thanks for that," he said, and she laughed.

He stared at her as she smiled, his features softening.

"What?" she asked, her grin falling.

He shook his head. "Nothing. Tell me more about your family."

She narrowed her eyes at him, unsure why he even cared, but continued, "My mom was always kind of a fragile woman. You would think raising two girls on her own would mean she was super strong or something, but it was the opposite. Alex and I were always taking care of her. And when Alex got sick, it kind of all fell on me. Now… I don't see her very often. I should, but," she sighed. "Every time I see my mom, it just tears the wound open again, even if it's actually healing. She has a boyfriend now, and I actually like him, so I trust him to take care of her."

Julian nodded, looking contemplative. Then, he asked, "Besides music, what else do you like?"

She stretched her legs out in front of her and said, "I'm in grad school, so I kind of only think about music. But…" She thought about it for a moment. "Well, in high school, I liked to draw sometimes. I was never very good, but it was a good stress reliever."

"Can you draw something for me?"

She worried her lip between her teeth. "Like I said, I'm not very good. It's been a little while since I've really worked on it."

"I don't care," he said. "Just draw something. Humor me."

She choked out a laugh. "Fine."

Setting down her mug on the coffee table, she stood and retrieved a stray notebook and pencil from her room. When she returned, she glanced at him, and she knew what she was going to draw.

Twenty minutes or so later, she sighed and set down her pencil.

"Can I see it?" he asked, his hair falling in his face, trailing shadows across his cheeks.

Suddenly, feeling a little bashful, she hugged the sketchpad to her chest. There was a mischievous glint in his eyes, and she narrowed her eyes.

"Do not try to take it from me, Sneaky," she said.

He shot his hand forward, snatching the sketchbook from her before she could even dart back. As soon as he saw what... who... she'd drawn, his face fell.

"What?" she whispered.

He looked at her. "You drew me."

She nodded silently. He studied the sketch for a few more seconds before he asked, "Is this how you see me?"

Her cheeks colored, but she replied, "Yes. What do you see?"

The wind howled outside, and his lips parted, his eyes still on the sketch. Finally, he said, "I see... I do not deserve for you to see me in this way."

She swallowed. "I'm sorry?"

He set the sketchbook down. "No, Evans. Don't be. This isn't your—"

She cut him off, "Please stop taking on all the responsibility. Please stop putting this all on yourself. I'm an adult. I am quite capable of making my own decisions."

"I know, but—"

"Stop," she ordered. "Just stop. If you want to stay, I'm going to make soup and watch a movie. If you want to go, go."

She stalked off into the kitchen and heated a can of chicken noodle. He was still on the couch when she returned. She handed him a bowl and spoon, which he accepted silently. Once the TV was on and one of Amelia's favorite cheesy rom-coms was playing out across the screen, she said quietly, "Thank you for staying. Today was weird, and I'm fine but... Thank you."

"You're welcome," he replied, his tone soft.

They ate soup and watched the movie, both of them scoffing at the ridiculousness of it. When the soup was gone and the movie was over, she looked at him and said, "I'm going to bed."

"I should go then."

She took a deep breath and said one word. One monumental, stupid word.

"Stay."

He pursed his lips, and she added, "I'm very tired and I'm sure you are too. I just want to sleep. But you're right. I don't want to be alone tonight."

She half-expected him to refuse her, but he only sighed and said, "Please tell me you don't have a twin bed."

She smiled slightly. "No, it's a double."

"Thank God," he muttered.

"I have an extra toothbrush if you need it."

"Ah. Do you have a stock for all your overnight suitors?"

It was a joke and a question. She flipped her braid over her shoulder and said, "Yes, there's a very long waitlist. You're currently holding up both Damen and Jared tonight."

His brows raised. "Two at once, then?"

She shrugged. "Maybe."

Something hungry flashed in his eyes, but it was gone quickly. He followed her to the bathroom, which mercifully had been cleaned not *too* long ago by Amelia. They brushed their teeth together, which felt both nice and weird.

Once they were done, she led him to her bedroom. He averted his eyes as she changed and she snorted. "Bashful suddenly?"

"Evans," he said, and there was a slight warning to his tone.

She realized she was currently topless and grabbed a t-shirt from her overstuffed drawer.

"There," she said. "I am clothed."

He raised a brow, and she chuckled. "Alright, half-clothed. I don't usually sleep in long pants."

Indeed, she wore short-shorts and an oversized t-shirt, and for some odd reason unknown to her, she didn't care that he saw her this way. She just crawled into bed and patted the space beside her.

He blinked, then began to undo the buttons of his shirt. To her slight disappointment, he wore an undershirt beneath it. Though, he did strip down to his boxer shorts and she didn't look away for a second. Not that she planned on making a move. The day had been weird, and she was truly exhausted.

When he climbed into the bed, they were inevitably close. He was tall, and the double bed wasn't exactly super spacious. She turned off the bedside lamp, and in the dark, his arm looped around her middle. It felt so natural, she almost forgot who he was, who she was.

She fell asleep to him murmuring something in her ear. She didn't quite catch it and was pulled under by unconsciousness before she could try to listen closer.

Chapter 12
Dangerous Feelings

THE NEXT MORNING, when Julian awoke, he found himself in a too-small bed, still wrapped around Rowan. Early morning light filtered into the room through the cheap blinds, illuminating the small space. He could tell she was awake by the slight tenseness of her body and the uneven rhythm of her breathing. Still half-asleep and nearly drunk off the scent of her, he murmured roughly in her ear, "Good morning, Evans."

"How did you know I was awake?" she asked, her voice equally raspy.

"Dunno," he muttered, brushing his nose against the soft curve of her neck.

Her breath caught, and he dutifully ignored how hard he was—and not only due to just having woken up.

"What are you doing today?" she asked after a moment.

"Work," he grumbled, remembering.

"What do you want to be doing?"

He sighed. "I'd like to work on my current composition."

"How many pieces have you composed?"

"Evans, I just woke up."

She tried to turn to face him, but before she could flip fully, he pulled her more snugly against him so she stayed put.

"Just a moment longer," he whispered into her hair.

"Okay," she breathed.

He stroked her stomach in lazy circles, and he heard her barely-held-back inhale as his fingers skimmed the waistband of her shorts. He gripped the hem of her t-shirt, bunching it in his hand. His cock twitched against her backside, and this time, her sharp breath was audible.

She arched into him, and he groaned softly, his palm flattening against her stomach. Slowly, she moved her hips, and he brushed his lips across her shoulder.

"You probably have things to do," she said breathily as he sucked gently on the soft spot between her neck and shoulder.

"Mhmm," he rumbled.

"Julian."

She had yet to say his name until now, and the sound of it on her lips was nearly his undoing. Just surreal enough that he tensed and said, "Don't call me that, Evans."

But as usual, she was all fiery defiance as she retorted, "Why, *Professor*?"

He huffed out a breath. "Fine. Just... don't call me that right now."

"Why, Julian?" she asked innocently, twisting to face him.

And the way she was looking at him as she said it—it

snapped any semblance of resistance he'd been trying to uphold. He moved, positioning himself so he was above her. He brushed his mouth over her torso, skimming her breasts, her nipples peaked under the t-shirt she wore.

He descended lower, and when she realized where this was going, she opened her mouth, perhaps to protest. But he cut her off, breathing, "Let me. Please."

He held her gaze until she nodded and whispered, "Okay."

He kissed her inner thigh and then began to slide those tiny shorts off, pulling her underwear with them. Her cheeks were flushed pink as he looked at her, and for a moment, she would not meet his eyes. He wondered if she was embarrassed or shy. She had no reason to be. Every inch of her, completely bare before him, was fucking perfect.

As he kissed her thigh again, he murmured against her skin, "Look at me, Evans."

Finally, she did, her eyes darkening as she saw him settled between her legs. He kissed her thigh again, then finally put his mouth on her.

At the first stroke of his tongue, she shuddered, her legs closing. With a firm grip, he held them open, and she let out a gasp that turned into a loud moan. At the second stroke, she was writhing under his touch. He laid a hand flat against her stomach as he devoured her, high on the taste of her and the sounds she was making. Still not letting up with his mouth and tongue, he slid a finger inside her. When he added another, she gasped his name.

He gripped her thigh with his free hand, glancing up at

her again. Almost immediately, her body arched off the bed, her fingers clawing at the sheets as she came.

As she floated down from the high, he sat back, still staring at her. Her cheeks were flushed, even more so than before, and her full lips were half-parted. For what could have been mere seconds or a few minutes, they said nothing, her gaze catching on his. And for what was not the first time, this thing between them felt oddly surreal. They were dangerous, these feelings, razor-sharp in their precision, just jagged enough to cut through any semblance of normalcy in his life. He didn't know what to call whatever was between them. There wasn't a word for it. At least, not one he would let himself use.

Rowan didn't want to be the one to break the spell. This morning had been...something else. She'd let him do what no one else had. Her past partners had only ever been interested in fucking her and leaving, caring little for her pleasure. But just now, she had barely touched Julian—and he had been happy to get her off without anything in return. Or perhaps not, given the sounds he'd made and the way he was looking at her now.

Eventually, the silence grew too heavy, loaded with words they could not say. When she spoke, her voice was barely a whisper as she said, "I didn't know... I didn't think it would be like that."

He stared at her. "No one has ever done that for you?"

Still half-dizzy, she shook her head.

"Have you ever been in a relationship?"

She took a breath. "No. Nothing serious ever."

He rose back up to her and tucked a strand of hair behind her ear. His expression was slightly closed off, and she shook her head. "Don't shut down," she whispered. "And please... Please don't regret this."

He took a shuddering breath. "I should regret this. But I never have, not one moment, not one kiss."

Something stupidly fuzzy lit up her insides. She felt warm and open and...

Oh God.

She was falling in love with him.

She wasn't sure how she hadn't realized it until now, but it was at that precise moment that the undeniable fact overcame her. He didn't feel that way about her—that much she was sure of. She had an inkling that even if he felt something beyond lust, he would never let it go anywhere. It was the right thing to do, of course, but she was beginning to not care about right or wrong when it came to him.

"Rowan?" He said her name softly, gently, as if he cared.

She realized she had gone quiet. His use of her first name was only dismantling her shields further.

"I shouldn't keep you," she said quietly. "If you have work to do."

He was watching her carefully, as if he could read her thoughts, like they were playing out on her face. She only hoped she was a better actress than she had been in the past.

"I'll go then," he said after a moment.

She nodded, and he got up from the bed, pulling on his pants and shirt then heading to the bathroom. Once she heard the sink running, she got up and pulled on a pair of sweatpants in lieu of the pajama shorts. By the time she'd braided back her hair, he was emerging from the bathroom.

They looked at each other, not speaking at first until he said, "I suppose I won't see you until term starts again."

She nodded, something inside her cleaving in two. She brushed past him and headed for the front door before he could see the tears forming in her eyes. She heard him following after her, and she had collected herself by the time they reached the door.

He faced her, and then, unexpectedly, he pulled her to his chest, his arms wrapping around her. They stayed like that for a minute or two before he drew back and leaned down, resting his forehead against hers as he said, "Don't think I don't care. Just because of... everything. I care about you, Rowan. Alright?"

She didn't know how he nearly read her thoughts exactly, but she said, "And does it matter if I care?"

He searched her gaze. "Of course. It always does. It matters more. I—"

But he caught himself, halting whatever he was going to say.

"You should go," she whispered, giving him an out, mostly because she was too afraid to hear what he would have said next.

"Alright. I'll see you later."

She let him go, but he paused just before he got to the door. "I'm still here. If something happens or you need..." He sighed. "I left my personal phone number on a note in the bedroom."

She suppressed a small smile. "Alright. Thank you."

He looked at her one last time then left.

Chapter 13
The Moon & the Stars In One

Rowan spent the next five weeks completely, utterly alone. Amelia called a few times and her mother video called her on Christmas. Rowan feigned a cold to avoid going home. She didn't feel like seeing anyone right now.

She didn't text or call Julian, though she came close several times. She supposed she wanted to prove to herself that she could stay away.

The day before Amelia was supposed to come back, she realized two things.

One, her period was five days late.

And two, she was really about to hurl.

Both of these things dawned on her in one horrible tandem moment, and she ended up swearing and rushing to the toilet. When she was done vomiting her breakfast up, she sat back and swore again loudly.

There was no fucking way. No goddamn, fucking way.

The condom had broken, but they'd had sex *once*. And she was on the pill. The odds were astronomically low.

She tried to ignore the nagging, anxious suspicion all day. But eventually, she relented and ventured out into the cold, wintry evening to the nearby pharmacy. She avoided the cashier's eyes as she checked out the pregnancy test. She felt like a high school girl trying to pretend it wasn't for her, that she was just "buying for a friend."

She wished that was the case.

Once she got home, she decided to sleep on it. Maybe she was being stupid and worrying about this was a waste. But when morning came and her stomach tripped over itself in anxious nerves, she knew she just had to take the test. It would be negative, and then she could relax.

She hauled herself from bed and padded to the bathroom, her breathing shallow. When she pulled the test out of the box, she stared at the pink wrapper for nearly five minutes before ripping it open. She read the instructions over twice and then peed on the stupid stick. After setting it down on a square of toilet paper on the counter, she washed her hands and didn't look at it for the allotted three minutes that instructions had said to wait.

When she finally forced herself to check the test, she froze completely as she saw the two tiny pink lines staring back at her. Her eyes widened, and a roaring filled her ears. After a moment, she shouted, "Fuck!" just as she heard the front door open.

She froze again.

"Rowan?" Amelia called from the living room. "Rowan, are you alright?"

She swallowed and shouted back, "Fine! I, uh...stained my underwear. I'll be out in a minute."

She heard Amelia set down her bag and then walk over to the bathroom door. She knocked and said, "Can I come in?"

"No, I'm completely naked," Rowan said, unable to hide the slight shake in her voice.

She heard Amelia sigh, and the doorknob began to turn. She lunged for it, but was too late, and she nearly crashed into Amelia as she stepped into the bathroom.

"Row, what the fuck—"

But she cut herself off as she saw the test sitting on the counter.

"Ami, get out."

"Rowan." Amelia's voice was stern and alarmed.

"Yes?" she whispered.

"Is that a positive pregnancy test?"

Rowan swallowed. "It's..." She took a breath. "Well, um, yeah. It is."

She was shaking slightly, and Amelia stepped forward, touching her arm.

"Row," she said gently. "It's okay."

"It's really not," she said softly, a few silent tears escaping her eyes and rolling down her cheeks. "Like, really, really not."

"Ami?"

They both looked to the doorway to see Samuel standing in the living room.

"Should I go?" he asked quietly.

Rowan wiped the tears from her face with the back of her hand, and Amelia replied, "Just go get some donuts from the grocery store that's further away."

Samuel nodded. "I'll be back in a bit."

Then, he was gone. Amelia looked back at her and said, "Row, you know what I'm going to ask."

Rowan shook her head. "It's not... It doesn't matter who."

"Um, yes, it fucking does," Amelia said incredulously. "You've been hiding something, and I..." she trailed off, shaking her head. "I have a bad feeling that I know what you're going to say. And I think *you* know that too."

Rowan left the bathroom, heading for the couch, needing to sit down. Amelia followed her. Once they were settled, Amelia looked her dead in the eye and said, "That night you stayed at Professor Lynch's apartment. You two hooked up, didn't you?"

Rowan closed her eyes. 'Hooking up' felt like a light way to put what they'd done. But still, she nodded.

"So, I'm assuming," Amelia said, "that the positive pregnancy test in there is his fault."

Rowan opened her eyes and said sharply, "It is not solely *his* fault. I don't know why it's all on him. He acts the same way. I'm an adult. I can make fully informed decisions."

"Yes, but he's your *teacher*," Amelia said softly. "Row, how long has this been going on?"

Rowan shrugged as nonchalantly as she could. "That depends on your definition."

"When did things first become different between you two?" Amelia asked carefully.

"I guess... a few weeks into the semester. I kissed him. And then it was kind of off and on. Most of the time, it wasn't like that, though."

Amelia shook her head. "I *cannot* believe I didn't realize it sooner. I only really suspected something when Sam pointed it out. The way Professor Lynch had talked about you and the way you looked when someone mentioned him."

"The way he...what?"

Amelia furrowed her brow. "That day before the recital when Sam talked to him in the hall. Well, he talked about you, and Sam noticed that something was different. He said Professor Lynch talked about you like you were the moon and the stars in one. He said... Well, Sam said Professor Lynch talked about you the way he talks about me."

Rowan looked away. "I don't think he thinks I'm the moon and stars or whatever."

"He better. Especially now."

Rowan looked back at Amelia. "I can't tell him."

Amelia narrowed her eyes. "You really should. Are you planning on getting an abortion?"

Rowan rubbed at her eyes. "I should."

Amelia tilted her head. "What you *should* do doesn't mean a thing. I shouldn't have asked anyway. You literally just found out."

"No, you're right. I need to think about it."

Amelia put a hand over hers. "You do whatever is right for you. Not for him, not for anything else, but what *you* want."

"This would ruin my life," she whispered.

Amelia met her eyes. "But?"

She took a deep breath. "But the idea of an abortion... I don't want... It's—" She heaved in a sudden sob.

Amelia pulled Rowan close to her in a tight hug and began to stroke her hair as she said softly, "If you want this, your career will be there when you're ready. I will be there.

Sam will be there. And Professor Lynch better fucking be there, or at least his hard-earned teaching money better be."

Rowan choked out an incredulous laugh. Oh God, what was he going to say? *If* she told him.

"It's going to be okay, Rowan, I promise. It really is," Amelia said into her hair.

It was odd and unsettling that a calm feeling overcame Rowan then. She knew she should not be feeling calm. She should be freaking out. She should be calling a clinic right now. But somehow, this moment and every moment to come felt intrinsically tied to the day she sat on the steps of a different university and talked about stars and sunsets with a stranger.

Samuel came back about twenty minutes later with fresh donuts. They ate them in near silence until Samuel finally said, "So..."

"Your hunch was right. Good job," Rowan said dryly.

Amelia gave her a look, and Rowan said, "What?"

Samuel sighed. "Have you, uh, told him yet? Your teacher, I mean?"

Rowan shook her head, staring at the crumbs on her plate as she replied, "Nope."

"You're going to, right?"

She shrugged, and Samuel exchanged a look with Amelia.

"She will tell him," Amelia said, looking at Rowan pointedly. "If only to get her share of his teaching salary."

Samuel nodded. "So, you're going to go through with this?"

Rowan let her head fall into her hands then mumbled, "It seems so."

She felt Samuel's gentle hand on her back as he said, "Hey, Rowan. Ami and I are here for you, okay? You're not in this alone."

She peered up at him. "Thanks, Sam. Truly."

He smiled widely. "This kid better be ready to be triple-parented at the least."

She felt a sinking in her stomach. They were both assuming Julian wouldn't want to be involved. And why would he? They hardly knew each other, even if it felt like he was the first person to *know* her in a long time.

Samuel must've seen it on her face, because he said, "Hey. I wouldn't rule him out just yet. Talk to him. I think he might care more than you give him credit for. Or at least, it seemed that way when I talked to him."

"Maybe," she said, shrugging again.

Amelia sighed. "Well, I was planning on watching movies all day before classes start again tomorrow."

"I'm in," Samuel said. "And I don't envy you two. Even my corporate burnout job is easier than music school."

Rowan laughed, though it felt hollow.

Chapter 14
He Needed to Know

THE ENTIRETY of winter break had been cold and sobering for Julian. He hadn't realized how much he had gotten used to Rowan being in his life until she disappeared for five weeks. Understandably so—she was on break, after all. They weren't friends, and he wasn't her boyfriend. He didn't even know what to call whatever was between them. There probably wasn't a word that existed for it, mostly because it was something that simply wasn't supposed to happen.

He hadn't given her his number expecting her to call, but he would be lying if he said he wasn't checking his phone much more than usual.

The only reprieve over the weeks had been the fairly quick decision to dismiss Jake Quinn from the program after what he'd done to Rowan. A short meeting between staff and administration had been enough to decide that, especially with a strong word from both Ethan and him.

Though, now that he would be seeing her today on campus again, he wasn't quite sure how to act. The responsible thing to do would be to break this off now. It had already gone much too far, but maybe he could still fix it. The problem was—he didn't *want* to. Even if it was wrong. Even if everything about their relationship was impossible.

When Julian arrived on campus at eight for a staff meeting, the Reisner building was already bustling with students. Julian nodded briskly at a group of them who waved as he walked to the conference room on the second floor.

Many of the music faculty were there already, milling about and snagging free pastries and coffee from the table in the corner. Julian lingered near the edge of the room, his arms crossed over his chest. Ethan winked at him as he entered before continuing what seemed to be a heated conversation with Leo.

"Ready to start up again?"

Julian turned his head to see Penny Thea standing to his left, a paper cup of coffee cradled in her hands.

He cleared his throat and replied, "As I'll ever be."

She laughed softly. "You're doing an excellent job with her. Rowan Evans, I mean. Her recital performance was quite impressive."

Julian raised a brow at Penny and said, "Everyone in the department seems oddly interested in her."

Penny raised her brows right back as she said, "Including you. But," she took a sip of coffee, "we're lucky to have gotten her. She was recruited elsewhere first, and from what I understand, she nearly went out to the East Coast."

Julian was just about to ask which school when a stern-looking woman with graying brown hair walked in. As the chatter died down, Julian realized she was the department head, Maggie.

The rest of the meeting could only be described as dull. As Maggie talked, one or two of the faculty even looked to be dozing off. By the end of it, he was ready to bee-line out of the room, but Maggie cornered him before he could.

"Julian," she said. "How are you getting on?"

He smiled tightly. "Fine. Good."

"I know you've taught before, but a place like Grandview can be a bit of an adjustment," she said knowingly.

"It can be," he said, meaning it. "But things are going well."

Maggie gave him what he thought was a slight smile. Then, she said, "I hate to spring this on you so abruptly, but Miranda's flight was delayed. She was vacationing in Spain, I believe."

Julian cleared his throat. "Do you need me to cover orchestra rehearsal today?"

"If you wouldn't mind? I'd ask Penny or Bill, but they both have meetings until eleven. It'll just be today. And don't worry about sticking to Miranda's schedule. You could just fill the time with technical exercises or section work, at least for today."

He steered his thoughts away from the fact that he'd be seeing Rowan sooner than he anticipated and said, "Of course, it's no problem. I'll head over now."

Maggie patted his arm lightly. "Thank you. I appreciate it."

She left, striding over to talk to Ethan. Julian glanced at his watch—he'd have to hurry to get to rehearsal on time.

Leaving the conference room behind, he made his way downstairs. A few students were already in the rehearsal room when he arrived, looking up curiously as he took his place in Miranda's usual spot.

He busied himself looking over a few notes Miranda had left for herself in the conductor's binder, forcing himself to keep his attention downcast, even as he caught a flash of fiery hair in his periphery.

Finally, once the room was nearly full, he cleared his throat and said, "Professor Lark's plane was delayed, so I'll be filling in, just for today. We're going to start off with warmups, and then I'd like to hear each of the first chairs run through the solos assigned to you before break. Then, we'll go from there."

A low murmur filled the room, and for just a moment, his attention landed on Rowan. Her hair was in two braids today, the vibrant copper a contrast to the rest of her. She looked...

Something was wrong. She was too pale, too withdrawn.

He tried not to watch too closely as she took a deep breath and assembled her flute, but he swore he saw her hands shaking. Something akin to irritation washed over him as he watched her. If something was wrong, why hadn't she told him? Even as he thought it, he knew it was stupid. Still, the jagged edge of worry and annoyance remained as he began warmups.

After that, a few of the other soloists took turns playing. As the trumpet first chair finished his solo, he watched Rowan's eyes flutter shut. She looked to be in pain. And as usual, he was sure she would say nothing.

"Evans?" His voice came out sharper than he meant it to, especially as he added, "Any day now."

Come on, Rowan, he thought. *Don't just soldier through. Let me help you.*

But instead, she did exactly what he thought she would. She swallowed hard and raised her instrument to her mouth.

But one shaky inhale later, she was still just sitting there, the mouthpiece of her flute hovering at her lips.

"Evans. You've been asked to play your solo," he said shortly, his patience thinning.

She took a short breath, and her voice was thin as she said, "I'm sorry, I need to... I don't feel well."

He narrowed his eyes, and he regretted the next words that fell from his mouth. "If you were in a professional ensemble, you'd need to push through."

Students were murmuring amongst themselves now, staring at her. The lights suddenly felt too hot as he watched her pale further. She grabbed her instrument case and began to push past the others in her row, heading for the door.

"Don't come back until you're ready to be professional," Julian found himself saying.

They were harsh words meant to build a wall between them again, because he was about two seconds from running after her and demanding what the hell was wrong.

She only muttered a tight, "Okay," before practically sprinting for the exit.

Once she was gone, he forced himself to look back at the varying expressions of the students before him—some looking frightened, some seeming mildly impressed. He didn't care.

He *didn't* care.

But as he picked up a pencil to make notes in Miranda's binder, it nearly snapped in his hand.

Thankfully, Rowan made it for the bathroom before she vomited up the remainder of her breakfast. Then, she sat on the cold tiled floor of the women's restroom for a long time, heaving in steady breaths. After a while, the door opened, and someone called, "Row?"

Amelia.

Rowan didn't know how she had known it was her in the bathroom. Maybe someone from orchestra rehearsal had told Amelia about her hasty exit.

"I'm over here," she said on a rasp.

She unlatched the stall door, and Amelia rushed over.

"Are you okay?" she demanded.

Rowan nodded, took a deep breath, and told Amelia what had happened. As she finished, Amelia's body went still as her expression grew livid. Under her breath, she said, "*Asshole.*"

And then, she stood and made for the door.

"Ami!" Rowan called. "Where are you going?"

Amelia turned. "To give that waste of space a piece of my mind."

Rowan felt her face drain of color, and she scrambled to gather her instrument as she said, "Ami, don't!"

But Amelia was already out the door. Rowan packed her flute up as quickly as she could and then hurried after her friend. She wasn't in the hall outside the bathroom, but Rowan assumed she was heading for Julian's office.

She sprinted up the stairs to the second level where the offices were but still only caught up to Amelia as she began pounding on Julian's office door.

"Ami, stop," Rowan said breathlessly.

But it was too late. The door was already swinging open to reveal an irritated-looking Julian, though his expression quickly turned alarmed as he saw Amelia, Rowan red-faced behind her.

Amelia pushed past him into the office before he could speak, and Rowan followed, hissing, "Ami, I'm serious. Stop."

Julian shut the door and opened his mouth, but then Amelia spit out, "You're a dick, you know that?"

Julian's features sharpened. "If this is about rehearsal today, it's not my problem. Evans needs to figure out how—"

"Oh, hell yes, it is your problem," Amelia cut in viciously.

She glanced at Rowan, who was looking at her imploringly.

"I'm sorry, Row," she said. "But he needs to know."

"Ami," Rowan puffed out.

Julian narrowed his eyes and said slowly, "Know what?"

Amelia's expression twisted in anger as she looked back at him and said, "Rowan isn't unprofessional. She's amazing and talented, and you're an idiot for not seeing that."

Julian's nostrils flared as he began, "Regardless, today was—"

"Today," Amelia snarled. "Today, Rowan was just trying to leave that auditorium so she could go vomit her guts up. Because she has fucking morning sickness. She's pregnant, asshole."

The last three words cut through the air like a sharpened blade, slicing through any semblance of stability in Rowan's world. From this moment on, she knew everything would begin to fall around her, burning and broken.

Julian actually took a step back, and she watched as his face slowly, very slowly, drained of all color. His gaze finally met hers, his onyx eyes wide.

"Ami," Rowan said hoarsely. "Go."

"I am not—"

"Amelia," she said sharply, ripping her gaze away from Julian to look at her. "Go. I'll see you at home later."

Amelia finally shut her mouth and nodded.

"I'm sorry, Row," she whispered, shaking her head. "He needed to know."

She left, shutting the door softly behind her. Rowan shut her eyes for a moment. When she opened them and looked back at Julian, he was still standing in the same spot, his hands slack at his sides.

They stared at each other for a moment, until finally, he broke the heavy silence and said, his voice breaking slightly, "Is it true?"

Rowan nodded, and his eyes fluttered shut.

"Dammit," he swore quietly.

She looked away, tears threatening at her eyes. They were again silent for what felt like a while before he said, "Were you really not going to tell me?"

She shrugged, still not looking at him. "Does it matter?" she said, her voice hollow.

She heard him take a step closer to her, felt the near-stifling heat of his presence as he said, "Rowan."

Still, she averted her gaze.

"Rowan, look at me," he said.

Finally, she raised her eyes to his.

"Were you afraid to tell me?" he asked quietly.

An incredulous smile lifted her mouth, and a silent tear slid down her cheek as she said, "Of course, I was. Because I knew you'd want nothing to do with all of it. You'd want nothing to do with me."

He stared at her, and she laughed hoarsely. "Go on. Deny it. Prove me wrong," she spat.

He was just looking and looking at her, still not speaking. She flared her nostrils and said shortly, "I'm not... I'm keeping it. If you even care."

The only sign he'd even heard her was that his eyes had widened again. She shook her head.

"I should go. Let you live your life," she said bitterly. "You don't want me ruining it."

She turned, but just before she reached the door, he caught her wrist. She whirled and said harshly, "What? Want me to keep my mouth shut? Done. I don't give a fuck."

"Rowan," he whispered. "Please."

She paused, a crack splintering in her at the rawness in his tone. He took her hand, and she flinched.

"I'm not..." He shook his head. "I don't know how this is going to work, but I'm not leaving you alone in this."

She took a deep breath. And then, she forced herself to

look at him as she said, "No one can know. Not yet. I want to try and continue in the program for now. What happened today won't happen again. I want us to act like nothing happened."

"I can't teach you anymore," he said quietly. "You know that."

"I don't want to be the screw-up who got herself knocked up by the teacher," she snapped, and it was his turn to flinch.

Her head was pounding, and she let out a puff of air. His hand had gone slack in hers as he said quietly, "I'm sorry. I'm so sorry."

Her lower lip wobbled, and tears spilled out over her cheeks.

"It'll be fine," she said, her voice breaking. "Nothing needs to change. Not yet."

"Rowan—"

"Please."

She stared at him, with wide, imploring eyes, and he swallowed and finally relented. "Alright. Alright."

She was still crying, and he took a tentative step closer. She bowed her head into his chest, and his arms wrapped around her. He was shaking too, she realized.

"I still meant what I said," she whispered. "You are everything... Everything I have been trying not to feel, to want or need, for so long."

As she looked up and searched his gaze, she expected him to deny or push her off again. Instead, he replied in a voice barely above a whisper, "You are the very thing I've been looking for for so long. Even with the consequences. Even with impossibilities."

"You're not running, then?" she dared.

"No," he vowed, his forehead pressing against hers. "No. Never."

They stayed like that for a few moments, absorbing the force of what was happening. Finally, she pulled back and said, "I should go."

He took a deep breath. "Come over later. We need to talk more...just not here."

She nodded. "Just, uh, text me your address then. I do have a car. I just try not to drive too much since gas is expensive."

He shook his head. "No, I'll pick you up. At seven, if that's alright?"

"That's fine," she replied, wiping her eyes.

He swept over to his desk and handed her a tissue. She muttered a thanks and took it, blowing her nose and wincing as her head pounded. His brow furrowed, and before he could ask what was wrong, she mumbled, "Just a headache."

He nodded, clearing his throat.

"I'll see you later," she said, picking up her instrument case and bag.

"I'll see you," he replied quietly.

She left him standing by the desk and staring out the window.

Chapter 15
The Stupid Tree

FOR A LONG TIME after Rowan left the office, Julian simply stared at the snowy tree just outside the window. He tracked the knobs in the trunk and watched a squirrel skitter over some of the higher branches.

He felt like he was floating, and perhaps, this stupid tree was the only thing tethering him to the Earth right now.

Eventually, he slumped in the chair behind his desk. It was a comfortable chair. He'd been lucky to get this office, with the big window and the natural light and—

A knock on the door had him nearly jumping to his feet. He wasn't sure he could talk right now, but he managed to call out, "No office hours today!"

A chuckle sounded from the other side of the door, and then it swung open. Ethan strode into the office like he owned it, sprawling in one of the chairs that faced the desk. His brow creased as he looked at Julian.

"What the hell happened to you?" he asked, snorting.

"Nothing, Ethan." Even his own voice felt far away.

Ethan leaned forward, bracing his forearms on his legs as he said, "Bullshit. You look like you just got whacked across the face, and not in the good way."

Julian didn't have it in him to even pretend to laugh at the crass joke. He merely blew out a breath and said, "It's nothing you need to be concerned about."

A strange look spread across Ethan's features. Julian couldn't quite read it, but he might have thought Ethan looked irritated or even angry. It was gone quickly, instead replaced by wry humor as he teased, "Does a certain student perhaps have you...strung out?"

Julian tensed but didn't trust himself to say anything. Not right now. Not with what she had just told him.

But as usual, Ethan had to push.

"Ah, I see," he said, wagging his brows. "It does have something to do with her, doesn't it?"

"I'm just tired," Julian deflected, his knuckles white in his lap.

"So," Ethan drawled, "you wouldn't mind if I finally made my move?"

Inhaling sharply, Julian said in a thin voice, "I meant what I said before. Keep her out of your escapades. She doesn't deserve that."

"Hmm, perhaps. Though, maybe it would be good for her, given how defiant she is. Plus, her mouth would look so pretty wrapped around my cock—"

"Enough."

Julian nearly shouted the word, standing abruptly and slamming his fist against the desk. He didn't even realize how ragged his breathing had become until the office had fallen silent. He shouldn't let Ethan get to him like this, not when there was so much at stake, but he couldn't let him talk about her like that.

And he wouldn't let Ethan touch her, wouldn't even let him near her now. She was his...his...

He didn't know what they were to each other anymore.

"I see I've hit a nerve," Ethan said quietly, though not gently.

Julian closed his eyes briefly before opening them and saying, "It's just been an odd day. I didn't mean to get angry."

Ethan laughed, standing too. "Oh, I think you did. But I do hope you remember to keep your feelings to yourself. For your sake and hers."

If he only knew...

"Right," Julian muttered, not even trying to deny it this time.

Ethan smirked triumphantly. "Well, I should get going. Drinks on Friday?"

Right now, Julian wanted to punch Ethan more than get a drink with him. But in a last-ditch effort to keep things normal, he grunted, "Sure."

After that, Ethan left, and that was when the full force of what was happening finally hit Julian, square in the face.

He'd gotten her pregnant. She was pregnant. With his child. *Their* child.

He had no idea how to do this, how to move forward or make things okay. But he did know, with absolute certainty, that he was going to do everything in his power to protect her from the shitstorm that was sure to soon hit them once it got out.

When Rowan got home later, after a grueling repertoire class, Amelia was waiting for her.

"I'm fine," Rowan said in a way of greeting. "It's all fine."

Amelia stepped in front of her before she could head to her bedroom.

"I need more than 'it's all fine.'"

Rowan sighed. "We're going to talk tonight. He's picking me up at seven, which is in two hours. So, I need to shower and take a nap."

"But what's going to happen?" Amelia pushed.

Rowan shrugged. "Nothing, for now. And before you call him an asshole again, that's my decision. I just want a little more time before it all changes."

Amelia looked down at her feet. "I get it, I guess. And what about you two?"

"What do you mean?"

"I mean... are you and him going to do this together? Like, as a couple?"

Rowan sighed. "I honestly have no idea, Ami."

"Do you love him?"

The question came out of nowhere, and it hit Rowan square in the chest as the answer tried to force itself from her lips.

Yes.

But she just muttered, "It wouldn't matter if I did."

Amelia shook her head. "It would. And Row?"

"Yeah?"

"The way he looked at you today when I, uh, shared the news... I see what Sam was saying. And I think that even though he's an asshole, you should give him a chance. But just one."

Rowan met Amelia's eyes and said, "We'll see."

Amelia nodded and finally let her pass. Rowan grabbed clothes and took a long, long shower. Then, she fell into bed, setting her alarm for 6:50 p.m.

Muffled voices woke her up. It was dark outside, and she let out a quiet groan at the ghost of the headache still lingering. She reached for her phone and swore as she saw the time.

7:15 p.m.

She raised her head a little as her bedroom door opened, and to her surprise, she saw Julian standing there. He'd changed, wearing dark jeans and a sweater, and he'd pulled his hair back into a bun like he had the night of the recital.

"Hey," he said. "Amelia let me in."

She rubbed her eyes and nodded. "Sorry. I must've set my alarm for a.m. instead of p.m. or something."

His features were unreadable as he said, "You can sleep if you need to. We can talk later."

She shook her head. "No, no. I'm coming."

He watched her closely as she hauled herself out of bed.

Her head spun as she stood, her body swaying. He was instantly at her side, holding her arm.

"Get up slower next time," he said.

"Yup, noted," she replied dryly.

Slowly, he let go of her arm, and she blinked against the light. Amelia was sitting on the couch, sheet music spread in front of her on the coffee table.

"Text me if you need anything," Amelia said sternly.

Rowan nodded. "I will. See you later."

Amelia eyed Julian, and he eyed her right back. She *had* gone off on him earlier today.

Rowan grabbed her bag and led Julian out into the hall, locking the door behind them. They walked in silence to his car, and he cranked the heat once they were inside. So he remembered the fact that she got cold easily.

He pulled out of the parking lot, and she watched the streetlights flicker by as he drove away from her complex. Snow floated down lazily, just a few flurries here and there.

"I'm sorry," he said after a few minutes. "About today at rehearsal."

"It's fine," she said, a little absentmindedly, tracing a finger over the fogged window.

She could feel his gaze on her but didn't look at him, not until they parked in front of his apartment complex, when he asked, "Are you hungry?"

She shrugged. "I suppose."

"You should eat."

She could hear the edge to his tone and, just like the night she'd stayed over, she had the vague sense he was fussing.

She forced herself to smile tightly. "I'll eat. Whatever you want."

He took a breath. "Alright. I was planning on cooking stir-fry. It's one of the few things I'm good at."

She nodded and said, "That's fine," as he turned off the car.

They got out, and she followed him. Once they were inside his apartment, she took off her coat, and he put it in the closet by the front door.

"The couch isn't wet anymore," he said. "So you can get settled there while I cook."

"Okay," she said, pulling her arms around herself.

He disappeared into the kitchen, and she sat down on the couch. Soon, classical music floated her way from a speaker he must have with him in the kitchen. She closed her eyes and listened to it, tapping her fingers along to the beat as the smell of ginger and soy sauce filled the air.

Before she knew it, she heard him say her name. She opened her eyes to find him standing in front of her.

"Is it ready?" she asked.

"Yeah," he said, and his voice sounded strangely hoarse.

She stood, and he led her to a small breakfast table, where he'd laid out two portions of stir-fry and rice, along with glasses of water. She smiled slightly at the orderliness of it all as he said, "What?"

"Nothing," she said. "It's just... You're very neat."

"Is that a bad thing?" he asked, raising a brow as he sat down.

"Not usually," she replied.

"And when would it be a bad thing?"

"I don't know. When something is out of order and you can't fix it."

She realized what it sounded like she was saying as soon as the words left her mouth. He shifted in his seat and only said, "You should eat."

She pursed her lips and sat down. They were quiet for a few minutes, just eating. Thankfully, any nausea kept itself at bay, and she was able to get through the meal without incident.

She took a deep breath and said, "So, um. We need to talk."

He looked at her, something cautious in his gaze. "Yes. Let me load the dishwasher, then we will."

She swallowed her last bite. "Gotcha."

He took away the dishes, and she wandered back to the couch. Unsurprisingly, he lit one of those cinnamon candles before he sat down next to her.

She cleared her throat, but he spoke first. "Rowan, I don't want you to think you have to worry about anything. I know being a grad student means you're probably tight on money, but I'm going to be there for you."

She nodded, thinking of the words Amelia had spoken earlier, about whether they were going to do this as a couple.

"And," he went on, "I don't want you to feel like you need to be pressured into anything. With me, I mean. I understand if you want to keep things..." He trailed off.

So what they'd said earlier today must have meant nothing to him. She swallowed hard and could only nod and say, "Okay."

"And as far as things at school," he said carefully. "We

can keep things normal, if that's what you really want, but not for long."

"I know," she whispered.

Because he could lose his job if neither of them said anything for too long. That danger was there, even at this point. But no one needed to know just how long this had been going on.

"We can work out more of the logistics later," he said heavily.

She could only nod. He was sitting on a cushion still, looking so, so far away.

"Do you want to go home?" he asked.

"No," she whispered. "I don't."

He met her eyes, still looking closed off, and said, "I have a few things to finish up. Do you mind?"

She shook her head and whispered, "No, of course not."

He cleared his throat and stood, heading for the bedroom. Then, he paused and asked, "Do you want me to turn the music back on? You seemed to like it."

She smiled tightly. "Yeah, thank you."

Once the music was playing, he turned without another word or glance and went to the bedroom, no doubt to sit at that desk she'd seen in there before.

She was still tired, and she laid down on the couch, intending to only close her eyes for a few minutes...

Julian sat at the desk in his bedroom, trying and failing to focus as the blue light of his laptop screen hurt his eyes. It was too warm in here. The food wasn't sitting well.

Everything was wrong. There was a wariness in her eyes when she looked at him now. A chasm stretched between them, widened by the words spoken tonight.

When something is out of order and you can't fix it.

As if she was a broken toy on the playground. As if he'd snapped her life in two. He supposed he had.

He stood, intending to go, and—well, he was not sure.

But when he went back out into the living room, she was curled up on the couch, asleep. She looked so small there, her legs tucked in and her brow just slightly creased. A chord struck deep within him, unexplainable feelings rushing through him so fast, he could hardly decipher them. He wanted to kiss her and shake her and demand *why?* Why choose me? Even if you didn't think this would be the outcome, why even risk anything to look at me like you have?

He realized he had been standing there, staring at her, for a while. Forcing himself to move, he draped a throw blanket over her, resisting the urge to smooth her brow. He turned off the lamp by the couch and went back to the bedroom.

She slept until he was nearly done with the work and already in bed, trying to read in an effort to distract himself.

"You can come in," he said as she knocked softly on the door frame.

She slipped into the room, staring at him, her large eyes shadowed with exhaustion and her braids coming undone.

"I didn't want to wake you," he said quietly in explanation.

She clenched her hands into fists and asked, "Can I have a change of clothes? And a toothbrush, maybe?"

He nodded and slipped out of the bed, wordlessly gathering sweatpants and a t-shirt, then handing them to her.

"In the cabinet, above the sink, there should be extra toothbrushes," he said, watching her carefully.

"Alright," she said. Her voice was so flat, so devoid of her usual spark.

He had done that. He had done this to her.

She went to the bathroom, and he sat back in the bed, picking up the book again and blinking back the burning in his eyes.

He only looked up when he heard her say, "What time do you have to be at school tomorrow?"

"I have to be there at eight. You?"

"Nine," she said. "Our lessons are my first class on Thursdays."

There was something so forced and pleasant about their exchanges now, and he hated it. He wanted things to go back to before, but they couldn't. They couldn't—and her life going forward was going to be intrinsically shackled to him.

She took a step forward and then another towards the bed. He watched her all the while, the book still in his hands. When she reached the edge of the bed, she folded back the blankets and climbed in. He stiffened, still gripping the book.

She took a breath and moved closer to him. He went utterly still as she took the book and set it to the side before she slid her legs around his hips, straddling him. He could hardly breathe as she looked at him, didn't know what to do with his body or where to look. They shouldn't do this again. He'd already caused her enough pain.

But eventually, he couldn't help but move his hands, skimming her waist. She placed her hands on his chest, her fingers curling in the fabric of his t-shirt. She began to move her hips, and he murmured her name. Softly. Imploringly. Begging her to stop and to also never let go.

"I want this," she whispered. "I want you."

A puff of air escaped him, and he tightened his hands on her hips. He wanted her. He wanted her so badly, it was making him shake. But there was still that stupid distance between them, and he didn't know how to bridge it. Didn't know if he even should, or if she even wanted him to try.

She kept moving her hips, grinding against his cock. Painfully hard and drowning in both guilt and the feel of her, he groaned. She let out a small noise, and he gasped, "Rowan, we—"

"Don't say we shouldn't," she breathed. "We've passed that bridge. I want to know what you *want*."

He huffed out a breath. "God, you. I want you. I want you so badly, it drives me out of my mind. But this isn't simple anymore."

"This was never simple," she said, her hand touching his cheek. "I want to know if what you said, earlier today in your office, was true."

He paused, and she held her breath. He could lie—probably should. The words had been true, but maybe she would be better off not being his completion. But with everything that had happened today, maybe...

Maybe it was too late. Perhaps they were already each other's downfall, and there was no coming back from it.

"It was true," he finally said.

Her eyes widened slightly, shining in the dim light. Something flickered across her face, and her lips parted, as if to say something. Instead, she leaned in and kissed him softly. The kiss quickly deepened, and her hips began to move again. He groaned against her mouth, skimming his hands underneath the t-shirt, palming her breasts. She let out a breathy moan as he ran his thumbs over her nipples, her back arching.

A low sound he almost didn't recognize escaped him, and he tugged her shirt off, throwing it to the floor. She tore at his shirt too, and it was off in an instant, tossed to the side. His mouth closed around her nipple, and she dug her nails into his shoulder, pleasure and pain making him tremble.

He looked up at her and murmured, "Sensitive?"

She nodded, and he hardly paused before swirling his tongue across her other nipple, gentler this time. She moaned, gripping his shoulder again. His hand squeezed her breast as he continued, and she gasped.

"Mhmm," he rumbled against her bare skin.

She tugged at the waistband of his sweatpants, and suddenly, he didn't care about restraint or the right thing anymore. He wanted to be inside her, to feel her tighten around his cock and make her moan his name. And by the way she was panting and writhing against him, he knew she wanted just the same.

He planted a quick kiss on her mouth, and then she

rolled off him momentarily, both of them stripping down to nothing before she settled back onto him.

She ground against him, gasping as he murmured, "So fucking wet."

She kissed him as she lowered herself, moaning against his mouth as he stretched and filled her. Her hands went to his hair, pulling out the ties and threading his fingers through it. As soon as she moved her hips, he hissed, "*Fuck.*"

She moved again, faster this time, and he said in a rough voice, "That's it, Rowan. Ride my cock."

His hand drifted between them, and she gasped as his fingers began to work her as she rode him. She began to shake, and she choked out, "Julian, please."

He groaned, the sound melding with her moans as she fell apart and soared in his arms. As soon as she looked back at him, instinct had him flipping her over on the bed, threading his fingers with hers.

And then, something changed.

The pace became slow, almost heady. Their gazes locked onto each other, and he felt as though he was tunneling into her eyes. His movements were unhurried and deep as her legs wrapped around his hips. His lips brushed hers, and he felt her breaths coming in quick gasps. Her name slipped from his lips, whispered like a prayer, like a plea. She was something holy, and all he could do was kneel at her altar. She had once said he held the power, but she was wrong. He was completely, utterly powerless in this moment, perhaps for every moment since he had met her.

A tear slipped down her cheek, and he kissed it away.

"Look at me," he said, his movements becoming a bit

faster, a bit more unchecked. He needed her to see exactly what she did to him.

And she did, holding his gaze as his body seized up and trembled. A low gasp slipped past his lips, and he came hard enough that his vision blurred. He gripped her hand tightly and let his head fall to her neck. She stroked a hand through his hair gently, and he knew that no matter what came, no one could take this moment from them.

Eventually, he pulled out and laid down next to her.

A while after, she murmured, "I'll be right back. Bathroom."

He nodded, brushing his thumb over her bottom lip. Words bubbled up as he tried to encompass what he was feeling. He pushed them away out of a lingering fear, even as she stared at him like he was sacred too. She finally looked away, pulling on the t-shirt he'd given her and padding to the bathroom on bare feet.

In the minutes she was gone, he managed to pull on boxer shorts and slump back down on the edge of the bed. He looked up as she paused at the doorway, her expression unreadable.

"You look far away," he said after a moment.

There was a confession and need in those words that he hadn't even really meant to show her, but he was exhausted, both physically and emotionally. He didn't have the energy to hide anything from her now.

She walked towards the bed and climbed in, whispering, "Come here."

He felt a little lost as he turned and met her gaze. But he laid down with her, facing her, their faces inches away. He reached out with a hand and slowly, gently caressed her cheek.

"Have you made a doctor's appointment yet?" he asked softly.

She sucked in a short breath and replied, "Not yet."

"I'll come with you," he said, and she shook her head.

"That's probably not a good idea."

But he only looked at her steadily and said, "I promised you wouldn't be alone in this. I meant that."

She bit her lip. "I'll let you know when I make it."

He nodded. "You should sleep."

She indeed looked exhausted, sleep tugging at her eyelids. She closed her eyes and, in the space between them, he laced his hand in hers. But he did not sleep, not at first, instead content to watch her drift off. There was a catch in his chest, and he pressed his lips on her forehead and whispered softly, "I'm going to take care of you. Both of you. I promise."

Chapter 16
This is Real

THEY WOKE up early the next morning so Julian could drop her off at her apartment before he headed to school. The drive was sleepy, and they were both quiet throughout it. As he parked in her lot, he glanced at her and said, "Don't forget to tell me. About the appointment, I mean."

She took a breath. "Alright. I'll see you later, I suppose."

She moved to get out of the car, but he grasped her hand gently, squeezing it tight once before letting her go. A silent, subtle goodbye until later.

She gave him a small smile and left, heading for her apartment.

Amelia was already up when she walked in, making breakfast. Well, 'making' a bowl of cereal. She whirled as soon as Rowan walked in the door and demanded, "How was it?"

Rowan sighed. "Good. Fine. He offered to come with me to my doctor's appointment once I make it."

Amelia made her way over to the couch, carefully

balancing her full cereal bowl as she sat down and patted the cushion next to her.

"I have to shower, Ami."

"Just a second," Amelia quipped.

Rowan sighed and joined her on the couch. Amelia set down the bowl of cereal on the coffee table and said, "I know this is probably scary for you, especially given that your dad was never around."

Rowan shrugged. Somehow, she had hardly thought of her absent father, but Amelia did have a point.

"I also think you need to be honest about your feelings for him, or you might regret it forever," Amelia went on.

"What feelings?" Rowan muttered.

Amelia gave her a look. "Row, c'mon. I know you feel something for him. And now is not the time to hold it all back. You're having his baby, for goodness sake."

Rowan screwed her eyes shut and said, "Now is precisely the time to hold back."

"Because you're afraid you'll scare him off?"

God, Amelia knew her too well. She opened her eyes and stared at her friend. Her voice cracked slightly as she said, "I can't lose him, Ami. And if this is the only way I get to have him, then that's fine by me. I'll deal with it."

She stood, done with this conversation, but Amelia called after her, saying one last thing. "He doesn't deserve you, you know. But I think if you told him you loved him, maybe you'll be surprised by the answer he gives you."

Rowan looked away and headed for her room. As she showered, she mulled over Amelia's words. But still, she decided against saying anything to him about it. It was too risky ,and things were still too shaky at a time when they desperately needed some semblance of stability.

After her shower, she vomited up nothing then called the local clinic that her student health insurance covered and made an appointment for the start of the next week. Her hands were shaking as she hung up the phone.

This was real. This was really, really happening.

Amelia had already left by the time she emerged from her room. She grabbed a granola bar and her coat, bag, and instrument case, then headed out. The air was frigid and biting, and she shivered the whole walk to campus. When she finally arrived, she headed for the private lesson rooms. When she reached the door, she took a deep breath and knocked.

"Come in," Julian said from the other side of the door.

She steeled herself and walked in. He had showered, and his damp hair was curling at the nape of his neck and around his ears as it dried. His shirt was unbuttoned slightly at the top, and she couldn't help but see the bare chest she knew was beneath. His eyes were shadowed, and he looked tired and stressed.

She tried to stop looking at all the details of him, tried to stop cataloging them. But as he looked at her, she had a feeling he was doing the same. Taking in her messy braid and soft floral shirt. Memorizing the blue of her eyes and itching to feel the fabric of her jeans where they curved over her hips.

Finally, she cleared her throat and turned, opening her instrument case and assembling her flute. She heard the piano bench creak, and once her instrument was ready, he played a note on the piano so she could tune. She did. He cleared his throat. She fidgeted with a string on the hem of her shirt. And then finally, he said, "Scales, Rowan."

She nodded and played through them, her hands steady and her breath keeping all the notes mostly afloat and smooth.

He nodded. "Good. We're going to work through some more technical exercises for the next couple weeks. Then, we can start thinking about a piece for the end-of-term recital...if you'll be participating?"

Those last four words were strained, and she knew why. She would be showing by then.

But she only nodded and said tightly, "Of course."

"Good," he said, but the word sounded hollow. "Let's start with the exercises, then."

He pulled out a few sheets and brushed past her to place them on the music stand. She tried not to lean into him as he reached forward and then moved away. Staring at the music sheets, touting the exercises they'd be working through, she asked, "Which one first?"

"Three," he replied.

She nodded and lifted her flute to her mouth to play through it. Once she was done, he said, "Again. Your breath support was a little weak."

He seemed to be falling back into their usual routine, relaxing a bit. She nodded and played it again. He furrowed his brow and walked over to her, pausing next to her before he said, "Something is up with your support. Play it again. I'm just going to feel your diaphragm if that's alright?"

She nodded, trying to avoid his eyes as she lifted her flute to her lips again. His hands were warm even through her shirt as he placed them lightly over her abdomen. She tried to ignore what the touch did to her. Tried and failed as she watched his gaze lower, felt his hand inch further down. Slowly, she paused and lowered her instrument. His hand was still resting on her stomach, his eyes on the same spot.

"Julian?" she whispered.

His breath shuddered out, and his gaze snapped up to hers as he said hoarsely, "I'm sorry. I wasn't trying to... I was just trying to check your breath support."

"I know," she said softly.

She tentatively placed a hand atop his. They stayed like that for only a few seconds before she pulled her hand back and whispered, "We should continue."

His jaw tightened as he said, "We should."

With what seemed to be a monumental effort, he pulled his hand away and said, "Try number six."

She did. And so, they continued with the lesson, maintaining as much a sense of normalcy as they could. Still, she caught him staring at her stomach a few times throughout the hour.

When they wrapped up for the day and she had cleaned and packed up her instrument, she said quietly, "Next Monday. At four-thirty."

He furrowed his brow, but then understanding dawned over his features. He nodded and said, "I'll be there."

"Do you have a class to teach or lessons then? I know it's not an ideal time, but—"

"Rowan. I'll be there," he said firmly.

She bit her lip and whispered, "Okay. I'll see you later."

"Later," he affirmed.

She left with no small amount of effort and headed to the coffee shop. She had just ordered a mint tea when she heard a gaggle of girls, including Helen, one of Julian's other students, whispering loudly in the corner. She casually took a seat close to them, put in earbuds without the sound on, and listened.

"I swear to God, it's hard to get through our lessons. He's so intense, and all I can think the whole time is how much I want to have his babies."

That was Helen.

"Why don't you?" one of the other girls giggled.

Helen sighed. "I just might. I mean, maybe he feels something too. He *did* help me with my stuff that one time."

"You mean, like, three months ago, when you dropped your shit all over the floor?" a girl said, laughing. "Really, Helen, you should let that go. He was just being nice. Besides, didn't you say he pretty much ran after..." The girl glanced up, and Rowan dutifully tapped her fingers, as if along to the music it looked like she was listening to.

"I don't know what exactly happened," Helen muttered.

"Remember that guy, Jake?" a girl said, and Rowan held in a flinch. "My roommate told me something crazy about why he left. That he had kissed..." Rowan assumed the girl was indicating her head. "You know. He was always talking about her. Well, apparently, she told him to stop and he didn't. Professor Lynch showed up and grabbed Jake and started yelling at him. And then you-know-who left with him."

"Left?" Helen whispered.

"To fill out a Title IX form or something, apparently."

"Which is probably what she did, since Jake's not here anymore," someone else pointed out. "What's your point, Ella?"

There was a pause, then Ella said, "I'm just thinking... If he's interested in a student, it might not be you, Helen."

If only they knew.

Helen scoffed and muttered, "No way," just as the barista called Rowan's name. She got up, and the girls immediately fell silent. She gave them all a small smile as she breezed past. They returned it, though she caught a gleam in Helen's eye as she looked at her.

As soon as she was out of the coffee shop, she swore softly. This was not good. People were already talking. People had noticed. And soon, when she and Julian inevitably had to come clean, everyone would know.

She drank the tea, threw it up in the women's bathroom, and then headed to her theory class.

The next Monday morning, after a tense lesson with Julian, she squirmed in her seat in orchestra practice. Thankfully, Professor Lark didn't ask for the soloists to play, and the rehearsal went fairly quickly. Afterward, she had a few classes, including the dreaded advanced theory class, and then she headed home. Amelia had promised she would feign a migraine and leave jazz rehearsal early so she could be there when Rowan left for the appointment.

Indeed, by the time Rowan was home, she was sitting on the couch, working on transposing a piece. She shot up when Rowan entered the apartment.

"Is he picking you up?" she asked immediately. "I forgot to ask."

Rowan shook her head. "No. He has to get back to school pretty soon after, so I told him I'd just drive separately."

Amelia nodded. "That makes sense, I suppose. Are you ready?"

Rowan shrugged. "I think so. I don't even know how these things work."

"I looked it up and—"

"Ami. I'll find out in like thirty minutes. I can wait."

Amelia chewed on her lip. "Okay, okay. Sorry. If it was me, I'd want to know everything."

Rowan felt a little guilty and said, "I don't *not* care. I just... I'm adjusting to it all."

Amelia smiled softly. "I know, Row. You're going to make the best mom, like actually. And you have time."

Rowan cleared her throat. "I should get going."

Amelia nodded but asked, "Have you eaten today?"

"A granola bar and tea, both of which I hurled," Rowan replied tiredly.

Amelia made a face and stood. "You need to eat. I'm buying chicken noodle soup from that café near campus. I have night class, but I'll put it in the fridge, and you better eat some."

"Ami, you don't have to."

"Yes, I do. Because I want to. Now, shut up and go to your appointment."

Rowan sighed, glancing at her phone. She did need to go. Once she grabbed her car keys from the little dish on the counter, Amelia hugged her quickly, and Rowan headed to her car.

Amelia left first, waving as she walked away. Rowan smiled slightly, waving back and then leaving herself. It was a twenty-minute drive to the clinic, but she managed to get there five minutes early. She didn't see Julian's car in the lot, but she decided to go in, knowing there would likely be paperwork to fill out before the appointment.

When she walked in, her hands clammy and shaking, a young-looking receptionist greeted her with a smile.

"Hello, how can I help you?" she asked Rowan.

"Um, I have a four-thirty appointment with Dr. Wright."

The receptionist beamed and nodded, asking, "Name and date of birth?"

"Rowan Evans, August third, 2000."

"Alright, Ms. Evans, I just have a few forms for you to fill out. Bring them back here when you're done, and Dr. Wright should be with you soon."

Rowan nodded, taking the clipboard of forms and a pen. Then, she paused and said awkwardly, "Um, I do have someone coming with me to the appointment. He's not here yet, but..." She trailed off.

The receptionist nodded knowingly. "Of course. If he gets here after you go back, I'll direct him in."

Rowan took a deep breath. "Thanks."

"Of course."

Rowan took a seat in the hard chairs of the waiting room and quickly filled out the forms. The air smelled like antiseptic lightly concealed by some sort of floral air freshener. She finished the last form and glanced at her phone, which read 4:35.

Maybe he wasn't coming. Maybe he'd changed his mind. It would be fine. She could do this on her own. She could...

She heard the receptionist speak, and she looked up to see Julian standing a few feet away, his hair windblown. He met her eyes and then strode over quickly, taking a seat next to her and saying quietly, "I'm sorry I'm late. I got caught up... A student was being difficult."

"Helen?" she guessed.

He furrowed his brow. "How did you...?"

But then, a nurse called her name from a door off the side of the waiting room. Rowan pursed her lips and stood, Julian following her. She dropped the forms off with the receptionist, who was shamelessly eyeing Julian. Rowan resisted the urge to slap her.

"Easy," Julian murmured in her ear. She glanced up at him, and he smiled slightly as he said in a low voice, "I'm not about to run off with the receptionist."

She couldn't help the small smile that surfaced. Then, they headed for the door, where the nurse was looking impatient.

"Follow me," she clipped out.

She led them to a small room, and the nurse handed Rowan a cup.

"Bathroom is down the hall, the first door on the left. We just need to confirm your pregnancy. We should have the results before the doctor even comes in."

Rowan nodded, a small feeling erupting in her chest.

What if the pharmacy test had been wrong? That would be good, right? Right...

She took the cup and headed for the bathroom. Julian took a seat in the chair in the room, waiting. When she returned, she handed the nurse the cup, and she disappeared.

Rowan sat in the chair next to Julian, bouncing her knee and clasping and unclasping her shaking hands. He glanced at her, and gently, he untangled her hands and took one of them in his, squeezing gently.

The nurse returned a few minutes later, and still, he didn't let go of her hand as the nurse said, "You are pregnant. The ultrasound will confirm how many weeks."

Rowan took a shuddering breath and nodded. Julian gripped her hand tighter, and she wondered if now, it was more for his sake than hers.

"Sit on the table, please. I need to take your blood pressure and pulse."

Julian released Rowan's hand, and she walked over to the examination table, perching on the end. The nurse took Rowan's blood pressure and pulse, her brow furrowing.

"Are you stressed?" the nurse asked, and Rowan shrugged.

"A little, I suppose."

Julian was watching closely as the nurse said, "Your blood pressure is a bit high, and so is your pulse. You're going to need to learn how to manage your stress, or it could cause issues down the line, or even cause you to miscarry.'

Rowan clenched her hands and nodded. Julian watched every movement of the nurse as she removed the blood pressure cuff and stepped back from Rowan. Then, she glanced at them both and said, "The doctor should be in soon. After he talks to you, I'll take you to a different room for the ultrasound."

Both Rowan and Julian nodded, and then, they were alone again. For a moment, she just stared at the wall of brochures, touting information about birth control pills, STIs, and pregnancy. After a couple of minutes, Julian broke the silence and said, "You'll listen to what she said...about managing stress?"

Rowan glanced at him. "I'll try. I am a grad student, though."

Julian's jaw clenched, but before he could speak again, there was a short rap on the door, and then the doctor entered. He was a middle-aged man, with silvery-brown hair and kind eyes.

"So," he said. "I'm Dr. Wright. I'll be with you through your whole pregnancy, and if you'd like, I can do the delivery. We'll get to know each other quite well."

He glanced at Julian and said, "I'll assume this is Dad?"

Julian nodded, though she noticed he paled a little. She realized this was the first time he'd been referred to as a father. The situation was becoming very real, very quickly.

Dr. Wright walked over to her. "The nurse told me your blood pressure was a little high. Said you were stressed. There are ways to manage that, but it'll be up to you."

She nodded and took a deep breath. "I'm a grad student. Stress is kind of a part of the job."

Dr. Wright smiled. "Grandview?"

She nodded, and he said, "That's where I went for my undergraduate degree. What do you study?"

She swallowed. "Music. I play the flute."

Dr. Wright smiled wider. "Ah, my girls both play the flute. Such a pretty instrument." Then, he sighed and said, "I know grad school is rough, but I think pulling back a little bit and finding some balance, at least while you're pregnant, is going to be pretty vital to ensuring things go smoothly here."

She could only nod.

"I'm just going to listen to a couple of things here," he said, pulling out his stethoscope.

Julian watched closely again, a sharpness in his features, as the doctor listened to her lungs and heart and then pressed on her stomach in a few spots.

"Alright. All sounds good to me, so I'll let the nurse know she can take you over for your ultrasound. It was nice to meet you both, and I'll see you in a few weeks."

"Thank you," Julian said quietly, and Doctor Wright glanced at him and said, "Were you in the Elgin Symphony Orchestra? About, oh my goodness...seven years ago?"

Julian's expression clouded slightly, but he said, "I was."

Dr. Wright smiled. "My wife and I saw you play, I think. Thought I recognized you somehow."

Julian nodded, and the doctor looked back at Rowan one last time before he left the room.

"I didn't know that," she said to Julian. "That you played in Elgin. I grew up really close to there. Batavia."

He smiled tightly. "Funny."

Though there was nothing "funny" in his expression nor his tone, especially as the nurse walked back in and led them to the ultrasound room. Rowan laid back and pulled up her shirt so the technician could squirt goo on her stomach.

"Sorry, I know it's cold," the woman said as Rowan flinched slightly.

"It's okay," Rowan said.

The technician adjusted her oval glasses and then pressed the instrument to Rowan's stomach, swirling it around as images began to blur on the screen above them. After a few seconds of charged silence, a small, steady *thump* began to fill the room.

"That's your baby's heartbeat," the technician said casually. "It looks like you're at about eight weeks, so I can't tell the sex yet."

Rowan barely felt like she was breathing as she stared at the grainy blur on the screen. Her hand was resting at her side, and she felt Julian take it, his own hand shaking.

She didn't dare look at him, not yet.

"Is everything else okay?" she heard him ask, as if from far away.

The technician nodded. "Yup. Everything looks perfectly normal."

Beside her, Julian released an audible breath. The technician sighed as she removed the instrument and flicked off the screen. Rowan kept staring at it, even as it went blank. That was, until the technician handed her a towel to wipe off the goop and then led them back out into the waiting room. Julian lingered close by as she made an appointment for four weeks from now. Then, they were done, heading out into the cold winter air.

They both paused, but then Julian moved or she moved, and he pulled her to his chest, breathing deeply.

"This is real," she said.

He nodded against her hair and whispered, "This is real."

She pulled back and said, "I know you need to get back to campus.'

He took a deep breath. "I do. I have a lot of work to do this week, but... Friday night. Can you come over?"

She gripped the fabric of his shirt. "Yeah, I can do that."

His brow creased, but then he let her go, brushing a hand down her cheek in farewell and then heading for his car.

She did the same.

Chapter 17
The Edge of a Cliff

THE WEEK WAS AGONIZINGLY slow and full of lots of vomit. At this point, she could hardly keep anything down, and Amelia was starting to get worried. On Thursday morning, she threatened to call 911 after Rowan threw up so forcefully, she had a ten-minute-long coughing fit afterward.

When she could finally breathe again, she said, "Ami, I'm fine. This is normal."

"I'm really about to call Professor McHotty and make him call an ambulance. Maybe you'll listen to him."

Rowan gave her a look. She had given Julian's number to Amelia a few days ago, just in case something happened and Rowan couldn't text or call him. She was beginning to regret that decision.

"Ami, this happens. Remember, you said you read that morning sickness can be really bad?"

Amelia shook her head. "You have to be able to keep *something* down. This just can't be good for you or the baby."

Rowan shrugged, resisting the sudden urge to cover her stomach with her hand.

"Row," Amelia said. "If you can't eat without hurling by the time the weekend is over, I'm either calling your doctor myself and making an appointment, or I'll drag you to the ER."

"I have to get to class," Rowan said, deflecting.

Amelia sighed and shouted at Rowan as she walked out the door, "I mean it!"

Somehow, Julian managed to get through Rowan's lesson on Thursday without slipping too much. He truly hadn't meant to the other day, but it was becoming near-impossible to maintain any sense of professionalism between them. He knew it was time to say something, to drop the ruse that everything was normal, but he was holding off, mostly out of fear for her. He didn't want her to get dragged down for this. He just needed to make sure she was okay.

Later that day, when he saw her in the coffee shop, he couldn't help but peer at her order and make sure she wasn't actually drinking coffee. She wasn't, of course. She always drank tea. Still, his overprotectiveness earned him a look from her—nothing too damning, since they were very much in public. It took no small amount of self-control to keep from moving closer to her as she said slyly, "See you on Monday, *Professor*."

She knew it too, by the way she smirked. He only glared at her as she left.

The rest of the day was uneventful, and he didn't get a chance to see her again before he left campus. Friday morning, Ethan stopped him in the hall.

"Julian," he said. "We still good for drinks tonight?"

He'd nearly forgotten he had agreed to that. He cleared his throat and said, "I'll have to cancel. I'm sorry, something came up."

Ethan raised a brow. "Are you going to elaborate on that?"

Julian paused. "Am I obligated to?"

"No," Ethan said, leaning against the wall. "But I know you well enough by now to know you're hiding something. I'm just curious to know what it is."

For a moment, he debated telling Ethan everything. Amelia knew, after all. Maybe it would help to confide in a friend. But even if Ethan was his friend and had been for many years... He had said such awful things about Rowan. How could Julian trust him with anything pertaining to her?

"It's nothing," Julian finally said.

Ethan's eyes narrowed. "Fine, then."

And with that, he strode away down the hall. Julian let out a long breath just as he heard a mildly familiar voice say, "Well, damn."

He turned to see none other than Amelia standing behind him, an overstuffed folder of sheet music in her arms.

"Amelia," he said slowly. "Do you need something?"

He was still wary of her, unsure where he stood in her mind.

After all, only a week ago, she'd stood in his office and accused him of being an asshole. Which, to be fair, he had been. But she was important to Rowan, so he didn't want to write her off.

Amelia shifted on her feet. "Um, can we talk? In your office, probably. It'll only take a sec."

He swallowed and nodded, leading her just down the hall. Nerves fluttered in his stomach—had something happened?

Once he shut the door, Amelia asked, "Does Professor Petrarch not know, then?"

Julian creased his brow. "No. Why do you ask?"

She shrugged. "Rowan told me you guys are friends, so I just wondered if you had told him."

Julian cleared his throat. "Like I said, no."

Amelia snorted. "Well, you're just all warm and cuddly, aren't you?"

"Amelia," he pressed. "Is something wrong?"

She scrutinized him for a long moment before she said, "That right there is the only reason I let you within ten feet of Rowan."

"What?"

Leaning back against the closed door, she said, a shade quieter, "Because you genuinely care about her. Despite how fucked up this whole thing is, that's pretty clear." She paused, then added, "She's not eating enough. The morning sickness, it's making it hard for her to keep anything down. I almost called 911 this morning. She sounded like she was choking because she threw up so forcefully. I know Rowan, and I know she'll probably try to act like everything is fine. So, I thought I'd tell you. Maybe you can help in some way I can't."

Fear sharpened his senses, but he forced himself to stay calm as he said, "Thank you for telling me. I'll see... I'll do what I can."

Amelia nodded and left without another word.

For the next hour or so, he rotated between worrying and working. He would get through a bit, and then he would remember the conversion he'd just had with Amelia, and his focus would slip. Around six, there was a knock on his office door.

Unsure of who it was, he stood and opened it to find Maggie standing there.

"Hi, can I help you?" he said.

She smiled warmly and gestured to the chairs and desk. "Do you have a moment to talk?"

He nodded, trying to conceal his wariness. She must've noticed, though, because she said, "Relax, Julian. This is going to be a positive conversation for the most part."

He cleared his throat, sitting at the desk across from her. She laid her hands flat on the surface and said, "So, I recently talked to John."

"How is he?" Julian asked, genuinely concerned.

Maggie grimaced. "Not very well. And he's decided that even if his condition improves, he won't be returning to teach."

"I'm sorry to hear that."

She nodded. "It's a tough blow for the department. But luckily, we have you. I'd like to offer you a more permanent position here. Tenure-track, full benefits...the works."

He stared at her for a moment, a little shocked. He hadn't expected an offer like this, at least, not one so soon. And there was also the matter of things the department didn't know about. Things that might cause them to retract such an offer.

"I'm honored," he finally said. "Can I take some time to think about it?"

She nodded. "Most definitely. I wasn't expecting you to give me an answer tonight. I'll email you the full contract as soon as I get back to my office, but I wanted to ask you personally."

"Well, thank you."

She laughed softly. "There's another thing too, if it isn't too much to spring on you."

He waited.

"John and Penny were both set to perform at the C.S.O. this spring. Obviously, John won't be able to, but I spoke with a few of my friends over there, and they would be happy to have you take over his visiting spot."

True shock coursed through him. He knew how big of a deal this was.

"Again, I would be honored," he said.

"Can I confirm with them then? There will just be a couple of rehearsals you'll have to attend."

He nodded. "Of course, go ahead."

She smiled and sighed. "Good. I'll let you think about the offer for now. Have a good weekend."

"You too," he said as she stood and left.

As soon as she was gone and he glanced at his watch, he swore quietly. It was nearly seven, and he'd told Rowan he would be there then. Quickly, he stood and began to gather his things, his mind whirring.

When seven o'clock came and went and she had still not heard from Julian, Rowan began to worry.

"Chill," Amelia said from the couch as Rowan started to pace. "I'm sure he just got caught up at school."

"That's what I'm worried about," Rowan snapped.

"What do you mean?"

She stopped walking. "The other day, at the coffee shop we always go to, I overheard Helen, you know, one of his other students, and some of her friends talking. At first, it was basically Helen just pining for Julian, but then one of her friends mentioned me."

"In what way?" Amelia asked.

Rowan shook her head. "It was just gossip, but the girl was basically saying she thought there was something between Julian and me."

"Which there definitely is," Amelia pointed out.

Rowan gave her a look. "Ami, not helping."

Amelia shrugged. "They're going to know soon anyway. I mean, you guys are going to have to come clean pretty soon, before you start showing. I think you're an idiot and so is he for not saying something to administration right away, but it's not my life."

Rowan took a heavy breath just as her phone buzzed in

her pocket. As soon as she saw it was Julian calling, she picked up.

"Hey," he said from the other line. "Sorry, I'm just leaving campus."

She took a shallow breath. "It's fine."

He paused. "Are you alright?"

"I'm fine."

There was another pause that told her he wasn't convinced, but he just said, "I'll head your way now, then, if that works."

"Yup," she said, probably a little too cheerfully, and then cut the call.

Amelia rolled her eyes as soon as Rowan looked at her.

"You are down so bad for that man, it's not even funny," Amelia said.

Rowan ignored her comment, muttering that she would be right back. She went to her room and, for once, packed an overnight bag. She debated throwing in some of her transcription homework but decided she'd finish it tomorrow. She'd already worked through most of it during her break between classes today.

Her phone buzzed again, just as she was leaving her room. Just a text, letting her know he was here.

She had the fleeting thought that maybe they should be more discreet about this, since there *were* probably students living in this complex. No music students that she knew of, but then again, she hardly interacted with her neighbors.

"Bye," Amelia called as Rowan headed for the door. "Be safe. And try to eat something!"

Rowan snorted. "We'll see," and then left before Amelia could reprimand her further.

The car was warm when she got in, and he was staring at an email or something to that effect on his phone.

"All good?" she asked.

He looked up, clearing his throat. "Yeah."

She narrowed her eyes. "You're sure?"

He pursed his lips. "They... I was just offered a more permanent position in the department."

At the expression on his face, understanding dawned over her. Now, soon, was the time for this charade to be over if he didn't want to jeopardize his job.

"I have some time before they need a final decision," he said. "But—"

"I know," she cut him off. "I know. We'll have to come clean before then."

He nodded and then pulled out of the lot.

"It's going to be okay," he said softly, glancing sidelong at her.

She only shrugged, and he didn't say anything for the rest of the drive.

"Amelia told me, you know," was the first thing he said to her as they stepped into his apartment.

"Told you what?" she asked warily. There were lots of things Amelia could have told him.

He cocked his head at her. "That you're hardly eating and keeping none of it down."

She sagged slightly in relief and replied, "It's just how it is."

He pulled off his coat and offered to take hers. She gave it to him, and once he'd hung them in the closet, he moved close to her, lifting his hand to her cheek. "Rowan, you need to take care of yourself. I meant that the first time I said it, and I mean it now."

Right. When he had berated her for her bloodshot eyes and lack of sleep, and then she'd kissed him. His eyes flickered, as if remembering that moment too.

"I am. I'm trying," she said heavily. "I'm just tired. And," she took a breath, "I'm scared, Julian. I don't like to admit that often, but right now... I'm terrified, and everything feels like it's balancing on the edge of a cliff, and I'm about to fall over the edge and crash."

"I'm scared too," he admitted quietly. "But I promise, if you crash, so do I. I'll be with you through it all."

"Thank you," she whispered.

He pressed his lips to her forehead then said, "Why don't we try to eat?"

He cooked and she sat on the couch, fighting nausea, but somehow, she managed to keep the pasta and bread down. They watched some weird documentary, and she fell asleep against his shoulder. She awoke in the bed, her head in his lap as he read, the salt lamp the only light in the room.

"You'll strain your eyes, reading in dim light like this," she muttered sleepily.

He looked down, tapping on the glasses perched on his

nose as he said, "My eyes are already strained. Being a musician has done that much."

She smiled hazily. "I like the glasses on you."

He chuckled softly. "And why is that?"

She narrowed her eyes and deadpanned, "Because it just really fulfills my student-professor fantasy. Makes you look more the part."

It was his turn to narrow his eyes as he set the book down on the table next to him. He took off the glasses too, setting them on top of the book. She shifted so she was lying on the pillows. He laid down next to her and leaned in, peppering kisses up her jaw. His lips were warm and soft as they met hers in a slow kiss. She gripped at the collar of his shirt and his hands threaded in her hair.

They moved closer to each other, and she hooked her leg around him. He made a low noise and pushed his hips into hers. Everything after that was slow and unhurried.

For the second time ever, they made love.

And as he stilled inside of her, she swallowed the words that were pushing to the surface. After she'd used the bathroom and they both brushed their teeth, he pulled her tight to him in the dark, kissing her neck softly and murmuring, "Goodnight, Rowan."

"Goodnight," she whispered.

Chapter 18
An Original Piece, Part Two

THREE AND HALF WEEKS LATER, Rowan sat in that same room in the clinic, Julian once again at her side.

The month had been a blur of classes, nausea, headaches, and weekends spent with Julian. She still hadn't told him she loved him, even if the words tried to surface nearly every time they were alone.

Julian was close to giving an answer about his position at Grandview, but she knew, deep down, he had only hesitated because of her.

At the check-up, Dr. Wright had given her some medication for the nausea, looking slightly concerned as she described how bad it had been.

"Are you two wanting to know the sex?" the ultrasound technician, a different one than last time, asked.

She glanced at Julian, who said quietly, "It's up to you."

Looking back at the technician, she nodded. The woman smiled and said, "Alright. Let's take a look."

She lowered the instrument onto Rowan's goo-smeared stomach, and an image slowly formed on the screen.

It was a baby now, undeniably so, not just a smudge of black and white and gray. The tech moved the instrument around and said, "Okay... It looks like you're having a little girl."

Julian's hand, holding hers, tightened. She glanced at him to find his eyes wide and glued to the screen. She looked back too as the tech said, "Everything looks to be in order to me, but the doctor will call you soon with the full results. Do you want me to print a picture?"

Rowan was about to say no, it was alright, but Julian spoke before she could, saying, "Yes."

She looked at him as the tech pushed a few buttons and then removed the instrument from Rowan's stomach. He didn't say anything, just brushed a thumb down her palm.

Rowan cleaned the goo off her stomach, and then the tech handed them a photo of the ultrasound. Of their daughter.

Rowan made another appointment at the front desk before they left. Once they were out in the parking lot, she said, "You can keep the photo."

He eyed her and asked, "Are you alright?"

Rubbing her eyes, she replied, "I'm okay."

"You're not regretting—"

"No," she said, cutting him off. "I want this. It's just a lot."

He sighed, glancing at the photo. "I know. I need to go, but I'll see you tomorrow at school."

"Alright," she said.

He kissed her forehead, such a simple gesture, and then left. She wondered if he knew how much it meant to her.

The next morning, when she walked into the practice room, that ultrasound photo wouldn't stop flashing in her mind, making her feel shaky and unbalanced.

Julian was sitting on the piano bench, facing her as she entered.

"Hi," she said quietly.

He nodded. "Get your instrument out."

She did so and glanced over curiously as he assembled his own.

"We're going to play together today," he said before tuning his flute. She followed suit, and then he placed a piece of sheet music on the music stand. It was a duet, untitled and unfamiliar to her.

"What is it?" she asked.

"A composition of mine. I want to see if it sounds how I want, with someone else playing. We'll just run through it a few times. Don't worry about being perfect, since you've never seen it before."

She nodded and lifted her flute to her mouth. He played the opening, then she played a completely different section before they wove together in what almost sounded like a dance, a game of push and pull until the melodies clashed together in a sweeping crescendo of sound. And then, the piece quieted and became slower and sweeter. Finally, the ending heightened again, that push and pull returning and ending on a trill.

As she lowered her flute, she realized...

This was them. He'd written them into music.

She turned to him, shaking her head. Emotion was overcoming her so strongly, and she was powerless to it. Despite where they were and what they were supposed to be doing, she looked at him and said, "I love you."

His entire body seized up. And then, he met her eyes, his expression hard, and said, "No, you don't."

She looked away, hurt already pulsing through in a painful beat as she whispered, "You cannot tell me what to feel and what not to feel."

When she looked back at him, he was still unyielding as he said quietly, but not weakly or softly, "You shouldn't be feeling that. I don't know what you want me to say, Rowan."

She stared at him, at the sudden coldness, and shook her head, turning and cleaning and packing up her flute with shaking hands.

"If you want an out, you have an out," she said sharply.

His nostrils flared. "I didn't say—"

"I heard what you said. Goodbye, Julian," she shot back and stormed out of the room.

She blinked back the tears threatening to surface and instead honed in her anger. He had led her on, led her to believe she made him feel. She had truly thought he'd reciprocate *something*. Anything.

She headed down the hall, towards the practice rooms, her breath shallow and her heart a quick, nervous beat. She felt sick as she opened the door to the practice room she'd reserved earlier. The lights were off as she entered, which was strange.

She flicked on the switch and blinked, her eyes adjusting. And then she saw the word, written in red paint on the far wall.

Whore.

She froze, just as the door clicked shut behind her. For a moment, she stood there, her shallow breath the only sound, until she heard someone *else* breathing. She whirled, and in through her panicked, half-blurred vision, she saw Jake standing there, a grin on his face—a smile that was strangely unhinged and devious.

"Hello, Rowan," he said. "You've had an interesting past few months, haven't you?"

"Jake," she said breathlessly. "What are you doing here?"

He cocked his head. "You ruined my life, Rowan. All because of a misunderstanding. The professors and administration decided to kick me out of the program, but I'm sure you've realized that. And you want to know who the biggest advocate for my expulsion was?"

She was silent. She didn't need to ask.

He smiled. "Oh, you know. That professor you've been fucking."

"You're wrong." Her hands were shaking so hard, she almost dropped her music folder.

He shook his head, taking a step towards her. "Oh, but I'm not. I know you go to his apartment and I know you stay the night. More than once, actually. What a naughty student and an even naughtier professor. In fact, I think it's my duty to report both of you, right after I finish up here."

"Jake, please," she whispered, the fear of uncertainty cresting in a tidal wave over her. "I didn't mean to hurt you."

"Shut that pretty mouth of yours," he said, lifting a hand and caressing her chin. She flinched as he went on, "And take your punishment."

That was when she realized the floor was wet. And it smelled like...

Gasoline.

Holy god in heaven, there was a thin stream of gasoline separating her and the door. And in Jake's hand was a tiny purple lighter.

Without another thought, another breath, she lunged for the door, but he caught her, shoving her hard against the far wall where the paint was. She gasped as he held her roughly, and she choked out, "Please, Jake. I'm pregnant. Please."

She saw the conflict momentarily flicker across his face, but it was gone in an instant, that terrifying smile returning. "Well, this will really be a lesson for the professor then. He made me lose everything. Now, I'll take everything from him."

He shoved her against the wall, and she screamed, half on instinct, half on purpose, a loud, screeching sound that she prayed someone would hear in time.

Jake smiled, flicked the lighter on, and dropped it, letting it catch on the line of gasoline. She screamed again, as loud as she could, as flames rushed around her in a half-circle.

She tried to lunge forward, but the fire was already

licking too high for her to get through. When she looked for Jake again, he was already gone.

The fire alarms and sprinklers weren't going off. Why, why, *why?*

He must have somehow disabled them in this hall. She would be dead before the fire spread into another area of the building and set them off.

"Help me!" she screamed, the sound tearing at her throat. "Fire! Help me!"

The door flew open, and she saw a wide-eyed girl, who backed away as soon as she saw the flames.

"I'll go get help!" the girl shouted. "I'll be right back!"

Rowan coughed as the smoke started to force itself down her throat. She pressed herself against the wall as much as she could, one hand flattening instinctually on her stomach. The piano caught aflame, and the fire spread into the hall beyond. Somewhere through the smoke and flames and blind panic, she thought she was at least glad she had said it. Maybe she was going to die, but at least he knew.

Vaguely, she heard footsteps racing down the hall as she began to cough again, uncontrollably so now.

"Did you call 911?" a voice frantically demanded.

"Yes, but, Professor, someone is in there!"

"Who?"

Rowan coughed ,and through the flames, she vaguely saw Professor Petrarch.

"A girl...with red hair in a braid and—"

"Rowan!" Professor Petrarch shouted almost immediately. "Rowan! Can you hear me?"

"Help," she gasped just as her vision began to tilt and fade.

Julian was walking through the main lobby, back to his office, when he smelled the smoke. He froze, narrowing his eyes and turning. No smoke alarms were going off, so maybe some idiot had just lit a cigarette inside.

An idiot.

Like him.

He might have just lost her now. It twisted his stomach to think about the way the spark in her eyes had sputtered out as soon as he had refused the words she had laid bare. He was just so damn afraid. It was selfish and stupid, and he'd probably just ruined everything.

He was just about to make his way up the stairs to the second level when he heard the screaming.

The hairs on the back of his neck stood up. He recognized that voice. He would recognize that voice in a room full of a hundred people.

Without a second thought, he broke into a sprint, following the scent of smoke that was growing thicker by the second. Commotion was blooming in the lobby around him as people realized what was happening. He didn't care, shoving people aside as he ran.

He had to be wrong. She was okay. She needed to be okay—

He skidded to a stop when he saw Ethan and another student backing away down the hall from a small wing of practice rooms nearly engulfed in flames.

He met Ethan's eyes, the truth written all over his face.

"We called 911," Ethan began, but Julian hardly waited for him to finish before frantically searching for a way into the room.

"Rowan!" he bellowed, the heat and panic making him sweat.

The firefighters would not make it in time, Ethan had to know that. And quite suddenly, he realized, he would rather die saving her than be here without her.

He loved her. He loved her. God, it was all he could think as he stared at the flames. He loved her and he could not —*would* not let her go.

He managed to get to the entrance of the practice room and kicked the door further open, darting into the room just as Ethan shouted, "Julian, no!"

The flames surrounded him, and the air was thick with smoke. He didn't care, not as he saw her slumped against the far wall. It would be nearly impossible to reach her from where he stood, but if he didn't try now...

This room was about to collapse, and then they'd both be trapped anyway.

Bracing himself, he forged ahead, choking back a scream as he felt his flesh burning. He just had to get to her. He kept repeating it in his mind, a tether through the pain.

She was barely conscious, limp in his arms by the time he managed to pick her up. He ignored the pain, ignored the seizing of his lungs, ignored the fact that the room was about to fall in on them. All he could do was focus on getting her out.

"Jake," she muttered, her voice thin and rasping. "Jake did this. He's probably still here..." She trailed off, coughing.

Rage bloomed in his gut, cutting through even the danger around them, but he shoved it aside quickly. He could worry about anger and revenge later, especially as the room groaned and the flames licked higher.

Sirens wailed in the distance just as he saw a small opening in the inferno. He hardly waited before rushing through it. Something hit his head, but he kept going, his chest wrenching at the whimper Rowan made. He knew it was hurting her. He was. *He* had done this. If he hadn't been such a coward, she would be safe, but now, as he broke out into the smoke-filled hallways, she was barely breathing, her eyes fluttering shut.

He didn't care about the people watching them as he collapsed with her on the floor of the lobby, didn't care about the consequences or the fallout as he gently gripped her face and begged, "Rowan, stay with me. *Please*, just open your eyes."

Glass shattered somewhere. A chorus of voices rose around them. His world narrowed as her lungs tried and failed to take in the air and as her ash-stained face grew too pale.

The sirens grew louder, and a breath caught in his throat. He didn't even realize he was half-sobbing until the EMTs surrounded them. He ignored their attempts to shove him onto a gurney, instead staying beside her as they shoved an oxygen mask over her mouth.

He followed her onto the waiting ambulance, and a woman insisted, "Sir, we need to treat you—"

"She's pregnant. Please, just help her," he said, and the woman's eyes widened slightly.

He put a shaking hand over Rowan's, and her eyes fluttered open hazily.

"Rowan," he gasped. "Please stay awake. I didn't mean..." He choked on a short sob. "I love you, Rowan Evans. Please, *please*, just stay with me."

Then, her eyes rolled back, and his world broke.

Chapter 19
Ruin

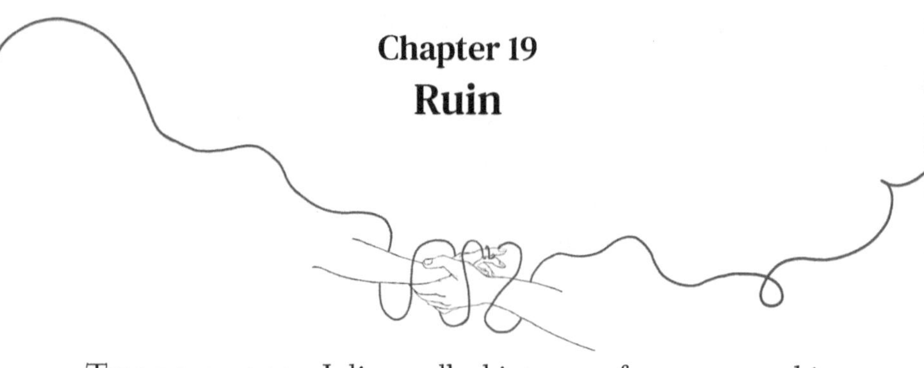

Two days later, Julian walked into a conference room, his arms covered in bandages and his chest still on fire. Despite the anxiety surrounding the very uncomfortable meeting he was about to have with Maggie and the Provost, he reminded himself it was nothing compared to what he'd felt in the last forty-eight hours.

It was why, as he sat down in front of the two grim-faced women, he repeated in his head: *She is okay. The baby is okay. Nothing else matters.*

Because in the end, it didn't. A miracle, the hospital staff called it, thanks to him. But he was no hero in this room.

The Provost glanced at Maggie, and she nodded, took a deep breath, and finally said, "Okay. We're going to need an explanation. Obviously."

I raised his gaze to her. "I understand if you need to fire me. But all I ask is that you keep her out of the blame."

"Are you saying the situation was against her will?" the Provost asked sharply.

He shut his eyes briefly, then said, "No. Not in any sense. I... She instigated things initially, but the last thing she needs is more stress right now. So, if you want to paint it that way, if that makes things easier for her, I don't care."

The Provost studied him for a long moment, then said, "I'm sure you understand that would be career death for you, even more so than if we let you go quietly."

He shifted. "I think you know we're past this being quiet."

"Because of Jake Quinn," Maggie interjected, glancing at the Provost.

The Provost ignored her. "Were you ever planning on saying something?"

"I was," he said heavily. "And I wanted to do so sooner but..." He paused, then decided to just be honest. "I was afraid."

"For yourself?" the Provost asked.

He shook his head slightly. "For her."

The Provost sat back in her chair, scrutinizing him again. Maggie sighed heavily and then said, "We need to move quickly and make a decision. It's why we called you here today, and I apologize for doing so when you're still recovering."

Julian nodded, tightening his jaw. He supposed this was it, the moment they fired him. But instead, the Provost asked, "Has she woken up yet?"

He froze, not expecting the question. Not expecting to be reminded of the last time he had seen her a few hours ago, so small and pale in that hospital bed, covered in tubes. He couldn't think of it, the way he'd had to force himself to leave her side. Still, he felt himself pale now, the air rushing too fast in his ears.

"No," he managed to say, his throat tight.

The Provost narrowed her eyes. "We'll give you another chance, Julian."

Even Maggie looked at her in surprise. Julian opened his mouth, but the Provost cut him off. "We'll keep this all as quiet as we can, highlight the crime in order to draw people's attention elsewhere. It will be easy enough, with the damage to the building. Rowan Evans will be assigned a new advisor, and in the future, concerning your students, you will keep your hands to yourself." She paused, and then, with a knowing look, added, "Though, I daresay, that won't be a problem now."

He shook his head numbly and rasped, "No."

The Provost stood. "Good, then. I assume you'll be wanting to head back to the hospital."

He nodded, and she left the room without another word, leaving him alone with Maggie. She eyed him before saying, "She was ready to fire you on the spot, you know."

He swallowed but dared to ask, "Why didn't she?"

Maggie folded her hands in her lap and held his gaze as she said, "I was there, in the lobby, when you carried her out of that room. I knew something was different as soon as I saw your face. After that, of course, it became clear to anyone with eyes and ears. And I think if Provost Ives thought you cared any less for that girl than you do, you would be without a job right now."

With that, Maggie stood and left too, obviously having nothing else to say to him.

When she came to, Rowan was in a too-bright room, and there were bandages all over her hands and arms. She blinked and coughed.

"Rowan?"

"Ami?" she croaked.

Amelia shot up. "I'll get a nurse."

Amelia left the room, and Rowan looked around. No Julian. Oh God, he'd literally walked through fire for her. What if he wasn't okay? What if...

Amelia came back with a short nurse, who said, "Welcome back, Ms. Evans."

"How long have I been asleep?" she rasped.

The nurse checked the IV bag next to her and said, "Just a couple days."

Rowan looked at Amelia, the movement making her head hurt as she said, "Julian. Where is Julian?"

Amelia shot back up. "Shit. He will be so mad he wasn't here when you woke up. I'll be right back."

"But he's okay?"

Amelia nodded. "He's alright. A few gnarly burns, but nothing too bad. They let him out yesterday, but of course, he didn't really leave much."

She left, and Rowan glanced at the nurse, her heart pounding as she said, "I... I'm pregnant. Is everything okay?"

The nurse smiled softly. "By some miracle, yes. Thank

goodness your partner was stupid enough to get you out of that room when he did, or things would be a lot worse."

At the confused look on Rowan's face, the nurse explained, "The news has spread among the staff here. A man willing to walk into a room on fire for someone..." She shook her head. "You're both very lucky to be alive."

Rowan took a shuddering breath, the sound rattling in her chest. The nurse frowned and added something to the IV bag. Rowan let her fingers slide over her stomach, a slight bump making itself known there. When she looked up, Julian was standing in the doorway.

"Hey," she breathed.

The nurse patted Rowan's hand. "Press the call button if you need anything. I'll be back in a bit."

"Okay," Rowan said distractedly, her eyes on Julian. The nurse brushed past him, and he slowly walked over to her. There were bandages on his bare arms and one on his left hand.

He sat down in the chair next to her and said, "Please don't ever do that again."

She looked down at her hands and said, "Okay. I'll try not to accidentally get myself locked in a room with a psychopath."

She glanced at him as he whispered, "Rowan, what happened in that practice room?"

After taking another rattling breath, she said, "When I walked in, the lights were off. I turned them on, and then Jake was standing there, that...word painted on the wall behind him. He backed me up against the wall, and that was when I realized there was gasoline on the floor. I tried to run, but he shoved me and then lit the gasoline on fire and disappeared. And Julian, he knows about us. Everything. I tried to get him to stop by telling him I was pregnant."

A mix of emotions had washed over Julian's face as she spoke, but it had mostly been anger. His features softened, though, at her last words.

"I told them," he said quietly. "I... I think they all knew there was something between us the moment I walked out of that room with you in my arms." She looked at him expectantly as he said, "They're not firing me. Naturally, you'll be assigned a new advisor, but I think, given the whole situation, they were feeling more lenient than they usually would."

"How am I even going to continue the semester? I've already almost missed a week."

He brushed a careful, gentle touch over her hand and said, "Don't worry about that right now. Besides, they'll be willing to work with you. They won't penalize you for something that was completely out of your control. And Rowan?"

"Yeah?"

He smiled tightly. "I'm fairly certain the hospital staff contacted the authorities as soon as you woke up. The police have Jake, but I could only tell them so much. They'll want to talk to you."

She shut her eyes.

"I'm sorry," he said. "I'm so sorry this happened."

She looked at him. "It's not your fault."

"If I hadn't said what I said, acted the way I did in your lesson, you could have been safe. You wouldn't have gone to that room and—"

"Julian," she cut him off. "I had the room reserved. This probably would have happened no matter what."

He only shook his head, running his uninjured hand through his hair. But then, he looked at her and asked, "Do you remember much of it?"

She shook her head. "Not much." He took a breath, and she added, "Just you telling me you love me."

He didn't look away or backtrack like she expected him to. Instead, his gaze was steady and he said, "Good. I wanted you to remember that."

"Really?"

He reached over, placing a gentle hand on her bandaged one. "I'm sorry for how I reacted at first. I was scared. I thought I'd ruined you, that maybe you'd ruined me too. Maybe a part of me still thinks that, but... I don't care."

She lowered her lashes and said, "I think we've been telling each other for a while; we were both just too afraid to say it out loud."

He nodded. "I know. You don't know how many times I stopped myself, told myself it would be better or easier if I didn't say it. But then, all I could think of when you were in that room was how I might never be able to tell you, how I was a stupid fool for not letting you in like I wanted. Because I want to. I love you, Rowan. I..." He shook his head. "You've been in my head since the first time I met you, years ago. I felt like I knew you somehow, even then."

"I know," she whispered.

They both looked towards the door then, at the sounds of radios rumbling and heavy feet on the floor. The police, there to question her.

Julian got up, standing at the edge of the bed, his arms crossed.

"Sir, we're going to have to ask you to leave while we question her," one of the cops said.

Julian looked the man over once, then again, and said coldly, "Don't stress her out more than necessary."

The cop narrowed his eyes but only said, "Alright."

The three police approached Rowan, one man and two women. One of the women sat next to her in the spot where Julian had been and said, "Hi, Rowan. My name is Officer Vernon. We just have a couple of questions for you. To start off, can you just tell us how you know Jake Quinn, and then let us know what happened on Monday morning?"

Rowan nodded and recounted every detail she could remember. When she was done, the cops asked her a few more questions then left, one of them saying something into their radio.

Julian and Amelia were in the room almost immediately after the cops left.

"Are you okay?" Amelia demanded. "They didn't say anything weird or—"

"Fine, Ami. I'm fine," Rowan said tiredly.

Amelia glanced at Julian and then said, "Sam is downstairs, but we can come back tomorrow, if you want?"

"I just need to sleep," Rowan said, exhaustion pulling at her.

"Of course. You should rest as much as you can," Amelia said. She walked over to Rowan and placed a light kiss on her cheek. "You scared me," she said quietly, meeting Rowan's eyes.

Rowan smiled softly. "I know, Ami. But I'm okay."

Amelia smiled tightly and said, "Sleep well. I'll be back in the morning."

She left, and Rowan and Julian were alone again. He walked over to her, slumping down into the chair next to her.

"You should go home and sleep," she said, but he shook his head.

"I can sleep here."

"Julian. Go home."

His jaw tightened, and she realized there were tears gathering in his eyes as he said, "I'm not leaving."

"You need to sleep—"

"You were hardly breathing," he said, nearly choking on the words. "You were in my arms and you were hardly breathing. All I could do in the minutes before the ambulance arrived was try to keep you awake. So, no, I am not leaving you alone. Not now, not ever... I won't keep making that mistake."

A tear escaped his eyes and tracked down his cheek. She reached out with a shaky hand and brushed it away. He leaned into her touch, taking deep, steadying breaths.

"Sleep," he finally said. "I'll be here."

She nodded, leaning back on the pillows and closing her eyes. He began to hum, something she recognized but couldn't quite remember the name of. She drifted off, listening.

Chapter 20
Always

Rowan sat on Julian's couch a month after the attack. She'd gotten out of the hospital after being there for nearly a week for her lungs. Both their burns were now just starting to fully heal. He was making some kind of soup in the kitchen, classical music floating around the room.

Rowan was starting back in-person at school on Monday after taking a few weeks at home. She'd mostly been able to keep up, practicing when her cough would allow and working through the mountain of late assignments. Julian was there whenever he could be, fussing and pissing off Amelia.

She was going to take her private lessons with her new advisor, a woman named Professor Thea, someone Julian claimed was a very brilliant musician. Rowan didn't really care who she was taking lessons with; she was just glad Julian had been able to keep his job.

What she was worried about was the gossip and the stares, which she knew was really stupid, given everything that had happened, but she couldn't help it. She knew Julian was keeping things from her when he said no one had made a big deal out of it all.

She rose from the couch, walking over to the kitchen.

"Is it ready?" she asked.

Julian turned, his brows raised. "Two months ago, you would have run away from this kitchen and straight to the bathroom."

She raised a brow too. "I assume being hungry is better."

His face softened. "It is. And it is ready. Let me just toast the bread."

She grabbed the slices of French bread before he could and threw them in the toaster. As soon as she pushed down the lever, she felt him come up behind her, his arms looping around her. He brushed his lips against her ear, and she grasped his hand.

And then...

She felt it. The slightest fluttering in her lower abdomen. She went still, waiting.

"What?" Julian said, and she could hear the alarm in his tone.

She said nothing, just moving his hand so it was pressed over the slight curve of her belly. He was hardly breathing behind her as she felt another quickening. The toast popped, and they both jumped.

"I can't feel her, not yet," he said after they'd both recovered.

"Soon, I suppose," Rowan murmured.

She turned, and he caught her chin, tilting it up and kissing her hard. She ran a hand through his hair, and he pulled back, only enough to whisper against her lips, "You're incredible."

She stared at him and said with a half-grin, "Means a lot coming from a professor."

He closed his eyes and huffed out a laugh.

"You're also insufferable," he said. "Must you always remind me what a bad, bad man I am?"

She raised a brow. "Maybe I like bad men."

"Like Damen and Jared?" he chuckled.

Ah, yes, her imaginary suitors. She was surprised he remembered that joke. It seemed like eons ago, when he had followed her home that night.

She smiled and nodded. "Yes, just like Damen and Jared, both bikers with lots of tattoos and ill-intentions. You made me miss out on a pretty wild night."

He sighed, resting his forehead against hers. "We need to eat. You're distracting me."

She laughed softly. "Are you that easily seduced?"

"Not usually," he said, pulling away from her and grabbing bowls. She snatched the cooling pieces of bread from the toaster and buttered them.

They carried it all over to the table, and as they both sat down, she asked, "Has Helen asked you about me? About us, I mean?"

Julian's brow creased, and he said, "Yes, and I told her it was none of her business. Why do you keep bringing her up?"

Rowan shrugged. "She has a thing for you. I've overheard her talking about it a few times."

"Ah. Jealous, are we?"

She swirled her spoon around in the soup and replied, "No. Just a little... wary. I have a feeling she'll want to corner me tomorrow."

She looked up, and his expression had darkened slightly. "Are you worried she'll do something?"

Something like what Jake did is what he didn't say.

Shaking her head, she said, "No, nothing like that. But gossip isn't fun either, especially when it's about you."

He took a sip of water and said carefully, "People do talk."

"And they have been, haven't they?"

He shrugged. "Does it matter?"

"The people who are going to talk the most are the students, and I have to interact with them on a daily basis. Plus, if anyone forgets, there'll be a nice little reminder for them every time they see me." She glanced down at her stomach.

"If it gets out of hand, just let me know," he said tightly.

She rolled her eyes and replied, "I'm not saying I can't handle it. And you going agro on any students who have an issue with me is definitely not going to help. I just want an idea of what I'm getting into."

"Going...agro?" he mused, his mouth twitching.

She sighed. "It means—"

"I know what it means, Rowan. I didn't think it applied to me, though."

She huffed out an annoyed breath at his stupid little half-grin and said, "You can be kind of intense. And as much as I know you probably want to go all macho, mega-protective mode right now, I'm going to need you to cool it. It will give people even more to talk about."

He nodded slowly. "Alright. I will try to avoid being so...agro."

She rolled her eyes again and began to eat. He chuckled softly, but she ignored it. She wasn't actually mad, but she did wish he'd take the whole gossip thing more seriously.

Once they were done eating, he cleared the plates away, insisting she go sit on the couch while he loaded the dishwasher. She relented, settling down in her established spot at the far end. Curling up in a blanket, she stared at the wall, nervousness churning in her gut, which eventually led to her feeling nauseous.

"Crap," she muttered.

"All good?" he called from the kitchen.

Swallowing a wave of nausea, she said, "I'm good. Just a little nauseous."

He paused then closed the dishwasher and strode over purposefully to the couch. He sat down next to her and said, "Focus on your breathing like we talked about."

Indeed, she had discussed with Dr. Wright ways to keep stress and anxiety at bay, factors the doctor thought were making her nausea worse. Julian's hand rubbed her back in gentle, calming motions. She forced herself to breathe in through her nose and out through her mouth until the nausea subsided.

"Okay," she breathed. "Danger zone passed."

Julian kept rubbing her back, and they stayed like that for a few more minutes. Then, he turned on the baking show they'd been slowly working their way through in between their constant streams of work.

She leaned against him, content to sit in near silence. When the episode finished, he tried to conceal a yawn, and she smiled.

"Tired?"

He sighed. "A bit, I suppose."

"We should sleep. I have my first lesson with Professor Thea tomorrow, and I don't think she'll want me showing up half-awake."

"No, she won't," he said. After a pause, he added, "I'll miss teaching you. You really are a phenomenal musician, and I say that as a teacher, not as..." He trailed off. They'd never really defined exactly what they were to each other. She didn't mind. There wasn't really a word that fit the situation. 'Boyfriend' was far too juvenile and light, and they weren't married. 'Partner' probably worked best, but even that felt too surface-level.

She nodded. "Thank you. It does mean something to me that you think that."

"I think it because it's true," he replied fiercely.

Her heart pounded in her chest at the fire igniting in his dark eyes.

"You are among the best I've ever taught, and part of me mourns the fact I won't be able to do that...to *be* that for you anymore."

She lowered her lashes, her gaze fixed on the floor. "I know."

"But," he went on, "I am happy to give up that part of our relationship for this."

Her eyes lifted, and she met his heavy gaze as she nodded. "I am too."

His eyes drifted to her lips as they parted, and she moved, straddling him. His hands immediately found their home on the curve of her hips, the touch familiar.

"I know you need to sleep," she whispered.

She could see that his pupils had expanded, even in the dim light of the room.

"I'll sleep later," he said roughly and then kissed her.

She moaned softly as he tugged her bottom lip between his teeth. Her fingers dug into his shoulders, and he released her mouth for a moment to tug off his shirt and hers. His hands went to her back, deftly unhooking her bra and tossing it to the side along with their shirts. He palmed her sensitive breasts gently, and she let her head fall to his shoulder. He tugged on her earlobe with his teeth, and she arched further into him.

"Pants off," he muttered, swallowing a groan as her hands immediately went to the top button of his jeans. She pulled them off and glanced up at him as she kneeled in front of him.

"Rowan, you don't have to—"

"Shh," she murmured. "Let me."

He began to protest again, but his words were quickly cut off as she put her mouth on his cock, teasing at first with just a brush of her lips. She wasn't an expert at this particular act and had never done it to him before, but she did her best, and he didn't seem to mind her inexperience, his hands threading in her hair and gasps slipping from his mouth as she took him in her mouth, hardly able to handle his size.

Eventually, he hissed, "Rowan."

She looked up at him, feigning an innocent expression. "What?"

"If you don't stop now..." He sucked in a breath as she rose and dragged off her sweatpants, straddling him again.

He kissed her, not minding where her mouth had just been. She rubbed up against him and then slid onto him, pulling back from the kiss to breathe, to moan, to gasp. He gripped her hips as she rode him, both of their breaths rasping and uneven. His hand drifted between them, and her head fell to his shoulder again as she gripped the couch cushion behind them and gasped.

"That's it," he murmured in her ear as she writhed against him.

His touch was mounting a storm inside her, the sensations ripping through her, destroying all semblance of reality. Destroying *her*. She dragged her fingers down his shoulders as the sensation increased, the pressure building and building and building.

"Come for me, Rowan," he said just as the pressure broke and red flashed in her vision. He groaned and hissed, "Thank fuck."

As soon as she came down from the heady high of it, she knew he was going to try to flip her over on the cushions, but she caught her breath and pressed a hand to his chest in a silent demand. He held her gaze as she began to move again, slower this time, relishing the power she held over him. Every hitched breath he took, every soft groan he let out, each ripple of pleasure across his face... It was all because of her.

"You're mine," she breathed.

He caught her lips and murmured against her mouth, "I'm yours."

She moved her hips, and then his head bowed and his body went taut beneath hers. She held him through it, as he whispered her name over and over again.

Thirty minutes and a shared shower later, they lay in his bed, Rowan leaning against a few pillows. Next to her, he propped up on his elbow, his hair still wet. She glanced at him and opened her mouth to say something, but then he reached out his hand and ran his fingers gently over the slight bump of her stomach.

They didn't talk about the baby often. She was a far-off reality, even as the weeks sped by. Of course, they'd talked through finances and some of the basic logistics. He wanted her to move in with him but hadn't yet found a good way to ask. She had told him that her lease with Amelia went until August and that she didn't have the money to cover two leases at once. He didn't really care—she could live here for free. Should, honestly, given what his salary was compared to hers.

She shouldn't have to worry, not any more than she already did. He wanted—needed—her to let him take on some of the burdens in her life. She was already doing enough, what with catching up on her work, practicing when he wished she'd rest, and growing their child.

Slowly, carefully, he lowered his head so that his ear was pressed against her belly. His eyes widened slightly, and his lips parted as he heard it.

"What?" she asked.

He glanced up at her. "She's kicking. I can hear her now, just barely."

His thumb brushed against her belly, and his vision became slightly unfocused for a second. And then, he began to speak, but this time, it was not to Rowan.

"My father...your grandfather...is a musician. So is my mother, and so am I. And your mom is the one of the best I've ever heard. I know that sometimes, the music can take us away, even from what's really important to us. Even if we don't want it to. It's like a sort of madness. You're probably going to grow up in a world surrounded by it. So, I want you to know, now and always, that regardless of the track record of my family, I'm not going anywhere, ever. I will always take care of you."

He finally glanced up at Rowan to find tears rolling down her cheeks.

"Always," he said softly. "I will always be here, Rowan."

She nodded, her lower lip trembling. He placed a kiss on her belly and rose back up, turning off the salt lamp. He pulled her against him, his arm looping around her middle.

"I love you," he whispered into her hair.

After a moment, she grasped his hand and replied, "I love you, Julian."

Chapter 21
A Conversation in the Coffee Shop

THE NEXT MORNING, Julian almost insisted on driving her to campus. She insisted right back that it would draw too much attention to her.

"Rowan," he sighed. "It's really not that big of a deal."

"Just not this first day, at least," she said.

"Are you ashamed of me?"

She looked away and said in a hushed voice, "No. And I don't think it's fair of you to ask me that. You know why I'm nervous, and it has nothing to do with the way I feel about you."

His expression softened, only slightly, as he said, "I was serious when I said you need to tell me if anyone gives you trouble."

"I can handle whatever happens."

"You don't need any more stress."

"I'm fine!" she shouted, splaying her hands.

He let out an incredulous, humorless laugh. "You nearly died! I almost lost you, both of you. And Dr. Wright was concerned at the last appointment. Did you hear a word of what he said?"

She lowered her chin. "Of course, I did."

Any more major trauma or stress could cause her to go into early labor, one that could endanger her. One that the baby would not survive. The doctor had been worried about her going back to school, but she'd insisted...and she'd hardly let the words hit that day at the appointment. She hardly let them hit now. Deep down, she knew Julian was warranted in his concern, but she couldn't bring herself to imagine that reality, or even entertain it.

Julian ran a hand through his hair and begged, "Please take this seriously, Rowan."

She scoffed. "Don't you dare insinuate that I'm not!"

"That's not what I..." He took a breath. "I know you care. I know. I just want you to take care of yourself right now, above all else. I'll drive you home if it makes it better."

She flexed her hands, which had been balled into fists, and nodded.

He sighed and picked up her bag before she could bend down and grab it. They walked outside and to his car in silence. The March air was brisk, but today was a little warmer than it had been, the first hints of a coming spring.

He drove her home and she refused to look at him. She knew she was being petty and childish, but she was too upset and scared to care.

When he parked, he said, "Look at me, Rowan."

Still, she refused.

"I'm sorry," he said.

She sighed and glanced his way. His expression was

earnest and open. He was being an adult, and she was being immature, probably just as he expected her to be at twenty-four.

"It's okay. You're right," she finally said heavily. "But I need to go."

He furrowed his brow but replied, "Okay. Please be safe when you walk."

"I will."

He brushed his knuckles down her cheek and said, "Good luck with Professor Thea. And...I love you."

Her lips parted. They didn't usually say it so casually, at least not up to this point. It was something that typically came up in more heated moments or soft ones, like when she was just about to fall asleep.

"I love you too," she whispered after a moment, then added, "I need to go."

He nodded, dropping his hand.

She got out of the car, avoiding a slick patch of half-melted ice on the sidewalk. She looked back once and found he was waiting to make sure she got to the door. She raised a brow, and he raised one right back.

"Fine," she muttered and headed inside. Only then did he drive away.

Amelia was already gone by the time she let herself in. She rinsed off quickly, changed, and then headed back outside.

The walk to campus was short, but these days, she kept running out of breath by the end of it. Today especially, with the anxiety churning in her stomach, she was nearly panting by the time she reached the music building.

She paused before mounting the short number of steps up to the door. After taking a few deep breaths and repeating, *it will be fine*, over and over again in her head, she walked up the stairs and inside.

As she walked through the main entrance area, she noticed one wing, the wing of the practice rooms where the fire had started, was still blocked off, with tarp and yellow caution tape all over it. She paused in front of it and only moved away when she heard a few people whispering.

As she turned to walk down the hall to meet with Professor Thea, she was met with stares. Some landed on her face, others on her stomach. She pasted a small smile on her face as she passed them.

"Knocked up by a professor..."

"Jake tried to kill her."

"Yeah, Dr. Lynch, the moody one."

"Who knows how long they've been hooking up?"

She let the whispers wash over her and flow down a river far, far away. Still, she nearly sagged in relief when she reached the room where Professor Thea was. She knocked twice, and a woman's voice called, "Come in, Rowan."

She took a deep breath and stepped into the practice room. A different, but similar, room flashed in her mind then. A room with a bright red word painted on the wall. A room where flames and smoke had almost consumed her whole. A room where Julian had risked his life to get to her in time.

Professor Thea looked Rowan over carefully and said, "Trauma is hard. I should know. My mother died in a car accident in front of me when I was ten."

Rowan furrowed her brow. "I'm sorry, Professor."

Professor Thea cleared her throat. "It was a long, long time ago. But things happened not so long ago for you."

Rowan shrugged.

Professor Thea sighed, her features made more stern by the way her raven-black hair was pulled tightly into a bun at the nape of her neck. She was thin and fragile-looking, reminding Rowan of a bird. But she had a hunch Professor Thea was anything but frail.

"Julian also informed me of what your doctor said, about the stress."

Rowan's expression must have shown her irritation, because the professor continued, "It's confidential, don't worry. He only told me because he knew we'd be spending so much time together. And I'm glad he did, because by the look on your face, you wouldn't have said a word about it."

Rowan looked down at her feet. "I suppose not."

Professor Thea sighed heavily. "You remind me of myself when I was young. And I appreciate your ambition, Rowan, I do. I will hold you to a standard, just like all my other students, but I'll be upfront with you. Until you are no longer in danger of hurting yourself or the baby you carry, I will be gentler with you. I want you to know that, and I want you to know that it's not a weakness to pull back right now. I saw your end-of-term recital. I know you're talented. You don't have anything to prove, not right now. Take care of yourself, learn to keep loving the music, and your professional career will be waiting when you're ready."

Rowan's eyes were burning in both shame and gratitude.

"I wish I could be a better student for you," she finally said.

Professor Thea shrugged. "Be whatever kind of student you want to be. I take all kinds."

And with that, they began. Rowan felt immensely better after the lesson and decided to brave the coffee shop for some tea and a pastry. Unfortunately, as soon as she stepped inside and saw Helen sitting there with her usual gaggle of friends, her resolve weakened. She avoided their stares and ordered her drink and food.

She had just gotten her usual mint tea and taken a few bites of a scone when Helen sauntered over to her. She swallowed a sudden wave of nausea as Helen asked, point blank, "Is it true?"

Rowan looked up. "Is what true?"

Helen laughed, a girlish giggle, and said, "Don't be coy, Rowan. Did you fuck Professor Lynch? I tried asking him, but he wouldn't say. I suppose he was ashamed."

Rowan swallowed and said steadily, "He wasn't ashamed. He said it was none of your business, which it isn't."

Helen's brows lifted. One of her friends joined her, the girl she'd heard called Ella. With her hands on her hips, Ella said, "I feel like it is kind of our business. You were probably getting favored for months because of him. I mean, why else would you hook up with a professor?"

Rowan lifted her chin and looked at Helen as she said, "Oh, I don't know? Because you want to have his babies?"

Helen's face turned beet red as she shot back, "Looks like you beat me to that pretty quickly. But I'm sure he'll get bored of you soon enough. Once you pop out a screaming kid and get fat and—"

"Shut up," Rowan hissed, standing.

Helen scoffed. "Excuse me?"

Rowan laughed coldly. "I said shut up."

"You have no right. You're just a slut who fucked her way into getting solos and who knows what else."

"Maybe I am."

"*Oh*, she admits it."

Rowan took a step forward, and Helen narrowed her eyes. Out of the corner of her eye, Rowan saw Amelia rush through the door before she turned her attention back to Helen and said, "I fucked my professor. Happy? But guess what? I got those solos assigned to me before I even met him. I worked my ass off to get where I am."

"She's a liar," Ella muttered to Helen.

The entire coffee shop had gone silent. Rowan stared at Ella. "I'm not. You can think what you want about me and you can gossip behind my back all you like, but I didn't fuck him for favors. And he didn't fuck me because he was bored."

"Likely," Helen said under her breath.

"Do you walk into a room that's on fire to save someone you think is 'boring?'" Amelia said from behind them.

"The firefighters got her out," Ella snapped.

Amelia smiled. "Professor Lynch has some pretty badass burn scars on his arms and his left hand from carrying Rowan out of that practice room. The next time you're checking him out, you can fact-check me on that."

Rowan was feeling majorly nauseous at this point, but she swallowed it back and said, "Move, please. Before I throw up my scone all over you."

Helen and Ella immediately darted out of the way, and

Amelia linked her arm around Rowan's as they walked out of the coffee shop.

As soon as they were out of sight, Rowan sagged and then ran for the nearest bush.

"Ugh, I am so sorry," Amelia said as Rowan finished hurling and sat back. "Are you okay? Do you want me to call Professor Lynch—er, Julian?"

Rowan had told Amelia to stop calling him "professor" last week, at least when it was just them.

She shook her head. "No. No, don't bother him. I think he has some important meetings today."

Amelia nodded. "Okay. Are you good to go to your theory class this afternoon?"

Rowan swallowed. "Yeah. I just need water and gum. Can you hand me my bag?"

She'd thrown it to the side when she'd hurled. Amelia retrieved it, and Rowan pulled out the water bottle and gum she now always kept on hand, just in case. Once she had gotten a drink and was chewing on a piece of mint gum, she stood, dusting herself off.

"Let's do this," she said, and Amelia grinned.

"That's the spirit."

As he was walking back to his office, Julian nearly walked right into Leo, the director of the jazz band. He was distracted—more distracted than he'd been in weeks. Half because of the worry about what Rowan would encounter today and half because of the ring sitting in his pocket.

He was still half-unsure about it, though not for any of the "normal" reasons. He just didn't want her to feel overwhelmed by him or think he was doing it out of any sense of obligation. He needed her to understand that, in a different circumstance, he probably would have done this even sooner. Which he realized sounded half-insane in itself, but that had always been the case when it came to her, to them.

Then, there was the lesson he'd just had with Helen. She had asked him to roll up his sleeves, and he had decided to be forthright with her about everything. Given her reaction, he was beginning to believe that Rowan was right about her.

"Julian," Leo said by way of greeting.

Julian gave him a curt nod. "Leo."

Leo studied him in a way that gave Julian pause, enough that he asked, "Is something the matter?"

Leo pressed his lips together, concealing a half smile. Or a grimace. Julian couldn't really tell.

"I overheard an...interesting conversation in the coffee shop this afternoon."

Julian narrowed his eyes. "Did you now?"

Leo chuckled. "Ethan was right, as usual. You are quite intense."

Julian sighed through his teeth. "If you need to say something, go ahead."

Leo laughed, putting a hand to his chest. "You've got the wrong idea. I have no issue with you, Julian. Sure, we're all a little wary of the situation with Evans, but it's mostly just morbid curiosity, at least on my part."

"Okay," Julian said slowly.

"And I thought I'd let you know what I heard, in case it gets out before she can tell you about it."

Julian froze. Leo had to be referring to Rowan, which meant something had happened.

"One of your other students... Ah, the girl with the blonde hair and the sour attitude?"

"Helen?" Julian said, recalling this afternoon and remembering what Rowan had said about her last night.

Leo snapped his fingers. "That's the one. Well, she cornered poor Evans as soon as she sat down. I thought it was going to be a real shit-show, honestly, but I must admit, she knows how to handle herself."

"Helen?"

"No, Evans," Leo said, smiling faintly. "I won't repeat it verbatim, but when Helen confronted her about, well...*you*, Evans pretty much stood strong. Told Helen exactly how it was and that she wasn't ashamed. In other words than that, but I'll let her tell you the details."

Julian swallowed, emotion blooming in his chest and tightening his throat. And quite suddenly, his decision about what to do was made.

She was strong. He had always known that. But the fact that she was willing to stand up for him, even now...

"Thank you for telling me," he finally said to Leo.

Leo patted his shoulder. "'Course. See you around, Julian."

Julian nodded at Leo and then strode off to find Rowan.

Chapter 22
Right Person, Wrong Time

Apparently, Helen had told people about Rowan's confessional in the campus coffee shop, because she heard someone shout, "I fucked my professor, happy?" as soon as she walked into her theory class.

Rowan ignored the boy, a bassoon player with bad B.O., and took her seat.

"That's enough," the professor, an ancient-looking man who everyone called Bill, shouted. "Not another word about it."

She pulled out her laptop to take notes and ignored the stares and whispers. After class, Bill called her name, and she took a deep breath and turned.

"Yes, Professor?"

His face was kind as he said, "Give it a week, Ms. Evans. They'll find something more interesting to gossip about, and then it will blow over."

She nodded. "Thank you, Professor."

He smiled, and then she left. When she stepped into the

hall, she saw Professor Petrarch speaking in low tones to someone she didn't recognize. A man who looked a lot like…

"That's her," she heard Professor Petrarch say, and the man turned to face her, his nostrils flared.

Oh God, that was Julian's father. It had to be. He had the same eyes and the same hair color and…

"So," he sneered, "you're the girl who nearly got my son fired."

She swallowed. "Mr. Lynch, I—"

"Let me say my piece, *girl*," he cut in.

Frantically, she met Professor Petrarch's steely gaze. He was supposed to be Julian's friend and had been kind to her before. But now, he was looking at her with near malice.

"I will make one thing perfectly clear," Mr. Lynch said. "I do not recognize you nor your bastard as my family. You will not be welcomed. Ethan told me about how you nearly got Julian killed and then almost cost him his career. Do you think of nothing but yourself? He is brilliant and you are nothing. Nothing, hear me? Just a whore who—"

"Stop," she cut in, and he stared at her, his cheeks turning ruddy.

"You dare?"

"I am not solely responsible in this situation. If you didn't know, it takes two people to make a baby."

"That's—"

"And I'm not a whore or a slut," she went. "I'm tired of people calling me that. I'm a woman who fell in love with the right person at the wrong time, and I am *done* apologizing for it."

He stared, his jaw clenched, but he was not looking at

her. She turned to see Julian behind her, staring right back at his father.

"Leave," he said to his father. "Now."

Mr. Lynch scoffed and said, "You can't be serious, Julian? She's a child, an irresponsible sl—"

"Do not," Julian warned, "say what I think you were going to say."

She watched as Julian's gaze shifted to Professor Petrarch, and he growled, "I can't believe you called him."

"Someone needed to talk some sense into you," Professor Petrarch said. "You nearly died because of her!"

"And I would do it a thousand times over again!" Julian shouted, taking a step closer to her.

His father glared at Rowan, shaking his head.

"I have my job. I'm alive," Julian said in a low voice. "I don't know what the issue is here."

His father's lip curled. "The problem is that you were willing to lose it all just because some student spread her legs for you."

Julian shot forward, but Rowan grabbed him before he could land the blow. He paused as her hand snagged around his wrist and turned to look at her, his face pale.

"Don't," she breathed. "Don't. You'll regret it."

Slowly, eyes wide, he nodded once.

"At least she's smart," his father mused.

Julian closed his eyes. Her hand was still around his wrist, but she let it go slowly.

"Go," he said roughly.

"Your mother would be so disappointed," his father said before turning.

Julian was breathing heavily, the rage palpable on his face as he looked at Professor Petrarch.

"You're a bastard," he snarled.

Professor Petrarch clenched his hands into fists. "I nearly watched you die, and for nothing. I mean, God, Julian, do you even love her? Or is it just that you want what you can't have? You were always looking for some grand adventure. Is she just another escapade?"

Julian stepped in front of Rowan, angling himself between her and Professor Petrarch as he said, "You're a horrible judge of my character if you think I would have walked into that burning room for any other reason." Professor Petrarch opened his mouth, but Julian cut him off. "Yes, Ethan. I love her. I don't give a fuck what you or my father think. You two can go to hell for all I care."

Professor Petrarch smiled slowly and said, "He was right. Your mother would be disappointed in you."

And then, he walked away too.

When Rowan was standing in the hall alone with him, Julian took a deep breath and asked, "Are you alright?"

She nodded. "I'm fine."

"Are you done with class?"

She bit her lip. "Yes, but I was going to go to the practice rooms for a while."

He shook his head. "For once, Rowan, I'm going to tell you absolutely not. We're going home."

She blinked. He'd just called his apartment home. For both of them. When she recovered, she said, "But I want to—"

"Rowan," he said tiredly. "Just come home with me. Please."

She pursed her lips and said softly, "Fine. Alright."

"I need to get my coat and bag," he said. "Walk with me."

She ignored the nerves at being seen with him in public and nodded. His hand brushed hers as she followed him out of the back hall and into the main lobby. A few... no, lots of people stared. Julian ignored them all, even going so far as to put his hand on her back as they walked up the flight of stairs to his office.

Once they were inside, he gathered a few papers, stuffing them into his briefcase. Then, he shrugged on his coat and stared out the window, his face drawn. She walked over and tentatively took his hand.

"Let's go home," she said softly.

His gaze swung to hers, and he asked, "Will you let it be home for you?"

Her mouth twitched. "Are you finally asking me to move in with you?"

"Was it that obvious?"

She raised a brow. "I need to talk to Ami about it, to work everything out since our lease doesn't end till August. But she did say she thought Sam could maybe find someone to replace his lease and take over mine."

Julian's face softened, just a bit, and he said, "Good. I want to see you every day."

She ducked her head, trying to hide a small smile, but he caught her chin, tilting it up.

"C'mon," she said, stepping out of his touch. "I want tea.

And those weird English cookies you have in your pantry right now."

"Ah," he said, brushing past her and opening the door. "They're actually Scottish."

"Why am I not surprised? Do you actually know any Scots, since you grew up there?"

She followed him out as he said, "I'm surprised you haven't asked yet, *mo ghràdh.*"

"What does that mean?"

He glanced sidelong as they walked and replied, "Look it up when we get in the car."

Fortunately, they escaped campus without any more incidents. She pulled out her phone as soon as they got into his car. She typed: *Scots to English,* and a translator popped up. She quickly typed in the word he'd said and then stared at the screen.

Mo ghràdh...my love.

Julian glanced at Rowan as before turning off the main road, asking, "Figure it out yet?"

She swallowed. "Yeah."

She looked up then as he parked, and he watched as she realized they weren't at his apartment, but at a small park near the lakefront. There was only one other car parked in the lot, no one visible in the area.

"I thought you wanted to go home?" she ventured.

He shrugged, trying to look nonchalant. "I changed my mind. And I like this park, especially at sunset."

A smile tugged at her lips. "Of course, you do," she murmured.

"Let's go for a walk," he said quietly. "Just a short one. I know you've probably been on your feet all day."

She nodded, and they got out of the car. He took her hand as they stepped onto the asphalt path that led down to the small, rocky beach.

"So," he said. "I heard you had quite the day, even before you met my wonderful father."

She snorted. "How'd you know?"

"Well," he began, "first of all, I had a lesson with Helen today, and she asked me to roll up my sleeves. And then, she asked me what happened the day of the fire. I figured she was trying to prove some point, so I decided to tell her. Sparing details, of course. She was quieter than normal for the rest of the lesson. And then, my colleague, Leo, told me of a rather interesting conversion he overheard in the coffee shop on campus."

She sighed. "It was pretty interesting."

They stepped off the path, which had faded into gravel, and onto the beach. There was a rickety wooden bench near a patch of grass, and they sat down on it, his hand still in hers.

"I'm sorry," he said softly. "That you had to deal with so much today. I shouldn't have downplayed it or dismissed it before. But I'm proud of you, for sticking up for yourself. And...for me."

Their eyes met, and she said, "I wish I could have met your father under better circumstances."

He sighed heavily, a mix of anger and something akin to sadness roiling in his gut.

"He's always angry these days," he said. "I haven't called him in months, and not because of anything to do with you. As much as I hate how he acted today, I can't say I'm too surprised. And the thing Ethan and my father said, about my mother being disappointed...don't think that's because of you. I think my mother would love you."

"Do you know where she is?"

He stared out at the orange and pink staining the horizon, remembering past sunsets shared with his mother, moments he would never get back. "Yeah. I don't know if she'd want to talk to me, though."

"Maybe she would now? If only to meet her grand-daughter."

He looked back at her. "You might be right. I think my sister would like you too. You and she are both so head-strong," he smiled slightly, looking down at the dark sand beneath them.

"I should tell my mother too," she said. "She'll freak out at first, but she adjusts quickly."

He nodded. "I'd like to meet her."

His fingers twitched, and he shifted on the bench as his eyes darted back to the setting sun. Now—he wanted to ask her now, but sudden fear made him pause. What if she said no? What if, again, he ruined things? He seemed to have a knack for doing so.

"Julian?"

"Yes?" he asked a little too quickly.

"Is everything okay? I mean, besides what happened today?"

He closed his eyes and took a deep breath, leaning his forehead against hers. He needed to be close to her as he did this, not kneeling on the sand. He was too unsteady, too damn in love with her to move away now. He reached into his coat pocket, and she glanced down. He opened his eyes, watching as she saw the silver ring clasped between his fingers.

Her breath caught, and her eyes widened in surprise.

"I know everything has been so shaky lately," he breathed. "And I don't want you to think I'm doing this just to provide some sort of stability. I'm asking you because I have never met someone who knows me so fully. I have never met someone who cares so fiercely and someone who lives in such a beautiful, reckless way. I have never once loved someone so deeply, never even considered sharing my life with someone in such a way. I love you, Rowan, and I want to always be there for you. No matter what. Will you marry me?"

She stared at his hand, at the worn silver ring set with a turquoise-green stone and the band engraved in Scots. And then she looked back at him, and he stared at her blue eyes, at the mouth he had now kissed countless times. He thought she might be about to say no, and he would be okay with that. He could wait, would wait years if she needed him to. But he just needed to know.

"Rowan?" he said in a crackling voice. "You can say no, but you're leaving me in suspense and—"

"I wasn't going to say no," she said softly, and his eyes widened.

"So...?" he ventured, his body still tense.

She smiled and brushed her lips against his as she whispered, "Yes. I will marry you."

A shaky exhale left him, and they both looked down as he slid the ring onto her hand.

"It was my grandmother's," he explained. "She gave it to me before she died. Told me not to give it away until my heart was no longer my own."

She shivered and he did too, both from cold and the feelings coursing through him.

"We should go," he murmured, pulling away and holding out his hand as he stood. She took it, and they walked back to the car. He watched the stars begin to emerge in the darkening sky as he drove.

Once they were at his apartment, he ordered delivery takeout, and they settled on the couch. She held out her hand, looking at the just slightly too-loose ring on her finger.

"We can get it resized at a jeweler's," he said. "I figured it might be a little too big."

"Okay," she said quietly.

He glanced down at his phone and muttered, "The food's here. I'll be right back."

Pressing a kiss to her forehead, he left. When he returned carrying the bag, she was staring at him, a soft, steady fire in her eyes. He swallowed hard as he set the bag down.

This was his fiancée. This was the woman he was going to marry.

They ate on the couch for once, and she teased him when he scolded her for spilling a little on the carpet. When they were done and the containers were thrown out, she said tentatively, "I have to be on campus at eight tomorrow. But I'll need to change, so we'll have to leave early again."

He smiled slightly. "I figured. Do you want to go to bed?"

She yawned in reply, and he laughed.

"I'll take that as a—"

But she cut him off, kissing him. He didn't laugh often, not fully like that. It set something off in her, some open chasm in her heart that only he could enter, one that he had only been able to see inside, ever.

He caught her in his arms, wrapping one around her, the other twining in her hair. When they finally broke apart, she was breathless. He laughed again, and she did too. Then, they were kissing again, and she truly wasn't sure where she ended and he began.

Eventually, when her breath came in panting gasps from the kissing and the standing, he scooped her up in his arms and carried her to the bed. They kissed some more, and then she lay in his arms, gently tracing the still-sensitive scars from the burns.

"I meant what I said today," he murmured. "I'd walk through fire a thousand times more for you."

She kissed his shoulder and whispered, "Forever a professor with a hero complex."

He snorted softly. "You don't know how much I wanted to kiss you when you said that to me."

"How inappropriate."

"Entirely," he agreed.

She fell asleep before even brushing her teeth. He woke her up a few hours later, and they dragged themselves into the bathroom to do so. He helped her into a t-shirt of his, and then they fell sleepily back into bed.

When the alarm rang in the morning, Julian groaned, turning over and slamming a fist on the snooze button.

"I have to get up," she mumbled.

"Mhmm," he rumbled, kissing her neck.

"Julian," she breathed. "We need to go."

He made a low, exasperated sound and said, "Killjoy," before rolling away from her and standing.

She sucked in a breath, her hand going to her stomach as she felt a soft kick, and his head immediately snapped towards her.

"What?" he demanded. "Is something wrong?"

She shook her head. "She's just kicking."

His alarmed face fell. "God, I thought..."

"No, we're good," she said, sitting up and wincing at the ache in her back.

He strode over to her side of the bed and helped her up, a little unnecessarily. She wasn't big at all yet, just whiny, but he was happy to fuss.

She pulled on her pants from the previous day, and he

handed her a granola bar before they left. She dutifully ate it in the car, staring at the ring on her hand all the while.

"Amelia is going to have a heart attack when she sees this," she mused.

Julian smiled slightly. "Amelia makes *me* nervous with how jittery she always is."

Rowan chuckled, taking a swig of water from the bottle he'd also grabbed before they left. He parked, and she sighed as she said, "See you later?"

"Talk to her about the lease," he said. "For me. But yes. I have work to do tonight, but if you want, you can come by and work on your homework while I do it."

"I will. And okay," she replied.

She stared at him, and he leaned over and kissed her softly before murmuring, "Go. You don't want to be late."

She pulled away reluctantly and got out of the car. When she stepped into her apartment, Amelia was predictably eating cereal on the couch, her earbuds in. She pulled them out as Rowan walked in.

"Hey, you forgot to tell me you weren't coming home," she said crossly.

Rowan sighed. "Sorry. I got caught up."

Amelia rolled her eyes. "What, Professor McHotty was *so* captivating that you couldn't remember to text me?"

Rowan sat down next to her and cleared her throat. "For once, actually, yes."

Amelia narrowed her eyes. "What's going on? Something's up."

She looked Rowan over, her gaze snagging on her left

hand clasped her lap. Slowly, she raised her wide-eyed gaze and whispered, "No fucking way."

Rowan couldn't suppress her smile. "As usual, it seems this is actually happening."

Amelia's mouth dropped open, and she screeched, "You're engaged?"

"Yeah, apparently."

"Oh my God. Holy shit. Okay, you need to change and brush your hair, but you are going to tell me everything on the walk over. And then, when we get to campus, you are going to find Helen straight away and rub that beautiful family heirloom-looking piece of jewelry in her stupid face."

Rowan snorted and stood, heading to the bathroom. Once she was done, she changed and then met Amelia at the door. As they walked, she told her. About Julian's father and Professor Petrarch, about how Julian finally had asked her to move in with him. Then, she told him about the impromptu beach trip, and Amelia cut in. "No way. He totally planned that."

Rowan shrugged. "It didn't seem like it."

"Well, he's a genius, so maybe you just didn't notice."

Rowan rolled her eyes as they stepped into the main lobby. She had orchestra rehearsal first, and she parted ways with Amelia as she headed into the space. She kept her head down as she assembled her flute. As they began warmups, she heard someone nearby whisper her name. She turned to see a petite blonde girl staring at her finger.

"Are you engaged?" the girl whispered.

Well, Rowan supposed now was as good a time as ever.

"Um, yeah," she whispered back.

The girl's eyes widened. "To Professor Lynch?"

"Also, yeah," Rowan said quietly.

"Hello, ladies!" Professor Lark called. "Can we have whatever conversation you're having later, please?"

The girl shrank back with a nod. "Yes, Professor."

But then, other people started to notice Rowan's finger and began to whisper amongst themselves. Helen's face turned beet red when she saw the ring. Professor Lark sighed loudly. "Alright. What is so very captivating that we need to pause rehearsal?"

"Rowan Evans is engaged!" a boy Rowan thought might be named Derek blurted out.

For once, surprise lit up Professor Lark's face as she said, "I see. Congratulations, Rowan. I'll be sure to give my congrats to Professor Lynch later."

Rowan's face warmed slightly as Professor Lark just about outed her to anyone who was in the dark about the latest gossip.

"Alright, let's continue!" Professor Lark shouted over the murmurs.

Chapter 23
A Slow World

REHEARSAL THANKFULLY FINISHED without any further incident, and Rowan avoided Helen on her way out. She had one more class, but not for another half hour. She stared at her phone and decided now was as good a time as any to finally call her mom. She pressed her contact and hit call, then waited.

"Rowan?" her mother said, picking up almost immediately. "This is an odd time for you to call."

"Hey, Mom. I have something to tell you. And...you might want to sit down."

There was a pause from the other end of the line, and then her mother said, "Oh God. You don't have cancer, do you?"

Rowan took a breath. "No, no nothing like that. It's good news. Just big news."

"Okay?"

"Um, so, it's a very long story that I really should have

told you a long time ago. But you remember how my advisor was switched right before the first semester started?"

"I do."

"So." She took a breath. This was a lot harder than she thought it was going to be. "I, uh...well. Don't freak out."

"Rowan, baby, just tell me. You said it's good news, right?"

She sighed. "Yeah. It is. So, I sort of ended up being in a relationship with him."

Her mother paused for a long moment, and then she began to laugh.

"Sorry," her mother chuckled. "I'm sorry, baby. It's not funny. But it's so like you to find someone when you really shouldn't."

"There's more. You're sitting, right?"

"Yes...?"

"I'm kind of four months pregnant. But it's fine, it really is. He's sticking around, and I know this sounds naive, but I love him. And he loves me, and he just proposed last night."

The longest pause in the history of phone call pauses ensued until finally, her mother said, "It's not naive, Rowan. I know you think I'll probably reprimand you for making my mistakes, but you know your own mind and your own heart. You always have. I know you wouldn't be sure about something if it wasn't truly what you wanted. I'll just ask one thing."

"Yeah?"

"I want to meet him. ASAP. Your spring break is next week, isn't it?"

Rowan sighed. She'd known this was coming, and she said, "Okay. I'll bring him home."

"How about Sunday evening? The first Sunday of your break, I mean."

"Mom, that's in like four days."

"And?"

She sighed. "Let me run it by him, just to make sure he's free then. I'll text you to confirm."

"Okay, good."

"I have to go. I have class in ten minutes, but... Thank you for not freaking out. I love you."

"I love you too, baby. See you soon."

"See you soon. Bye."

Rowan ended the call and steadied her shaking hands. She hadn't told her mom about the fire. She'd long ago taken her mother off her emergency contact form, instead using Amelia. Her mother didn't need to be alerted to every little thing, big things either. Rowan would let Amelia use her discretion on what to tell her mom. She was glad her friend had let Rowan decide about telling her mom about the attack.

Rowan stood from the bench she'd been sitting on outside and headed to class. When it was over, she walked up to Julian's office. She heard voices inside, so she waited, slumping against the wall. The voices became raised, and she strained to hear.

Professor Petrarch was inside. She was almost sure of it.

Julian glared at Ethan, his chest heaving. The man he'd thought was his friend had stormed into his office ten minutes ago, and quickly, he'd watched everything he had hoped wasn't true about Ethan become a reality.

It hurt to hear the insults, to know that his former friend thought so little of him, but what had caused him to snap was when Ethan had brought up Rowan.

"I always knew she was a bit of a slut, especially for you, but I never thought she'd be this stupid."

Now, he held Ethan's hard gaze and spat, "Get out."

Ethan's expression sharpened, but he said nothing more, flinging the door open and stalking out into the hall. Julian froze as he saw Rowan standing there, her hand curving over her belly as Ethan stopped short in front of her.

"Ethan," Julian warned, his patience lost now.

Julian watched as Ethan's eyes darted to the hand over her stomach and to the ring on her finger before he left without a word. Julian's brow furrowed. Something felt very wrong about the way Ethan had looked at her. He just wasn't quite sure what it was.

He pushed the worry away and glanced at Rowan, saying, "We should go."

"Okay," she said, her hand still clasped on her belly. Her voice was thin, as if she'd also sensed how strange Ethan's expression had been.

Julian went back into his office momentarily to grab his bag and jacket and then joined her in the hall. They walked in a tense silence to the lower level. Once they were out of the music building and in the parking lot, she finally asked, "What did he want?"

"The same as my father," he told her hollowly. "Mostly trying to convince me not to go through with this. Insulting us."

"Why does he hate me so much?"

He furrowed his brow, shaking his head. He honestly didn't know. Beyond the crass comments, he hadn't thought Ethan actually cared about Rowan.

"I don't know," he said. "I think he might just care about me in the wrong way, like my father."

She nodded, looking up at the pink-hued sky. He stared at her for a moment, taking a deep breath, but then he turned, feeling a pricking sensation on the back of his neck.

The first thing he saw were Ethan's familiar hazel eyes. Then, the gun. The gun in Ethan's hand. Pressing to Julian's head. The barrel was cold against his forehead, and for a moment, his mind went completely blank.

Rowan turned then, her entire body going ramrod straight as she looked back at him and saw the gun pressed up against his head.

Ethan had moved so quickly, neither of them had even seen him approach. Rowan's breath started to come in short gasps, and Julian's eyes met hers. He just needed to neutralize the situation and get her out of here. That was suddenly all he cared about—getting her away from Ethan and to safety.

He raised his shaking hands slowly and said in a low voice, "Ethan. Put the gun down."

Rowan's hand went to her pocket, to grab her phone, but Ethan said coldly, "I don't think so, Rowan."

"Please," she breathed.

Julian held her gaze, pleading with her to stay where she was and to stay quiet.

"Put the phone down and slide it over to me," Ethan said to her, oddly calm.

She obeyed, and Julian watched her so, so closely as she knelt, kicked the phone over, and then stood back up.

"Good," Ethan said. "Now, I want you to get in the running car three spots down. It's navy-colored, not too hard to miss."

"Rowan," Julian said quietly. "Do not do what he says."

Silent tears were streaming down her cheeks as Ethan pressed the gun barrel harder into the side of Julian's head.

"Why?" she gasped. "Why are you doing this?"

Julian held his breath as Ethan smiled slowly. "It seems that Julian got in more than one man's way," he said with a cock of his head. "I tried everything to separate you, even persuading that idiot boy, Jake Quinn, to try and kill you," he chuckled. "Because I thought, if I can't have you, no one can. But that failed. So, this seems to be the only way."

"You," she breathed. "You disabled the fire alarms and sprinklers. You knew to be there when the fire started."

"Smart girl. Just not quick enough to get it."

"Ethan," Julian growled, rage and terror mingling, making him shake.

"Shut up," Ethan snapped. "I gave you everything. You would have never gotten this job without me."

For the smallest of moments, Rowan's gaze flicked behind him and Ethan. Julian almost thought someone might be there, but he said nothing. Neither did Rowan at first, not until she said hoarsely to Ethan, "I'll go with you."

Julian felt the world slow.

"Good, Rowan," Ethan said.

"Just let me say goodbye," she said.

Ethan's jaw tightened. "I'm not moving this gun."

She sucked in a breath. "Fine. Just let me say goodbye."

Julian's body seized as she moved closer to them—not in fear for himself, but for her, moving so close to the gun Ethan held to his head.

"Rowan," he warned. "Do not go with him."

"I have to," she whispered, her breath uneven. "I'll be fine. Trust me."

She said the words so softly, soft enough that he wondered if something else was going on here.

"Take off the ring," Ethan ordered.

She obeyed, slowly slipping it into Julian's coat pocket. As she slid her hand out, Julian's phone in her hand, Ethan moved, pointing the gun at her head as she stepped back.

And if the world had slowed before, now, it stopped. Everything stopped. Nothing was real as Ethan advanced towards her.

"Ethan," Julian said, his voice cracking. "Stop."

"Put the phone down. Now," Ethan barked at her.

She shook her head, and he moved forward, pressing the gun to her head. A sort of choked gasping noise escaped

Julian as he watched the metal barrel dig into her forehead. Her blue eyes were wide and shining with tears.

"Ethan," he begged, unable to move or breathe, helplessness overcoming him like a tidal wave. "*Please.*"

"Take the phone from Rowan, or I'll do it. I meant what I said. And maybe it will be even sweeter to see you suffer."

Sirens sounded in the distance, and Ethan dug the barrel of the gun harder into Rowan's head. She was trembling as she met Julian's eyes, and Ethan mused, "Looks like someone sounded the alarm already. Ah, well. On your knees, Rowan."

Even as the police cars flew down the main road towards the lot, Julian saw something like acceptance pass over her features. She knew what was coming, knew that he could not save her now. So much good his savior complex did her as she kneeled on the asphalt and he was helpless, just steps away from her.

He could try to push Ethan away, but that gun barrel was directly against her forehead. And somehow, he knew Ethan was no longer playing. Something had broken inside of him, his eyes wild and his expression twisted into something unhinged that Julian did not recognize.

Rowan met his eyes as she whispered, "I love you. Always."

"No," Julian gasped. He had to do something. Stop this, take the bullet for her. Anything, *anything* but this. It could not end like this.

Ethan smiled, his crazed stare fixed on Rowan. "Yes," he said.

A gunshot went off, the sound slicing through the air.

Both Rowan and Ethan dropped to the ground as Julian roared her name.

No.

Please.

She was still on the ground, and blood was spreading rapidly across the asphalt. If it was hers... If Rowan was—

He rushed towards her and fell to the pavement hard enough that his knees cracked. He reached for her because he had to hold her. He had to know. Then, Rowan raised her head, just slightly, just enough, as Ethan met his eyes. Julian held his friend's hate-filled gaze as he died next to Rowan on the asphalt.

It didn't matter that there was blood on her as he pulled her trembling body into his arms and said through heaving gasps, "Oh God, Rowan. I thought... Oh God."

Because for a moment, the world had ended. And even though it had just been a split second, when he thought the blood now covering them had been hers, he could hardly breathe for it.

The officers were rushing towards them, and he saw Amelia hot at their heels. Vaguely, he wondered if she had been the one to raise the alarm and call 911. More sirens wailed as ambulances pulled into the lot. Julian was rocking Rowan as they shook. It was all he could do.

Soon, officers were all around them, checking Ethan's nonexistent pulse and then converging on the two of them. EMTs crouched down next to them just as a crowd from the music building gathered, many of the students covering their mouths with their hands as they saw Ethan's body on the ground of the staff parking lot.

An EMT crouched down in front of her and Julian and gently asked, "Are either of you hurt?"

"She's pregnant. About four months. There was another incident before this, so her doctor was worried about stress." His shaky voice felt disconnected from his body, as if he was underwater.

"Rowan?" the EMT was saying, and Rowan met the woman's hazel eyes. "Rowan, we're going to take you to the hospital so the doctors can run some tests and make sure your baby is okay."

Rowan's voice was hollow as she said, "Okay."

With an edge to his voice, Julian told the EMT, "I've got her," as he cradled her in his arms and lifted her off the blood-soaked asphalt. He could not let her go, not yet. He had to make sure she was real and alive and safe.

"Is she okay?" Amelia demanded from nearby.

The EMT replied, "Your friend is just in shock right now. We're going to take her to the hospital, just to make sure she's alright."

"Call me," Amelia rasped. "Okay? You need to call me, Julian."

"I will," he told her, barely registering that he spoke to someone else as Rowan curled a hand in the material of his jacket.

He glanced down at her and said, "It's going to be okay."

That felt like a lie. Nothing felt okay right now. He wanted to kill Ethan all over again and save him and rewind time and clean all the blood off Rowan himself. He wanted to rage and bellow and sob like the world was ending. Because for a moment, it had.

But he couldn't... *could not* fall apart right now. Not when she was holding his gaze like an anchor, as if he was the only thing still tethering her to the Earth.

He only looked away when the EMT insisted he set her down on a stretcher. The ambulance ride was a blur, and soon, they were at the hospital. The next thing Julian knew, doctors were rushing around Rowan. He bit back the urge to shove them away, reminding himself they were not Ethan and were not here to hurt her.

"How far along did you say she was?" one of them asked.

"Sixteen weeks," Julian replied, his eyes hardly leaving her. She was curled up on the hospital bed like a child, her hands pressed protectively around her belly. Eyes wide open, she took in breaths that were too slow, as if she was actively trying not to hyperventilate.

"Her records say there was smoke inhalation and burns?"

Julian was entirely distracted but managed to reply, "Another attack, orchestrated by the same person."

"Rowan?" the doctor, an older woman with dyed blonde hair said. "We're going to do an ultrasound, okay?"

Rowan took another shaking breath and nodded. The world was finally beginning to settle around him, but the lights were too bright here, and there was still blood on both of them. It was in her hair and staining his hands, like some kind of sticky, gory paint.

He was not usually an overly anxious person, but he felt himself nearing the edge of what might be panic as the doctor rolled over the ultrasound machine.

He just needed...

He had to hold on.

The familiar cold goo was dumped on Rowan's stomach, and then the instrument came, spreading it around her slightly rounded belly. Julian's hand encased hers. He was still shaking.

"The baby is in some distress. No contractions, though," the technician said.

Rowan felt a fraction of the tension in her chest loosen. The baby was okay for now. She just needed to stay calm, a feat she had been attempting since they had arrived at the hospital what felt like hours ago.

"Good," the doctor sighed. "We'll keep her overnight to monitor."

Then, she left, and the nurses came to help gently clean the blood away. Julian looked reluctant as he let go of her hand to let them work. But he watched them closely, his jaw set as they wiped away the gore.

After that, sleep claimed her mercifully fast, and she slept until four in the morning. Julian was awake when she opened her eyes, staring at the beeping and blinking of the machines above her. But his gaze shot to her once she stirred, and he immediately asked, "How are you feeling?"

"Better," she croaked.

He looked exhausted, but his voice was gentle as he said, "I should go get the nurse. I'll be back in less than a minute, alright?"

"Alright," she whispered, holding his gaze.

He stood, his chest rising and falling in what she thought might be forced slowness before he left the room. True to his word, he returned with the nurse quickly. A few minutes later, they did another ultrasound, and then the doctor came in.

"Okay, crisis averted, it seems," she said. "But you need to be on bedrest for at least a week. And I mean it," she added with a glance at Julian. "After that, you're going to need to be very careful. Call your doctor if anything at all feels amiss, even if it doesn't seem like an emergency."

She nodded, and the doctor glanced at her watch. "I'll get your discharge paperwork started. You should be out of here within an hour."

She left, the nurse remaining and taking out the IV. Once she was gone too, Julian said, "Amelia said she and Sam can pick us up."

Right, because Julian's car was still in that lot, the pavement stained with now-cool blood.

Julian must have seen it all on her face, because he took her hand and said, "I'm so sorry, Rowan. I should have done something, I should have seen this coming, but I'm an idiot and I—"

"Julian," she whispered, cutting him off. "Don't do this to yourself. There was nothing either of us could do."

He shook his head. "I had absolutely no idea he was capable of something like this. Until a few weeks ago, Ethan was my friend. Or, I thought he was."

"No one saw this coming," she said.

He let out a heavy breath and kissed her hand, his breath trembling against her skin.

An hour later, Julian helped her into Samuel's car, who had apparently come to stay with Amelia last night.

"Hey, Row," he said in greeting as she sat down. Then, as Julian got in on the other side, Samuel said, "Hi, Professor."

Julian nodded once and said, "Thank you for picking us up. And Amelia, thank you for knowing what to do."

Rowan heard Amelia take a quick breath, and then she said, "Of course."

They drove, mostly in silence, and in the quiet, Rowan relived the moment she had seen Amelia across the lot. In her mind's eye, she saw her friend's eyes widening as she saw the gun in Professor Petrarch's hand. Saw her covering her mouth and backing away, raising her phone to her ear. Amelia had known what to do when Rowan had been helpless, standing on that pavement.

Samuel broke the heavy silence, saying, "I found someone to take over my lease for the rest of the year, so Rowan, you're free to move out if you want."

She nodded. "I'll email our landlord tomorrow."

"Nope," Amelia said. "I'll do it. You aren't supposed to be doing anything, I assume."

"Bed rest. For a week," Julian said evenly.

Amelia sighed. "There you go."

Rowan rolled her eyes, but the movement felt forced. "I'd hardly constitute sending one email as work."

"Well, too bad."

Rowan paused then asked, "Did you call my mom?"

Amelia twisted to look at her and said, "I was wondering when you'd ask. The... It was all over the news. So, yeah, I called her and told her you're fine. She just said to call as soon as you were feeling up to it and that she still expects you and McHotty to come over for dinner."

Rowan's eyes flicked to Julian's face as he raised a brow and said slowly, "McHotty?"

Amelia's face colored slightly, but she held her ground. "Yup. It's your nickname. And I'd bet good money that half the girls in the music school call you something similar."

She saw Samuel smile tightly in the rearview as they pulled into the lot of Rowan and Amelia's complex. Rowan moved to get out, but Amelia said, "I'll get your stuff, Row. Just give me a few minutes. I'll be right back."

Rowan conceded, sitting back in the seat. Amelia left her, Julian, and Samuel in the car alone. A slightly awkward silence ensued until Julian asked, "So, Sam, you were a music student in undergrad?"

Samuel cleared his throat and said, "Yeah, I played the saxophone. But I got really burnt out by the end, and I have a minor in the tech field. So, now I'm just a lackey for a big corporate company."

"There's nothing wrong with that," Julian replied. "This field can be a lot, even if you love it."

Samuel sighed. "Yeah. It can. Is it true you got your master's and doctorate at Juilliard?"

"I did. In composition. I got my teaching certificate soon after and worked in a temporary position at the University of Sierra Hill. Then, I played in an orchestra for a short while before coming here."

Samuel nodded. "That's impressive."

Julian lifted a shoulder, but said, "Thank you." He sounded so tired.

They sat in a more comfortable silence for a few minutes before Amelia returned with a stuffed duffel bag. She hefted it into the trunk and got back into the car, breathing a little heavily.

"Do *not* let Rowan carry that bag," she puffed out.

"I wasn't planning on it," Julian replied, glancing at Rowan with a look that said, *Don't even try to fight us on this.*

She sighed through her nose but didn't protest. The drive over to Julian's apartment felt longer than normal, and she kept drifting off. By the time they got there, she was nearly half asleep.

"Row?" Amelia said. "You awake back there?"

"Mhm," she mumbled.

"I can get the bag if you want to help her up?" Samuel said, and Julian murmured something in agreement.

She clumsily undid her seat buckle. The door to her side opened, and Julian scooped her up.

"This is not necessary," she mumbled into his chest.

"I don't care, *mo ghràdh*," he said. "And for the record, it is."

Amelia chuckled tightly, and Rowan heard her say, "I'm going to have to warn you never to speak whatever language that is around other girls. It makes your Irish accent stronger."

"It's Scottish," Rowan mumbled, closing her eyes as Julian carried her up the stairs. "And it's very sexy, I know."

"I'll remember you said that," Julian muttered.

She smiled, and then the next thing she knew, she was being set down on a bed that smelled like laundry detergent and a hint of cinnamon. His bed. *Their* bed.

She vaguely felt Amelia peck her cheek and tell her she'd email their landlord as soon as she got home. Then, the bed bowed slightly as Julian laid down next to her. Her eyes felt heavy, but she forced them open to look at him.

"So," he said. "You told your mother?"

She nodded hazily. "She wants to meet you. As soon as I'm off house arrest, we'll go for dinner."

"Bed rest, not house arrest," he corrected.

"Same difference," she muttered. "At least we're on spring break so I won't miss much."

"Rowan," he said tentatively. "Are you sure you want to go back this semester? You can always wait until next fall."

She shook her head, burying her face in a pillow. "No. It would be a waste. There isn't much of the term left."

"I just don't know if it's a good idea."

"Julian, please don't fight me on this right now."

He shifted, brushing a strand of hair from her face as he said, "Alright. We can talk about it later. You should try to sleep."

She sighed, her tired gaze sweeping around the room. "There's no room for a crib in here," she muttered.

He kissed her forehead. "I know. I've already started looking for a better option. My lease ends towards the latter half of July, so...perfect timing."

Because her due date was in August.

Her hand curled around her belly. Professor Petrarch had compromised everything twice now. Julian somehow read her thoughts, because he whispered, "He's gone. He won't hurt us anymore."

"Are you sad?" she asked quietly. "He was your friend."

Julian let out a heavy breath. "I think I'm mourning the man I thought he was, but the person he became... I am not sad he's gone."

There was a pause, a heavy silence filling the air, and then he asked quietly, "You saw Amelia approach, didn't you? That's why you took my phone. Not to try and call 911, but to distract him, to buy us time."

She met his eyes and nodded.

He shook his head slightly. "Everything stopped when he pointed that gun at you."

She put a hand on his chest. "It was my turn to be heroic."

His breath shuddered, and he pressed a hand over her heart. She fell asleep counting the steady beats, sure he was doing the same.

The End

"I Love You, I'm Sorry"—Gracie Abrams

"Madness"—Muse

"Silhouette"—Aquilo

"Make This Go On Forever"—Snow Patrol

"Look After You"—The Fray

Chapter 24
Maybe We're Cursed

Five days passed in a blur. Julian only let her leave the bed to go to the bathroom, shower, and change.

She curled up on the couch and called her mom later that afternoon, promising her that she and Julian would be over the next weekend. Julian tossed the sheets in the washer and then cleaned up the bathroom and kitchen as she talked.

When she hung up, he slumped next to her on the couch, smelling faintly of sharp cleaner.

"We need to talk about next week," he said.

She shrugged. "What about it?"

"I think you should take the rest of the term off."

"No," she said with a shake of her head. "No, not when we're so close to being done. I want to finish in two years, like I planned."

"Plans change."

She glanced at him. God, she knew they did, but she wasn't going to relent on this. "Julian. I'm going back."

He stared at her for a long moment, then said, "If

284

anything goes downhill, or God forbid, anything else happens, promise me you'll step back?"

"Okay," she assured him. "Okay."

"And you need to promise not to push yourself too much either. I don't give a damn about the expectations of grad students. You can worry about being ambitious later."

She looked away, and he pushed, "Promise me."

"Okay. I promise," she said.

He pulled something out of his pocket. Her engagement ring, she realized. She'd almost forgotten that Professor Petrarch had made her take it off. The subtle reminder of those moments had her trembling as she placed her hand in Julian's and he slid it back onto her finger, snugger now.

"I got it resized," he said quietly. "Well, Amelia did it for me, but she used my credit card."

"Those hard-earned teaching dollars have to go somewhere," she said, but her voice was unsteady.

"And there's something else too," he said.

She glanced at him, brows creasing. "What?"

"I called my mother while you were sleeping the other day. She wants to meet you."

Rowan blinked. "Really?"

Slowly, he nodded. "She lives in Aurora, close to your mother. I figured we could make a weekend out of both visits."

"I'd like that," Rowan said with the smallest of smiles.

"My sister will be there too—or at least, that's what my mother told me."

Rowan's lips parted. "Oh."

"Is that alright?"

She huffed out a breath. "Yes. Of course. I'm just already nervous about meeting them."

"It won't be like meeting my father," he assured her.

"Have you talked to him since...?"

"He texted me. Told me he was sorry and had no idea about Ethan. I didn't reply."

She took his hand, and he cleared his throat. "It's fine. I'll, uh, talk to him when I'm ready. If that day ever comes."

"I know," she said softly. "You're not required to have a relationship with him. But if you do, that's perfectly okay too. There's no right way to navigate this."

He furrowed his brow. "Sometimes, I forget how young you are."

She snorted softly. "I'm not that young. Besides, you shouldn't say things like that. Makes you sound like a creepy old man."

"I am not old," he said.

She raised a brow. "I dunno, thirty-four is getting up there."

He sighed. "What I meant was that you're very wise for your age. It was supposed to be a compliment."

He glanced over at the laundry room, where the washer had gone quiet.

"I'm going to throw the sheets in the dryer. I'll be right back," he said, kissing her head. "Lay down. You're still on bed rest."

"For one more day."

"Yes. For one more day. Lay down."

She rolled her eyes and muttered, "So demanding," as he walked away.

"I heard that!" he called from the tiny laundry room.

She heard him start up the dryer, and then he was back. She bullied him into turning on a TV show and letting her sit up. She knew he had work to do, but he sat with her anyway. She woke up later on the bed, folded between clean sheets, Julian breathing evenly next to her.

When they pulled into the parking lot on Monday morning and stepped out onto the asphalt, Rowan froze, her eyes on the spot that was just a little darker than the rest of the lot. Julian's mind flashed to the gun digging into her head as she whirled, her breath coming in quick gasps. He caught her arms and pulled her to him.

"Breathe," he ordered. "Breathe, Rowan. You're all right. We're safe."

The words were just as much a reminder for himself as they were for her.

She nodded once into his chest, trembling faintly as she clung to him. After a minute or so, she untangled herself from him and said shakily, "I'm f-fine. It was just a bit of a shock."

"I can park somewhere else next time," he said gently.

"No, it's fine."

"They have counselors in the music building right now for anyone anxious about the attacks this year. You should go talk to one of them."

She shook her head immediately, what he surmised was a

jerk response. Accepting help was not something that came easily to her. His being here didn't change that. Still, he reminded her, "It's not a weakness to seek out help. I might go talk to one of them myself."

A *small* lie—he was required to go talk to the counselors and admittedly was not thrilled about it. But if she thought he wanted to go, maybe she would too.

She pressed her lips into a thin line. "My mom tried to get me into therapy so many times after Alex died. It was rough, but I made it on my own."

"You don't have to."

She closed her eyes briefly. "I know you have a class to teach. We should go."

"Will you consider it? Talking to someone?" he pushed.

"I'll consider it."

He wanted to say more, wanted to fix this in a way that was impossible. He could not turn back time, could not figure Ethan's true, twisted intentions out sooner and save them both. So, instead, he just nodded and took her hand as they walked up the steps to the back entrance. There were already quite a few people in the main lobby, and as they emerged into the space, heads turned.

Hundreds of eyes landed on both of them, but mostly Rowan, as they walked towards the stairwell. No one said anything, and the lobby grew oddly hushed.

"Ignore them," he said in her ear. "If you want, you can go to my office and hang out before your lesson."

She glanced at him with wide eyes and then out at the lobby. "I think I'll take you up on that," she muttered.

They walked upstairs together, and when they entered

the hallway to his office, they ran into Bill and Leo. Both men were talking in low tones, but they quieted and turned when they saw her and Julian.

"Welcome back," Bill said tightly.

"We were all on spring break, Bill," Julian said dryly, avoiding his pitying stare.

Leo sighed. "Take some sympathy for once, Julian. We all know what happened, and we're very glad you and Rowan are alright."

"Thank you, Leo," Julian said in a calm voice, even though he was feeling anything but calm. In truth, he wanted to punch the wall and cry and shout all at once.

But without another word to either man, he opened his office door. Before Rowan stepped inside, she turned to them and said softly, "Thank you."

Julian watched as both Bill and Leo nodded, giving her tight smiles. Then, she followed Julian inside the office. He shut the door, leaning a hand against the wall and closing his eyes. It was all he could do not to let loose the tidal wave in his chest in some form or another.

"Julian?"

He opened his eyes and looked at her as he said, "Let's not get tangled up in any more disasters, alright?"

"We can try. But we seem to attract trouble. Maybe we're cursed."

He didn't laugh at her weak attempt to lighten the mood, but he crossed the short distance to her and pressed his lips to her forehead.

"I have to go," he murmured against her skin. "But once you're done with your classes, text me. I'll probably be here, but you can work on your homework or something while I sort through all this damned paperwork."

He pulled away, and she met his eyes, brushing away a strand of hair that had fallen in his face. "I will."

His hand found hers, squeezing it once before he let go. Then, with great effort, he let go and left her in the office.

He could feel eyes on him the entire walk to the classroom. Before, they had been a mix of curious and disdained, but now, they all stunk of cloying pity. He hated it almost as much as he hated the fact that he was going to have to stand in front of his students and pretend to be fine.

After Julian left, Rowan pulled out the transcription work she was depressingly behind on and worked for the hour before her private lesson with Professor Thea.

When nine o'clock came around, she sighed, grabbing her bag and instrument. She could feel the baby moving, and she brushed her fingers over the tiny bump as she muttered, "Shush. I have things to do."

The bump did not listen.

As she walked downstairs, she kept having to tell herself not to put her hand on her stomach. It would only cause people to stare more.

By the time she knocked on the door to the practice room, she was already tired. Professor Thea took one look at her and ordered, "Sit down. On the piano bench."

Rowan opened her mouth to protest, but Professor Thea clipped out, "Now, Rowan."

She relented, sitting down. Professor Thea stood in front of her, hands on her narrow hips.

"You can't catch a break, can you?" she finally said, though her voice wasn't cruel or teasing. It was gentle, sad, even.

Rowan looked at her hands pressed into the bench at her sides. "It feels like that sometimes."

"Why don't you take this time to go talk to one of the counselors?"

Rowan raised her gaze, shaking her head as she said, "No. I'm fine."

Professor Thea sighed, looking her over before saying, "It's called dissociating, Rowan. You feel fine because you're forcing your mind to separate yourself from what happened to you. And it will catch up with you eventually. Our lessons going forward will be much more productive if you talk to a counselor, even just a few times."

"But Professor—"

"Go to the counselor or go home. Those are your options today."

Rowan closed her eyes. "Alright. I'll go."

She stood, and Professor Thea said, "They're nice. All the staff are required to go... Yes, including your fiancé," she added. "It'll do you more good than harm."

"Where are they?" she asked warily. "The counselors, I mean."

"Main floor. There are a few rooms they've taken over right off the lobby."

Rowan picked up her things and said, "I'll be ready later this week. I promise."

"It's not about being ready. It's about being able to commit your mind fully. And right now, I don't think a single person in your position, no matter how talented or brilliant, could do that. Go talk to a counselor. Get some rest. We'll check in at your next lesson."

Rowan clenched her jaw but nodded. She headed to the lobby, which was much emptier, thanks to it being in the middle of a class period. A table near the back of the lobby was set up with two women sitting behind it, chatting quietly. They both looked up as Rowan approached.

"Can we help you?" the woman on the right asked. Her lime-green glasses were as distracting as the enormous earrings she wore.

"Um, do you have a session available? I have time now, but I can come back if not..." She trailed off.

The other woman, with huge blue eyes and a soft face, said, "Most of the counselors are available. You can have your pick," she said with a smile. "Can we just see your student ID?"

Rowan pulled it out, handing it to the woman. As her large eyes skirted over the grainy photo and name, she sucked in a breath.

"Rowan Evans," she stated.

Rowan fidgeted. "That's me."

The woman handed her back the ID, checking something off on a piece of paper. "I'm glad you decided to come try a session. And we're all so glad you're alright. I'll be right back.

Do you have a preference? Some of the girls have preferred talking to women."

Rowan shook her head, her hands clammy as she said, "No, whoever is available is fine."

The blue-eyed woman nodded, hurrying back and sticking her head into a doorway. The other woman, the one with the green glasses, glanced at Rowan and asked, "How far along are you?"

"Oh. Um, four months, almost five."

The woman smiled. "That's wonderful. Do you know if you're having a boy or a girl?"

"A girl," Rowan said, her hand twitching.

The other woman returned, and the one with green glasses said, "Good luck. And congratulations," she said, her gaze flicking to Rowan's stomach.

"Thanks," Rowan said, a little absentmindedly as she passed the table and followed the blue-eyed woman to a room. The fluorescents were off, the room instead lit by a soft lamp. A diffuser was plugged into the wall, emitting a mist that smelled like lavender and something else she couldn't place.

"Hi, Rowan," the counselor said, a warm smile on her face. "My name is Dr. Westin, but you can call me Lucy. Please, sit."

The door closed behind Rowan, and she took a seat in the chair facing Dr. Westin. The counselor seemed to be waiting for Rowan to speak first, so Rowan took a deep breath and began to speak, hardly registering the words leaving her mouth.

"My twin sister died when we were eighteen. Cancer. I took a gap year between high school and college because of it, and my mom tried to get me to see a therapist for months. I never went then and I was fine. It took time, but I figured it out. And then, I came here, and I almost died twice. I'm having a baby, and I almost died twice. So did my fiancé. We should probably both be dead; it was just luck. Alex would have probably laughed at how ridiculous this year has been for me. First, I get knocked up by my teacher, and then, someone commits arson right in front of me and *then*, Julian's friend tries to shoot us in the parking lot..." She trailed off, realizing she was rambling.

The therapist didn't balk, though. She only asked, "Was Alex your sister?"

Rowan looked up from where she'd been staring at her hands and said, "Yeah. I think I want the baby to have her name as a middle name."

She wasn't sure why she told the therapist that. She hadn't even talked to Julian about it yet. It was just something she intrinsically knew she wanted, had known, since she saw the two pink lines on that pregnancy test in late December.

The therapist smiled softly. "I like that. Is Alexandra the full version of her name?"

Rowan bit her lip. "It is."

"I'm wondering," Dr. Westin began, "why you decided not to go to therapy after your sister passed away?"

Rowan shrugged. "Alex was always so calm and cool. I tried to be like that too. But my mom used to say we were like fire and ice, two sides of the same coin but different. When Alex died, I felt numb, and then I was angry. It was like I was carrying both of our emotions, both of our personalities.

Going to therapy didn't feel like something she would do. So, I didn't."

"And now? Why are you here?"

"Well, my teacher basically told me not to come back until I tried this out."

Dr. Westin smiled tightly. "I see. Well, let's just start off with: what are you most worried about?"

Rowan paused and thought about it. Then, she replied, "I know this probably sounds stupid and petty, given everything that's happened, but the gossip and the stares are what bother me the most. It just feels like it'll never let up. I mean, I get it. A professor and student relationship is pretty scandalous, especially given…" She gestured at her stomach. "But it was never like that to me. I mean, sure, I knew it wasn't exactly what we were supposed to be doing, but in any other situation, there would have been no doubt."

"No doubt about what?"

"That I love him. That I have for a long time, much longer than I even admitted it to myself. And despite how much people talk and how strange I know the situation must look, the way I feel and the way he feels are the only things that have really ever mattered to me."

"So, the gossip bothers you because people aren't validating your feelings?"

She shook her head. "It bothers me because it makes me feel like I did something wrong, even when I know that there is never anything wrong with loving someone as much as I love him."

Dr. Westin sat back in her chair. "Is it true that he walked into a room on fire to save you?"

Rowan raised a brow. "He is never going to live that down, but...yes. He did. We both have the burn scars to prove it."

"Prove it?"

"People didn't believe it at first, especially some of the students. I guess they didn't think it could be true that someone like him cared for 'someone like me' in that way." She shook her head. "As if my worth is determined by that."

Dr. Westin smiled. "I'm glad you recognize that about your worth."

Rowan shrugged. "I had a life before him, you know? I still have a career ahead of me, even if it might not go exactly as I expected."

"When are you due?" she asked.

"August. I haven't decided if I'll start the next term right away or take a break. I don't want to take a gap year, but I have a feeling Julian will encourage it, especially given what's happened recently."

"He's very protective of you."

Rowan chuckled softly. "He likes to fuss."

"Don't you think he has a reason to?"

Rowan blinked. The therapist was waiting for her to respond just as a dam cracked inside of her. Of course, he had a reason to be worried. Lots of reasons, actually.

"I..." Rowan's voice crackled. "I know he does. But accepting that means accepting everything that's happening, accepting everything that could *still* happen."

Her hand went to her bump on instinct, and this time, she didn't have the wits to stop it.

The therapist nodded. "I think you're both going to have

to work through a lot, but the most crucial thing you can do right now, for him and yourself, is to let each other in. Lean on one another. Because the truth of it is, very few people are going to really understand what you've been through, but your fiancé has been there every step of the way. Even without speaking to him, I'm fairly certain he probably has similar fears as you do. Share those fears and keep opening yourself up emotionally, even if it's just a little bit each day."

Rowan nodded and glanced at the clock as the therapist smiled knowingly.

"Yes, we're about done," she said. "But I'll be here for the rest of the month. I'd suggest you come back a few times if you can. If not, just try and hold onto what we talked about today. You're obviously a very bright young woman who is very mature for her age. Just don't let those positive qualities hold you back."

"Thank you," Rowan said quietly. "I...might come back. I'll have to think about it."

"No worries, Rowan. Thank you for trusting me today."

"Yeah," Rowan said a bit awkwardly. "Have a good day."

She stood, grabbing her bag and instrument case as the therapist replied, "You too."

Rowan left, her body trembling with nervous energy. She felt a little light-headed, so she sat down on a bench and scarfed down a protein bar just as most of the classes let out and the lobby filled with people.

"Hey, Row!" she heard Amelia call. Her friend rushed over and said, "Hey, I have to get to class, but...the landlord approved the transfer! You just have to go to the leasing office and sign something."

Rowan smiled, though it felt forced. Amelia furrowed her brow and sat down next to her.

"You okay?"

"I'm fine. I just had a session with some counselor. It was weird."

Amelia sighed. "I'm supposed to go this evening. My mom pretty much blackmailed me into going. Offered a couple months' worth of grocery funds if I went two or three times."

"Well, that's nothing to scoff at," Rowan said, her tone lightening.

Amelia laughed. "Yeah, well, we don't all have smexy Scottish flute players to cook for us."

"Smexy Scottish flute players?" a voice mused behind them, and Amelia swore loudly as they saw Julian standing there, his arms crossed over his chest. "Are you ever going to get tired of coming up with demeaning nicknames for me?"

Amelia swore again and said, "Why do you *always* have to show up at the most inopportune times?"

Julian's face was impassive, but Rowan caught the flicker of amusement in his eyes and the twitch of his lips. Relief swept through her at even the hint of anything but worry on his face. He had hardly smiled since that day.

"Ugh, you are so boring," Amelia said. "I have to get to class. Row, please tell him to stop looking at people like he's about to vaporize them."

She stood, and Rowan said, "I'll try."

Amelia flashed a grin and then sauntered away, her tiny hips swinging. Julian sighed, and Rowan stood up too, crumpling the wrapper from the protein bar in her hand.

"I have to go too. Theory," she said.

"You're making a face," he said lightly. "What's wrong with theory?"

She tried for a smile. "It's my most boring class."

"I teach music theory this semester."

Raising a brow, she said, "Too bad I couldn't have been in your class. I bet it would be a lot more interesting for everyone if I was there."

"They will never in a million years allow you into a class I'm teaching again," he replied. "But I agree. My students are very interested in hearing about you, especially the one class of undergrads I teach."

"And what do you tell them?"

His mouth kicked to the side. "Not much. Usually, I just tell them my personal life is none of their business."

"Ah. And how does that go over?"

He shrugged, snatching the empty wrapper from her hand and tossing it into the garbage bin next to him. "Well enough, except when they decide to get cocky. There's this grad student, a bassoon player, who once shouted something very interesting in my repertoire studies class."

"'I fucked my professor, happy' guy?" she said, a small laugh escaping her. It felt odd to laugh, like using a stiff muscle.

"The very same."

She shook her head. "Well, I need to go spend some quality time with him. He's in my theory class."

"Ah. Good luck."

She nodded and went to leave, but then she turned and said, "When you go to the counselor, which, by the way, I know is mandatory for you to do, ask for Dr. Westin. She's very nice."

He blinked. "You went?"

"Professor Thea pretty much made me. But yes. I went." She sighed, glancing at the time on her phone. "I do need to go. I'll see you later."

"Alright. Be safe," he said softly.

She nodded and then headed for class. 'I fucked my professor, happy?' guy was in her usual spot, and the only seats left in the lecture hall were now near the top, since everyone had the habit of spreading out their stuff across two or three seats. She was breathing heavily by the time she reached a row of open seats. Sitting down, she pulled out her laptop, and rested a hand on her stomach, still catching her breath.

The class was boring but a little more interesting as she imagined what Julian would be like when teaching it.

After the allotted two hours passed, she gathered her things and headed for Julian's office. When she knocked, he shouted, "Come in!"

She pushed open the door to find him engrossed in his computer. He looked up at her as she closed the door and sat, but she said, "Keep working. I'm just gonna text my mom to confirm about this weekend, and then I have a paper to start."

"Good luck. I don't envy you with the paper. But feel free to use the desk—where it's not covered in papers."

She pulled out her phone to text her mom and said absentmindedly, "A messy desk. Probably stresses out your orderly brain."

He let out a short laugh and went back to his work. She

sent a text confirming they were good for Saturday brunch, and then, she set her laptop on the end of his desk and began to write. They both worked through eight p.m. Finally, when she rubbed at her temples one too many times, trying to banish the headache forming, Julian said, "Okay. We're going home now."

"I'm so close," she muttered. "I just need to finish formatting the works cited."

He sighed and carefully snatched the laptop from her.

"Hey!" she exclaimed, but he only held up a hand, telling her to wait.

She rolled her eyes, the movement making her head headache throb even more. Five minutes later, he handed her the laptop back, her references page finished and perfectly formatted.

"I'm fairly certain that is not allowed," she said.

"And I'm fairly certain you were told by multiple doctors to take it easy. You've been working for hours, and I know you have a headache. It was just medical intervention on my part."

She scoffed, standing and stretching her fingers before pulling on her jacket. He did the same, and they headed out of his office and down to the parking lot. In the dark, she couldn't see the blood stain. That made her feel better—for now, at least.

Chapter 25
A Nudge from the Universe

SATURDAY MORNING CAME, and she and Julian left Chicago early to try and avoid rush hour traffic to Batavia. He turned on something different than classical music as they drove, some alternative rock album. She thought she recognized a few of the songs. The car ride felt easy and casual, and her hand rested on her bump nearly the whole way, tapping to the music.

After a while, when they were exiting the freeway, she said, "I want her middle name to be Alex."

Julian glanced sidelong at her before making a right turn onto a familiar road. She'd taken this route many times. Well, fewer times than she probably should have, but it was what it was.

"I like that," he said after a moment. "What about the first name?"

She sighed. "I literally have no idea."

"My grandmother, the one who gave me the ring, her name was Callie."

A small smile lifted at her lips as she said, "Callie. I like that."

"Is Alex short for Alexandra?"

"Yeah," she said as the GPS instructed him to *turn left onto Deerpath Road.* "Okay. Here's the deal. My mom has a boyfriend named Cameron. He's really nice, but he's really nosy, and he's probably going to ask us a lot of questions. He kind of lacks a filter. So, just be prepared to be forced to probably overshare a little."

"And your mother?"

Rowan shrugged. "When I talked to her on the phone, she seemed surprisingly chill about the whole thing. So... hopefully, she still feels that way."

Julian smiled. "Alright."

She rolled her eyes. "Do you *ever* get nervous?"

He raised a brow, turning into her mom's neighborhood. "I am very nervous right now. Until quite recently, your mother only vaguely knew I was your teacher. I almost expect her to be a little cold to me, at least at first."

"I don't think she will be. Oh, uh, park on the street, just in case."

He nodded, doing so and then turning off the car. They both looked at each other, and Rowan said, "It'll be fine."

"Are you telling me or yourself that?"

"Both?"

Julian indicated with his head to where the front door had opened, the glass door revealing her mother standing behind it, a soft smile on her face. Rowan took a deep breath.

"Let's go."

She opened the car door, and Julian got out too, snatching

a bouquet of flowers from the back. He'd insisted on picking them up from the grocery store before they'd left, despite her protests that it was completely unnecessary.

But as soon as her mother opened the glass door, she smiled even wider as she saw the flowers.

"Hi, Ms. Evans," Julian said calmly, pleasantly. "I'm Julian."

Her mother laughed a little. "Oh, I know. You didn't have to bring flowers."

He shrugged. "It seemed appropriate."

She laughed again. "Funny, Row. He's funny. I like that. And you, Julian, just call me Abby. We don't need any of the fussy titles or surnames."

She winked at Rowan and mouthed, *Professor*.

"Mom," Rowan groaned. "He totally saw that. And can you please let us in?"

Her mother took a step back. "Of course."

Cameron was waiting in the hall, brows raised as he saw Julian. In recent years, Rowan supposed Cameron had begun to see her as his own daughter, or at least his responsibility.

Her mother took the flowers from Julian, and in a flurry, she hugged Rowan, and Julian shook Cameron's hand.

"Oh my goodness, you're showing already!" her mother exclaimed, adding, "You look so beautiful, Row. It suits you."

Rowan smiled tightly. "Thanks, Mom."

"We should eat!" Cameron said. "It's all ready. I figured you guys would be hungry right away after your drive."

She smiled at Cameron, walking over and giving him a quick hug. "Thanks for cooking, Cam."

He chuckled, leading them into the dining room. "You

know I'm the only one around here who can. Julian, do you cook?"

Julian made a "so, so" motion with his hand, but Rowan said, "Yes, he can. A few levels above me, at least."

Cameron huffed out a laugh. "Well, you can pretty much only cook instant ramen and canned soup, so that's not very promising."

Julian laughed as they sat down. Her mom and Cameron were on one side of the table, and she and Julian sat next to each other on the other. Rowan went for the bowl of fruit before her mother could start some sort of gratitude circle, something she loved to do on holidays.

Julian glanced at the food. "Are we good to just go for it?"

Cameron barked out a laugh. "Yeah, go for it. All you."

Julian glanced at Rowan, and she raised a brow.

"Go for it," she said with a grin.

He chuckled and loaded his plate with the breakfast items spread before them—eggs, bacon, fruit, toast, and mini cinnamon rolls.

Once they had all served themselves, Cameron took a long swig of orange juice and said, "Well. Where do I even start?"

Rowan took a bite of scrambled eggs, fighting a smile.

"I looked you up, you know," he said to Julian. "Pretty hefty credentials, I have to say, Juilliard and whatnot. And then to land a teaching job at a school like Grandview? Very impressive."

Julian nodded. "Thank you."

"But," Cameron went on, and Rowan braced herself,

"what I really want to know is how the hell you two became a couple."

"I told Mom, Cam," Rowan pointed out. "And I'm sure she told you."

Cameron shrugged. "That was just an itty bit of detail. I want to know how he went from being your teacher to your fiancé."

Rowan glanced at Julian, brushing his hand under the table in assurance. Cameron stared at them both, waiting, and finally, Julian cleared his throat. "It was not planned."

Cameron barked out another laugh. "Obviously. I mean, she was going to have a completely different teacher. It's why she went to Grandview instead of Juilliard. And then, you show up at the last minute. I mean, what are the chances?"

"Juilliard?" Julian said, looking at Rowan again. "You didn't ever tell me you got into their program."

She shrugged. "It never felt important. I didn't go there."

"Row," Cameron whined. "He's not cracking."

Rowan shook her head. "Cam, I really don't know if you want or need to know the details."

"Ah, c'mon," he said, glancing at Rowan's mother, who was smiling as she took a sip of her coffee, as if she was enjoying this just as much as Cameron was.

Rowan sighed. "Alright. You really want to know?"

"That's what I said, isn't it?" Cameron chuckled.

"I kissed him first," Rowan said boldly.

"Of course, you did," Cameron said, shaking his head. "You've always burned a little too hot for the life you were given. But what then? Did you keep teaching her?" he asked, looking at Julian.

Julian took a sip of water and said, "For a while."

"Damn. And you still have your job?"

"I do."

"Well, I suppose that's good, given the fact that you have a kid coming—" Cameron cut himself off, tilting his head, his gaze landing on Julian's hand and then his arms as he rolled his sleeves up.

"What is it?" her mother asked.

"I worked as a firefighter for most of my life," Cameron said. "And those scars you have, Julian... Those are from some pretty nasty burns."

His attention swiveled to Rowan, to her hands, and his brows rose.

"Row, you did not have those the last time I saw you."

"There was a fire at Grandview a few months ago," her mother muttered then exclaimed, "Rowan, why didn't you say anything?"

Rowan thinned her lips. "I didn't want to worry you. And there was already so much going on."

"Was it the same person?" Cameron asked quietly. "Between the fire and the shooting, I have to ask."

Julian's jaw was tight. "It was. A colleague of mine, as I'm sure you know from the recent news broadcasts. He orchestrated both attacks."

"Jesus," Cameron said. "At least he's gone now."

Julian nodded, and a tense silence followed until Rowan broke it. "Mom, I've been thinking of baby names."

Her mother's face smoothed out a bit. "What are you considering?"

"Well, I've always known I want Alexandra to be her middle name."

Her mother's lips wobbled as she said, "Your sister would've loved that. And what... What about a first name?"

Rowan glanced at Julian, and he answered, "My grandmother's name was Callie, so that's a contender."

Her mother smiled, recovering. "I love that. What's your accent, Julian?"

"Scottish. I grew up in Edinburgh, but my parents are both musicians, so we moved to the States for their work when I was fifteen."

Rowan lifted her hand. "The ring was his grandmother's."

Her mother snatched her hand from across the table, pushing Rowan's belly into the wood.

"Mom," she winced. "Um, you're kind of crushing my stomach."

"Oh, sorry," her mother said, letting go of her hand with a small laugh. "We don't want that. By the way, how are you feeling, baby? I know you said in your text that the doctors were a little worried."

"I'm fine, Mom. I just needed a week to sleep and chill."

Her mother looked at Julian and said sternly, "You make sure she's taking care of herself. I know how Row can be. Sometimes, she needs to be reminded to slow down."

Julian sighed. "Believe me, I know. I'm doing my best."

They finished up eating, Cameron asking Julian questions about his schooling, particularly about his time at Juilliard. Once they were done and Rowan went to help clear the dishes, her mother stopped her.

"Go sit on the couch, baby. You too, Julian. Cameron and I have got this."

"You're sure?" Julian asked.

Her mother smiled. "I'm sure. Go relax. I know that's probably a novelty for you, being a professional musician, but you look like you need it."

Julian chuckled softly. "Thank you."

They went over and sat on the worn leather couch. A fluffy, gray cat rubbed against Rowan's leg, and she called, "Mom! I didn't know you guys had a cat?"

"Just picked her up from the shelter last week," Cameron said from the kitchen. "Her name's Lulu—which I didn't pick out, by the way. The name came with her."

The cat jumped right into Julian's lap, and he scratched it between the ears and under the chin with a smile.

"You're a very pretty girl," he murmured.

Rowan smiled. "You're a cat person, huh?"

He glanced at her. "Sort of. The last time my family had a cat was when I was ten."

Rowan petted the cat's back, her hand brushing against Julian's as she did. A look passed between them, and her mother sighed loudly from the kitchen. Rowan looked at her to see her hands on her hips and a faint smile playing on her lips.

"I knew I was right to trust you on this," her mother said.

Rowan raised a brow. "Um, thanks?"

Her mother laughed as Cameron started the dishwasher. She walked over, sitting on the armchair to the side of the couch. Cameron took a seat in the chair by the fireplace, and her mother said, "The fact that you two don't even realize what you're doing tells me everything I need to know."

"And what are we doing?" Rowan asked, bracing herself for the answer.

Julian's hand brushed hers as her mother replied, "Love has a look. You both have it. I was worried he might not, or at least not to the degree I know you deserve. But I'd almost say—"

"I'd say you've got him tied tight around your little finger, Row," Cameron finished for her mother.

Julian's cheeks were actually a little pink as he said, "You're not wrong."

Rowan laced her fingers with his, the other hand on her bump.

"Can I take a picture?" her mother asked suddenly, and Rowan groaned.

"Mom..."

"Just one! You don't mind, do you, Julian?"

"I don't mind," he said, smiling slightly as Rowan gave him an imploring look.

Her mother sighed. "Good. Lulu, off!"

The cat didn't move, and Cameron strode over with a cat toy that had been lying around to coax the cat off Julian's lap.

"Okay, smile!" her mother said.

Julian's arm looped around her, casually but tight enough that she knew he was feeling something deeper too. And as the stupid flash of her mother's phone camera went off and she exclaimed, "Oops," the moment did feel somehow surreal. Julian pressed a gentle kiss to her forehead, and Rowan's cheeks colored, though she couldn't help the soft smile, the real smile, that rose to her mouth. The camera made that stupid, fake shutter noise, and she honestly didn't care. In fact, she wanted this moment captured.

"So cute!" her mother said, sitting back down. "I'll send these to you, Row. You're going to want them."

Julian's arm stayed draped around her for the next hour or so as they chatted with her mother and Cameron. When she glanced at the clock and saw it was nearly four o'clock, Rowan said, "Okay, we have to go. I'm meeting Julian's mother and sister tonight."

"Ooh, double whammy," Cameron said. "Good luck, Row. They'll love you, I'm sure. Right, Julian?"

Julian nodded. "I'm sure they will."

There was a flurry of goodbyes and hugs, her mom telling her to not shut her out again. Rowan promised to give her more frequent updates, and then they were out the door. The air was warmer, and she could smell rain. As they got into the car, Julian said, "I liked them."

She snorted. "I'm glad you had fun. Cameron definitely liked you a lot."

"And your mother?" he asked as he started the car.

"I think she did. If anything, she's just happy to see me happy."

Julian pulled the car away from the curb. "I'm glad. And I'm happy you could see them after so long."

She nodded, and he took a breath and said, "Alright. I haven't seen my mother or Lena in years, so this might be a little awkward at first."

"It's fine," she assured him.

"And my mother is a very level-headed woman. She can

sometimes come across as cold, but it's almost never personal. Lena is similar."

"Good to know," Rowan said.

"This will be fine."

She glanced at him as rain began to patter against the windshield. "It will be. Even if it doesn't go as you hoped, I'll be right there."

He took a slow breath. "I know."

A mere ten minutes later, they were in front of a small, well-kept house. The lights were on inside, but the curtains were drawn. Julian turned off the car.

"Okay. Ready?" he asked.

"I am."

He got out of the car, and she did too, taking his hand as they walked to the front door. He knocked three times, and Rowan heard footsteps. Then, the door swung open to reveal a tall woman with dark hair and sharp cheekbones. Behind her, a girl who looked a little older than Rowan stood, smirking. She looked like Julian—they both did, even more so than his father.

"Hello, Julian," his mother said coolly.

Julian tightened his grip on Rowan's hand, more for his sake than hers, as he said, "Hi, Mom. This is Rowan."

His mother surveyed Rowan, from the worn oxford shoes she wore to the casual floral dress and the bump of her stomach. She was assessing, like she always did. Julian had half a mind to tug Rowan back to the car then and there, but then his mother said, "Come in. It's nice to meet you, Rowan."

Rowan smiled and gently let go of his hand as she replied, "It's nice to meet you too."

They walked into the entryway, and Julian took a quiet, shaky breath. He had never been in this house, the place his mother had escaped to after she had left them. He had seen her a few times since she had left that awful day, but it had always been brief; after a performance of hers he had attended in an effort to make things right, or just a quick call on her birthday.

The house was small but neat, exactly what he had expected. There was art on the walls, some of it framed, some of it pasted on. It was a lot like the decor in his own apartment. He tried not to think about that too much. He was more like his mother than he wanted to admit.

A standing piano was against the wall to the left, along with several music stands. To their right was a formal dining room, which he had a feeling was hardly used.

"Hi," a familiar voice said loudly, a shock to his system. Lena was standing in front of Rowan, holding out a hand. "I'm Lena, but I'm sure Julian's already told you that."

Rowan shook Lena's hand and nodded. "He did."

"Good to know he still remembers me."

He stiffened, but Lena said, "Oh, cool it, Julian. Bring your fiancée into the kitchen. We want to get to know her."

Rowan caught his eye for just a moment, and he nodded. They followed his mother and Lena into a softly lit kitchen. A candle that smelled like fresh laundry was burning on the counter, and a spread of cheese and crackers was on a platter next to it. At least they had tried.

"Help yourself," his mother said. "Oh, and Rowan, please don't call me Mrs. Lynch. Cara is fine."

Rowan nodded. "Thank you for letting me know."

Lena pulled out a bottle of wine from the cabinet, and Julian eyed it. He *had* told them Rowan was pregnant, which he supposed didn't mean the rest of them couldn't drink. Before he could decide how he felt about it, Lena noticed his expression, snorting before she said, "Yes, yes, I know pregnant women aren't supposed to drink. But that doesn't mean the rest of us can't. Do you like pinot noir?"

Julian tensed, clenching his jaw as he nodded. The last time he had seen Lena, she hadn't even been legally able to drink.

Lena poured three glasses and then said to Rowan, "I bought some of that weird sparkling apple juice if you want it?"

Rowan smiled. "That would be great. Thanks for thinking of it."

Lena looked her over, from the tip of her toes to the top of her head. Silently, she poured a glass of the sparkling juice and handed it to her. The tension in the room was thick.

Rowan took a sip of the juice but coughed as Lena asked, "How on Earth did *you* manage to snare my brother?"

"Lena," Julian warned. He could understand Lena's anger at him, but he wasn't about to let her take it out on Rowan.

Lena shrugged and his mother took a sip of wine, watching silently. Waiting.

"I want to know," Lena said. "And I want to make sure you're not with her just because you got her knocked up," she added, looking at him.

"I wouldn't be here if that was the case," Rowan said steadily.

Lena's gaze swung back to her as his mother spoke. "These things do happen. A student-teacher relationship is an intimate one, especially in a music setting."

"Yeah, but look at her," Lena said harshly.

Julian opened his mouth, fully ready to say they were leaving, but Rowan beat him to it, asking, "And what do you see when you look at me?"

Lena looked a little taken aback, and his mother sat up a little straighter in her seat, almost as though she was intrigued.

"I see softness," Lena finally said. "I see someone who crumbles easily. I see...not who I'd expect Julian to bring home. I mean, he's never brought someone home. Not once."

Lena was brutally honest and to the point, he knew that, but this was nearing a line.

"I may not look the part," Rowan said quietly after a moment. "But I was willing to take a bullet in the head for him."

Julian couldn't help the flinch that tore through him.

"So, it's true. About Ethan?" his mother asked.

"Of course it's true. It was all over the news," Julian gritted out.

His mother folded her hands in her lap. "Well, one never knows what to believe. And you didn't go into detail when you called me."

"What exactly happened?" Lena asked, her expression sharp.

Next to him, Rowan placed a casual hand on the edge of the counter, but Julian noticed it right away, glancing at her to find her face a shade too pale. He had known today was going to be a lot for her, despite the number of times she insisted she was feeling fine.

Immediately, he said, "Lena, please move so Rowan can sit down."

"Alright, calm down," Lena muttered. "She's pregnant, not sickly."

He held out a hand to help Rowan as she hauled herself on the high-top chair, repositioning so he was behind her. He glared at Lena and said, "Lena, I'm going to need you to stop assuming things."

She raised her hands, glancing at his mother as she said, "What did I do?"

His mother was eyeing Rowan, her expression just slightly softer than before. She ignored Lena and instead said, "Julian told me what happened, that you were in a fire. Sparing the details, of course, which is so like him. But that had to have been hard on your pregnancy."

Rowan met his mother's hazel eyes and nodded. "I hate it, how fragile everything feels. But...after the fire and then what happened with Professor Petrarch," she cleared her throat, "I'm supposed to be cautious."

His mother smiled, a rarity for her. "Us ambitious women never like feeling vulnerable. Children will do that to us, though."

Rowan took another sip of the sparkling apple juice. "I'm

sorry if we got started off the wrong way, but I'm not some mistake Julian made, even if people seem to like to treat me like I am."

Lena's gaze snagged on Rowan's finger, and she asked Julian quietly, "Is that Grandma's ring?"

"Yeah," he said, reaching over Rowan's shoulder, grasping her hand and sliding a gentle touch over her palm.

I'm sorry for this, he tried to convey to her.

"Do you remember what she said when she gave it to you?" Lena asked.

"I do," Julian replied, holding his sister's gaze. "And I didn't give it away lightly."

Lena took a long sip of wine and said, "Alright. I'm sorry for misjudging you guys. Can we stop bickering and eat?"

"If you behave, we'll stay," Julian said softly, but not gently, to his sister.

Lena rolled her eyes. "I get it, Julian."

She sauntered over to the oven and pulled out a dish with a hot pad and set it on top of the stove.

"It's basically just potatoes and meat," she explained to Rowan.

"Scottish fare, *mo ghràdh*," he murmured in Rowan's ear.

His mother must have caught the phrase, because she said, "I see you still remember some Scots, Julian."

"Just a bit," he replied as casually as he could, holding a hand out for Rowan as she slipped off the chair.

They sat around a dark wood table as Lena served them hearty portions of the casserole and brought out glasses of water.

"Thanks," Rowan said as Lena set the glass down in front of her.

Lena paused and said, "A gun to the head, huh? That's pretty metal."

"Honestly, it didn't feel like it at the moment, but thanks," Rowan replied, her voice tight.

Lena's brows raised as she circled to the open seat next to Julian. She took a few bites, her brow furrowed. "Well, thank you. For being willing to save him like that."

Rowan bit her lip, shrugging as she glanced at him. "I suppose we're even now on the heroics."

His mother looked up from her plate. "What do you mean?"

Julian sighed; he had hoped telling them about what exactly had happened in the fire would be avoidable. But he supposed at least his mother deserved to know, so he rolled up the sleeves of his sweater. His mother sucked in an audible breath at the angry, mottled scars covering his arms.

"What happened to you?" Lena demanded.

He rolled down his sleeves. "There was a fire, as you know. We figured out later that Ethan had orchestrated it. But his accomplice, a former student of mine, trapped Rowan in a room covered with gasoline and lit it on fire."

"And you, what? Walked into a room that was on fire?" Lena asked.

"That is the short of what happened."

"Christ, Julian," Lena muttered.

"Your father contacted me, you know," his mother said quietly, and his stomach dipped. "I haven't talked to him in almost ten years, and he called me to tell me you'd made an enormous mistake and he needed me to fix it."

"And?" Julian said, his leg bouncing twice.

His mother straightened in her seat. "And I didn't trust a word that came out of his mouth. You don't make mistakes, Julian. You never have. You make promises, and I have never seen you break one. Quite obviously, you and Rowan have made a promise to each other, and she is the first person I've seen with you who I am sure would not break her promise either."

"Thanks, Mom," he said quietly, meaning it.

"And," his mother added, "I will not be isolated from my grandchild. Not if I have any say in it."

"Good," Rowan said. "Because I want you to be in her life."

"A girl, then?" Lena asked.

Julian looked warily at Lena and nodded. She smiled, warmer this time, and said, "You're going to be a dad. Like for real, for real."

"For real, for real," Julian echoed.

Lena chuckled. "I have to say, I never saw this day coming. I thought you'd be a loner forever."

Julian glanced at Rowan, and he thought about what her mother had said earlier, about how love had a look. He supposed he agreed with her.

They lingered for only fifteen minutes or so after dinner was over before Julian said, "We should get going. We have a decent drive back."

Lena sighed. "I get it, you want to leave."

Rowan watched as Julian glared at his sister, and she glared right back. Cara simply strode to the entryway. She squeezed Rowan's hand first before embracing Julian.

"Keep me updated," she said as she pulled away from him. "As much as you're able. I know you're busy, and so am I."

"I will, Mom," he said.

Lena faced him and said, "It's nice to see you again, big brother. And...congrats. You've checked off two life milestones, and it only took you thirty-four years."

Julian snorted softly. "Goodbye, Lena."

Lena rolled her eyes. "It was nice to meet you, Rowan. Sorry about earlier."

Lena gave no explanation and didn't backtrack. Rowan figured she wasn't the type of person to usually apologize for her actions.

"Alright, goodbye," Julian affirmed, taking Rowan's hand and leading her out the front door.

It was raining softly, and they carefully rushed to the car. Once they were inside, Julian pulled away from the curb before she could even speak.

"I'm sorry," he said as they turned out of the neighborhood. "I knew it might be weird, but I thought Lena would be a little more civil than that."

"It's okay," she replied. "I liked your mom. I think I might even like Lena, once we warm up to each other a bit more."

Julian scoffed. "Good luck with that." She yawned, and he glanced at her. "You can sleep. It's not a short drive."

Shaking her head, she muttered, "I shouldn't."

"Sleep, Rowan. We'll be back before you know it."

She closed her eyes...just for a moment. And when she opened them again, Julian was parking in front of his apartment complex. She groaned softly at the ache in her neck. He got out of the car, and before she could reach for the door handle, he opened it for her.

"I've got it," she muttered.

He held out a hand for her, the rain coming down harder now, running in rivulets down his face. A single, dull yellow street light shone above him, making his eyes look black in the backlight. She paused, something pulling taut within her—a string she swore she'd felt that day on the steps outside of Sierra Hill. A nudge from the universe, letting her know that this moment was integral in some way. Important. Sacred.

"Rowan," he said hoarsely.

She took his hand and stepped out into the cool spring rain. The car door was shut in a flurry of motion before he kissed her, thunder crackling in the distance.

"We should go inside," he murmured against her mouth.

Lightning split the sky apart above them, white light flashing in his eyes. She let him lead her inside, both of them dripping water across the floor, and into his apartment. *Their* apartment.

The second she started shivering, he tugged her towards the shower and ran the water warm. She stepped out of her shoes and then, gently, carefully, he tugged at her soaking dress. She pulled off his shirt, running her hands down his chest. The rest of their clothing followed, creating little puddles on the bathroom floor as steam filled the air.

They stepped into the shower. He ran soapy hands down her back and over her chest. She did the same. Once they were done, he snatched two towels from the rack. She relished the sight of him with the towel slung low on his hips as he collected the wet clothes, threw them in the washing machine, then took a few paper towels to the wet floor.

As he finished mopping up the puddles, he glanced up at her, his expression unreadable as he said, "You're staring, Evans."

"Mmm, really?"

She didn't even scold him for the use of her surname. In fact, it ignited something in her—a feeling from months ago in a practice room with him, when she'd crossed a line she shouldn't have.

He stood, tossing the sopping paper towels in the trash can. "You should get some rest."

"I will."

He swallowed. "I don't know if it's a good idea. I know the doctor said to be careful about—"

"It's been nearly two weeks, Julian," she said. "They said no sex for five days, just for extra precaution."

He sucked in a breath. "I know. I just... Are you sure?"

She nodded silently, holding his gaze. His expression shifted, but before she could read it fully, he scooped her up in his arms, the towel nearly sliding off her. She grumbled a bit as he walked to the bedroom. He only kissed the tip of her nose and said, "Whiny."

She reached up, flicking his cheek just before he set her down gently on the bed.

"That wasn't very nice," he murmured, leaning over her but not putting any weight on her.

"Sorry," she said with a small smile.

"And that didn't sound sincere," he breathed against her neck.

She looped her legs around his hips, and he huffed out a breath before his tongue flicked over her skin. Her breath caught, and he raised his head to look at her.

"You're okay?" he whispered.

She held his heavy stare and replied, "I'm okay."

It was all the permission he needed. Gently, slowly, he pushed into her, his hand grasping for hers. He didn't look away from her the entire time, even as her eyes began to flutter shut at the pleasure. His lips hovered over hers, catching her moan as she shattered under his touch. Then, without breaking the kiss, he rose up, leaning against the headboard so she was cradled in his lap. And when he broke too, his eyes widening and his muscles tightening, she bowed her forehead against his, her fingers digging into his back.

They stayed like that for a few minutes once it was over, breathing heavily. Finally, he let her down, and they lay next to each other on the bed.

"Thank you for today," he said after a while. "Thank you for letting me into your life."

"It's what I wanted but thought I could never have," she said softly.

Julian searched his gaze before he replied, "It was inevitable, no matter what had happened."

Chapter 26
Must Be Nice

On Monday morning, as Rowan ate a piece of buttered toast, Julian glanced at his phone, and then said, "Oh, just so you know, we're going into the city on Friday night."

Her brows rose as she swallowed. "Why?"

"I was invited, along with Professor Thea, to play at the C.S.O. Just a guest appearance."

She nearly choked on the bite she'd just taken, and he looked at her, alarmed.

"Chew," he commanded.

She took a drink of orange juice. "Um, when were you going to fucking tell me this?"

He merely shrugged. "I got invited months ago. There were other things to worry about."

"I don't give a shit! Julian, the Chicago Symphony Orchestra? You do know how big of a deal this is, right? I mean, you have to."

"I suppose," he said.

She rolled her eyes. "Leave it to you to be so nonchalant about this."

He ignored the comment. "I have two guest tickets, so I figured you could bring Amelia if she's free."

Rowan grinned, shaking her head. "She's going to think this is so funny."

"But she can't come if she keeps giving me nicknames."

"They are also funny."

"They are not."

She shoved at his arm, and he glared at her. She sighed. "Alright, alright, I'm going. Just let me use the bathroom."

"Didn't you just ten minutes ago?"

She rolled her eyes, setting the plate in the dishwasher. "I'm pregnant. Or have you forgotten?"

"No," he said flatly.

"You're in a mood today," she muttered as she headed for the bathroom.

When she emerged, he was holding her jacket, and she shrugged it on over the green dress she wore. She'd taken to dresses because they didn't have the funky elastic waistbands she hated so much and they still gave her room to breathe.

They got into the car, Julian morosely silent. He didn't speak for most of the drive, until she glanced at him and asked, "Okay, what's wrong?"

He kept his eyes on the road. "Nothing."

"Julian, c'mon. Don't deflect with me."

"You do it often enough."

She sighed. He was acting like this—defensive and cold—because he was hurting. She didn't know why, but she knew him well enough by now to know the ice wasn't directed at her.

"I'm sorry," she said patiently, then waited.

He parked in the further lot, avoiding the one where Professor Petrarch had almost shot them both and died. By the time he shut the car off, he was already getting out, slamming the door and grabbing his bag from the back. She got out, a puff of air escaping her as the baby started to kick lightly.

Julian locked the car as soon as she shut the door and got her bag and instrument. She hurried after him.

"Julian."

He didn't look back. She huffed out a breath and grabbed his wrist. He whirled, and she saw the angry tears in his eyes as soon as he did. His jaw was tight and his cheeks were flushed.

"Slow down," she commanded.

"I'm going to be late. I need to go."

She took a step closer, not really caring if anyone saw what she was about to do as she took his hand and pressed his palm to her bump, where the baby was currently kicking up a storm.

His cold, distant expression became slightly unfocused then softened a fraction. He shut his eyes, a single tear tracking down his cheek. He wiped it away hastily with his free hand, and then he looked at her and said, "It's Ethan's birthday. He would have been thirty-eight today."

She nodded, not saying anything, not judging.

He went on, "It's horrible that I even care, but he...he was my friend. I've known him since Juilliard. I think I'm just having a hard time separating him, my friend from school, from the person who put a gun to your head."

"I know," she whispered. "And you know that's okay, right?"

He looked away, pulling his hand from her belly. Then, he took a deep breath and said, "I do need to go. I have a class starting in ten minutes."

She nodded softly. "Alright."

They walked together in silence to the Mitchell Center, skirting around the parking lot where she knew fading blood still darkened the asphalt. They passed the taped-off hall, the sound of construction workers banging around somewhere inside. Fixing and repairing the room where she'd collapsed against a red-painted wall and nearly died. A room where Julian had walked through flames.

The counselor's table was still set up at the back of the lobby. Helen was babbling to one of the women there, but she turned as Rowan and Julian approached the nearby staircase. Rowan saw her decision to move towards them a moment later, and she murmured so quietly that only Julian could hear, "Go straight to your class. Helen is walking towards us."

He nodded and took off, walking briskly down the hall that branched off to the right of the stairs. She glanced back at Helen, who had caught up to her, a look of mild disappointment on her face at Julian's speedy departure. Still, she said shortly, "Hey, Rowan."

Rowan turned, bracing herself.

"Is it true Professor Lynch is playing at the C.S.O. on Friday?"

Rowan reeled in her annoyance that even Helen had

known about the performance and replied, "Yeah. With Professor Thea."

Helen sighed. "Well, tell him I'll be there."

Rowan raised a brow. "Why don't you just tell him yourself in your lesson later today?"

Helen shrugged. "Maybe I will. Are you going to be there?"

"I will."

"Must be nice," Helen mused.

Rowan narrowed her eyes. "What 'must be nice?'"

"You know, the favors. The free concert tickets and who knows what else."

Rowan took a breath. "I should go."

"To his office?"

"What, do you want to come along?" Rowan said flatly.

Helen shook her head. "No. He won't be there anyways. I'll just ask him my question later, in our lesson."

And with that taunt, Helen left. Rowan watched her go until someone said from behind, "She just gets bitchier by the hour."

Rowan turned to see Amelia grinning behind her on the stairs. Rowan snorted. "Apparently so."

"Is it true? About the C.S.O.?" Amelia demanded, taking Rowan's hand and tugging her to a small bench on the side of the stairs.

"Yup. And guess who didn't tell me until *this* morning."

Amelia rolled her eyes. "He did not."

"He really did. But good news is, if you're free Friday, you can come with me. He was given two guest tickets."

"You sure you don't want to take Helen?" Amelia mused.

Rowan rolled her eyes. "You didn't hear? She already has a ticket."

Amelia barked out a laugh. "Oh my God. She is so obsessed with your fiancé, it's not even funny."

"Tell me about it."

Amelia checked her phone and then said, "I can go on Friday. I'll just skip my last class, since I assume we'll be driving with McHotty early."

Rowan shook her head incredulously. "He also told me if you keep giving him nicknames, you can't go."

"This isn't a new nickname," Amelia said innocently.

"Fair enough," Rowan muttered. "Oh, by the way, I'm going to the leasing office soon. I meant to go this weekend, but we had the big 'meet the family' day on Saturday, and then I was exhausted on Sunday."

Amelia shrugged. "It's fine, no rush. Just let me know when you want to move all your stuff out. Not that *you* will be lifting anything. And before you tell me that you're a big, strong, independent woman... I know you are. But you have doctor's orders to take it easy."

"I know. I wasn't planning on fighting you on it."

Amelia lifted her chin victoriously. "Good, you're learning. I have to go, but text me about Friday. And please bring your moody professor over some time. I miss you."

"Miss you too, Ami," Rowan said. "But go. You don't want to be late."

Amelia snorted. "Maybe I do. Leopold was in a mood last week, and I have a horrible hunch the dark times are not over yet. But...you're probably right. I'll see you later."

"See ya," Rowan replied.

She glanced down at her phone to see it was already almost nine, so she headed down the hall for her lesson with Professor Thea. Thankfully, the professor didn't send her off to the counselors again. In fact, she didn't even mention it.

They started working on a piece for the end-of-term recital after running through an annoying number of technical exercises and scales. Towards the end of the lesson, Professor Thea said, "I assume you'll be at the concert on Friday evening?"

Rowan nodded. "I will. Congrats, Professor."

"Thank you, Rowan. But I'm surprised you didn't mention it earlier."

Rowan shook her head and said in an exasperated tone, "He—Professor Lynch, I mean, didn't tell me until today."

Professor Thea barked out a laugh, shaking her head too. "Why am I not surprised? Did he happen to 'forget' the part about him playing a solo as well?"

Rowan balked. "You're not serious?"

Professor Thea's eyes crinkled in amusement. "I am."

Rowan rubbed at her forehead and said, without really thinking, "Men can be so insufferable sometimes."

Professor Thea chuckled. "They really can be."

Rowan looked at the professor and asked boldly, "Do you think I should be upset? That he didn't tell me, I mean?"

Professor Thea's brows rose in surprise at the question, but she answered honestly, "In any normal year, probably. But this hasn't been a normal year for either of you, has it?"

Slowly, Rowan shook her head and replied, "No. It hasn't been."

Professor Thea nodded. "There you go."

Near the end of the day, Julian headed to one of the private practice rooms for his lesson with Helen. He had grown wary of her, knowing how he treated Rowan. But she was still his student and deserved just as much attention as any of his others.

Today, she swept in, wearing too much floral perfume as usual and a slight smirk on her face.

"Professor," she began, "I wanted to congratulate you. On the C.S.O., I mean."

He gave a subtle nod. "Thank you, Helen."

Her cheeks pinkened as she assembled her flute. "I already have my ticket."

"I appreciate the support," he said, pasting a smile on his face. "Shall we get started?"

Helen opened her mouth then shut it, wavering.

"Something the matter?" he asked, raising a brow.

She lifted a shoulder before taking a sharp breath and asking, "Will she be there?"

Julian thought he was fairly sure who 'she' was, but he decided to play dumb, saying, "You're going to have to be a little more specific."

Helen gripped her instrument tightly. "Rowan," she said, her voice strained with the effort of sounding pleasant.

He fought the urge to look skyward for patience and replied, "Yes, she will be."

Helen's face deepened in color, but she looked him dead in the eye as she asked in a too-loud voice that oozed forced confidence, "Do you love her?" Then, after a beat, she added, "Professor."

This time, he couldn't help his gaze from rising to the ceiling, asking someone, *anyone*, for patience. When he looked back at Helen, he decided to just be honest. Maybe that would keep her at bay.

"Yes, Helen, I do," he said steadily.

"But Professor, she's—"

"And this conversation is entirely unnecessary and inappropriate for our lesson."

"Is that what you told her?" Helen asked quietly.

He paused before he said stiffly, "We should continue with the lesson."

Thankfully, Helen didn't push further than that. The rest of the lesson was awkward but manageable, and soon, he was back in his office.

An hour into answering emails, his mind wandering to Rowan, footsteps sounded outside. Standing, he strode to the door and opened it, relief settling through his body as he saw her in the doorway, looking a shade surprised.

"Good," he said quietly. "I was hoping it would be you."

He stepped aside to let her in and then shut the door behind them, slumping down in the office chair behind the desk. Rowan set her things down and then walked over to his side of the desk, leaning against it and facing him, waiting. He ran a scarred hand through his hair; she was waiting for him to speak first.

"I'm sorry for not telling you about the concert sooner,"

he finally said. "Professor Thea informed me you were...irked about it."

Indeed, she had. Just a quick conversation in the staff lounge, as most of his interactions were with his colleagues now. He supposed they were wary of him now—as if he was going to jump any of their students too. Or perhaps it was just pity. Likely a mix of both.

Rowan nodded, searching his eyes. "A bit."

"It wasn't on purpose," he said after a moment. "Besides the few rehearsals Professor Thea and I had, I hardly thought about it. With everything else, it kind of fell to the back burner."

"Were you sneaking off into the city?" she asked with a raised brow.

He smiled tightly. "No. I mean, I went to rehearsals a few times, but it was quite a while ago. I'll be going on Wednesday night. It's the only reason I actually remembered to tell you."

She clasped her hands. "I understand. I do. But I want you to tell me these things. I want you to be excited to tell me stuff like this."

"I know," he said heavily. "I know. I'm sorry."

"It's alright. Just don't do it again," she said, a hint of teasing in her tone. She was always trying to lighten the room, always trying to make things easier for everyone else, even at the expense of her own comfort or happiness.

"I'm also sorry for running off and leaving you alone with Helen this morning," he added on second thought.

She shrugged. "I told you to. What was her question?"

His brow creased. "Question... Oh."

Rowan bit her lip. "What did she say?"

"Well, for one, she was very excited to tell me she'll be at the concert on Friday. Which isn't too strange; a few of my students are going, I think."

"She told me too. I think she was excited to rub it in my face," she said lightly.

Julian shook his head and huffed out, "Sorry."

"It's not your fault. What was her question, though?"

"It was not something that was appropriate for her to be asking me in a lesson. Or ever, really."

Rowan looked oddly nervous, but she met his eyes as he said with a small smile, "She asked if I love you. I told her I do."

"And that was it?"

He sighed, looking out the window. "I think she probably wanted to say more, but I shut her down."

"Why is everyone so obsessed with us?" Rowan said. "It really has made things much harder than they need to be."

Julian glanced back at her, his mouth twitching. "It seems like that sometimes, doesn't it?"

"I suppose I did get knocked up by my professor. Dunno what I expected," she mused.

She'd said something similar months ago in anger, and he felt his stomach dip with guilt that was still slowly fading.

"I'm sorry you have to deal with all—"

"Stop saying sorry," she said, cutting him off. "Because I'm not. I'd deal with a hundred bitchy Helens if it came to it. And I've been thinking..." She took a breath. "I think you're a little angry with me for getting Professor Petrarch to put the gun to my head."

He clenched his jaw, but she went on, "But I would do it again, just like I know you'd be an idiot and walk into another room on fire for me. It's what we do. We save each other."

He stared at her. She was...

Everything. She was infuriating and fiery and soft all at once, and he didn't want to wait one more second before showing her just how he felt.

"I want to marry you. As soon as possible," he said.

She blinked in surprise but recovered quickly as she shot back, "How does next weekend work?"

He grinned, the expression tight on his face but not unwelcome as he replied, "I'm pretty sure that Leo, the director of the jazz program, has a license. To officiate weddings, I mean."

She chuckled. "That's random."

"A little, but I can ask him if he's free?"

"Bombs away," she said, smiling. "Go for it."

Julian pulled out his phone, and she laughed.

"Are you actually asking him, like right now?"

His eyes scanned the phone screen as his fingers tapped against it, sending a text to Leo and hoping the man didn't think he was crazy. And maybe he was, but nevertheless, Leo confirmed he was free next weekend and that, yes, he did still have that license. Thirty seconds later, he set the phone down. "It's done."

They both looked down as the phone buzzed, and Rowan rolled her eyes. "Don't you professors have better, more important things to do than texting each other like teenage girls?"

He caught her eye, a gleam in his as he said, "Probably, but he said yes. The first Saturday of April."

She sighed. "I wish I could wear a pretty dress. I didn't ever have big, white wedding fantasies as a kid, but it would be nice to actually look good in the pictures."

He leaned forward in his chair, pressing a quick kiss to her stomach as he said, "You're beautiful, Rowan."

She swallowed as he sat back, glancing at his computer.

"I'm sure you have stuff to do," she said. "Go ahead. I have another dreaded paper to finish up."

"Fine. But we go home by nine."

She pushed off the desk and took a seat in front of it. "Fair enough."

Friday afternoon, Rowan stood with Amelia in her old bedroom. Truly her old bedroom now, given that she'd signed her name off this lease and onto Julian's on Thursday. Amelia was fussing with Rowan's hair, which she'd curled and pinned into a bun.

"Ami, the wind will mess it up anyway."

"Ah, ah, not if I work my hairspray magic!"

Rowan pushed her off. "I probably shouldn't inhale the fumes. That stuff is pretty potent."

Amelia rolled her eyes. "Okay, mom. God, your kid is going to be so mega sheltered between you and Mr. 'I-save-my-lover-from-a-fire.'"

Rowan made a face. "Lover?"

"Well, you weren't engaged at that point, and let's be real —you guys were never a boyfriend-girlfriend type of couple. You're both too fricking intense."

Samuel stuck his head into the bedroom and said, "Just a warning, Ami. I'm pretty sure he heard the nickname. So, can I have your ticket?"

"Yes, please hand it over to him," Julian drawled, walking into the bedroom, his hands in his pockets.

Amelia narrowed her eyes. "It technically wasn't a nickname. I was just stating the obvious."

"I feel like the 'Mr.' at the start kind of makes it a nickname," Samuel pointed out.

"Whatever. Can we go? If you two are done staring at each other like a couple of teenagers at prom. I mean, seriously, you've seen each other in dressy clothes before."

Rowan blinked. She had been staring at Julian—at the dark, fitted suit and raven-black curls of hair smoothed back into a bun—and he'd been looking right back at her.

"We can go," Julian said.

Amelia bounced on her heels. "Good. Because I want to get food before the concert."

Julian looked mildly amused, and Samuel was chuckling as he said, "You're so predictable."

Amelia walked over and flicked Samuel's nose before kissing him on the cheek. "I am just making sure my friend doesn't pass out during the standing ovation. For all of your information, Rowan told me she ate a PB&J today."

"And?" Samuel said.

Julian huffed out a breath. "It's three in the afternoon and that's *all* she's eaten."

Rowan scoffed. "I had a busy morning."

Taking her hand, Julian muttered, "All the more reason."

Amelia followed them, grabbing the fancy purse she hardly ever used on the way out.

"I'm riding in the front!" she called as they walked outside. Julian gave her a look, and she laughed. "I'm kidding, I'm kidding! God, take a joke for once, Mc—"

"Ami," Rowan said in warning, but she was smiling as she got into the car.

The short drive consisted of Amelia showing Rowan stupid memes on her phone until Julian eventually turned on that rock album they'd listened to while driving to her mom's house.

As soon as the third song finished, Amelia said loudly, "Damn, I didn't know you could be cool!"

"Only sometimes," Julian said dryly. "I'll park in the garage closest to the concert hall. There are a few restaurants around here."

"I know," Rowan said. "I've been to the C.S.O. before. Alex and I used to save up all our Christmas money when we were younger so we could go once a year."

Amelia fell quiet, and Julian glanced sidelong at Rowan as she fidgeted with the skirt of her dress.

"What was her favorite?" he asked.

"Tchaikovsky, Symphony No. 6," Rowan answered immediately. "It was played at the first C.S.O. concert we went to when we were, like, twelve."

"It's a good one," Julian said.

"What are you playing tonight?" Amelia asked.

Julian pulled into the parking garage and took a ticket. Once he was parked, he said, "Ravel."

"Which one?" Rowan asked carefully, though she had a suspicion she knew.

"*Daphnis and Chloé*," he replied.

Rowan raised a brow at him. "And you were not going to tell me you're playing the flute solo in fucking *Daphnis and Chloé*? That's a big deal, like a really big deal."

He nodded and said a little sheepishly, "I thought I'd surprise you."

Amelia laughed. "You know she could have just looked it up online."

Julian opened the car door and said, "Yes. But I know she wouldn't have."

Rowan rolled her eyes, opening her car door. The air was warmer than it had been but still cool, and she shivered in her thin jacket. She had worn it for style, not warmth, she supposed.

"I'll walk with you until you get to wherever you decide to go for dinner," Julian said.

"It's going to be a long-ass dinner," Amelia said. "It's barely four."

Julian's brow creased, and he said, "When I get there, I'll ask the conductor if you can come back for a bit before the performance."

"You don't have to—" Rowan began, but Amelia cut her off.

"Um, yes, please."

"I'll text you if it's a go," he said to Rowan as the three of them began to walk.

Rowan felt his warm fingers brush her cold ones as he said, "You should have worn something warmer."

"It's fine," Rowan muttered, suppressing another shiver.

"She always does this," Amelia said. "Says 'no, I won't get cold!' and then steals my coat by the end of the night because her teeth are chattering."

They crossed a street, and Amelia stopped in front of a café-looking restaurant and said to Julian, "We leave you here. It smells like bread in there. Good bread."

"It smells like a dirty river," Rowan said, wrinkling her nose.

"Past the smell of dirty river," Amelia added. "Somewhere in there, I smell the bread."

Julian let go of Rowan's hand and said quietly, "Be safe. I'll see you soon."

She nodded. "If I don't see you before, good luck. And tell Professor Thea I say so too."

"I will," he said before tilting her chin and kissing her quickly.

As he pulled back, Amelia muttered, "PDA much?"

But he was already gone, striding away down the sidewalk towards the concert hall a block away. Amelia turned to Rowan and said, "Okay. Food time."

Rowan nodded. "Food time."

Chapter 27
The Concert

THEY ORDERED soup and lots of bread and spent an hour talking about pretty much nothing. After a quick visual sweep of the restaurant, Amelia mostly made fun of Helen for a good thirty minutes before Rowan's phone buzzed. She glanced at it and read the text from Julian:

It's a go. Someone will go to the front entrance and open it for you in about five minutes. Just confirm my name with them and they'll let you in and show you where to go.

Amelia looked at Rowan expectantly, and she said, "We can go back. But we should leave now."

"Fuck yeah," Amelia exclaimed, and a woman close by with two little boys shot her a dirty look. Amelia groaned. "Please do not be that type of person once you have the kid, Row."

Rowan shook her head. "Nah, she'll probably have a sailor's mouth."

"Good," Amelia quipped. "Now, let's go. Oh my God, Helen is going to be so jealous."

"Yeah, and she'll have another reason to hate me. She's always talking about all the favors I get."

They stood as Amelia said, "Well, this is kind of a favor. How many music students get to go backstage at the C.S.O.?"

"I suppose," Rowan grumbled.

They left, venturing out into the cool, windy night. By the time they reached the entrance to the concert hall, Rowan was shivering again. A man was waiting there, right behind the glass door. He opened it and said, "Can you just confirm the name of the musician you're here for?"

"Julian Lynch," Rowan said, her voice rough from the cold.

The man nodded and smiled, stepping aside to let them in. "Just follow me," he said. "They're warming up right now, but once they're done, there'll be a short break before the concert starts and you need to take your seats."

They followed him down a hall and past a door marked: Staff Only. Then, they passed through another door he scanned a card to open, the lock clicking as they stepped backstage. Musicians milled about, drinking water, stretching their hands and chatting. Apparently, they were done with warmups.

Amelia craned her neck to find Julian, spotting him talking to a short older man near the front of the room. He turned as they approached.

"Hey," Rowan said.

"You're still shivering," Julian said in greeting, his brow furrowed.

She was, but she turned her attention to the older man as he said, "Ah, and who are these two young ladies?"

Amelia stuck out her hand first and said, "I'm Amelia Minch. It's nice to meet you...?""Hector," the man replied with a smile, shaking Amelia's hand. His attention shifted to Rowan. "And I'm going to assume you're Julian's fiancée?"

She raised a brow. "How'd you know?"

His eyes crinkled, and he replied, "I would be concerned if he was looking the way he is at someone other than his fiancée."

A small smile tugged at her lips. "I'm Rowan Evans. It's nice to meet you."

The man cocked his head. "Rowan Evans?"

Julian glanced at Hector as she said, "That's me."

"Ah. I have a friend, Gella Dessin. She's a professor at Juilliard. I'm sure you know who she is, Julian?"

Julian nodded, and Hector went on, "I understand Gella wanted you as her student in the graduate program. She'll be so interested to hear you're at Grandview now. Pleased, I'm sure."

Rowan felt a little sheepish as she said, "I would have loved to work with her. I actually came to Grandview for John Higgins, but he fell ill right before the start of the semester."

"Ah, I'm sad to hear that," Hector said. "So, you ended up working with Penny... Professor Thea, I mean?"

Rowan looked down at her feet, and Amelia smirked.

"Am I missing something?" Hector said.

Julian glanced at Hector. "I was actually her teacher for the first semester."

Hector's bushy gray brows rose as he laughed. "My god. What an interesting story I'm sure that is."

"Another time, Hector," Julian said as the conductor called ten minutes.

"We should go find our seats," Rowan said, her cheeks burning.

Julian nodded, kissing her forehead and murmuring, "See you later."

"Good luck," she said. "Not that you really need it."

He shook his head. "Given my track record, I might."

"Okaaay, let's go," Amelia said, tugging on Rowan's hand. "Bye and good luck, S.S.F.P."

It took Rowan a minute to realize what the acronym meant.

Smexy Scottish Flute Player.

"Really, Ami?" she laughed as the same man who'd led them in showed them to the auditorium.

"What?" she said, feigning innocence.

"I'm gonna start calling Sam 'corporate sex god,' or something like that."

"Ew, no."

"See what I mean?"

Amelia ignored her, squinting at the seat number on her ticket then at the quickly filling rows of seats.

"We're over there, in the middle," Rowan said, pointing.

"Thank God you've been here before. The way they organize these numbers is so confusing."

They sat down after taking programs from one of the

people milling about and helping people find their seats. Amelia found Julian's picture in the program and said, "He looks, like, really stressed in this photo."

Rowan glanced at it, her brow furrowing. He did. It wasn't super noticeable unless you were really looking at it.

"You think it was taken in January?" Amelia asked. "You knew, around the time I, uh, gave him the news?"

"Don't remind me of that day," Rowan muttered just as the musicians began to walk out onto the stage.

"Sorry, not sorry," Amelia said.

Rowan spotted Julian as soon as he walked in next to Professor Thea. They sat next to each other, and a cacophony of randomized notes began to fill the concert hall as the musicians warmed up one last time. The conductor walked out, and the patrons around them quieted, as did the musicians. And then, it began.

They opened two shorter pieces, both newer ones Rowan didn't know as well. She relaxed into her seat, letting the music float around her, occasionally looking at Julian. When they were done, most of the musicians filed off the stage for the fifteen-minute intermission. Rowan made a beeline for the restrooms, though there was already a long line when she arrived. Thankfully, it moved quickly, and she was back in her seat with five minutes to spare. Amelia had stayed put, engrossed in the program when Rowan returned.

"Apparently, that Hector guy we talked to has been a member of the C.S.O. for a long time," Amelia said in greeting.

"Mm, that's cool," Rowan said.

Amelia glanced at her. "Stop fidgeting. He'll do fine. I bet they'll want to kick out their first chair and replace them with him."

Rowan ignored Amelia, placing a hand on her stomach and muttering, "Please, go to sleep."

Amelia raised a brow. "She's kicking?"

"Yup."

"Woah, what if she, like, kicks to the rhythm of the music?"

Rowan gave Amelia a look that said, *I would not like that as much as you think I would.*

Snorting, Amelia turned, looking behind them, then immediately turned back.

"What?" Rowan asked.

"Helen and her girl group are a few rows behind us."

Rowan thinned her lips, but thankfully, the musicians began emerging as intermission came to a close. Once they were all in their seats and poised, the conductor raised his hands, and the first act of *Daphnis and Chloé* began. The music was almost haunting and supernatural in theme, and Rowan let herself float into it. Act two heightened in intensity, with the trumpets marching through in a staccato-like sound. Then came act three, where she knew the flute solo was.

Amelia gripped her hand, and Rowan smiled slightly in the dark as Julian began the solo. The rhythm was floating, a back-and-forth flirtation of melody. She reveled in the music, in the skill he wielded, in the power of the notes and rhythms.

He didn't falter once, each note supported and smooth. And when he was done, the audience clapped as the music moved into an explosive ending. When the piece was over, the musicians bowed, most people in the concert hall standing. The conductor motioned for Julian to come forward, shaking his hand before Julian bowed slightly.

Someone whistled from behind them, and Amelia said in Rowan's ear, "I think that was Ella."

But Rowan didn't care, not now, as Julian's gaze somehow found hers in the enormous crowd. She smirked and blew a kiss, and he tilted his head forward in acknowledgement.

Finally, when the musicians cleared off the stage, she and Amelia shuffled out of the concert hall with everyone else. They waited in the lobby and Rowan noticed Helen and a few other of Julian's students, along with Ella, were also lingering.

Her phone buzzed, and she glanced down at the text from Julian.

Should I come out to the lobby? Or meet you outside?

She glanced at his students and Ella and texted back:

You should come out. There's a group of admirers waiting for you.

Her phone buzzed, and she snorted as he replied:

. . .

Oh, joy.

But sure enough, about five minutes later, as most people were beginning to clear out of the lobby, he emerged.

"Professor Lynch!" one of his students, a girl Rowan recognized but didn't know, called.

His gaze immediately landed on Rowan, but she mouthed, *Say hi.*

He nodded and walked over to his group of students, who gathered around him, going on about how amazing his solo had been and asking what it had been like. He entertained their babbling for a few minutes, like a good teacher. Then, he said something that made Helen frown, and he strode over to Rowan and Amelia. Helen noticed them and whispered something in Ella's ear. Maybe it was their presence, or maybe it was the fact that she was just so insanely proud of him, but as Julian approached, she threw her arms around him as gracefully as she could with the belly. He caught her, sweeping her off her feet with one arm, his instrument case in his other hand.

"That was fucking phenomenal," she said as he set her down.

"Means a lot coming from a student," he teased.

She shook her head. "Shut up and take a compliment."

He grinned. "Thank you."

"Better."

"Yeah?"

She nodded, and he leaned down and kissed her, his hand on the back of her neck. They broke apart just as Amelia coughed. Rowan glanced at her as she said, "That was some major PDA, guys. And I had to stand here awkwardly the entire time."

"Apologies," Julian said, not sounding even a little bit sorry.

As they turned to leave, Helen, Ella, and the others were still in their spots, gaping a little as Amelia waved bye.

"Okay," Amelia said as they stepped outside. "Never mind. Enduring the PDA was totally worth the look on Helen's face."

Rowan couldn't help her laugh, and even Julian smiled a little at the words.

Amelia dozed off on the drive back, Rowan having to shout her name to wake her up when they dropped her off.

"Good job, Professor Genius," Amelia muttered as she left the car, slamming the door behind her.

Julian sighed. "She's never going to stop with the nicknames, is she?"

"Probably not," Rowan replied.

"So," he said as they drove home. "Penny... Professor Thea has a huge garden in her backyard. She said some of the flowers are starting to bloom already."

"Oh?"

"I thought it might be a nice place for the ceremony," he said softly.

She glanced at him as he parked the car, smiling as she said, "That works for me."

"Good. Because I already confirmed with her that next Saturday will be a good day."

She huffed a laugh. "Of course, you did."

In the dark, he took her hand and said, "Thank you. For coming tonight, for being there for me. It means more than you know."

"You really did amazing," she said.

"I tried."

"Who knew you could be so humble?" she whispered.

He stroked his thumb down her palm as he glanced outside at the starry sky. "Who knew? Quite the oddity for an asshole like me."

"I meant it when I called you that," she said.

"I know. I was being one."

"I also meant that kiss. I know I said it was a mistake later on, but no matter how much I told myself it was, I never really believed that."

"I should probably be smited by some god of morality for saying this, but I'm glad you did it."

"I know," she murmured, staring up at the starry sky now too.

They stayed like that for a long while, until Rowan started to get too cold and they went inside.

Chapter 28
Broken Pieces

THE WEEK WAS long and busy.

Rowan had slept through most of Saturday until Julian made her get up, insisting she needed to move her legs "once or twice at least." Sunday, she'd called her mom and told her about the ceremony next Saturday. Julian had done the same. Cara couldn't make it—she had some sort of performance that afternoon—but Lena, for better or worse, would be there. Thankfully, she wouldn't have to interact with Rowan's mother or Cameron, because much to her mom's chagrin, they had previously planned a short vacation next weekend—with nonrefundable tickets.

So, it would be her, Julian, Amelia, Samuel, Professor Thea, Leopold, and Lena.

Probably a disaster in the making.

Rowan was mostly worried about Amelia interacting with Lena. They could both hold their own, even when they were wrong. Which was the problem.

"Lena is...nice," Rowan said to Amelia as they sat in the

coffee shop on campus on Thursday during their lunch break.

"Okay, that was not convincing at all," Amelia said around a mouthful of panini.

Rowan shrugged. "Okay...she takes some getting used to, I'll admit. Just try not to get into a fight in the middle of my wedding."

"I know, I know," Amelia assured her. "I'll be nice."

"Good."

"I still can't believe you're getting married to your former teacher in your current teacher's backyard."

Rowan glanced at her hand, at the ring there, and said, "Yeah, me neither."

"You want this, though, right? I know everything happened really fast, and it was all really intense."

Rowan looked back up at Amelia and nodded. "I want this. I don't know... This sounds lame, but I feel like this is one of the best decisions I've ever made. And I've made some pretty questionable decisions."

"Like kissing your professor."

Rowan snorted. "Yeah. Like that."

Amelia sighed. "Okay, I have to go, but text me if something comes up later or...anything."

"I will. See you later."

Amelia smiled broadly and chirped, "See ya."

She left then, leaving Rowan sitting alone at the square table. She ate the rest of the sandwich she'd forced herself to buy and then sat back, sipping her herbal tea. To her surprise, Julian walked through the door a few minutes later, heading for her table immediately.

"Hey," she said. "You good?"

He nodded, looking a little distracted as he said, "I had to let my class out early. I figured I'd find you here."

Her brow creased as he sat down, and she asked, "Was everything okay?"

He sighed, running a hand over his face. "Mostly."

"What does that mean?" she asked flatly, nervousness already making her feel a little nauseous as she fiddled with the lid of her cup.

He huffed out a breath, not looking at her as he explained, "Someone had a panic attack. A girl who saw Ethan get shot."

Her hands stilled. "Is she okay? The girl."

He chewed on his lip and then replied, "I think so. She was one of Ethan's students. But the counselors are still here for the week, so I got her to one of them. Everyone was way too riled up to continue with class, so I just let them out early."

"Are you okay?"

He shrugged. "I wasn't the one who had the panic attack."

"Julian," she said quietly, and he finally looked at her.

"I'm fine," he said shortly, holding her gaze.

"You don't have to be."

"I kind of do," he muttered, then added, "I should go."

"Hey. Don't shut me out," she said quietly, barely concealing the tremor in her voice. The reminder of Professor Petrarch had shaken her more than she'd thought it would.

"You have class, don't you?" he asked wearily as he stood.

She rubbed at her temple, deciding to let his deflecting go for now. "Yeah, I do."

"Headache?"

She stood too and said, "It's nothing. Just the usual. Do you need to get coffee, or can you walk with me?"

"No, I don't need any. Let's go."

As they left, an older woman eyed them closely. Rowan thought she recognized her face but didn't quite know why. As soon as they were out of the coffee shop and out of earshot, Julian said quietly, "That was Provost Ives."

"She was looking at us funny."

Julian huffed a short laugh. "Yes. She was, of course, on the committee deciding whether to let me keep my position here or not. She was...wary of the situation. Understandably so."

"I see," Rowan said. "And that all happened right after the fire?"

"Yes. The morning of the day you woke up."

"You were barely out of the hospital at that point!" she hissed.

He sighed. "The situation needed to be addressed before the gossip escalated. They needed to make a decision quickly before outside sources inevitably impacted what they had to do."

"Before people started to call for your dismissal, you mean."

They made their way up through the front door of the music building, and he nodded. "Precisely."

She pursed her lips. "I have to go. And just so you know, I'm going to stay here late tonight. I really, really need to get in some practice hours before the end-of-term recital."

He looked like he wanted to protest, but he said heavily, "Okay. Check in before you start, though."

She rolled her eyes. "I'm not going to drop dead between now and eight p.m., but okay."

He flinched visibly, his entire body going taut. Her lips parted, but then a tour group walked through the front doors, the tour guide nearly shouting into the megaphone. Julian only muttered, "Have a good class," and then he was gone, striding away towards the staircase.

She was rooted in her spot for a few moments until the tour guide shot her a look that said, *Move, please.*

Rowan forced herself to unfreeze and walk to the lecture hall. She ignored a few whispers and stares as she sat down, a hand on her stomach. Just a moment. She needed just a moment to breathe.

She had talked about being dead. Just a joke. And he had flinched. Reality felt like it was crashing loud, so loud, in her ears, like waves against rocks. She always forgot everything that had happened. She had to forget to survive and move forward. They both had to.

But he had faced her death twice in the last five months. She had nearly died in his arms, pregnant with his kid. She had watched another professor, a man they'd both trusted, point a gun at his head and then turn it on her.

She had been joking, but he had flinched. And now, she was shaking, unable to steady her breaths. The baby was kicking, as if sensing the distress.

She needed to calm down. She had to breathe, if only for

the daughter she hadn't yet had. Another major incident, and she could lose her, the doctor had said. She took a shaky breath, and someone from behind said, "Rowan? Are you okay?"

Rowan took a breath. Tried. She tried to count backward in her head—tried to feel the rough fabric of the seat she was in.

"Professor!"

Her vision was blurring. Oh God, she needed to calm down. Oh God, oh God, oh God...

She blinked through tears she didn't know she'd been crying as footsteps hurried her way.

"Bill, what's going on?" a voice asked.

Professor Thea.

She thought that might've been Professor Thea.

"Penny, thank God," Bill said. "Can you sit with Rowan for now? I'm going to try and find Julian."

Rowan tried to breathe. She really, really did. She tried to keep a grasp on reality, but all she could see was that flinch. All she could feel was the heat of fire and the cold, metal barrel of a gun pressed to her head.

There was a flurry of movement, and then a cool, dry hand laid over hers.

"Rowan," Professor Thea said gently. "Rowan, I need you to lift your head and look at me."

Rowan tried to speak, gasped and choked on the word she tried to form.

"Rowan, don't worry about anything except looking at me. I just need you to do that."

She forced herself to lift her head. Cool metal touched

her forehead as she did so, or at least she thought it did. But then, gentle brown eyes met hers through the tears. Not Professor Petrarch's eyes. Not Jake's.

"That's it, Rowan," Professor Thea said softly. "That's it. Just keep looking at me."

Her breathing was still labored and quick, and Professor Thea didn't look away as she said, "Rowan, is it okay if I put my hand on your chest? You can do the same to me, and then we can breathe together, alright?"

Somehow, Rowan managed to nod. Her hand was shaking as she lifted it. Her fingers trembled and twitched against the top of Professor Thea's chest, but the professor's hand was warm and steady as it pressed to the same spot on Rowan's chest.

"Now, follow the movements of my breath."

Rowan felt a wave of panic wash over her. She had said something similar to Alex once.

"Rowan, I need you to take a breath," Professor Thea said. "Just one, and then we'll go from there."

"C-c-can't," she gasped.

"Yes, you can," Professor Thea said sternly. "You can and you will."

Rowan thought she might've heard a door open behind her, might've heard footsteps and heavy breath. For just a split-second, Professor Thea's eyes flicked behind her.

"Rowan," she said. "Take one breath. Just one to start."

She tried. With a rasping push, she took one slow intake of air. She let it out as Professor Thea nodded at someone, breaking eye contact with Rowan as she murmured, "Only about five minutes."

"She started breathing funny as soon as she sat down," a quiet voice said from behind her.

"Rowan," Professor Thea said. "I'm going to move now, just down a row. But Julian is here, and he's going to take my place, okay?"

"Okay," she gasped.

She tried to take more breaths as Professor Thea stood and the familiar smell of cinnamon washed over her. Gentle hands touched her shoulders as Julian's face came into view.

"Hey," he whispered. "Just keep doing what Professor Thea said. One breath at a time, okay?"

"I'm s-s-sorry," she stuttered out. "I-I t-tried."

"Shh," he murmured. "Just breathe. That's all you have to do."

His finger began to make slow, circling motions over her arms, and she took a few more slow breaths.

"That's it," he said. "That's it. Good girl."

She sniffled, and he pulled out a pack of tissues from his bag. It was so typical of him that she let out a noise between a sob and a laugh. He handed a tissue to her, lifting the armrest between them up and scooting closer so he could wrap an arm around her.

"Feel my chest rise and fall," he murmured. "Try and copy the motion."

She did. A few minutes or maybe even an hour passed before her breath came evenly and slowly and her vision cleared. She was still shaking slightly as she lifted her head to look at him and whispered, "I didn't mean for this to happen."

"I know you didn't, *mo ghràdh*," he said in a rough voice.

Someone had dimmed the lights in the lecture hall at some point, but she didn't think they were alone. Someone was talking in low tones a few rows down.

"Do you think you can walk to the car?" he asked, taking his thumb and sweeping it across her cheek to wipe the tears still rolling down her face.

"I can't go yet," she muttered. "I was going to rehearse today and—"

"Rowan."

Both his hands were cupping her cheeks now as she sucked in a breath.

"Rowan, look at me."

Her darting gaze found his dark eyes as spoke again. "We're going home now, and that is okay."

Her lip trembled. "I didn't think it bothered me so much. I wanted to be strong. I wanted everything to stay the same. I tried so hard to pretend I felt normal."

He nodded, utter understanding in his eyes as he said in a crackling voice, "I know."

"I can walk," she finally said. "We can go."

Her legs trembled as she stood and her head felt light. He scooped up their bags along with her instrument case. She leaned against his arm as the spots in her vision finally cleared.

"Okay?" he murmured.

"Yeah."

Her voice sounded flat, as if she'd used up every last bit of emotion in the last hour. She kept her eyes downcast as they walked down the stairs that led to the main level of the room. Most of the students had cleared out, but she recognized the two who remained: Ella and another girl from Helen's friend group.

Ella's face was drawn and she was biting her lip, but her voice was soft as she said, "I hope you feel better, Rowan."

Rowan could only nod.

About an hour later, she was curled up on the couch at home, two blankets bundled around her to keep the shaking at bay. An untouched mug of tea sat in front of her, still steaming. A room over, she could hear Julian's voice rumbling. He'd insisted on calling Dr. Wright, despite her weak protests that she was fine.

"A panic attack. It lasted nearly an hour," she could hear Julian saying. There was a pause and then, "No, not that she's said. And where was I? Teaching a class... Yes, she was in class."

There was another pause, longer this time, then Julian sighed loudly and said, "Yes. I understand."

Silence followed, and she heard the door creaking.

"Rowan?"

She looked up. Julian was standing in the doorway of the bedroom, his hands slack at his side. He looked tired.

"Yeah?"

"I know I asked earlier, but Dr. Wright wanted me to check again. No cramps or pain, right?"

She shook her head. "No."

He nodded and walked over to the couch, sitting down heavily next to her.

"He wants you to take the rest of the semester off."

"No," she said instantly.

"Rowan...he might be right."

She took a breath and said, "Sitting here alone all day is only going to make things worse. I won't have anything to distract me, and I won't have anything to aim for. I don't work like that. I never have."

Julian met her eyes, still not touching her as he said, "I just want you to be okay. I want to fix this, and I can't."

She swallowed. "I've always been broken. Don't try to put the pieces together, especially not now. Just accept me as I am."

"Always," he vowed, closing the distance between them, moving close enough that their foreheads touched as he whispered, "I love you."

"What if loving me is starting to break you too?" she murmured.

"Then I'll be broken. I'll shatter. I don't care. I have never cared what this did to me, what *you* do to me."

She tilted her head so she could look into his eyes. "Neither have I."

It was reckless, what they were to each other. She knew it always had been, and maybe it always would be. But it wouldn't ever matter, not enough to stop this force of nature between them, anyway.

"In sickness and in health?" she said.

His mouth twitched. "Yes."

"I believe the correct answer is, 'I do.'"

"You Americans and your weird, scripted ceremonies."

"Do you not have weird, scripted ceremonies in Scotland?"

"Well, yes," he laughed softly. "But they're much more beautiful."

She rolled her eyes. "Of course, they are. Have you ever even been to a Scottish wedding?"

He nodded and said seriously, "Yes, when I was fourteen and I married a sheep herder's daughter."

At the look on Rowan's face, he grinned, his hands cupping her cheeks as he said, "I'm joking, Rowan."

She huffed out a breath. "How the hell was I supposed to know? You've never told me much about your past relationships."

His thumbs stroked over her cheekbones as he said, "Because there isn't much to tell. We moved around the U.K. until we immigrated to the States and settled in Chicago. Then, my parents split, and relationships seemed like a horrible idea in general. After that, music took up everything. All of my time, all of my energy and emotion. I had a girlfriend for a month and a half in undergrad. She broke up with me because she said I didn't give her enough attention, and I probably didn't. After that... A few partners here and there, but nothing that turned into anything."

"I didn't think you'd have been a hookup type of person," she said with a slight teasing tone, despite the silly bite of jealousy souring any humor she felt.

He shook his head. "I wasn't, really. I mean...yes, a few times. But it never felt right."

She bit her lip and admitted, "I was kind of promiscuous

when I was at Sierra Hill. I think it was a way for me to avoid how I was feeling about Alex being gone. Nothing ever stuck. I mean, I think some of them wanted to try and make a relationship out of it, but I always pushed them away."

His gaze was steady as he said, "Selfishly, I'm glad you never gave any of them a chance."

She smiled a little. "There was only one person I ever really remembered in that way. Honestly, I hardly knew them."

There was a gleam in his eye, and he asked, "Oh really? Was it one of your bad-boy biker suitors?"

She sighed, feigning thoughtfulness as she replied, "Actually, no. He was probably a little old for me. At the time, I thought he was a PhD student."

"Mm, how shocking to find out he was actually a professor."

"Shocking indeed. Scandalous, even."

He grinned, though it fell as she let out a short puff of air, her hand going to her belly.

"Rowan? What's wrong?" he pressed.

She shook her head. "I think it's fine. She's just kicking harder than usual."

Relief flooded his face, and he said, "That's good. Dr. Wright said if you keep feeling her move, that means everything's probably fine."

She nodded. "Good."

Julian moved one of his hands so it was resting on her belly, stroking gently.

"She is really moving today," he murmured.

"Probably protesting about the lack of oxygen earlier."

"Mhm, is that right?" he muttered, and Rowan had the distinct feeling he wasn't talking to her. He began to hum softly, something that almost sounded like a lullaby, his fingers making small, circular motions.

He hummed for nearly an hour until Rowan's phone buzzed and she saw that Amelia wanted to call.

"She probably heard what happened today," Rowan muttered sleepily.

"You should talk to her," Julian said.

"I know, I'm just tired. But alas..."

She began to get up, but he shook his head, rearranging the blankets around her and then standing and stretching before he said, "Stay here. I'll go to the other room and work."

"Alright," she replied, feeling a little guilty. She'd just taken up nearly his whole day because of her freakout. She knew he always had work to do.

Once he was gone, shutting the bedroom door behind him softly, she picked up her phone and called Amelia, who picked up right away and demanded, "Why did I hear from Ella that you had a panic attack during your theory class today?"

"Um, well, because I did."

"Holy shit, Row."

"I'm fine now, though, seriously."

"You're sure? You're not currently going into early labor and just not telling me?"

"Nope. I am not."

Amelia sighed into the phone. "Okay. Well, good. Oh, Sam says hi."

"I'm sure he enjoys seeing you more," Rowan said.

She vaguely heard Samuel shout, "I do!"

"Am I on speakerphone?" Rowan asked.

"Yeah, I was home alone, and I lost my earbuds."

"Oh, bummer."

"Row. You're acting very nonchalant about this. I mean, as usual, but still."

Rowan paused and then asked, "How else do you want me to be?"

"I don't know—"

"I can't *breathe* half the time, Ami. I can't think about it all without falling apart. And I can't. That is just not something I can afford right now. Because if I fall apart, if I let myself go there like I did when Alex died, nothing will survive."

"I'm sure Julian will be there no matter what."

"Exactly. That is exactly my point. If I fall apart...if we lost the baby or something happened to me, I don't know." She shook her head, even knowing Amelia couldn't see it.

"You think he'd go down too," Amelia said softly into the phone.

Rowan only whispered, "I *can't* fall apart."

There was a crinkling noise, and Rowan half-laughed, half-cried, "Are you eating right now?"

Amelia sniffed, and then Rowan heard chewing before she said, "Times like these require candy."

"Lemme guess: caramel and chocolate?"

"Maybe." Amelia sniffed again and then said, "I don't understand, Row. I don't think anyone but you and McHotty ever will, but I trust you. Just know I'll be there for you."

"Thank you, Ami. And I'm going to tell him you called him that again."

"Please, don't. I don't want to be uninvited to your wedding, which is like...the day after tomorrow?"

"Apparently," Rowan said, smiling a little.

"Okay. You do have some sort of dress, right?"

"Um. Well..."

"Row! Oh my God, we are going shopping tomorrow night. You can't just wear one of your weird little potato sacks."

Rowan scoffed. "They are not potato sacks. They are maternity clothes."

"Same difference."

"I am so going to make fun of you when you have a kid someday."

"Oh God, emphasis on someday."

"That is exactly what I thought six months ago."

"You just had to have a sleepover with your grad advisor."

"You just had to leave me drunk in the rain," Rowan retorted.

"Mm, it worked out for you. Maybe you should be thanking me."

Rowan yawned and said, "Maybe later. But now, I need to eat and go to bed."

"Ugh, same. Except I need to finish a paper and prepare something for my stupid, dumb undergrad lesson tomorrow."

"I should probably do that."

"Eh, questionable."

Rowan sighed. "Alright, goodnight, Ami."

"Thank you for calling me, Row. I miss you."

"I literally see you almost every day, but I miss you too."

Amelia snorted, said, "Goodnight," and hung up the call.

Rowan set the phone down, then picked it back up and checked her email. One of her students was apparently sick and wouldn't be at her lesson tomorrow morning, which meant she could get some work done in Julian's office instead.

She padded into the kitchen and found an instant ramen cup in the back of a cabinet. She turned on the burner, boiling water and pouring it expertly into the cup before covering it.

"That is not dinner."

She turned to see Julian leaning against the counter, his hair pulled back in a bun. He must have put it up while he'd been working.

She shrugged. "It was quick and I didn't want to bother you."

"You can bother me."

"Doesn't mean I should. I know you have work to do."

The timer above the stove went off, and she turned, uncovering the ramen cup and stirring the noodles.

"Do you have a preference for band color?" he asked from behind her.

"Are you going tomorrow?" she said, her back still to him.

Soft footsteps sounded and he said, closer now, "Mhm. I figured silver since your ring is, but I wanted to run it by you."

She twisted around. "Silver is good. Apparently, I'm going dress shopping with Amelia tomorrow."

His mouth quirked up in a half-smile. "I don't feel bad for procrastinating on the rings now."

She chuckled and said, "I don't think we're procrastinating. I think we're just busy, and we decided to have a wedding with very little time to plan."

He brushed a strand of hair from her face. "You're okay with it, how fast it's happening?"

She smiled. "I'm okay with it. I'm happy, Julian. I know today made it seem like I'm not, but..." She trailed off.

"Good days and bad days," he murmured. "We have them both."

"Exactly," she said. "I'm going to eat my noodles now."

He raised a brow at the ramen but didn't say anything, letting her through to the kitchen table. She ate, and he made a sandwich before he joined her. "I've been looking at places. To move, I mean."

She took her last bite and asked, "Like...two-bedrooms?"

He set down the remainder of his sandwich and said, "Like two-bedroom houses."

Her eyes widened slightly as she said, "You do know I'm kind of broke."

A smile played on his lips. "Yes, I know, but I'm not. And I have a very steady job with prospects to become tenured. There's no reason for us to live in shitty apartments. Plus, a house will be safer for the baby."

She squirmed in her seat and said, "As long as you're sure."

"I'm sure."

"I can help...a little. I mean, once I'm not in school, I can definitely help."

He tilted his head. "Rowan, I don't think of it like that. I'm happy you're willing to chip in, but we'll really be fine if you don't for a while. Besides, it's going to be both our money very soon."

"Right," she mumbled, standing. She threw the empty ramen cup away and then said, "I'm going to get ready for bed. I know it's only like eight-thirty—"

"Eight-forty-five. And go. You need to sleep. I can work out here."

She sighed, "Okay," and then headed for the bathroom to get ready. Once she was in bed with the lights off, she was asleep in minutes. Vaguely, she heard Julian come in at some point and get into bed. She thought he might've kissed her shoulder, but then she was asleep again.

Chapter 29
Beautiful, Scripted Ceremonies

On Saturday afternoon, Rowan stood in front of a huge mirror in Professor Thea's house and sighed. "I look so...pregnant."

Amelia snorted. "I wonder why."

"Does it look bad?"

The dress they'd picked out was pale blue and cinched under her breasts before flowing down to her ankles. Simple and soft, but elegant. She wore sandals, a somewhat new pair she'd bought last summer, and her hair was curled but flowing over her shoulders.

"Nope," a voice said from behind. "You look like a perfectly blushing bride—which is really deceiving, by the way."

Both she and Amelia turned to see Lena approaching in a fitted black jumpsuit and large gold bangles. She stuck her hand out to Amelia and said, "I'm Lena, Julian's sister."

Amelia surveyed Lena then shook her hand. "I'm Amelia."

"The friend?"

"Yes, I am," Amelia said coolly.

Lena narrowed her eyes, and Rowan said, "Can you two *try* to be civil? Just for today. And next time you meet, you can go after each other all you want."

Amelia stared and stared at Lena before she said flatly, "I like your bangles. And your accent is cool."

"Stronger than my big brother's," Lean replied, her tone equally as flat.

"Ladies," Professor Thea said from the doorway, wearing a fitted navy dress. "Everything's ready, so it's your call, Rowan."

Rowan took a breath. "Yeah, I'm ready."

"Your mother couldn't be here, so if you want me to walk you down the aisle, I can," Professor Thea said. "I planned to accompany Oliver on piano, but he can handle the music solo if need be."

"Oliver?" Rowan echoed.

Penny smiled softly. "Ah. My nephew. He's a violinist and is in town, so I asked him to play today with me. I hope you don't mind?"

"Of course not," Rowan said, meaning it. Professor Thea was already doing so much by letting them have the wedding here last minute.

"Is there actually an aisle to walk down?" Lena asked, her lips twitching.

Professor Thea shrugged. "Somewhat. Just the path that leads to the archway."

Her garden was indeed beautiful, full of flowerbeds that were just budding and neatly trimmed bushes. Rowan had surveyed it when they'd first arrived at the enormous Victorian house a few hours ago. She'd only briefly talked to Leopold before he and Samuel disappeared with Julian to some room on the main level and Amelia dragged Rowan to the guest bedroom upstairs to change and do her hair. Later, they weren't having any sort of reception, just dinner out with Amelia, Samuel, and Lena.

But now... Now, it was time.

"You don't have to do that," Rowan said to Professor Thea. "And I really appreciate the offer, but I think I want to just walk alone."

"Well said," Lena said, and Amelia shot her a look, to which she went, "What?"

"There is nothing wrong with a parent or loved one walking the bride down the aisle," Amelia replied.

"It's archaic," Lena shot back.

"Please," Rowan said. "Just be civil today. I swear, just today, and then you two can bicker all you want."

Lena rolled her eyes, but Amelia just took Rowan's hand and said, "Let's do this."

Rowan took a breath. "Let's do this."

The air smelled like freshly mowed grass and spring rain as Julian stepped out into the garden. The sun was just barely hidden by puffy gray clouds scattered across the sky, and Leo and Samuel were all standing under the small white archway, chatting with an auburn-haired man covered in tattoos who looked about Julian's age, perhaps a little younger.

"Hey," Leo said by way of greeting. "So, this is all kind of random."

Julian managed a smile. "I know, but thank you for doing this."

Leo shrugged. "Why not? I've never used the license beyond my sister's wedding, so might as well."

Julian glanced at the stranger, who was holding a violin. He stepped in before Julian could speak and said, "I'm Oliver. Penny is my aunt... I'm in town, so she asked me to play. Hope you don't mind."

"Not at—"

But Julian stopped mid-sentence as Samuel nudged his arm, Rowan at the edge of the garden.

She held a bundle of wildflowers and was holding back a small smile. Oliver quickly stepped to the side, joining Penny as she played a simple, sweet piece on the keyboard she'd set up on the patio. She had asked Julian what she wanted her to play this morning, and he'd told her it was totally up to her and what she had currently prepared. He supposed that was good, since he hadn't been expecting her to have a playing partner.

As the soft melody filled the garden and Rowan strode towards the archway, Julian's smile fell slightly as she stepped in front of him.

His lips parted as she murmured, "Hi."

"Okay!" Leo said. "Hello, everyone. Random group of people, but hey, whatever floats your guys' boat."

Julian saw Amelia roll her eyes out of the corner of her eye and he pursed his lips, biting back a smile.

"So, Julian emailed me some funky, but very sweet Scottish vows literally last night. I did not have time to memorize said vows, so," he pulled a piece of slightly crumpled paper from his pocket, "here we are. I'm not really sure how to do this, so I figured we'd just alternate every few phrases."

Lena muttered something, but Julian ignored it as he took Rowan's hands.

"Okay," Leo cleared his throat. "Let's go."

Julian glanced at him, a brow raised.

"Uh, Rowan, repeat after me, got it?" Leo said, wincing.

She nodded and said softly, "Got it."

Her eyes were locked with Julian's as Leo said, "I take you, my heart, at the rising of the moon and the setting of the stars."

Her breath caught slightly as she heard the words, but she repeated them in a steady voice. Julian's chest felt tight and loose all at once.

"Great. Julian, your turn... To love and to honor, through all that may come."

Julian's hands tightened around hers as he repeated the words.

"Through all our lives together, in all our lives may we be reborn, that we may meet and know," Leo said, his voice a little softer.

He watched as Rowan swallowed and then repeated the words, her voice becoming hoarse. Then, Leo said the last lines and Julian repeated them, the entire garden silent.

"And love again, and remember."

"Bands, Samuel," Leo said, and Samuel pulled out a small black box that contained two silver wedding bands. He handed them to Leo, who handed Rowan the one for Julian first. She slid it onto his finger with slightly trembling hands. He did the same, his hands steady.

"Okay," Leo said. "Go ahead."

Amelia snorted, and she heard Lena mutter, "Go ahead?"

But Julian didn't care. He caught her chin with a gentle grip, tilting it up and pressing his lips to hers. The kiss was somewhat chaste, but it wasn't short, and he thought he might've heard Leo clear his throat at one point.

When they finally broke apart, Samuel whistled and Amelia screeched, "Woohoo!"

Even Lena was smiling, shaking her head with her hands on her hips.

There wasn't really much to do after that, except to thank Leo and Penny for the space and their time. Penny accepted the thanks graciously and said, "I'm happy for you both. Truly. After such a year, it's good to see some real joy."

Rowan simply replied, "I'll suppose I'll see you on Monday."

Penny smiled. "I'll see you on Monday, Rowan." She nodded at him. "Julian."

But just before they left, Lena paused, glancing at Julian and asking, "Who the hell is that?"

He followed her gaze to where Oliver stood, packing up his instrument. His lips twitched at Lena's expression, and he said, "Penny's nephew. He's in town, apparently, so she asked him to play."

"And you let him crash your wedding?"

"*He* can hear you, you know."

Lena stiffened as Oliver stood, smirking. A sort of long-lost brotherly protectiveness rose up in Julian as Oliver looked at Lena, a spark in his hazel eyes. But he reminded himself that, unlike all those years ago, Lena was an adult now. She could handle herself, and handle herself she did.

"And I care because?" she snapped at him.

Oliver's dark brows rose. "Well you're friendly, aren't you?"

Julian glanced at Rowan, and she pressed her lips together, suppressing a smile as Lena and Oliver glared at each other. Even Penny looked amused, and Amelia was covering her grin with her hand. Neither Lena nor Oliver seemed to notice.

"And your name is?" Lena said, eyes narrowing.

"Oliver," Penny's nephew said, tilting his head. "And I assume you're somebody's sister or friend or girlfriend."

"Right," Lena said sharply. "Because that's all I'm worth, being someone's 'girlfriend or sister.'"

"Or friend," Amelia chirped, half-laughing.

Lena didn't even spare her a glance. "Well, *Oliver*, we have a dinner to go to. And unfortunately, you're not invited."

Oliver snorted. "Yes, how unfortunate that I won't get to spend more time with you and your pleasant demeanor."

"*Ok-ay*," Rowan said, her smile breaking through now. "We *do* need to go. But Oliver, if you really want to come along—"

"Absolutely not." Lena's voice was firm. "Our party is full."

"Fine by me," Oliver said, eyes still held on her.

Rowan's eyes flicked to Julian's, and he shrugged, as if to say, *What do you want me to do?*

"Um, it was really nice to meet you, Oliver," Rowan stepped in. "And thank you for playing."

"Likewise," he said, finally looking away from Lena.

Lena stared at Oliver for a few seconds longer, something indecipherable in her sharp expression before spinning on her heel and walking out of the garden towards the driveway.

Penny shook her head, chuckling and glancing at Oliver, who didn't react aside from a slight tensing of his jaw.

Julian shifted his attention back to Rowan as she said with a half-grin, "Shall we?"

"Mhmm," he murmured, taking her hand.

They left, Samuel and Amelia driving together and Lena insisting on going with Rowan and him. He saw Amelia mouth *good luck* to Rowan just before they got in the car. Rowan only laughed and shouted, "See you at the restaurant!"

"Thank God, I'm starving," Lena said. "I mean, could you guys not even afford a cheese platter?"

"Lena," Julian warned. "If you are just going to be a pain in my ass, please go home."

She smirked. "I've always been a pain in your ass, big brother."

He rolled his eyes, getting into the car. The drive to the restaurant consisted of Lena babbling about the drama of the group she played for in the city and him shooting amused looks at Rowan. By the time they arrived twenty minutes later, Lena was griping about her hunger again.

Just before they stepped out of the car, Rowan ventured, "So, Lena, about that guy—"

But Lena only snapped, "Nope."

And that, apparently, was that.

Once they sat down, Rowan, Samuel, and Amelia were all looking warily at the fancy decor and white tablecloths.

Lena snorted loudly and said, "You three look terrified. Don't worry, I looked it up beforehand, and the majority of the entrees are only, like, twenty dollars."

"If you need me to cover—" Julian began, but Amelia cut him off.

"No way, McHotty. I am not having you pay for my meal on your wedding day."

Lena's brows raised. "McHotty?"

At the same time, Samuel said, "Doesn't the couple normally pay for everyone's food at the reception?"

"Yeah, if it's catered," Amelia said. "Which this is not."

"*McHotty?*" Lena was guffawing. "Oh my God. You are never going to live that one down, Julian."

He glared at Amelia. "You couldn't have laid off with the nicknames, even today?"

"Nope," Amelia said with a smile before taking a sip of ice water.

A waiter came around then and said, "Hi, folks. Looks like we're celebrating something today! Baby shower?"

Amelia choked on her water, and Samuel clapped her back as Lena said sweetly, "Shotgun wedding. Her father was real upset when he heard the news that his daughter was knocked up out of wedlock, so he didn't even show up to the ceremony."

The waiter's eyes widened, and she said tightly, "Oh. Um, can I get you folks started with some drinks?"

"I'm good with water," Samuel said, and everyone chorused in agreement.

"Are we ready to order then?" the waiter asked warily.

"Sure," Julian said, glaring at Lena.

They all ordered, and once the waiter was gone with the menus, Julian said, "Really, Lena?"

Lena only shrugged. "Technically, Rowan's dad was not at the ceremony."

"Yeah, because Rowan's dad is a deadbeat," Amelia muttered.

Lena's brows raised. "Hm, interesting. Were your parents not married?"

"Nope," Rowan said. "My dad was completely out of my life by the time my sister and I were four."

"Sister?"

Julian's hand found Rowan's under the table as she replied, "My sister died of leukemia when we were eighteen. We were twins."

For once, Lena's face softened as she said, "Oh. I'm sorry."

Rowan cleared her throat. "It's fine. I mean, it's not, but it is what it is."

"As is life," Lena said evenly.

A tense silence followed, and then Amelia broke it, asking, "Rowan, have you thought of baby names? For your 'out of wedlock' child?"

Samuel chuckled, and even Julian's mouth twitched.

"Don't you want it to be a surprise?" Rowan ventured.

"Hell no. You know I hate surprises," Amelia shot back.

"Me too," Lena agreed.

Amelia shoved Samuel's shoulder, and he added quickly, "Yeah. Me three."

"Well, for a middle name, Alexandra," she said, the conversation mirroring the one they'd had with her mother and Cameron as she glanced at Julian.

He nodded and said, "Callie, for the first name."

"Grandma's name," Lena said quietly. "That's nice."

"Thanks," Julian said evenly, just as the salads arrived.

The rest of the meal, they had light conversation, mainly revolving around more gossip about Lena's fellow symphony members. During the latter half, Samuel talked about some of his corporate job drama.

"Everyone thinks the secretary, Mindy, is getting down with our manager, but nothing's happened yet...so," he shrugged, "who knows."

Lena picked at the remainder of her pasta and said, "Hmm, sounds so familiar."

"Okay, time to go," Julian muttered, rising from his seat.

They'd already paid their bills and had been lingering ever since. Amelia stood up too, stretching and yawning. "Rowan, when can you come by and get the rest of your stuff?"

"Oh, crap. Um, next weekend?" she replied, glancing at Julian, who nodded.

"That works for me."

Once they were outside the restaurant, Amelia and Samuel both hugged Rowan.

"Congrats, Row," Samuel said. "And I'm glad you gave him a chance."

Julian glanced at Rowan, brow furrowed, and she said in his ear, "I'll tell you later."

Samuel shook Julian's hand, and Amelia awkwardly high-fived him. When Rowan laughed, Amelia muttered, "What? It'd be weird to hug a teacher."

They left, and Lena followed Rowan and Julian to the car, complaining about her sore feet. They let her talk throughout the entire ride back to their apartment, where her car was parked. When they finally arrived and got out of the car, she hugged them both.

"Congrats," she said. "And...thanks for letting me be there. I know we haven't been on the best terms since everything happened, Julian. But both Mom and I were happy you reached out again."

Julian nodded but only said, "Drive safe, Lena. Watch out for drunk drivers."

She grinned. "Always the overprotective big brother, aren't you? And Rowan," she met her eyes, "take care of him."

"I will," Rowan said. "Thank you for coming."

Lena ducked her head in acknowledgment and then headed for her car.

"Tired?" Julian asked carefully.

Rowan took his hand. "Not yet. Let's go up."

His gaze roamed her for a moment before he murmured, "Alright."

When they turned the lights on in the apartment, everything was the same, yet nothing was, not anymore. The bands on their fingers were a testament to that.

As soon as their shoes were off, Rowan led him to the bedroom—the bedroom where everything had changed on a snowy night in December. Julian stepped close to her, his hand threading through her hair as he asked, "What did Sam mean earlier, outside the restaurant?"

She put her hands on his chest as she replied, "When I first found out I was pregnant, I was...I was scared. I didn't know whether to tell you, and he encouraged me to. He had talked to you in the hall, the night before the end of fall term recital."

"I remember," Julian murmured.

"Amelia told me Sam said you talked about me the way he talked about her."

Julian's brow raised, but he smiled as he said, "I don't think I even knew it at the time."

His hand drifted to her back as she reached up, running her fingers through his hair. He made a low noise, the sound igniting her. She guided him backward to the bed, her hands slipping back over his hard chest and undoing the buttons of his shirt. Then, her hand drifted lower, and he groaned. A moment later, she pulled off his belt, undoing the button and zipper on his pants before straddling him. Her dress was still on, pooling around her legs.

She leaned forward, kissing him softly. They both sucked in a sharp breath as she slid onto him, joining their bodies. As she started to move, he swore softly, and she smiled.

"Something funny?" he asked, his voice rough and raspy.

She shook her head, not breaking eye contact with him as she rolled her hips forward again. He made a breathy sound that turned into a groan as she did it again.

"Rowan," he muttered, pleading.

She didn't let up, and his hands fisted tight in the fabric of her dress.

"Please... I can't...hold on," he gasped.

There was something wild in her eyes as she commanded, "Don't come, not until I say."

A puff of air escaped his lips, and his head fell against her neck as he nodded silently. She kept up a steady pace, her hips moving somewhere between languid slowness and frenzied quickness, just enough that he was barely holding on to the order she'd given him.

When she adjusted the angle slightly, he felt the moment she began to let go of all semblance of control, gasping, "*Julian.*"

"Please," he choked.

"Yes," she moaned as her breath became ragged. "Please."

He gasped her name as they fractured together, soaring until they crashed down together on the bed, limp-limbed and panting.

He lifted his head, a small smile playing on his lips.

"You liked the control, didn't you?"

She brushed the heated whisper of a kiss against his cheek. "Maybe I did."

Chapter 30
The Recital

APRIL FLEW by in a blur of lessons, class, and teaching. Weekends became progressively busier, and Rowan's back started to ache as the weight of her belly began to fight against her. By the second week of May, a couple of weeks before the dreaded and cherished end of the semester, she was utterly exhausted.

The campus coffee shop was crowded with students cramming in their final papers and studying for exams as she stepped inside the Thursday before the last week of the term. Amelia was meeting her, as usual, but she wasn't there yet. Rowan found a seat, not bothering to order anything. She'd brought her own lunch, courtesy of Julian, and opted for her water bottle instead of spending five dollars on tea. As she took a sip of water, her eyes flicked to the front door where Helen and Ella were entering, in the middle of what seemed like an argument.

Rowan hadn't spoken to Ella since her panic attack in

March, and Ella hadn't sought her out, but Rowan caught her own name as Helen slid into a seat, looking sullen. She tensed as Ella strode over to her, dragging Helen along.

They stopped in front of Rowan's table, and Ella looked at Helen expectantly.

"Hi, do you two, uh, need something?" Rowan asked after a moment.

Helen shifted on her feet and finally said, "I'm sorry for being a jerk to you this semester. Ella told me about what happened in class back in March, and I..." She took a breath. "I didn't think it affected you that much, everything that's happened. You always seem so cool and collected...but I'm sorry if I contributed to your stress."

Rowan pursed her lips. "Thanks, Helen."

Helen gave Ella a look that said, *Can I go now?*

Ella rolled her eyes and shrugged. Helen made a beeline for the door, and Rowan asked Ella, "Why now? I had that panic attack months ago."

Ella shrugged. "She hasn't bothered you since then, right?"

Slowly, Rowan shook her head.

"She feels bad, even if it doesn't seem like it. So do I."

Rowan stretched her fingers and said, "Don't waste your time feeling guilty. It won't do any good. And besides, I'm not ashamed. Not anymore."

Ella nodded. "I'm glad. I'll see you around, Rowan."

"See you, Ella."

Amelia had been lingering by the counter, and she sat down with Rowan as soon as Ella left. "Well, that was weird."

Rowan watched Ella leave and said, "A little, but not necessarily a bad thing."

Amelia shrugged. "At least we know Helen will totally leave you alone now."

"Yeah," Rowan said, suppressing a yawn.

After taking a bite of the cookie she'd bought, Amelia asked, "Did you guys get the house? The one close to campus, I mean."

Indeed, she and Julian had been trying to nail down a place in the past month. They'd found one that was pretty much perfect a few weeks ago—one-story, two-bedroom, decent neighborhood and close to campus.

"I think he was supposed to get a call from the real estate agent today," she replied, pulling out her sandwich.

"Are you nervous?"

Rowan laughed. "Not really. I mean, there are other houses out there."

"True," Amelia said, shoving the last of the cookie in her mouth. She sat with Rowan as she finished her sandwich, and then they both walked, arm in arm, back to the music building.

That evening, Rowan knocked on Julian's office door, her feet aching and a headache blooming right behind her eyes.

"Just a moment!" he called, and by the tone of his voice, she could tell he didn't realize it was her.

She knocked again and said loudly, "I am very tired and I need to sit down. Like right now."

A moment later, the door swung open to reveal an also tired-looking Julian. He smiled a little as he saw her and said, "Sorry. I was supposed to have an office hour with one of my students."

"Oh," she sighed. "Should I go hang out in the student lounge for a while?"

He shook his head. "I literally just got the email that they needed to cancel. Oh, and by the way, we got the house."

She blinked, staring at him.

"You're serious, right?"

He nodded. "Completely."

"Well, shit," she said, laughing a little as she sank into the chair in front of his desk.

His smile grew wider as he mused, "Indeed. We can go now. I finished up about twenty minutes ago."

She shut her eyes and muttered, "I should really practice."

"You should really not," he said, and she opened her eyes to glare at him.

"The recital is in less than a week."

"It is, but I can tell you're exhausted."

She groaned but relented, taking the hand he held out.

The night of the final recital of the semester finally arrived, and Julian was thankful for it. He knew that the last few weeks had been grueling for Rowan—and for him too, preparing all his students—and they were both ready for a break.

He gathered a small group of his students in a backstage practice room and helped them warm up and tune. When they'd finished, he made to go find Rowan, but Leo intercepted him.

"Ready to go out?" he asked.

Julian hesitated, and Leo chuckled as he said, "She'll be fine, Julian. Exemplary, actually, I'm sure. We should go."

He relented, letting Leo drag him out to the row of professors. Once they were seated, he checked his phone, an odd feeling of anxiety settling over him. He didn't have any missed messages, so he slid it back into his pocket, trying to ignore the feeling.

Leo had turned to him and was just about to speak when Julian saw Helen burst through the auditorium doors, weaving through the crowd.

"That's one of your students, right?" Leo ventured as she rushed towards them.

"Yeah," Julian muttered, standing in his seat.

"Professor Lynch," she said between breaths as she reached him, "you need to come backstage."

"What—"

"It's Rowan. I think she's gone into labor, but I don't know for sure. She was freaking out, and it seemed like she was in pain and—"

"Take me to her. Now," Julian cut in, his voice stern even as it shook.

Helen swallowed, glancing once at Leo before she led Julian through the crowd and out of the auditorium to the backstage entrance. A small commotion had bloomed in the dimly lit area by the time they arrived. The crowd of students parted as Julian rushed towards Rowan. He felt cold as he knelt next to the chair she was in.

"Rowan," he said, still catching his breath.

She met his eyes, her fear and panic mirroring his own as she said, "I think I'm having contractions."

"I called the paramedics," Provost Ives said from behind. "They should be here soon. Just make sure she keeps taking deep breaths."

"Thank you," Julian said, barely turning away from Rowan to look at the Provost.

Rowan hissed in pain, and Julian held onto her hand, letting her squeeze it tightly.

"It's going to be okay," he said, though his voice was shaking.

"She's too early," Rowan gasped.

"It's going to be okay," he repeated. It was all he could do to repeat the words, as if that would make it true. "The paramedics should get here soon."

A short sob escaped her, and he commanded gently, "Breathe, Rowan."

It felt too soon and not soon enough as heavy footfalls approached and an unfamiliar voice shouted, "Out of the way, everyone!"

Three EMTs circled him and Rowan, one of them already ready with a stretcher.

"How far apart are the contractions, honey?" one of them gently asked.

Rowan lifted her tear-stained face and said, "I don't know. My water just broke, though."

The woman exchanged a look with one of her partners as they asked, "How far along are you?"

"Thirty weeks," Julian answered instantly, his heartbeat pounding. He knew this wasn't good—he had been privy to enough worry from Dr. Wright about her ability to carry to term to know just *how* bad this was.

"We need to get her to the hospital, ASAP. The baby is probably going to need support," the woman said before she looked at Rowan and said, "Just keep taking deep, deep breaths. We're going now. Can you stand for just a minute?"

A small whimper escaped Rowan as she nodded.

About forty-five minutes later, Julian held onto Rowan's hand as he walked briskly beside the gurney she was on. The doctor they had met twenty minutes prior wanted her to have the baby in the operating room, just in case they needed to do an emergency C-section. They would likely have to take the baby away to the NICU right away.

The enormity of what was happening hit Julian like a battle ram as they entered the operating room. He forced herself to breathe, to focus on the weight of Rowan's hand, to count the seconds and minutes—to count fingers and toes they might never get to hold if things went any more wrong than they already had. He savored them now, imaginary digits in his mind.

Through all of this, through the terror and the guilt, he had hardly gotten the chance to let himself imagine the reality of the baby. Now, as the chance was slipping through their fingers, panic captured him wholly.

His face was masked, the rest of him clad in scrubs as they stepped into the operating room. He could see the fear in Rowan's clear blue eyes as he let go of her hand and the doctor looked at her. "Okay, Rowan, I'm going to need you to push now."

She sucked a deep breath but rasped, "Okay."

Julian stayed right beside her as a strangled sound clawed up from her throat, and the doctor said, "Good. Let's try another one."

She choked on a sob, and Julian murmured in a voice much calmer than he was feeling, "You're okay, Rowan. You're doing amazing. I'm right here."

"Marissa, get ready," she heard the doctor murmur to someone before he said, "Okay, Rowan. One more, and then she's out."

Rowan did as the doctor said, letting out a gasp. The doctors waiting in the corner suddenly converged, and Julian craned his neck.

"Julian," she said desperately.

"We've got breath sounds," someone said.

"Okay, little fighter, let's go," another murmured gently.

Julian didn't hear the baby cry, couldn't even see her.

"Julian," Rowan was sobbing.

"Rowan, try to calm down," a doctor in a mask said as a door opened and closed and footsteps rushed away, taking the baby with them. "We're taking your baby to the NICU," the doctor added. "They're going to do everything they can for her there. But right now, I need you to take a few breaths."

"Doctor!" the nurse called.

The doctor ducked back around the table, and Julian asked hoarsely, "What's wrong?"

"She's just bleeding a little more than normal," the doctor said, his voice muffled.

Then, Rowan's eyes crossed, and Julian said her name sharply just before she lost consciousness.

Chapter 31
A Thread in the Universe

WHEN ROWAN WOKE UP, the first thing she saw was sunlight streaming in through a window. Julian shouted for a nurse.

Her vision began to clear just as a nurse and a doctor entered the room.

"Hi, Rowan," the doctor said. "How are you feeling?"

She blinked a few more times. "I feel okay. Where… Where is my baby?"

The doctor's face softened. "She's hanging on. She's one little fighter. We had to give her something for her lungs last night, but she's recovering well."

"How long have I been asleep?"

The doctor glanced at Julian and nodded. She looked at him, at the dark circles under his eyes and the pallor of his face as he said, "Two days."

"You started to bleed a little too much after labor," the doctor explained. "We had to put you under and patch you up. You'll be fine, but your body was under an immense amount of stress. You just needed to rest."

Two days. God... So much could have happened in two days.

After the doctor left and the nurse checked her blood pressure and changed out the IV bag, Julian handed her a plastic cup of water. She sipped it slowly through a straw. When she was done, he said, "She's very small. They were worried about her lungs, but her brain and heart are fine."

"When can I see her?" she asked.

Julian took the cup of water and then laid a hand over hers as he said, "Soon. You need to rest more, though."

She shook her head, but he started to stroke her hair as he murmured, "Just rest, Rowan. I'm right here, always."

She fell back asleep, a protest still on her cracked lips.

Five days later, Rowan was feeling mostly normal. The surgery hadn't been very major, and after a few days of mostly sleeping, she was nearly recovered.

But until today, the doctors hadn't let her out of bed to see Callie, who still needed to be in an incubator.

"They said she's breathing really well today," Julian said as he wheeled Rowan down the hall. "The nurse said they might even be able to stop using breath support soon."

"It is so unfair that you've seen her and I haven't," Rowan said quietly.

She heard Julian take a breath then say, "I know."

They arrived at the entrance to the NICU then, the nurse handing them both masks before she let them inside. Rowan's eyes flicked over incubators of preemie babies, all tiny and covered in tubes. Julian stopped in front of one, and Rowan's gaze landed on the name sticker.

Callie A. Lynch.

Then, she lifted her eyes to the baby inside. *Her* baby.

Dark-brown eyes blinked hazily at her, and Rowan breathed, "You didn't tell me her eyes were open."

"Just yesterday," he said softly. "I thought I'd surprise you."

"She has your eyes."

"But your nose and mouth."

She glanced back at Julian for just a moment in wonder, and he nodded, understanding the instant adoration in her eyes. "I know."

A nurse approached. "Hey, Mama. Glad to see you're feeling better."

"Yeah, me too," Rowan said, her eyes still on Callie.

"Would you like to hold her?"

"Can I?" Rowan asked, ripping eyes away from Callie to look at the nurse.

The nurse nodded. "The skin-on-skin contact is actually good for them, once they're stable enough to be outside the incubators. I've seen it help a lot of babies get through rough patches."

Rowan could only whisper, "Then, yes."

Julian helped her sit in one of the cushy chairs nearby, and the nurse gently opened the incubator, careful of the tubes as she carried Callie the short distance over to Rowan.

"Her head is still very fragile, so just be careful," the nurse said. "And try not to put too much pressure on the wires."

Rowan nodded, her heartbeat thudding in her ears as the nurse handed over the baby. Her tiny body was warm, and she looked straight up at Rowan as she was passed into her arms.

"Hello, Callie," Rowan whispered.

Julian crouched next to the chair, peering at her too. Two pairs of identical brown eyes met, and a smile broke across Julian's face. A thread in the universe that had tugged at Rowan nearly four years ago pulled taut...and settled in place.

Bonus Track

"Daphnis et Chloé"—Ravel, Chicago Symphony Orchestra

Epilogue: Four Years Later

Rowan's leg bounced erratically as she said into the phone, "How is she? I know how things can get when I'm gone."

Julian's chuckle lightened the nerves fluttering in Rowan's stomach almost immediately as he replied, "She's fine. Didn't even cry when I dropped her off at daycare this morning."

"And you have your tickets loaded onto your phone, right?"

"Rowan," he said. "I may be older than you, but I'm not *that* old. I know how to use a mobile app."

She snorted. "I don't know. You almost messed up the rideshare that one time."

She heard him sigh, though she knew he wasn't actually annoyed, especially as he asked, "Are you doing okay? The hotel is fine and—"

"Yes, yes," she said, fidgeting with the hem of her shirt.

He paused, then said, "You'll do great, Rowan. I know you will."

"This is a big deal. I mean, London? I don't know, maybe I shouldn't have agreed to play the recital."

"Yes, you should have," he said steadily. She heard a faint knock, and he called, "One moment!"

"A student?"

"Presumably. I have to go, but we'll see you very soon, okay? I love you."

"Love you too," she said softly. "Be safe. And give her a kiss for me."

"I will."

"Okay...bye."

She could nearly hear the smile in his voice as he said, "See you soon," and then the call ended, leaving her alone in the hotel room.

The next morning, she got up early and headed to the hotel lobby as soon as eight o'clock hit. She resisted the urge to pace, instead checking her phone. Amelia had just sent her *way* too many pictures of turtles. She and Samuel were on their honeymoon in Hawaii this week—they'd finally gotten married a little over a month ago.

I get it. There are lots of turtles.

· · ·

A typing bubble popped up, then Amelia replied:

Killjoy.

But then, a small voice called, "Mama!"

Rowan shot up just in time to see Julian setting Callie down on the polished floor of the lobby. She rushed towards them, catching Callie in a tight hug. She pulled back and frowned, looking up at Julian. He raised a brow.

"What did I do?" he asked.

She shook her head. "You figured out how to braid her hair. They're actually pretty good."

"I showed him," Callie rasped proudly, tugging at her own auburn hair.

Rowan smiled. "Did you now, bug?"

She beamed and nodded, bobbing her head so her purple little kid glasses nearly fell off her nose. The poor vision had been the only lingering effect of her premature birth. Rowan figured it would only be exacerbated by the fact that Callie was already spending time staring at sheet music in front of their standing piano at home.

"Shall we?" Julian said. "I know you probably need to get ready."

Rowan nodded, standing. He gave her a quick kiss, though she could see in his eyes that he wanted to linger. She smirked and flicked his nose before taking Callie's hand while he hauled the suitcases behind him.

Hours later, Rowan stood on a small, brightly lit stage, her heart pounding in her ears as she trilled the final note of a twenty-minute solo. There was a heavy pause, and her stomach churned before the audience erupted into applause. She searched the rows of seats as people stood, finding Callie atop Julian's shoulders. He was beaming, holding onto her little legs as she clapped voraciously.

She found them afterward in the lobby of the concert hall, Julian chatting with an older woman as Callie fidgeted beside him. As soon as he saw her, he grinned, kissing her cheek and murmuring, "You're amazing."

Her cheeks warmed as he pulled back. She glanced at the woman, who was smiling softly. She looked vaguely familiar, and Rowan realized why as Julian said, "Rowan, this is Gella Dessin. I don't know if you remember, but she's a professor at Juilliard."

Rowan nodded, holding out her hand. Gella shook it and said with a tilt of her head, "I cannot believe Grandview got you. I would have loved to teach you."

Rowan smiled. "It would have been an honor."

"Out of pure curiosity, why did you choose Grandview?"

"I went to be taught under Dr. John Higgins, but he fell ill right before my first semester started," Rowan replied.

Gella sighed and said sadly, "Yes, I heard he passed away

recently. A shame; he was so talented and much too young. Who was your advisor then?"

Rowan glanced at Julian, still smiling as he said, "I was. For a time, at least."

Gella's brows rose as she glanced at Callie and connected the dots.

"Well, I suppose life works in strange ways," she finally said. "And looking at you two... It makes me wonder if maybe some lines are meant to be crossed."

Rowan felt Julian's hand brush against hers in a simple, innocent gesture. Callie whined and tugged at his shirt as Rowan smiled and said, "I wouldn't recommend it. But it worked out for us."

And it had. It really had.

Acknowledgments

When I set out to write this book, I initially only wanted to write a rom-com. But I quickly discovered, I might actually be totally incapable of doing such a thing.

The first draft of The Lines We Cross pretty much ripped itself from my brain and onto my laptop in about a week, and I discovered that I had written something that half-terrified me. For two years, I reread, rewrote, edited, and tried to convince myself I had done something completely crazy and that no one else would ever want to read it. But the story and its characters kept coming back to me. That was my first sign, and perhaps the push I needed, to finally show it to someone.

On that note, my first thanks goes collectively to MK Ahearn, Ky Venn, and Allyn Hamrick. The three of you were the first eyes besides mine to see this book and your reactions were much more than I could have hoped for. I found that—yes—I was a *little* messed up for writing this book, but fortunately, that had ended up working in my favor. My love for Rowan and Julian became yours and I cannot think of anyone else I'd want to trust this story with.

To my editor, Alexa, at the Fiction Fix, thank you for pushing me to work this manuscript to its fullest potential. And by the way, I was very happy when you asked to include memes in your reactionary comments. It made me laugh in between the grinding of my teeth and crying I did while editing.

To my partner, Ryan. You probably remember the week that I wrote the first draft of this well, because I barely talked to you and barely left my desk. Honestly, I probably wouldn't have had you not reminded me that I really did need to eat, stretch, and (please) shower. You're the logic to my chaos; and that includes reminding me that I am loved even when my mind tries to convince me otherwise.

If you're reading this, hi, Mom and Dad! Thank you (?) for insisting on reading every book I write despite the fact that they continue to get spicier and spicier. But in all seriousness, the love for music that you passed onto me from my first piano lesson on inspired much of this book. And Dad specifically, thank you for your insight into the rigors of music school. Go Wildcats and go trumpet majors!

Finally, a brief note to you (the reader) about me (the author).

Trauma is hard. I should know. And unlike Penny Thea, I won't tell you *why* I know that, but I will tell you that a large part of the reason that I wrote this story the way I did was in order to explore the way that love and trauma intersect. I often hear people say you need to be healed and whole in order to reciprocate in a loving relationship. I call bullshit on that. The right person will be with you each step of the way, and you will do the same for them (a reminder for myself and anyone else out there who sometimes doubts that). I also know Rowan is a very independent character—often to a fault—and I want to remind you that there is nothing wrong with asking for help. Help doesn't need to change the trajectory of your world, and it probably won't, in all honesty. But you are not a burden for struggling and you deserve to let someone help you carry whatever is weighing you down.

Thank you for reading. Thank you for feeling.

And keep an eye on Lena and Oliver for me...

About Rachel Tork

Rachel Tork is the author of fantasy romance and contemporary romance books, including The Lines We Cross and the Evening Star Saga. She adores rainy days, Reylo, and early mornings snuggled on her couch.

She writes quick-paced fantasy with snarky, yet flawed, characters, as well as deeply emotional romance that proves love really can conquer all.

You can follow Rachel on Instagram and TikTok at @racheltorkauthor

www.ingramcontent.com/pod-product-compliance
Lightning Source LLC
Chambersburg PA
CBHW061106310726
48974CB00002B/421